Against the Rain

Dawn of Alaska
Book 5

Naomi Rawlings

Alaska

Southeast Alaska
(Alexander Archipelego)
Canada
Stikine River
Juneau
Hoonah
Petersburg
Sitka
Wrangell
Pacific Ocean
Iskut River
Ketchikan

To Nathan, for your love of humor and people and those around you, and your determination to do what's right. I love you.

Description

What if the one woman he was taught to despise is the one he's meant to protect?

Yuri Amos has spent years watching his family suffer at the hands of Sitka's most ruthless businessman, Preston Caldwell. When Yuri discovers that Caldwell's daughter is hiding secrets, he knows he should walk away. But he can't.

Because Rosalind isn't like her father. She's quiet, intelligent, and far more trapped than anyone realizes.

But the deeper he steps into Rosalind's world, the more complicated his feelings become, especially when she begins to stir hope for a future neither of them can have. Because once he crosses the line between protector and something more, there's no turning back.

From a USA Today bestselling author comes a frontier family saga with a slow-burn, forbidden romance, a protector hero, and the kind of love that risks everything for a brighter tomorrow.

Want to be notified when my next book releases?
Sign up for my author newsletter.
(Subscribers also receive a free novel.)

1

Sitka, Alaska; December 29, 1888

Everyone looked so very happy.

Rosalind Caldwell shrank deeper into her coat as she stared through the frosted glass, watching as men and women twirled around the dance floor. Muted music from the three fiddlers filtered outside, creating an air of happiness despite the dark Alaskan night and the snow falling around her.

In the center of the room, one of her oldest friends, Bryony Wetherby Amos, danced with her new husband, Mikhail.

She looked beautiful with her long red hair curled with a hot iron and woven with flowers sent from California. Her hair splayed against her cream-colored dress as Mikhail twirled her in his arms, the expression on his face filled with love.

Mikhail twirled Bryony again, and her wedding dress fanned out as she laughed. The music swallowed the sound of her laughter, but Rosalind didn't have to use her imagination to know how vibrant and free it sounded.

And Mikhail . . .

Rosalind swallowed. Hopefully her future husband would look at her like that.

The problem was, that wasn't how marriages worked in her world. She tried to picture the faceless stranger her father would choose, who would one day call himself her husband. Perhaps he'd be older, a seasoned politician or a wealthy businessman with a calculating mind and an eye for connections. Or maybe he'd be young and ambitious, willing to do anything to climb higher in society.

She just hoped he wasn't cruel.

She forced her gaze back to Bryony and Mikhail. Bryony tipped her head back and smiled into her husband's eyes, and Mikhail leaned in close, murmuring something against her temple.

"You're allowed to go inside, you know."

She jumped at the sound of the voice behind her, then sucked in a breath and turned around.

Almost as though she'd conjured him, Yuri Amos stood a few feet away, his dark hair dusted with snow, his suit coat open despite the cold. "Yuri, what are you doing out here?"

A crooked smile tilted one side of his mouth. "Making sure you don't catch your death of cold, it seems. If you do, I'll have to haul you inside and set you next to the stove. Then my siblings will notice what I'm up to, and Evelina will fuss until I promise to knit you a scarf, Kate will lecture me on frostbite and propriety, and Alexei will demand to know why you froze in the first place. It's much simpler to make sure you don't get frostbite in the first place. Trust me on this."

"I'm perfectly warm." It wasn't a lie. Her fur coat and hat kept her warm in the ways that counted.

The cold loneliness that crept into her chest as she watched Mikhail and Bryony dance was another matter entirely.

She ran her eyes down Yuri's lithe form and over the shoulders that were neither too wide nor too slender but seemed to fit perfectly with his narrow hips. "You, on the other hand, seem to have forgotten your coat entirely."

He shrugged, his breath fogging in the air. "I'm conducting an experiment. I want to see how long I can last before Evelina calls me an idiot."

Her lips tilted up into a quick smile before she could stop them. He was always doing that, finding little ways to make her smile. Never mind that she had little in her life to smile about.

"You still don't have to stand out here." He nodded her direction.

"I do, and we both know why." The smile dropped from her face, and she glanced back through the window, her throat growing thick as she watched Mikhail plant a kiss against Bryony's temple. "Bryony looks so very happy with your brother."

"She is."

Her throat tightened even more. If Bryony had married into any other family, Rosalind would have been inside celebrating with her. But not the Amoses. "I'm glad. She deserves to be happy."

"So do you." The soft words filled the night, and she could feel the warmth of Yuri's gaze on her. It hadn't left her since he'd appeared.

Just what was he hoping to learn by studying her for so long?

Nothing good, she was certain. Just like she was certain nothing good would come of the two of them being alone out here in the dark.

"I'm going to San Francisco," he suddenly announced.

He was? She moved her gaze back to his, then forced herself to take a long breath while her mind filled with questions. *How long will you be gone? Why are you leaving? Will you return quickly?*

She didn't want to think about why any of those things mattered, so she shoved the thoughts aside and forced herself to focus on the practical aspect of his absence. "Do you have January's installment to give me?"

"Yes."

She nodded toward where his hands were tucked into the pockets of his suitcoat. "Did you bring everything with you now?"

"I would have, had I known you were coming."

Right. He wouldn't have expected to see her here. "Then we need to set up another time to meet. When do you leave?"

"Next Tuesday, unless the ship is late coming into port."

It was Saturday night. That only left her with Sunday and Monday. "I'll see if I can move my visit to Millicent's up to Monday afternoon, and I'll sneak off to meet you after I have tea with her."

He gave a single nod of his head. "The usual time and place?"

"Yes."

"I'm not sure how long I'll be gone." Yuri's breath cast another plume of white between them. "I'm guessing two weeks, maybe three. I'm sure Alexei will set my mail aside for me, but if something in San Francisco takes longer than I expect, do you want me to see if Bryony can meet you at the beginning of February?"

He might be gone that long? What would he be doing?

She clamped her lips shut. It wasn't her business. Not any of it.

Just answer the question, Rosalind. It was simple and straightforward, and he deserves an honest response.

"No," she found herself saying. "I don't think so. The fewer people who know about this, the better."

Yuri raised his eyebrows. "I thought Bryony was your friend."

"She is, but she doesn't need to know everything."

Silence stretched between them, as thick as the snow piling at their feet. A new song from inside filtered through the cracks around the window, laughter mixing with the fiddlers' tune.

"You should come to San Francisco." Once again, Yuri's words seemed to come from nowhere, bold and unexpected against the frigid night.

She found herself flinching at the offer. "You want me to run off? With you?"

How could the idea sound so very foreign when she'd been thinking the same thing only moments before he'd joined her?

But Yuri hadn't factored into her plans earlier. "You want me to run off—with you?"

"Not with me." He held out his hands, as though that might somehow make him look innocent. "I just want you away from here. We'll get you a new name, a ridiculous hat, and you can claim to be an heiress from Boston. No one will suspect a thing."

He sent her a crooked grin, and for one small moment, she let herself imagine being on the ship as it pulled away from Sitka, the icy air stinging her face as lightness filled her chest.

But the dream shattered before it could fully take form. "I can't leave. Things aren't ready."

"You've been saying that for the past year." Yuri shoved a hand into his hair. "Just come with me. San Francisco is a big enough city for you to disappear in for a month or two while you figure out where to go next."

Her pulse pounded at her temples. "If you think my father won't have men searching for me at every port city on the

Pacific Ocean the day after I disappear, then you don't know him very well. If I leave, everything needs to be perfect. If it's not perfect and I mess up just one detail . . ." She broke off, her fingers curling into the thick fur of her coat.

She couldn't afford the price her father would demand if she failed.

"Maybe you need to think more about what God can do to help you leave than about how afraid you are," he said.

She blinked at him. "What?"

Yuri rubbed the back of his neck. "Sorry. I probably shouldn't have said anything."

She took a step closer. "No. Don't apologize. I want you to explain yourself."

He shifted in the snow. "I was reading in the Bible about fear, and God brought me to Isaiah chapter forty-one and verse ten. 'Fear thou not; for I am with thee: be not dismayed; for I am thy God: I will strengthen thee; yea, I will help thee; yea, I will uphold thee with the right hand of my righteousness.' So I was thinking, maybe instead of being scared to leave Sitka, you should ask God to strengthen you, because the Bible promises he will."

She silently repeated what she could remember of the verse, committing the reference to memory. Isaiah 41:10. She could certainly do with less fear in her life. She'd have to look the verse up and read it when she got home.

"I meant what I said earlier too." Yuri's voice turned soft and low. "It's not just Bryony who deserves happiness. You deserve to be happy too."

Did she? It certainly sounded good to hear him say so. Perhaps that was why she was half in love with him. He was always nice. Always kind. Always gentle.

Those were traits that didn't exist in her father's world.

If she ever did leave Sitka, if she ever truly decided to walk away from the life her father was carefully planning for her, she would have to do it without anyone knowing . . .

Including Yuri.

She turned toward the water, staring at the dark waves lapping the shore. "I'll meet you on Monday. At the usual time. I should be able to talk Father into letting me have an extra visit with Millicent, especially with the holidays, and I'll sneak off to visit you after I'm at her house. Bring everything you've received with you."

She took a step back, then turned and strode off into the night.

For a few seconds, she thought Yuri might follow, or at least call after her for leaving so abruptly.

But he didn't. He stayed where he was, watching her as he leaned against the wall of the warehouse-turned-ballroom. And she could swear she felt the heat of his gaze on her the entire way back home.

It was a ridiculous notion. There was no possible way for him to see her after she rounded the first corner and turned up the hill leading to her family's mansion on the far side of town. But she still felt as though his eyes were on her.

The house was dark when she reached it, just as she'd known it would be. She'd been careful when planning how to sneak out for a glimpse of Bryony's wedding reception.

She headed around the back of the mansion to the kitchen entrance, just to be certain Father wasn't up late in the parlor.

But after she turned the doorknob and let herself inside, she found a form shrouded in shadows, his hands folded tightly on the table.

"Father?" she rasped, every last bit of warmth draining from her body.

He said nothing as the door clicked shut behind her, only watched—as though he'd been counting every second she'd been away.

2

Sitka; Monday Afternoon

She was late—really late.

Yuri pulled his coat tighter around his chest, the damp wool doing little to block the wind that cut in from the ocean. Rain slanted down from the sky, cold and relentless, soaking through the fabric of his cap and beading along his collar. A few droplets even slipped down his neck and onto his back, causing him to shiver.

The tide was out, leaving long stretches of wet sand under the gray, heavy sky. But the angry waves still surged farther up the beach than usual, frothed into angry white tips by the wind.

Rosalind had been late many times before, but never this late.

He exhaled sharply, his breath a faint ghost against the rain, and turned his gaze back toward the forest. The spruce trees loomed dark and dripping at the edge of the shore, but there was no sign of a figure hurrying toward him, shoulders hunched beneath the heavy mink coat she always wore.

Where was she?

Why wasn't she here?

Had something happened?

His stomach twisted. He hated the way he worried. Hated how he couldn't stop thinking about Rosalind Caldwell's well-being whenever something didn't go as planned. Hated that he couldn't simply head to her house and ask if everything was all right, like he could do with every other person in the town where he'd grown up.

But Rosalind was different. He'd known it the first time he'd laid eyes on her.

What was he going to do if she didn't come?

He had letters to give her before he left, and he had to be on a ship in less than twenty-four hours. That wasn't exactly something he could delay.

So where was she? And how long was he supposed to wait?

One hour? Two? Until supper?

He trudged across the sand, his boots sinking into the wet softness, and headed to where a log had fallen at the edge of the beach. He sat and stared out at the horizon, rain pummeling his hat and coat.

She was nearly an hour late at this point. Common sense told him she wasn't going to come, that he should get up and make the long walk back to town.

But for some reason he didn't quite understand, he couldn't force himself to leave.

FEAR THOU NOT; *for I am with thee: be not dismayed; for I am thy God.* Rosalind pressed her lips together and squeezed her eyes shut against the pain radiating up her arm. *I will strengthen thee; yea, I will help thee; yea, I will uphold thee with the—*

The grandfather clock standing against the far wall of her father's study let out a small chime. Another quarter hour had passed, making her forty-five minutes late to meet with Yuri.

"Does that hurt, dear?"

At the sound of Dr. Hollis's voice, she forced her eyes to open, but that only allowed her to see her father standing next to the doctor, glaring at her as though it was somehow her fault that her arm had been injured.

In fact, he probably did blame her for the injury. She could almost hear him telling her that her arm wouldn't have been hurt had she not flung it out to protect her face from his hand Saturday night after she'd returned from spying on Bryony's wedding reception.

Perhaps she shouldn't have tried to protect herself, but it had seemed like a good idea at the time. A bruise on her face meant her father wouldn't allow her to leave the house until it was healed. A bruise that could be concealed by gloves and long sleeves? She could at least go about town with that.

Still, she hadn't been prepared for just how hard her father would strike her, or for him to get even angrier and strike her wrist multiple times when she shielded her face from his attack.

Her ribs were bruised as well, but Dr. Hollis didn't need to know about those.

The damage to her wrist was bad enough. Deep-purple marks wrapped around the joint with faint yellow marks trailing up her forearm. And the swelling made it hard to bend her wrist and even some of her fingers.

If only she'd held her whimper at breakfast, when Father asked her to pass the bowl of potatoes. But the bowl had been so heavy, and the pain in her wrist had only grown worse over the past day and a half.

"Miss Caldwell?" the doctor asked again, a touch more firmly. "I asked if your wrist hurts when I press here?"

Rosalind blinked and refocused her gaze on the older man kneeling beside her chair. His fingers were pushing just below the joint, but even the gentle pressure was enough to send sharp stabs of pain slicing up her forearm.

"Yes. It hurts."

Dr. Hollis shifted, his wire spectacles sliding lower on his nose as he studied her wrist from a different angle. "The good news is I don't believe the bone is broken, but the joint is certainly sprained. I recommend using a sling for at least two weeks, perhaps three."

Two weeks? "No." She pulled her wrist away from the doctor and cradled it against her chest.

"No?" her father barked.

She swallowed, her heart thudding against her ribs. She could feel the eyes of both men on her, and she dropped her gaze to her lap. "Surely it's not that bad. I'll just rest it."

"A sprain that isn't immobilized properly can take far longer to heal." Dr. Hollis ran two fingers lightly over the swelling. "You don't want that, do you? I'll wrap it and provide you with a sling. With any luck, you'll have full use of it again within a few weeks."

But Father wouldn't let her out of the house if her arm was in a sling. He never let her out of the house when she had an injury that others could see. "Surely the sling doesn't need to be on for that long if I'm careful. I promise I'll keep it still."

Dr. Hollis adjusted his glasses. "Miss Caldwell, I'm sure you will try your best to protect your wrist without a sling, but I really must insist—"

"She'll wear it," Father snapped. "Wrap her wrist, bind it, do whatever is necessary. I won't have her injuring herself further with foolish behavior."

"But Father—"

"Do not try me, Rosalind."

Rejoice in the Lord always: and again I say, Rejoice. That was the verse her mother had always used when something difficult happened, not a verse about fear. Then her mother had told her to find something good about her situation, be grateful, thank God.

But the verse about rejoicing seemed horribly trite at the moment.

Oh, why did she have to be here in the first place? Why had God given her a father who thought nothing of striking her when he was angry?

Freya's father yelled when he grew angry, but he didn't hit anyone. The same was true of Jane's father. As for Millicent's father, well, she wasn't even sure he yelled. He always seemed calm and gentle, even when correcting Millicent or one of her brothers.

"This will only take a moment." The doctor reached into his bag and retrieved a roll of bandages and a long, wide strip of fabric.

She nodded stiffly, unable to speak. Her eyes drifted to the grandfather clock again. She was nearly a full hour late. Was Yuri still on the beach waiting for her, somehow hoping she was coming?

He probably was. That seemed like just the thing he would do, never mind the rain. And here she had no way to even send him a note explaining what happened.

The doctor wrapped the bandage around her lower arm and hand, then reached for a strip of fabric. He draped it down the front of her chest to gauge the appropriate length before looping it back behind her neck and tying it.

She slid her arm inside without being instructed to do so, and the doctor added more material to the sling, allowing her arm to rest a little lower.

"There now," he said softly. "That's not so bad, is it? Keep it elevated when you can. No lifting, and try not to jostle it. Send for me if the pain gets worse, and I can fit it with a splint. Otherwise I'll return in two weeks to check on it."

She studied the bandage. It covered the bruising but hadn't done a thing to help the pain. Maybe if she was extra careful and rested her hand constantly, she could remove the sling early. Then she could at least go to Millicent's next week for their usual monthly visit. She might not have a choice about missing her time with Yuri today, but she genuinely enjoyed visiting with Millicent every month before sneaking off to meet him. It was the one visit a month Father allowed her without asking her a bunch of questions first.

The doctor turned to pack his medical bag, and Father stepped forward, resting a hand on her shoulder. "Thank the doctor, Rosalind."

"Thank you," she whispered, trying to find a way to be grateful for the doctor's ministrations, even though she didn't want to be confined to the house.

Dr. Hollis's eyebrows furrowed, his gaze moving between them for an overly long moment. "You said you hurt your wrist this morning when you tripped on the stairs?"

"I'm afraid I am terribly clumsy." She didn't even think twice before letting the lie roll off her tongue, not with her father standing there. "My foot tangled in my petticoat, and I missed the bottom step."

"Yes, a most unfortunate accident. We appreciate your coming to the house on such short notice, doctor. Foster will show you out now." Her father nodded toward the door, where their longtime butler stood in the open doorway.

How long he'd been there, she didn't know. He might have been standing in that same spot since first showing the doctor into her father's study. His facial expression gave nothing away as he moved to the side, allowing Dr. Hollis to precede him into the hallway.

The door shut with a quiet click, but her father didn't move, and neither did she.

He let the silence linger between them for an unnaturally long time, his hand still clamped on her shoulder before he finally said, "See that something like this doesn't happen again, Rosalind."

There was nothing for her to do other than agree, but oh how she hated nodding her head. How she hated the fact that her injury would end up hidden, and his actions would once again be concealed from everyone in town.

Was it wrong of her to hope that the truth of her father's actions would somehow be made known? Her mother would say so. Her mother would say that she was living in a grand house with expensive dresses and a lady's maid, and she needed to be grateful that her every last need was provided for.

But Rosalind wasn't sure she could be grateful for very much longer.

3

Yuri sat with his back to the cookstove, soaking in the warmth from the fire as he plunged his spoon into a bowl of borscht. Rain pummeled the ground and streaked the windows in a steady, relentless batter that didn't seem inclined to stop any time soon.

The kitchen itself seemed incredibly small these days, especially with all of his family members crammed around what he'd once thought was a rather large table.

The table had fit him and his original seven siblings well enough. But now that three of them were married, and his sister-in-law Maggie had brought her two young half siblings into the marriage, there was no question that both the table and the kitchen itself were too small to host them.

They had a dining room, but it had always felt too austere and formal for a regular meal, so they crowded into the kitchen anyway, boots thudding against the floorboards, spoons clinking against bowls, and laughter filling the room. And in another seven or eight months, the room was going to be even more crowded, because both of his sisters and Sacha's wife, Maggie, were pregnant. Kate's baby was going to be born first, sometime around the beginning of June.

Yuri shivered, still not quite able to shake off the chill that had seeped into him earlier.

An hour and a half. That's how long he'd waited for Rosalind in the secret cove.

No, it was more like an hour and forty-five minutes.

"It's your last meal here." His half-Aleut, half-Russian brother, Ilya, tore off a piece of bread from where he was seated at the table beside Yuri. "I thought you were supposed to pick what we're having for dinner. Or does Evelina only do that for Alexei and Sacha and Mikhail when they leave?"

"I asked Yuri what he wanted," Evelina said from several places down the table, then pressed a hand to her stomach, which hadn't even started to grow round yet.

Ilya turned back to him and dunked his bread into the borscht with the type of bored look that only a thirteen-year-old could muster. "Of all the things you could have picked, you told Lina to make borscht?"

"I like borscht." Yuri tore a chunk of bread from the slice on his own plate and mimicked Ilya by dunking it into his soup. "And Lina's bread. I won't be able to have either in San Francisco."

Evelina sent him a bright smile. "Thank you, Yuri."

"You're welcome," he said around his mouthful of food. Though to be honest, he couldn't really claim to taste the borscht.

Just like he couldn't really claim to be paying attention to the conversation Maggie, Sacha, Mikhail, and Bryony were all having on the opposite side of the table.

He'd even lost track of how many times he'd bumped elbows with his brother-in-law Nathan, on his right, and it must have been a lot, considering how crowded they were.

Because his mind kept traveling back to that dratted cove. If only he knew why Rosalind hadn't—

"Maybe you should have sent Mikhail to San Francisco." Ilya leaned forward and looked at Alexei, their oldest brother, who was sitting at the head of the table. "He always picks a bear roast on his last night."

Alexei dabbed his face with his napkin. "Like Yuri, I happen to like borscht—and Evelina's bread."

Ilya scowled into his soup. "I still think Yuri should have requested bear, or at least venison."

Laughter erupted from the other side of the table, and Yuri slanted a glance at his large, burly brother Sacha, who wore a grin that spread from ear to ear. Mikhail sat beside him, the back of his neck and the tips of his ears red as he slowly shook his head.

"Wait." Bryony leaned closer to Mikhail, then peeked around him to look at Sacha. "Did he just say what I think?"

"Yes." Mikhail pressed his lips into a firm line, but Bryony's cheeks turned a bright shade of pink.

"Sacha, behave." Sacha's wife, Maggie, nudged him with her elbow.

Sacha only smirked. "They're newly married. Someone needs to say it."

"Do I even want to know?" Alexei murmured.

Jonas, Evelina's husband, loosed a chuckle from the other end of the table. "I don't think I've ever seen Mikhail look quite so guilty."

"He's not guilty." Sasha sent Mikhail a wink. "Just embarrassed."

Mikhail set down his drink, everything about his movements measured and patient. "One of these days, Sacha, someone is going to throw you into Sitka Sound."

Sacha held up his hands. "You've been saying that for years, and yet here I am. Dry."

"How unfortunate," Nathan said as he reached for another slice of bread. "I have a feeling Sacha could use a good dousing."

Kate shook her head. "Stay out of it, darling, or you'll be the one tossed into the sound, and don't ask how I know this."

"That's the key to survival in this family," Evelina said around a mouthful of bread. "Stay out of things and don't ask any unnecessary questions."

"I can confirm this strategy works." Jonas raised his mug in agreement before taking a sip. "And seeing how I was the first one to marry into this family, while you and Kate haven't even been married a year, I would know." He sent Evelina a wink.

Mikhail, meanwhile, continued to glare at Sacha, as though he truly was contemplating whether he could drag their giant, lumbering brother out the door and toss him into the sound in the middle of winter.

Honestly, Yuri wasn't sure which brother would end up in the water if Mikhail tried it. Probably both of them. Sacha might be bigger, but as a frontier guide, Mikhail was fast and strong in his own way.

"In this case, though, I have a feeling Sacha's just saying what everyone else is thinking." Jonas set his mug on the table with a thunk.

"I highly doubt *everyone* is thinking that." Mikhail shot a sharp look down the table at Jonas.

"Maggie's thinking it," Sacha said.

"I am not," Maggie said primly, even though red bloomed across her cheeks.

"Maggie's *absolutely* thinking it," Sasha corrected, winking at her.

Mikhail dragged in a breath through his nose and took a

deliberate sip of his drink, while Bryony sat in silence beside him, her cheeks just as red as Maggie's.

Nathan chuckled and shook his head. "And to think, Yuri, that you'll be leaving all this behind when you go to San Francisco. Don't get too used to the peace and quiet."

"I wouldn't dream of it." Yuri looked around the crammed table. The truth was, he might actually miss all of this. In fact, he was quite certain that he would. For all the times he'd begged Alexei to send him off on a business trip over the years, now that he was on the brink of leaving, he suddenly wasn't sure he wanted to go. Was this how his brothers felt whenever they needed to leave too?

But someone needed to go to San Francisco to buy the ship Alexei wanted, and there were too many things going on in Sitka for Alexei to go himself, especially now that Rosalind's uncle was the governor of Alaska.

So it would have to be him, and he was supposed to be excited, confound it.

"I can write to you." Sacha leaned closer to the table, that teasing grin still plastered across his face. "I'll make sure to include every single embarrassing thing Mikhail does while you're gone."

Mikhail leveled him with a look. "I have *never* done anything embarrassing."

"Is that so?" Sasha drummed his fingers on the table. "Then perhaps you'd like to explain why you nearly *toppled over backward* in your chair this morning when Bryony touched your arm."

"The chair was unstable."

Bryony raised a brow. "It seemed perfectly sturdy to me."

Sacha grinned. "It's not his fault, Bryony. Love makes a man forget how furniture works."

Alexei sighed, rubbing a hand over his face. "I cannot believe this is the conversation we're having over dinner."

Kate smirked. "What did you expect? Manners and polite discourse? Half of this table is made up of Amos men."

Alexei exhaled slowly, probably trying to summon a bit of patience. "I keep thinking they'll grow out of this at some point."

"We won't," Sacha quipped.

"Not ever. The house would be far too serious." Yuri let out a mock shudder and glanced around the table. Everyone was smiling—other than Alexei, and he never smiled.

Oh, hang it all. He really was going to miss his family while he was in San Francisco. What would it feel like that first night in the hotel where he knew nobody? He couldn't remember the last time he'd eaten a meal by himself. There was always someone in the house eating with him, even if it was Maggie's six-year-old half-brother, Finnan.

Was he supposed to eat every meal by himself in the hotel restaurant? He wasn't going to know what to do—not that he'd ever admit that to Alexei.

Hopefully after that first night, he'd at least have businessmen to eat with.

But that still wouldn't be the same as sitting at the table he'd eaten at for his entire life, laughing with his family.

And here he was, starting to feel homesick before he'd even left home.

He was being ridiculous. San Francisco was a large city bustling with people upon people upon people. Surely he'd find someone interesting there, or maybe ten someones. It couldn't be that hard to make friends.

But there was someone who wouldn't be in San Francisco.

Yuri dragged his gaze back to his bowl of half-eaten soup.

If only he had a way to contact her.

He shoved a hand through his hair. Maybe he was just conjecturing that something was wrong. Maybe there was nothing wrong and she simply forgot about their meeting, since it was usually on a different day entirely.

But what was he going to do about her letters?

The night of Mikhail's wedding, she'd said she didn't want Bryony to know about them, but it was starting to feel like he didn't have a choice. Should he pull his newest sister-in-law aside after dinner, explain the letters, and ask her to meet Rosalind on the usual day and time in his stead? Rosalind might not show up, since she knew he'd be out of town, but maybe she'd go to the cove anyway, just to spend a little time by herself. She always seemed to enjoy the walk out there.

Besides, it just might be easier for Rosalind to keep her typical schedule. It was already hard enough for her to get away from her father, but he was used to Rosalind visiting Millicent once a month. What her father didn't know was that Rosalind and Millicent's visit took up only half the time Rosalind was gone. Walking out to the beach where she typically met Yuri might be easier than changing her schedule and then needing to answer her father's questions.

"You've been quiet tonight, Yuri."

Yuri snapped his head up to find Alexei watching him.

"That's not like you."

"I'm just thinking," Yuri muttered, reaching for his drink.

"Don't hurt yourself," Sacha snapped.

Yuri rolled his eyes. "I *am* capable of deep thought from time to time."

"That's debatable," Mikhail murmured.

"No, Yuri's right." Evelina sent him a sickeningly sweet smile. "He had a deep thought just last month at Thanksgiving."

"Exactly." Yuri puffed out his chest. "And I've been recovering ever since."

Bryony shook her head. "You're all impossible."

Kate smirked, then reached over and squeezed Nathan's arm. "At least my husband was raised properly."

Nathan grinned. "That's why I married into the family. Someone needed to bring civility to this lot."

Bryony snorted. "I think you failed."

Laughter erupted around the table, but Yuri barely heard it. He was back to thinking about Rosalind and the letters.

BY THE TIME the meal was finished, Yuri still hadn't decided whether to tell Bryony about Rosalind's letters. Everyone around him was cleaning up, but he stood against the hutch, drinking a second cup of tea and observing the activity when Mikhail came up beside him.

"Can I talk to you for a few minutes?" Mikhail's voice was low and severe.

Too severe. Yuri didn't need some other serious thing to deal with, at least not until he'd figured out what to do about Rosalind's letters. He tilted the side of his mouth up into a smirk before even looking at Mikhail.

"Talk to me? Why? And why do you look so serious? Wait, don't tell me." Yuri snapped his fingers. "You spent the day with Alexei, didn't you?"

Mikhail rolled his eyes. "Just meet me in Alexei's study."

He widened his eyes. "That does sound serious. I'd best bring my tea with me. Sounds like I might need some liquid courage for this conversation."

Mikhail just shook his head and left the kitchen muttering

something under his breath that Yuri wasn't sure he wanted to hear.

Yuri lingered in the kitchen a few seconds longer, then pushed himself off the hutch and followed Mikhail down the hallway. He had no clue what his brother wanted to talk to him about, and he'd only been half joking about bringing the tea with him for courage.

Alexei's study was quieter than the rest of the house, closed off from the chatter and laughter still coming from the kitchen.

Yuri would have closed the door behind him, but Bryony rushed into the room before he could shut it.

"Did he tell you? I'm so sorry, Yuri. I didn't mean to do it. It was an accident."

"Didn't mean to do what?" Yuri swung his gaze to Mikhail, who was standing beside Alexei's desk holding a letter.

"Bryony accidentally opened one of your letters this afternoon."

That's what this was about? A letter? He'd already received all six of Rosalind's letters for the month of December, so whatever Bryony had opened would be harmless.

So why did Bryony and Mikhail look so serious? "That's all right, love." He flashed Bryony a smile, trying to set her at ease. "You're more than welcome to read my mail, either on accident or on purpose. I'm not writing any—"

His mouth closed the moment he saw the return address on the outside of the envelope. No. This couldn't be. He'd already gotten Rosalind's letter acknowledging her donation to the orphanage in New York City this month.

So why was Mikhail handing him a second letter with their return address?

Yuri reached out and took it. Sure enough, the top of the envelope had a clean slice right down the middle.

What did the letter say?

It didn't matter. He didn't know what any of the letters said. Just because they were addressed to him didn't mean they actually belonged to him. He'd been helping Rosalind with her letters for three years, and he'd never read a single one. That had been her only stipulation when she'd come to him asking for help.

"Are you talking about the letters already?" The study door opened, and Sacha stepped inside.

Alexei followed behind Sacha and sent Mikhail a glare. "I told you to wait for us."

Mikhail scowled right back. "You shouldn't have disappeared to the office after supper."

Alexei didn't bother to answer Mikhail. Instead he turned to Yuri. "So? What do you have to say for yourself? Why is there a letter addressed to you but clearly meant for Rosalind Caldwell? And why does it mention a twelve-hundred-dollar donation?"

"Twelve hundred dollars?" Yuri squeaked. That's how much the donation was? He took a gulp of tea, never mind the liquid was still hot enough to scorch his mouth.

"Sit." Alexei jabbed his finger at the chair in front of his desk. "You'd better start explaining."

"There's nothing to explain. It's not my letter, and I don't know anything about it. Bryony shouldn't have opened it, but it was an honest mistake. I'm sure Rosalind will understand."

At least he hoped she would. Still, it felt like he'd done something wrong. The only thing she'd asked of him was that he not open the letters, and here one had gotten opened, even if it was by accident.

"Wait." Yuri set his cup on the desk and stood right back up, his eyes narrowed on Alexei. "You just said the letter mentioned a twelve-hundred-dollar donation. How would you know that unless you read it?"

"Of course I read it." Alexei shoved a hand his direction. "You're getting mail intended for our enemy but addressed to you."

"Rosalind's not our enemy. Her father might be a snake, but she couldn't be more different from him, and you still had no business reading her mail."

"I'm the one who read it, at least at first." Bryony twisted her hands in front of her skirt. "It really was an accident, though. I promise. It was in a stack of other mail, and I didn't realize it was for you—or her—or whoever the letter's actually for until I'd opened it and started reading."

Yuri dropped his head into his hands. "It's for her. I don't have anything to do with what's in the letters. I just mail them and receive them every month under my name and with my address so that her father doesn't find out."

"Them?" Alexei snapped. "You mean there's more than one letter, and you get and send them every month?"

He pressed his eyes shut. Why had he just said that? "Never mind. It doesn't matter."

"Actually, I think it does matter." Alexei took a step closer to him. "Is Rosalind only donating to this one charity, or are there more? And how large are the sums?"

"And why are you involved in any of this?" Sacha scratched the side of his beard.

"Is it her father's money?" Mikhail asked. "Because if it is, and he doesn't know what she's doing with it, and you're somehow involved, that sounds like a recipe for another lawsuit."

"Or maybe Caldwell will find a way to skip the lawsuit and toss you into jail like he did with Sacha and Mikhail," Alexei muttered.

Yuri gripped the back of his neck. It wasn't as bad as all that, was it?

"We're looking at this two different ways. You're seeing it as a harmless donation receipt and a thank-you note for monies donated throughout the year, but it doesn't change the fact that you're sending and receiving these letters in secret for the daughter of someone who wants to ruin our family." Alexei pointed back to the chair in front of the desk. "Sit back down and start talking."

Yuri glanced around the room, taking in his brothers and Bryony, who was standing against the wall, as far away from the commotion as she could manage. They weren't going to let him leave until he told them everything.

Perhaps it was because they loved him. Perhaps it was because they were a close family that always tangled themselves in each other's lives. Or perhaps it was because they weren't a family that carried secrets.

Whatever the reason, he saw no way out of this—other than starting at the very beginning.

He pressed his eyes shut. *Dear Father, please help Rosalind to understand what I'm about to do.*

Then he opened his mouth and started talking.

4

San Francisco; Four Days Later

He was a failure. There was no other word for it.

The *Alliance* rocked gently beneath Yuri's feet as it crept through Golden Gate, the strait that separated the peninsula to their north from the bustling city of San Francisco to their south. It was a narrow strip of water, only maybe a mile and a half wide, but it protected both San Pablo Bay and San Francisco Bay from the rough waters of the Pacific Ocean.

Not that the ocean was rough today. It was calm as glass, with a brilliant blue sky and gulls circling above.

If only he could force his mood to match the cheerful weather. But how could he when he still felt as though he'd betrayed Rosalind?

If a brother or sister be naked, and destitute of daily food, and one of you say unto them, Depart in peace, be ye warmed and filled; notwithstanding ye give them not those things which are needful to the body; what doth it profit?

God had led him to that passage from the second chapter of

James three years ago. Rosalind had asked him to send and receive a single letter for her every month, a charitable contribution she hadn't wanted her father to know about. The Sunday after she made her request, the priest at St. Michael's had delivered a sermon on helping those in need.

So Yuri agreed to help Rosalind donate to a charity every month, and eventually the number of charities she supported grew to six. Each month, Yuri would send six donation letters from Rosalind, and the organizations would send six letters back to him acknowledging the donations. Occasionally, she'd made a one-time donation elsewhere, but for the past year, her list of charities had been the same.

The Bible was full of verses about helping the needy and delivering them from affliction. James 2:15–16 wasn't the only one. Matthew 25:35–36 and 40 said, *For I was an hungred, and ye gave me meat: I was thirsty, and ye gave me drink: I was a stranger, and ye took me in: Naked, and ye clothed me: I was sick, and ye visited me: I was in prison, and ye came unto me . . . Verily I say unto you, Inasmuch as ye have done it unto one of the least of these my brethren, ye have done it unto me.*

And Psalm 82:3–4 said, *Defend the poor and fatherless: do justice to the afflicted and needy. Deliver the poor and needy: rid them out of the hand of the wicked.*

Yuri had taken those verses to heart and spent the last three years trying to be a living example of them. And the entire time he was sending Rosalind's letters, he couldn't help thinking of Alexei. He'd done the very thing these verses spoke of after their father and stepmother died at sea eleven years earlier. Alexei had been in San Francisco, a year away from completing his studies in naval architecture, and had dropped everything to come home. His fiancée, Clarise, left him a few months later, choosing to move back to Washington, DC, with all its refinements rather than stay in Sitka with

Alexei. And still, Alexei had stood by their family, never wavering once.

So for the past three years, Yuri had been happy to help Rosalind and show the love of Christ to others. But at some point, he'd also wondered if maybe Rosalind needed help. She wasn't poor or hungry—there was no question about that. But some of those verses talked about helping the needy and afflicted, and people could still be needy if they had money, couldn't they? It certainly seemed that way when it came to Rosalind. Of course, it would make more sense if he knew exactly what Rosalind needed.

He didn't, but at times he had an almost overwhelming conviction that simply being her friend and sending the letters for her was helping her in ways she couldn't quite express.

So that's exactly what he'd done, and from time to time, he asked her if she wanted help leaving Sitka.

She didn't seem to care that he wanted to be her friend and had answered with a hard no any time he'd brought up the possibility of her leaving her home. He was succeeding in only one of the things he was trying to do, and even that had changed three nights ago when Bryony had accidentally opened one of Rosalind's letters.

The memory still caused a sour ball to form in his stomach.

Another thing he'd never done was ask Rosalind where her donation money came from. At the beginning, he'd assumed she was giving a bit of her own money and that the donations were tiny enough they wouldn't make much difference in the day-to-day operations of the first charity she'd supported, the orphanage in New York City.

Now Rosalind was supporting multiple institutions, and he'd long had a suspicion that the donations were for more than just a dollar or two. But he hadn't known for certain until he'd read the letter Bryony had opened. It had thanked Rosalind for her contributions throughout the year, totaling twelve hundred dollars. Since Yuri knew that Rosalind sent that organization a letter every month, it wasn't hard to deduce that each donation was a hundred dollars.

One hundred dollars.

That was four to five months' worth of wages for the average man.

Where had Rosalind gotten that much money?

Her father's bank account, like Alexei and the rest of his brothers suspected?

That was the most obvious answer, but if Preston Caldwell knew what his daughter was doing with his money, there would be no need for her to hide her correspondence.

Now Alexei was worried about would happen if Caldwell discovered a member of the Amos family had been secretly helping Rosalind send his money off to various charities, and he was probably right to be concerned.

Yuri rubbed the back of his neck. Could Caldwell legally accuse him of theft or money laundering or some other Finnancial crime? The powerful businessman had had no trouble having both Sacha and Mikhail charged with crimes they hadn't committed.

The captain shouted down from the deck, ordering his crew to prepare to dock. The men around Yuri flew into action, lowering the sails and removing the deck boards that covered the gangway stored underneath.

More shouting sounded from the shore, where men had gathered near an open slip on the wharf to help moor the ship. The helmsman pointed the nose of the *Alliance* directly at the opening, and the ship crawled forward with all but one sail furled.

The pier in front of them was alive with movement. Longshoremen in work-worn coats hauled crates from incoming vessels.

Merchants haggled over shipments of goods, and dock hands rolled barrels down the gangways. There were even a handful of cranes removing cargo from ships by hoisting crates high into the air, then swinging them onto the wharf and slowly lowering them.

Just past the wharf, a sprawling maze of warehouses lined the harbor, followed by a glut of factories. Houses and hotels and other buildings occupied space on the hillside farther away from the water, and the city's bright energy hummed in the air.

Hopefully it would be infectious. Hopefully it would pull his mind away from how he'd failed Rosalind.

Alexei had certainly given him enough things to keep himself busy in San Francisco. His first order of business was to procure three shipping contracts. Alexei had been writing to factory owners, and it seemed as though three of them were ready to sign two-year contracts to have the Sitka Trading Company ship their goods from California to Japan and China. Hopefully getting the contracts signed wouldn't be too hard.

And then there was the barge. Made of iron and steel, it had been badly damaged in a storm, and Alexei was trying to buy it at a good price, hoping that the cost of the ship plus repairs would be less than the price of a seaworthy ship. It was currently at the Farnsworth Shipyard, and Yuri was supposed to make an offer on it.

Yuri wiped his slick palms on the legs of his trousers as the *Alliance* slid into its space alongside the wharf.

When he'd volunteered to come down to San Francisco, he'd expected Alexei to tell him no, just like he'd told him last fall when they'd needed to send someone to Ketchikan.

But he hadn't.

Yuri glanced at the wharf again and the city rising on the hill beyond it. Three shipping contracts and a damaged barge. He could do this. He wasn't about to fail his brother.

KLAWOCK, Alaska; Two Days Later

"Why are you packing? I don't understand." Alexei stood on the beach in the small Tlingit village of Klawock, which sat on Prince of Wales Island, one island south of Baranoff Island where Sitka was located. His gaze swept over the shoreline where dozens of people were busy packing their belongings and loading them into canoes. Everywhere he looked, people were moving. Women packed woven baskets with clothing, blankets, and household goods. Men disassembled wooden drying racks and carried supplies toward the beach, and children gathered what they could, their small hands clutching toys or tools.

"Are you leaving?" he asked, even though the answer was obvious. "Now? Fishing season will be underway in a few months."

Tlákwsháa, the oldest elder of the clan, knelt on a mat that contained a ceremonial rattle, several Chilkat blankets, and various other items. He didn't look up as he picked up a worn raven headdress and wrapped it in a piece of deerskin, then tucked it into a cedar box.

"The soldiers said we need to leave."

So the rumor was true. He had a hundred things to do in Sitka, but when word had reached him that the people of Klawock were uprooting their village, he'd wanted to come check for himself.

"What soldiers are you talking about?"

"The ones who came here with the governor." Tlákwsháa reached for a sprig of dried hemlock gum, placed it between his teeth, and began to chew slowly.

"Soldiers came here with the governor?" He hadn't heard

anything about that, just that the clan was moving to a different location.

The elder merely nodded. "Navy men. On boats. We need to leave before summer."

Alexei's fingers curled at his sides. "But why?"

"The government needs this land." The elder's words were muffled slightly by the gum, but his tone remained even as he wrapped a strip of leather cord around the box and cinched it tight.

It didn't make sense. The government had plenty of land. More than they knew what to do with. Alexei's gaze flickered to the nearest totem pole. Its carvings told the story of the clan's lineage, and it had stood there long before any American official had set foot in Alaska. And somehow Simon Caldwell thought he had the right to take this land?

"I find it hard to believe that they need this land right here when there is so much other land." Land that didn't have totem poles or longhouses. Land that hadn't been home to a clan of people for several centuries.

"It's the island they want." Tlákwshάa reached for the Chilkat blanket. "The governor asked the village of Kasaan to leave too."

He had? It had been over a year since Alexei had visited the small Haida village on the opposite side of Prince of Wales Island. He'd had no idea any of this was going on. "Why do they want the village?"

The old man shrugged. "Do you think the new governor told us anything? If I had to guess, it's the cannery. I think they want to expand it and increase the number of fish they take out of the bays and streams every summer, but I do not know for certain."

Alexei looked around again, at the longhouses with their sturdy walls and elaborately carved beams, each one of which had taken over a year to build. Smoke still curled from the roofs, but fishing nets hung where they had been left to dry, and wooden racks that held salmon during salmon season didn't even hold a single fish.

He didn't like any of this. This was the very island Preston Caldwell had been trying to get his hands on last summer. The former governor, Milton Trent, had been only minutes away from signing an order leasing the island to the Alaska Commercial Company. Had the secretary of the interior and two senators not barged into that meeting, the Caldwells' company would have had full control of the island.

And now that Preston's brother, Simon, was the governor, they were trying once again to remove all natives from the island? Even though Secretary Gray had told them no? Had they found some way to bring the secretary of the interior on board with their plan?

And was it really to expand their fishing operations? Or was there something more going on?

"I don't think you should leave this easily," Alexei muttered.

The man paused his packing. "Do you think I want navy ships to come here and fire cannonballs into our village like they did in Angoon?"

Alexei winced. The bombardment of Angoon haunted the tribes of southeast Alaska. Several years ago, the navy had rained cannon fire on Angoon after a dispute in which a man had died and the government had refused to compensate the village. While no one had been killed, the village had burned, and the food stores the clan had saved for winter had been destroyed. The clan had survived, but barely, and only by relying on help from other Tlingit villages.

"Do you think I want to watch our homes burned and our food stores destroyed?" Tlákwsháa pulled the Chilkat blanket into his lap, smoothing a ripple in its fringe. "We will leave."

"But where will you go? Did you sign a treaty giving you land somewhere else?"

The elder stiffened, his hands tightening around the blanket. "Your government won't offer us a treaty. They say we have no right to the land. And even if they did offer, we wouldn't take it. The other elders and I have seen what your American treaties did to the tribes to our south. And if we were to sign a treaty, we would have to leave our home and go somewhere far away, never to return. Your government says we will be paid for our troubles, but maybe we will and maybe we won't."

Alexei couldn't argue. The Russians had maintained a good relationship with the tribes of Alaska, viewing them as equal trading partners and often intermarrying. But the US government had a far different Indian policy, and the tribes of Alaska were well aware of how the Americans had treated other tribes in the past. But unlike its treatment of the tribes from other regions in the United States, the government didn't even acknowledge that the native Alaskans had any right to the land. The government's official position was that since the United States had purchased the land from Russia, the Alaskan Indians had no claim to any of it.

"It's not my government," Alexei muttered.

Tlákwsháa's gaze held steady, his teeth working slowly on the hemlock gum. "Isn't it? You live here. You follow its laws, register your ships, submit yourself to its regulations. It is your government, and it is your country, but it is not mine."

Alexei's chest tightened. "Russia was my country."

Tlákwsháa finally set the folded blanket atop the cedar box and looked him full in the face. "Then maybe you should consider returning to Russia."

"I can't do that."

Tlákwsháa studied him for a long moment, his cloudy eyes once again seeming to see too much. "If it is your country, why not?"

Alexei opened his mouth, then closed it. How could he explain? He had been a boy when Russia sold Alaska. And his father, grandfather, and great-grandfather had lived in Alaska for nearly a century before that. He had no ties to Russia, not when his family had built a life here. Even if the government did not belong to him, the land did.

"Perhaps I don't consider myself American or Russian," he rasped. "Perhaps I consider myself Alaskan."

Tlákwsháa placed the folded blanket in another box. "One day, you will have to decide where you stand too, as an Alaskan. Now I need to pack."

The elder shifted on the mat, showing Alexei his back. It was just as well. There wasn't anything more he could say, and certainly not anything he could do.

He turned back to the small boat he'd sailed down from Sitka for the sole purpose of checking on Klawock. He'd send a letter to the secretary of the interior the moment he returned to Sitka.

The wind off the water pummeled his face as he retraced his steps to his boat. The ocean was awful choppy for sailing, but he didn't care. He'd sailed rougher seas, and he needed to get back to Sitka and start asking questions, because he fully intended to find out why the governor had given an order to clear this island. Then he would put a stop to it.

5

Sitka; One Day Later

She was a fool for coming.

Rosalind stared at the sound, the waves wild and gray, frothed with tips of white from the raging ocean. She couldn't see the ocean from where she sat on the log just inside the edge of the trees where she usually met Yuri. The mountains shielded the small cove in this part of the sound from any views of the open water, but the ocean would have to be roaring and angry to push such large waves into the sound.

In the summer, seals would often gather here, and she sometimes came early to watch them play. But there had been fewer and fewer seals of late. Her family's company, the Alaska Commercial Company, hunted them on islands far to the north of Sitka, and the number of seals they were allowed to legally harvest each summer was rather controversial. Many sailors felt as though too many seals were being hunted and were lobbying Washington, DC, to have the quotas reduced.

A gust of wind whipped down the mountain to her west,

driving rain into her face and causing her to shiver, even beneath her fur coat. The mountains surrounding her were covered with snow that started about a third of the way up, but other than the week of Christmas, when it had snowed three times, most of the winter had brought icy rain to the valleys and waterfront that quickly turned to snow at higher elevations.

She probably shouldn't have come. Not given the rain and wind. Not given the fact that there was no way for her to be remotely comfortable as she sat atop the damp wood.

Not given the fact that Yuri would not be coming to meet her, seeing how he was over a thousand miles away.

Fifteen hundred, to be exact.

Though she wasn't going to admit to looking it up.

And that just made her an even bigger fool for coming to a meeting place where she had nothing to think about other than the fact she was sitting in the rain missing someone she wasn't supposed to be missing.

She'd taken the sling off yesterday, a full week earlier than the doctor had instructed, and she wasn't going to think about how badly her wrist ached, nor was she going to put that dratted sling back on. She wanted to move about freely.

When she looked at how Millicent and Jane and Freya moved about town, the liberties her father allowed her seemed ridiculously small.

But if she wanted even that much freedom, she couldn't bear any proof of his outbursts. She'd learned that after her mother died, when her father had suffered his first fit of violence toward her.

A bruised cheek, a sprained wrist, a turned ankle, or anything else another person might notice would confine her to the house for weeks at a time, and sometimes even to her room, if her father thought the servants might gossip.

So yesterday she'd taken off her sling, simply to prove to her father that she could visit Millicent today.

And she had. It had been a pleasant visit, filled with the goings-on about town. People were still talking about the Amos-Wetherby wedding, and apparently Mikhail Amos had been seen traipsing up Castle Hill holding his new wife's hand. Not allowing his wife to grip his forearm as he escorted her up the hill like a gentleman, mind you. And not even with one palm clasped firmly in the other. No, their fingers had been laced together in public, no less. Mrs. Traverton had seen it herself and was scandalized.

Millie had claimed Mikhail Amos's actions were improper, but something about the way he'd held Bryony's hand in public made Rosalind's heart hurt.

She wanted to marry a man who would lace his fingers with hers and not care who saw it or what they said. Someone who would lean down and swipe a strand of hair away from her eyes when the wind was blowing. Someone who would look at her with tenderness and not mind waiting if it took her longer than expected to ready herself for church.

Something told her that the man her father would eventually marry her off to would do none of those things. He probably wouldn't even notice if she were alive. He'd have multiple houses, and he'd stuff her in one of them and then go about his business as usual—which would probably include visiting his mistress on a regular basis.

Or maybe he'd have more than one mistress.

Her father had never been like that, not while her mother was alive, but after she died . . .

Rosalind shifted on the wet log. She wasn't sure how to describe what had changed in her father after her mother's death. She only knew that he was no longer the man she'd grown up with as a girl.

Another gust of wind tore over the water, rattling the tree branches above her and sending a fresh spray of rain across her face.

She should leave. This was foolish. The damp was seeping into her bones, and she didn't want to spend another week confined to the house if she came home with a cough.

She wasn't even sure why she'd come in the first place.

The simple explanation was that she came on this little excursion every month when she visited Millicent. Millicent didn't know where she went or why, only that she left. It took a good thirty-five minutes to walk to this abandoned little cove, and another thirty-five minutes to walk back, and that gave her about fifteen minutes each month to exchange letters with Yuri.

If she suddenly stopped visiting Millicent while Yuri was out of town, someone might be able to piece together whom she was meeting, and she couldn't afford to have rumors about her and Yuri floating around.

She tried to tell herself that was the reason she was sitting there, getting wetter and wetter while the letters she typically exchanged with Yuri every month weighed heavily in her pocket. That everything about their monthly meetings was practical and transactional. That Yuri Amos was nothing more than a means to an end.

Come to San Francisco. She could still recall the sound of his voice, still feel the snowflakes landing on her cheeks and see the way the warm light from the warehouse window had almost illuminated Yuri's face, but not quite.

She'd wanted to say yes. For a fraction of a second, that had been all she could think about.

But then she remembered the letters and the money and how she couldn't possibly leave Sitka without also leaving the money her mother had left her. Leaving meant the charities that she donated to every month would suddenly stop receiving her donations, and some of them were quite generous.

Her mother's solicitor had left her a small inheritance in a separate investment trust until Rosalind turned eighteen. Her father had always dismissed it as trivial—a small lady's fund earning interest—so he'd never bothered to put his name on it. But unfortunately the account was at the same bank in Washington, DC, where her father, her uncle, and the Alaska Commercial Company held all their other accounts. They moved large amounts of money through the bank every year, and she had no doubt that if her father really wanted to get access to her money, he could.

The key was allowing him to believe the money in her trust was too trivial to matter.

Her solicitor reported to her directly, meaning that as long as she limited her correspondence with him so it wasn't frequent enough to be alarming, her father would leave her and her money alone.

She'd thought of trying to change banks and solicitors several times, but that would be hard to do without traveling back to Washington, DC, and she hadn't had an occasion to go —at least not one that wouldn't alarm her father.

Even if she did change banks, her father might still find a way to get his hands on her money. Her current solicitor, Mr. Holloway, had served her mother faithfully. He probably feared her father, but he didn't go out of his way to curry her father's favor. That made him more reliable than most men in Washington, DC—solicitors, bankers, and politicians alike.

But if she up and disappeared from Sitka? The first way her father would try to track her would be through her money. The bank Mr. Holloway worked for would likely force him to turn over all of her Finnancial information within hours. Even if her father couldn't put his name on her account—and she wouldn't put it past him to bribe the bank to do exactly that—he'd still be able to see what city and bank Mr. Holloway sent her money to, and she'd have little choice other than to ask her solicitor to send money.

What else would she use to pay for an apartment and food?

Having her father track her down would be so much worse than staying in Sitka, doing what she was already doing and dreaming that one day a man with kind brown eyes, a constant smile on his lips, and a thatch of hair that was always falling over his brow might—

A rustling sounded in the woods behind her.

Every muscle in her body went stiff.

It was a ridiculous reaction. An animal was probably making noise and—

"Rosalind?"

She turned to find Bryony moving through the woods, then stood.

What was her friend doing here? Her heart thudded against her ribs.

"Are you all right?" Bryony rushed forward, then clasped her in a hug, holding her tight against her chest, wayward strands of her red hair tangling in the fur of Rosalind's coat. "Yuri was so worried."

"Yuri?" Rosalind swallowed, trying to understand just what Bryony's presence here meant. "Did he tell you about our meeting? I told him not to say anything."

Bryony gripped her shoulders and pushed her back just far enough to look into her eyes. "I think he'd have been quite content to keep everything a secret if you had met him last week as planned. He was quite worried when you didn't come."

She pressed her eyes shut. Of course, he'd have been worried. He was too kind to shrug off a missed meeting. That was why she'd chosen him to send and receive letters for her in the first place.

That, and he was her father's enemy, meaning there would never be any occasion for Yuri to divulge to her father what she was doing with her inheritance.

"I wanted to meet him, but I hurt my wrist, and the doctor came to call when our meeting was set. I had no way to let him know."

Bryony stepped back. "You hurt your wrist? How?"

"Oh, it's nothing to fret over. It's almost better, see?" She pulled off her mitten and extended her left arm, twisting her wrist to show her friend. The trouble was, twisting it sent a fresh stab of pain through her arm, and she sucked in a breath.

Bryony's brows pinched as she looked at the wrist that was still a bit bruised and discolored. "It doesn't seem all that healed."

"It's healed enough to be out of a sling."

More questions filled Bryony's eyes, but she didn't voice them. Bryony had stayed with her for a few days after returning from the expedition where she'd met Mikhail last November. Her friend had pieced together just how quick her father was to use his fists when he was angry, but Rosalind wasn't going to admit anything, not aloud, at least.

Another gust of wind tore across the water, whipping a strand of Bryony's coppery-red hair across her face. She shoved it away, then met Rosalind's eyes. "Come back to the Amoses' with me."

"What?" Rosalind blinked. Where had that question come from? "I can't. Father will be furious."

"You can," Bryony insisted. "We'll have you on a ship away from here in a day or two, and you'll never have to face your father again. You can go somewhere and disappear and—"

"Did Yuri put you up to this? It will never work." She was already shaking her head. "He'll be able to track me."

"Not if we're careful."

Again, she shook her head. She wanted to leave, yes, but she couldn't abandon her inheritance and leave the charities she supported with nothing. If she was going to leave, she needed to find a way to do so while still protecting her money, and at the moment, that seemed utterly impossible.

"Did Yuri explain what usually happens?" Rosalind pulled the letters from her pocket. "I need you to mail these for me. Hopefully it won't look suspicious when you go to the post office, since the return address shows Yuri's name."

"I doubt it." Bryony took the letters and fanned them out, briefly studying the addresses before stacking them up and sliding them into her satchel. "Yuri says you give him letters that get mailed to the same places every month. Whoever sees them probably assumes he left them to be mailed in his absence, and that I'm doing it as his sister-in-law."

"Yes, you're right, of course." She blew out a breath, trying to calm the racing in her heart. "That doesn't seem very suspicious now that I think about it."

Bryony pulled another stack of letters out of her satchel and extended them. "Yuri said these are for you."

"Thank you." She took them, then stilled. One of them was open.

In the three years they'd been doing this, Yuri had never once opened one of her letters. That had been part of the original agreement when she'd first gone to him for help. What had caused him to—

"It was me," Bryony blurted.

"What?" Rosalind jerked her gaze back up.

"I opened it on accident. It was in a big stack of letters that I was going through, and I'm afraid I opened it and started reading before I realized it was addressed to Yuri. But even though the envelope was addressed to Yuri, the letter itself was addressed to you. You can see why I had questions."

Coldness swept through her. "Does anyone other than you and Yuri know about the letters?"

Bryony nodded. "The whole family knows."

"The whole family?" She could hear the panic creeping into her voice, and she didn't know how to stop it.

"Please don't be upset." Bryony reached out and settled a hand on her arm. "They're just donation letters. Sending money to these charities is nothing to be ashamed of."

She didn't answer. Instead, she shoved the letters into her pocket and backed away. "No one except for Yuri is supposed to know."

But if the rest of the Amoses had been told about the letters, how many people now knew? Twelve? Thirteen? Maybe even fourteen?

"Rosalind? It's all right." Bryony took another step forward. "None of us are going to tell your father."

"No, it's not all right." Nothing about the situation was even close to right.

"Rosalind, please. Let's sit back down on the log. We need to figure out how to get you away from your father. I know he was the one who hurt your wrist. You won't be able to convince me otherwise."

She just shook her head again, then took another step back. "No. No, I don't want to sit and talk to you. I don't want to do any of this."

Then she turned and ran.

6

An Hour Later

Alexei shoved open the door to Governor Simon Caldwell's office without waiting to be announced. He didn't care that it was almost time for the governor to leave for the evening, nor did he care that one of the governor's clerks rushed after him, telling him he couldn't enter. He didn't even care that his boots left muddy tracks on the rug due to the rain.

He'd arrived in Sitka less than an hour ago, and as far as he was concerned, he'd already waited too long to start demanding answers.

"You ordered the entire village of Klawock to leave Prince of Wales Island?"

"Alexei." The governor looked up from where he sat behind his massive desk working through a stack of papers, then placed his pen carefully into its inkwell. "How nice to see you. I was just about to send a messenger to your office to arrange a meeting, and yet here you are."

"Here I am," he growled. "Explain yourself."

"I'd love to." The governor picked up a sheet of paper that had been lying on the corner of his desk and held it out for him. "You are hereby barred from visiting the villages of Klawock, Kasaan, Ketchikan, Wrangell, Petersburg, Unalaska, Barrow, or anywhere else."

"What?" Alexei strode forward, once again not caring that his boots left scuffs of mud on the rug. A quick glance at the paper told him it said something about either halting contact with tribes or registering as an Indian agent or both. "You can't stop me from trading with villages I've been working with my entire life."

"But I can." Simon folded his hands over the polished desk, his thin lips pressing into something that wasn't quite a smile. "You see, the Department of the Interior is paying quite close attention to the tribes in Alaska. They're under the rather mistaken assumption that they have some sort of claim to Alaska, and the government wants that corrected."

Alexei tossed the paper back on the desk. "They were living and working here long before you arrived."

"We paid Russia for every inch of this land."

"Yes, and the Tlingit, Yupik, Inupiat, Aleut, Athabaskans, Haida, and any other tribe will tell you the land was never Russia's to sell."

A flicker of something he couldn't quite read passed over the governor's features—there and gone in less than a second. Then the man reached for the heavy brass letter opener on his desk. He turned it absently in his fingers, studying the dull gleam of metal. "Perhaps you're right, but the Indians won't claim the land is theirs either. They don't view land as something that can be owned, only used. What a shame for them."

It was a shame. Over the past century, that difference in mentality had caused far too many tribes to be taken advantage of, not just in Alaska, but everywhere.

"Since the Department of the Interior wants the Alaskan tribes to be consolidated into already-established towns, they've decided to limit outside contact with the tribes." The governor set down the letter opener with a thunk. "They don't want any negative influence on the tribes, you see. Don't want them communicating with anyone who might try to persuade them that they have a claim to the land—or tell them not to leave a village they're being ordered to leave."

Alexei picked up the piece of paper again and looked at it a little closer. "It sounds like you're saying I need to become an Indian agent in order to have contact with the tribes. What form do I need to fill out for that?"

The governor chuckled, then reached for another a short stack of papers. "You can apply, but you'll never be accepted. Your views of the natives are too . . . ah, compassionate."

The form was three pages long and filled with questions. Alexei's eyes landed on a question halfway down the first page. *What's your view of using government boarding schools to assimilate the next generation of Indian children into American culture?*

He crumpled the paper in his hand.

The governor chuckled again, then leaned back in his chair. "That's what I thought. The policy goes into effect at the beginning of February."

"The beginning of February? That's less than a month."

Governor Caldwell shrugged, brushing an invisible speck of dust from his sleeve. "Best say your good-byes then."

"And if I don't follow this order?" There was no way the government could enforce such an absurd restriction, not considering the vast, remote landscape of Alaska. He'd likely be able to visit all of the villages on that list without anyone from the government ever finding out.

"You can test me if you want, but I don't advise it." The

governor reached for his pen and dipped it into the inkwell. "The people who do usually lose."

Alexei's jaw tightened. He turned and strode toward the door. His hand was already on the knob, ready to wrench the door open, when the governor called him back.

"Oh, and Alexei, one more thing."

Alexei turned to find the governor holding out another stack of papers.

He walked back to the desk and swiped them out of the man's hand. "What are these? More forms for me to fill out?"

"No. It's the cancellation of three ship building commissions." The governor tapped a finger against the top page. "I've found a shipyard down in San Francisco that can do the work instead."

Alexei's fingers clenched around the stack as he scanned the official, neatly inked lines. "You're canceling . . ."

His throat tightened as his gaze trailed over the top page that referenced three different contracts with different ship names and specifications. The Amos Family Shipyard had been scheduled to build all three of the government vessels at various points over the next two years.

Not anymore.

Part of him wanted to ask why, but he already knew the answer.

Just like he knew fighting would be useless.

$$7$$

San Francisco; One Day Later

Yuri didn't have three signed shipping contracts.

He had eleven.

He'd been in San Francisco only four days, but he'd learned almost immediately that the docks were marvelously fun. They were always busy, with ships arriving and leaving at all hours. The warehouses employed people who worked through the night, illuminated by electric lights on the docks and a mixture of gas and electric lighting inside the various warehouses.

It turned out all a man had to do was stop and spend an hour or so talking to one of the smaller vendors or warehouse owners, and he could come away with a shipping contract that was good for two or three years.

He was starting to see why Alexei wanted that metal barge so badly. He wasn't sure he could offer another vendor a shipping contract unless they actually had an additional ship they could use to fulfill it.

Good thing his brother had all but purchased the barge already.

Things had been going so well at the docks that when Yuri finally made his way across the city to the Farnsworth Shipyard that afternoon, he half expected to find a gleaming vessel just waiting for a bit of polish.

Instead, he found himself staring at a sinking bucket of rust that would need an unimaginable amount of work.

The Farnsworth Shipyard itself was something of beauty. A massive dry dock dominated the yard's center, where a brand-new iron-hulled vessel rose from the scaffolding. Cranes and hoists loomed over it, their long arms swinging materials into place, and a small army of workers swarmed the ship, some hammering rivets, others welding seams, and others securing steel plates to the ship's frame.

He didn't need to have a degree in naval architecture to know the ship was a marvel of engineering. Smooth steel plating stretched along its hull, catching the afternoon sun.

The vessel had money behind it. A lot of money.

He now understood why Alexei had been so impressed with Harold Farnsworth and his shipyard. Of course, it didn't hurt that the man had a lovely daughter Alexei had been writing to for the past six months. Alexei claimed they were just friends, but if the two of them were to marry, it would give Alexei access to a new world of innovation in the area of naval architecture.

What a pity the ship Farnsworth was trying to sell them wasn't worth two pennies.

The *Emberfall* sat in a neglected corner of the yard, a rusting heap that no one seemed in a hurry to fix. Its hull was streaked with corrosion and rust, proving that the vessel had been neglected in disrepair long before its shipwreck.

A gaping hole in the stern bore evidence of a brutal collision, and the metal plating was warped and buckled where something massive had struck it. The deck above the hole sagged too, and a thin layer of stagnant water pooled in the lowest parts of the hull.

Yuri exhaled slowly. Just what was he supposed to tell Alexei? He understood why his brother wanted an iron- or steel-hulled vessel. The shipping industry was moving away from smaller wooden ships like the ones their family built and toward large barges and freighters that could transport four times the cargo.

But they couldn't purchase the *Emberfall*. No bank would lend them money for such a mess, and fixing it would probably cost more than their trading company and shipyard made in a year.

A man in a tailored suit and polished shoes approached. Yuri didn't need anyone to tell him this was Harold Farnsworth. The man looked far too clean and professional to spend much time in the loud, dusty shipyard.

"Mr. Amos." Farnsworth extended a hand. "I trust your journey to San Francisco went well?"

Yuri gave his hand a swift shake. "It did."

"I told my manager to get me when you arrived. I'm sorry he didn't. I wanted to show you the *Emberfall* myself." Farnsworth gestured toward the barge, a smooth smile fixed on his face. "What do you think of her?"

"Looks like she needs a good bit of work, but I have to say, I'm rather impressed by your shipyard. I see why Alexei speaks so highly of it." Yuri nodded toward the elegant new ship rising in the dry dock.

"Ah, thank you." The man gave him a smile that looked a bit more genuine and less polished. "She's a work in progress. We're always trying to improve things around here, but when I think back to where we started with only one dry dock and three workers thirty years ago, I have to say we've come a long way."

They certainly had. Yuri scanned the shipyard again. There was one thing he didn't understand, and it was probably best just to come straight out and ask it. "With all the resources and workers at your disposal, why not restore the *Emberfall* yourself?"

"We've switched to building only steel ships. It's a superior metal to iron, as I'm sure you know. We build two a year—each one made to order and spoken for before the first rivet is driven into the hull." Farnsworth gestured toward the workers swarming the pristine vessel. "The *Black Marlin* will be heading to Shanghai this spring."

That was a convenient excuse for trying to sell his family a leaky bucket of rust at an inflated price. "So what happened to the *Emberfall*, and how did you end up with her if you don't want anything to do with iron vessels?"

"She was a storm casualty, and the owner owed me a bit of money. I said I would take the ship as compensation and had it towed back here before deciding there was too much damage for me to repair it myself. I need it to be gone as soon as possible. We should already be laying the keel and starting on the frame for our next ship, which we usually do right here, where the *Emberfall* is sitting. I know she's a bit old, but most of the iron is solid. I'd say she's got another decade or so in her. And for a man like your brother who's looking to expand his fleet, she could be a fine investment."

Farnsworth's "investment" idea would still cost his family thousands of dollars. And no matter how thoroughly they repaired the hole in the hull, the rust climbing the frame and joints would take the ship at some point. Yuri wasn't enough of an expert in iron-hulled ships to predict exactly when that might be, but claiming the ship would last a decade was overly optimistic.

It would cost Alexei less to build a sixth vessel in their fleet.

"The iron itself is still quite valuable." Farnsworth said, probably because he didn't know what to do with Yuri's silence. "And the structure can be reinforced. She just needs the right man willing to put in the work. I'm willing to strike a good deal to have it out of my hair."

Farnsworth flashed him another smooth smile.

Yuri made a small humming sound, his gaze drifting from the *Emberfall* to the *Black Marlin*. It wasn't that difficult for a shipyard that worked with steel to repair an iron vessel. All the tools would be the same, only the metal would be different.

"Mr. Farnsworth! Mr. Farnsworth!"

There was so much activity in the shipyard, it took Yuri a moment to spot the speaker, a short, slender man in a suit as ill-fitting as Farnsworth's was pristine. He waved a letter in the air.

"I just received word from the Hollisters." The man stopped beside Farnsworth, his chest heaving as though he'd just run a mile, though Yuri suspected he'd come from the office building inside the shipyard.

"And?" Farnsworth held out a hand for the letter.

"I don't know." The man, likely Farnsworth's personal clerk, handed it over. "I didn't read it."

Farnsworth tore the envelope open and scanned the contents, then crumpled it in his hand.

"I assume they refused your offer?" the clerk asked.

"They're fools." Farnsworth's lips pressed together in a flat line. "They've no reason to refuse it. It's a perfectly good offer."

The clerk winced. "Ah, for you, yes. But I'm sure they don't want to sell their shipyard for a pittance of what it's worth."

Farnsworth was trying to buy a shipyard? Yuri rubbed the back of his neck. Why? He already had a beautiful one.

"They should sell it for a pittance. With Dwayne Hollister dead, they'll lose the business." Farnsworth dragged a hand over his mustache, then nodded at Yuri. "Sorry to bore you with this, Amos. We've been trying to acquire a small shipyard now that the owner is dead. He had four daughters and no sons. No one there knows how to build ships."

"The foreman knows a great deal." Farnsworth's clerk pressed his spectacles higher onto his nose. "He did that repair work on the *Houston*, remember?"

"That's not the same as having an owner who understands shipbuilding."

"Perhaps, but they'd be foolish to sell so soon for the price you offered."

Farnsworth scowled, then shoved the crumpled letter back at his clerk. "Raise my next offer by three hundred dollars."

The clerk shook his head. "That will still be less than half of what the shipyard's worth."

"Yes, but it will be three hundred dollars more than I offered them last time."

"You should offer more. If they put the shipyard up for sale on the open market, they'll be able to get a much better price, and then you'd be competing against other offers."

"Hollister has been dead for five months, and they've yet to try to sell it. That leads me to believe there's a good chance they'll take one of my offers without looking at other options."

"Yes, sir." The clerk left, and Farnsworth turned back to Yuri.

"Sorry about that interruption, Amos. So where were we?"

Nowhere. They were absolutely nowhere. The last thing he was going to do was buy the *Emberfall*, but he had a rather sudden interest in finding this Hollister family and touring their shipyard.

8

Sitka; Two Days Later

Her father hadn't found out. Rosalind's heart had pounded when she returned home with the letters from Bryony burning in her pocket, but her father hadn't suspected a thing.

Rosalind knelt beside the small hearth in her room where the rug met the corner floorboard. She pried the floorboard up carefully, then slid her newest stack of four letters into the narrow cavity beneath. It wasn't much space, but she liked to keep her letters for at least a couple months before burning them in the fire, just in case she needed to reference one later.

She pressed the board back down and smoothed the rug over it, then rose to her feet and glanced around. The room was quiet, her writing desk was in order, and her bed was neatly made.

But she listened for a moment, just to make sure no one was lurking outside her door, then moved to the window seat that overlooked the small garden behind the house and picked up her copy of *Pride and Prejudice.*

Everything about the letters made her unbearably nervous. It was so very impossible to do anything without her father learning of it, and part of her was amazed she'd secretly managed to donate money beneath his nose for three years. Now that the Amos family knew what Yuri was doing for her, would her father find out?

She knew what would happen if he did. He'd find a way to strip from her the trust account her mother had left her, never mind that it was in her name. Her father was very good at getting what he wanted, and she had no doubt he was powerful enough to bribe the owner of the bank in Washington, DC, into putting his name on her account.

Then he'd transfer the money out.

And if he didn't do that exact thing, he'd think of something else.

If Yuri were here, he would probably tell her not to fear because God was with her and could make her strong, like that verse in Isaiah talked about. But she wasn't sure how to be strong when it came to her father, wasn't sure how to be anything other than fearful.

Sometimes she felt like Joseph from the Bible, cast into a pit and then sold into slavery for years and years. God eventually brought Joseph out of slavery and made him a powerful man. Was that what the verse in Isaiah meant? Would God one day deliver her from everything if she trusted him instead of being so afraid of her father?

A knock sounded at her bedroom door. She recognized it as Foster's, but she found her body tensing anyway, her fingers tightening around the novel she'd opened but hadn't yet started to read.

"Come in." She tried to appear calm as she turned to face the door.

The long-time servant poked his head inside the doorway. "Miss Rosalind, your father would like to see you in his study."

Sweat slickened her hands. "He would?"

"Yes, miss." Though the words were simple, there was something soft about how he said them.

Foster had been with her family for as long as she could remember, and though the man did her father's bidding without so much as a blink, he was still kind beneath his starched shirt and straight suit.

"I wouldn't worry overmuch," he added. "He's in a good mood."

She pressed her lips together. Hopefully he was right about her father's mood. And hopefully he would still be in a good mood after their conversation.

Still, the dull ache in her wrist increased into a sharper pain as she headed toward the door. Foster followed her down the stairs to the study with the heavy oak door at the end of the hall.

At one time she could have told Foster that she would be right down, then taken a few minutes to compose herself before going to see her father. But those days were so long ago, they seemed like another lifetime, and she didn't even try to buy a few extra minutes for herself.

Foster knocked for her, and her father's voice called out. "Enter."

Foster turned the knob, and she took a steadying breath, then lifted her chin and stepped inside.

The study was warm, the fire in the hearth casting flickering light across the dark-paneled walls lined with bookshelves. The scent of tobacco lingered, mixing with the faint aroma of brandy from the glass her father held as he stood near the window, one hand in his pocket, staring out over the town below.

Rosalind kept her back straight as she waited.

He didn't turn but rather kept his gaze riveted on something outside. "As I'm sure you're aware, our family name has taken a bit of disparaging since Thanksgiving."

She frowned. It had? How so? Her uncle was the governor, and the Alaska Commercial Company was running smoothly and making a profit—it always did with her father at the helm.

"I'm talking about the harassment lawsuits the Amos family filed." He turned to face her then, his eyes dark and sharp.

She swallowed. Was this what Foster had meant by saying her father was in a good mood? Surely the butler had misread him.

"People are starting to talk. Your uncle came down too hard with the forced searches of the Amoses' ships last fall, and now they're wary."

They had every right to be wary. Her uncle had made no secret of using his new position as governor to serve himself first and foremost. "I see."

"I don't think you do." Father took a slow sip from the glass. "That woman lawyer—Evelina Amos Redding—has just filed three more harassment cases against our family."

Were they really against their family? Or against the governor's office? The first two had been aimed at her uncle, one for ordering the Revenue Cutter Service to search all Amos ships entering Sitka and hold them as long as possible, forcing them to miss deadlines and lose profits. The other had been of a similar nature but was filed by a blacksmith whose business license her uncle had refused to renew after the blacksmith refused to renegotiate prices for his government jobs.

The entire town had been taken aback when the Amoses filed that first lawsuit against her uncle for searching their ships just before Thanksgiving, but Rosalind had thought it a clever move. It had forced him to scale back, at least in public.

She didn't know anything about these new lawsuits, though. "Is there something I can do to help?"

Her father walked to his desk. "Yes. Your uncle and I have decided we need to do something that will foster the towns-folk's goodwill."

She blinked. "You have?"

"We received word just last week that Andrew Carnegie has awarded a grant to establish a library in Sitka."

"A library?" The words left her before she could temper her tone. "That's wonderful."

"While your uncle and I certainly appreciate Carnegie's generosity, his grant alone is insufficient." He set down his brandy glass with a thunk. "We need additional funds to ensure the library meets the standards befitting a town of Sitka's stature. So we've decided to make a rather large donation ourselves."

"That sounds like an excellent idea."

"Then you understand why it's important you hold a position on the newly formed library committee."

"A library committee?" Once again, the words slipped out in a rush, her smile rising before she could stop it. "You want me to serve on a library committee?"

"This isn't fun and games, Rosalind." Her father pinched between his eyebrows and drew a slow breath through his nose. "The entire town will be watching, and I need someone on the board to demonstrate that our family is committed to Sitka's advancement and ensure our name is properly associated with the library's success."

"Yes, sir." The picture was becoming clearer now. She wasn't going to have a seat on the committee because she loved books or might be good at helping to organize and structure

Sitka's first library. She was going to serve on the committee to make sure her family looked good.

Still, she couldn't help but be excited. A library. Right here in Sitka. She only hoped this wasn't the type of project that would take years to complete, that the inhabitants of Sitka would be able to start lending books in short order.

"The first meeting is in two days. I expect you to attend."

"Of course." She could hardly wait. Not only would she get to pick out books for a library, but she'd also get time out of the house. She was tempted to ask how often the library committee was scheduled to meet—if they could meet every week, or even twice a week, rather than once a month.

After a building was procured and books were ordered, would the library expect committee members to catalog and shelve them? She could volunteer to do so. That might get her out of the house for days.

And then, once the library was open, maybe she could volunteer to serve as librarian. All in the name of being a good library committee member, of course. All for the sake of keeping the Caldwell family name in good standing with the townsfolk.

"I suggest you wipe that silly grin off your face." Her father scowled at her, then picked his brandy back up and took a sip. "This is a serious endeavor, and the first thing I need you to do is make sure the library is named after our family."

"Oh." She tried to hide her grimace. "I'm not sure I'll have complete say over the name. I assume everyone on the committee will have an equal vote."

His eyes flashed. "Then it's your job to convince them of the merits of naming the library after our family."

Were there merits to it? Would the Caldwell Public Library somehow be able to serve the community better than the Sikta Public Library or the Alaska Public Library?

"Don't hesitate to remind the other committee members that we're donating a large sum of money. See that it gets done, Rosalind. At the first meeting."

So that's how things were going to be. Her fingers curled around the fabric of her skirt. "Yes, Father."

He studied her a moment longer, then lifted one brow and angled his head ever so slightly toward the door. "That will be all."

She didn't need to be told twice. She headed toward the door with the careful, well-mannered steps her father expected to see. Only when she was out of sight did she let out a slow, shaking breath.

The library committee. She wanted to be excited, but nothing her father wanted from her was ever as simple as it seemed.

Just what would happen if she couldn't manage to get the new library named after her family?

9

Sitka; One Day Later

"Eleven shipping contracts?" Alexei leaned back in his chair, his hands steepled as he studied Yuri.

He hadn't expected his younger brother to return from San Francisco so soon. Yuri had been gone less than two weeks, and when he'd arrived earlier that afternoon on a ship that a different company owned, Alexei had worried the trip had gone poorly. But he'd let the rest of the family greet Yuri before pulling him aside and telling him they should speak in the office above the warehouse.

Sacha and Mikhail had decided to join them, so here they were, gathered in the large office space littered with desks and tables and bookshelves, with windows on two walls that overlooked both the sound and the shipyard.

But before Alexei could ask how the trip had gone, Yuri had reached into his satchel and pulled out a stack of papers, then proclaimed he hadn't gotten just the three shipping contracts he'd been sent to procure; he'd gotten eleven.

Eleven.

"What did you do?" Sacha slapped Yuri on the back. "Hold those poor merchants at gunpoint and force them to sign?"

Yuri shrugged Sacha's hand away. "Don't be ridiculous. All I did was talk to them."

"I go to San Francisco and talk to merchants at least three times a year, and I've never gotten eleven contracts." Alexei was always quite pleased with himself if he came away with two or three, and sometimes that took several weeks of work.

"Do you really, though?" Yuri cocked an eyebrow at him.

"Do I really what?"

"Talk to them? Ask about the children hiding behind their desks or compliment their wives when they stop by the office to share lunch with their husbands? Do you ask them where they're sourcing their goods? If they own the farms producing the wheat and barley and grapes you want to export for them?"

Alexei stiffened. "I don't see what that has to do with anything."

Mikhail barked out a laugh. "Looks like it has more to do with things than you think. Because this contract here is completely legitimate, and it's good for three years." Mikhail set the contract he'd been reading down on the desk.

"Well done, little brother." Sacha slapped Yuri on the back again. "Maybe next time, you and Alexei should go to San Francisco together, and you can teach him a thing or two about charming businessmen into signing shipping contracts."

"I don't need any training." Alexei drummed his fingers on his desk. "I've been procuring shipping contracts for our family for over a decade."

"Yes, but have you ever procured eleven?" Sacha sent him a wicked grin. "On a single trip?"

How many times was Sacha going to mention those dratted

contracts? Alexei leaned forward, grabbed the stack of contracts off his desk, and flipped through them.

Just as Mikhail said, they seemed to be legitimate.

"I suppose sometimes it pays to be a little less businesslike and a little more friendly." Yuri looked straight at him, that boyish grin he'd never quite outgrown plastered across his face. "You should try it sometime, Alexei. Just like you should try smiling every now and then too. 'A merry heart doeth good like a medicine.'"

"Sure. I'll start working on that—as soon as I find a way to carry all the extra cargo we're now legally obligated to ship for the next two to three years." He'd been tallying the numbers as he flipped through the contracts. It was a lot of cargo, an awful lot. "Please tell me the *Emberfall* will be seaworthy in another month, or two at the latest."

"Ah, about the *Emberfall*." Yuri rubbed the back of his neck, the tips of his ears turning pink.

He'd known something seemed too good to be true. "Why do you sound like you're about to tell us something we don't want to hear?"

Sacha smirked. "Probably because he is. Go on, Yuri. Out with it." He made a rolling motion with his hand.

Yuri cleared his throat and shifted, suddenly rather preoccupied with the tips of his shoes. "Well . . . the *Emberfall* was . . . uh . . . not exactly what I was expecting."

Alexei pressed two fingers to his temple. "Define *not exactly* what you were expecting."

Yuri let out a long breath, then plopped himself down in one of the chairs across from the desk. "It was old, Alexei. Really old. I'm guessing maybe from the 1840s, and it was already a rusting pile of scrap metal. Even if it hadn't been caught in a storm, it would have had holes rusted through the hull by the end of the year. But it hit a rock, and now a gaping hole takes up half the stern. I might not be a naval architect, but given how the deck was sagging above the hole, I'm pretty sure the collision damaged the internal structure. And that doesn't account for any damage that might have happened to the boiler system."

Alexei leaned forward, a headache starting to form. "You're telling me we *don't* have a sixth ship for our fleet?"

"I'm telling you that it would take months to repair the *Emberfall*, and we'd have to pay for it completely on our own. No bank would Finnance such a dilapidated ship. And even if we somehow scrounged up enough money for repairs, the ship will last only for another year or two. Farnsworth claims it will still be on the sea a decade from now, but it won't. So I made a different investment."

Sacha chuckled, a great, hearty sound that seemed entirely too jovial for the increased pounding in Alexei's head. "Now this I have to hear."

Alexei ignored the throbbing in his head and glared at Yuri. "What. Did. You. Do?"

Yuri grinned. "I bought our family a second shipyard."

"What?" Something wasn't making sense. Yuri hadn't just said what he thought . . . had he?

Sacha slapped his hands onto the desk. "Oh, that's grand. Real grand. You went down to San Francisco to get three shipping contracts and a barge, and instead you come back with eleven contracts and an entire shipyard?"

Yuri stiffened. "Don't make it sound like I'm an idiot. I got the shipyard for less than what Farnsworth was asking for the *Emberfall*."

Alexei sucked in a breath through his nose. Calm. He needed to stay calm. "You *bought* a shipyard?"

"Well, I haven't *bought* it yet. Technically, I just made the offer." Yuri adjusted the cuff of his sleeve, as though this was all perfectly reasonable. "But the owner's in a bind. It's a small operation, nothing like the Farnsworth Shipyard, but the Hollister family is struggling. Their father died five months ago, and no one in their family knows enough about shipbuilding to keep it running. They were relying on the foreman, but Harold Farnsworth made him an offer he couldn't refuse, and he was set to leave at the end of the week. We're getting an excellent deal on the shipyard, I promise, but we're not stealing it out from under that poor family. The Hollisters will have enough money to live on from the sale, and the best part is, there's already a ship in the dry dock that the Hollisters owned. It was damaged and undergoing repairs when Mr. Hollister died, and it's been sitting there unfinished ever since."

Alexei dragged a hand over his face. "This ship is part of the sale?"

"Yes. And it can probably be repaired in about a month. Then we can use it to fill our extra contracts."

He had no words. Absolutely no words.

Just how much of a disaster was this shipyard? If it was cheap to buy, then it was probably in the same condition as the *Emberfall,* meaning it might cost thousands of dollars before they could even begin building ships down there. And how easy would it be to get commissions in a new town where nobody knew him?

"Are you angry?" Yuri asked. "Please don't be angry. You *did* send me to San Francisco to get more shipping contracts and find another ship, remember?"

"I told you to buy the *Emberfall.* Not an entire shipyard."

"But the *Emberfall* was a wreck. And besides, even though the Hollisters' shipyard is small, San Francisco has access to iron and steel that we don't have here in Sitka. It's possible we could one day expand. And honestly, there's a huge opportunity for a shipyard down there that specializes in wooden ships anyway."

"What do you mean?" Mikhail asked.

"I mean corporations are moving to these giant metal barges, but smaller businesses still have wooden ships. Yet fewer and fewer places want to repair them, or even know how to. Farnsworth certainly isn't interested. He wanted to convert the Hollisters' shipyard so it could build at least one, if not two, steel ships every year."

"Wait. This is the second time you've mentioned Farnsworth in conjunction with the Hollisters' shipyard." Alexei scrubbed a hand over his face. "Please don't tell me he was trying to buy it."

"Oh, ah . . . about that." Yuri scratched behind his ear, then released a torrent of words that included how he'd become aware that the shipyard existed and how he'd felt uncomfortable even listening to Farnsworth's plans. He then went on to express his dislike of Farnsworth, and he used no shortage of words for that either.

Alexei pinched the bridge of his nose. "I'm contemplating marrying Farnsworth's daughter. Did you have to give him a reason to hate me?"

"You are?" Yuri grinned. "You said Laurel was just a friend."

"She was. Six months ago when we started exchanging letters."

"And now she's more?" Sacha asked, a teasing glint in his eyes.

"Maybe." He sighed, thinking of Laurel with her clear green eyes and a pleasant smile and a knack for baking delicious desserts. "I enjoy writing her, at least. Did you give her the letter I sent along with you?"

Yuri nodded. "The Farnsworths invited me to dinner to

discuss the price of the *Emberfall*. I made sure to give the letter to Laurel before I told Farnsworth we wouldn't be buying his ship."

"How thoughtful." He tapped his fingers on the desk. "What did Farnsworth say when you told him you made an offer to purchase the Hollisters' shipyard?"

Yuri shifted. "I didn't exactly volunteer that information, and Farnsworth didn't ask."

"No. I daresay he didn't." Because the last thing the shrewd businessman would have expected was for happy-go-lucky Yuri to buy a shipyard out from under him.

"Laurel seems nice, though," Yuri added. "Too nice for that household, really. It's like she doesn't fit."

Those had been his exact thoughts when he'd visited San Francisco last summer and decided to start writing her.

"I approve of the marriage." Yuri sent him a wink.

Alexei just shook his head. "I haven't proposed yet—and I might not ever be able to, considering what you just did."

Yuri only grinned again. "A smart businessman will respect everything I just did. If Farnsworth doesn't, then maybe you're better off not marrying into the family."

"Maybe." Alexei narrowed his eyes at his younger brother. He wasn't sure whether to thank him or strangle him. Maybe both. "You really should have spoken to me before making an offer on that shipyard."

"If I had sent a telegram asking if I could buy a shipyard and then waited in San Francisco for your response, would you have let me do it?"

"Absolutely not."

"Exactly." Yuri crossed his arms over his chest, looking far too pleased with himself. "That's why I didn't ask."

"How lovely." Alexei stood. "Now if you'll excuse me, I need to pack."

Mikhail laughed. "Planning to head to San Francisco, are you?"

"Hopefully on the ship Yuri came in on. I'm not going to sign a banknote to purchase a shipyard I haven't seen with my own eyes." And he should probably talk to Farnsworth and try to smooth things over so he could still write to Laurel.

"Do you want me to come with you?" Sacha stood.

Alexei eyed his brother. "Do you really want to leave Maggie with her expecting?"

"No, but this won't be a long trip, will it? And I'm the one who knows how to build and repair wooden ships."

Alexei bristled. "I'm a naval architect. I know how to build ships."

Sacha slung an arm around his shoulder. "And when was the last time you picked up a hammer and drove a wooden peg into the hull of a ship?"

"Fine. Come with me, then." Alexei shrugged him off, then jabbed a finger at Yuri. "I'm in the middle of doing our semiannual audit, making sure the shipping manifests match our warehouse inventory and sales revenue. You should be able to finish it by the time I return."

Yuri let out a groan.

"You'll also need to answer as much correspondence as possible while I'm gone," Alexei continued.

"Perfect. Just what I dreamed of doing after conquering San Francisco. Battling ledgers instead of merchants."

Alexei sent him a dark look. "I cannot afford to get behind. And if, by some miracle, we do end up purchasing this second shipyard, I'll expect you to be the one who moves to San Francisco to run it."

"Me?" Yuri's eyes widened.

"Who else do you think wants the job?"

"But I—"

"Do you want me to go to the library meeting for you?" Mikhail asked. "The first one is tomorrow night."

"Library meeting?" Yuri's brows furrowed. "Since when does Sitka have a library?"

The library. Alexei had forgotten. *Drat.* "Since Andrew Carnegie decided to donate money for us to start one. Several businesses have also made donations, including ours. I've been named the president of the library committee, but you can fill that role for me, too, while I'm gone."

"Me? Mikhail just offered." Yuri shoved a hand at Mikhail.

"Yes, but this will be good for you. Think of it as training for when you're running the new shipyard."

"But . . ." Yuri opened his mouth, likely about to protest, but the outside door to the office banged open, and a trio of light footsteps rushed up the stairs.

"Yuri!" Freya Eriksson was the first to reach the top of the steps, followed by Jane Henshaw and Millicent Duret.

"They told me you were back, but I didn't believe it." Freya rushed toward him, whisps of golden hair flying from her bun. "Rosalind said you'd be gone for several weeks."

"The most marvelous thing has happened." Jane practically skipped across the room toward Yuri, a wide smile plastered across her face. "The town is going to have a library!"

"Yes, Alexei was just telling me about it." Yuri sent Alexei a glare over the top of Jane's head.

"Mr. Carnegie himself donated some of the money." Millicent came to a stop beside Yuri.

"So I've heard," Yuri muttered.

"And the Caldwells also made a large donation!" Freya clasped her hands together and tucked them beneath her chin. "Isn't it wonderful?"

"It certainly sounds wonderful." Yuri sent Freya a wink.

"Sitka has needed a library for years. Alexei was just telling me that I'm to have a spot on the committee."

"You are?" Millicent beamed. "That's so wonderful. Rosalind is going to be on the committee too."

Yuri stilled. "She is?"

"Yes," Millicent nodded. "Her father got her the position, but it's perfect for her. You know how much she likes to read."

"I'm glad to hear she'll like the job."

"Where do you think the library will be built?" Freya asked.

"Do you think it will be big?" This from Jane, who had sidled between Millicent and Yuri.

"I hope it has large windows to let in the light for people who want to sit there and read," Millicent said.

Alexei shook his head. The library committee position had gone from something Yuri despised to something he seemed genuinely happy about, and all because he'd seen how excited his friends were about the idea.

"You all right?" Sacha's meaty hand landed on his shoulder. "I thought you wanted to see about leaving on the ship that just came in."

"I do." Alexei exhaled slowly, dragging a hand over his face. "I just—" He shook his head, watching as Yuri leaned in to catch every word the women said.

Alexei didn't understand it. He never had. But somehow Yuri could navigate a room full of people with effortless charm and make himself useful in ways that had nothing to do with ciphering numbers on a ledger or drawing blueprints.

Or rather, he was useful when he wasn't burning bridges with a shipbuilder as significant as Harold Farnsworth and getting them tangled up purchasing a shipyard that might be more trouble than it was worth.

10

Rosalind hurried down the east staircase, careful not to trip on the hem of her skirt as she rounded the landing. She was never late, but here she was, running almost five minutes behind because she'd ordered her lady's maid to take extra care with her hair. She couldn't arrive at the first library committee meeting looking like a girl without a single idea in her head. She needed to present herself as a polished professional woman. One who had ideas worth listening to. Otherwise she'd never get the committee to agree to set up a temporary library while they made arrangements for a more permanent one—and she'd never be able to get them to agree to name the library after her family either.

Oh, she hoped that last part wouldn't be too hard. Her father would be furious if the library ended up named after a different patron.

She reached the lower hall, then straightened herself into a more dignified posture and slowed her steps lest she get in trouble for racing past her father's office.

The smell of pipe smoke drifted from beneath the heavy

wooden door. She was about to knock and then poke her head inside, just to let him know she was leaving, but the sound of her uncle speaking caused her to pause.

". . . I told the customs office those contracts were already spoken for," he was saying. "By the time the Amoses get wind of it, they'll have nothing left to bid on. And that's after I canceled three of the ship commission contracts earlier this week that the previous governor had given them."

Rosalind's hand dropped. The Amoses? Why were her father and uncle discussing them? Her family had already done enough to make the Amoses' lives miserable.

Her father spoke next, and she leaned closer to the door so as not to miss anything. "Just how much money do you think the loss of those ship commissions will cost the Amoses?"

"Ten thousand a year for each of them, I'd think. So they've already lost three that would have been in their revenue predictions, then an additional three that I'm not even letting them know about until we have another bid accepted. That leaves us with sixty thousand total in lost revenue, maybe more."

Her father let out a deep chuckle. "That's a nice, large figure. It might not be enough to bankrupt them just yet. But it's a start."

Rosalind fisted her hands at her side. She was so tired of this. Why was her father always looking for a way to harass the Amoses? They were the kindest, most upstanding family in all of Sitka.

Or at least, that was how it seemed from her perspective. She didn't know them very well. Being friends was impossible considering how much her father hated them. But she knew enough to tell that they were much different from her father. That was part of why she'd gone to Yuri and asked for help with her letters.

"Your favorite Marshal paid me a visit today." Uncle Simon's voice filtered through the door again.

A quiet clink followed, the sound of glass against glass, likely her father pouring himself brandy from the decanter. "Don't tell me Hibbs wants more money."

Her breath froze in her lungs. Were they talking about what she thought? Bribing the Marshal?

"You guessed that rather easily." Dryness crept into her uncle's tone.

"He always wants more money." A soft thunk sounded. If she had to guess, her father had just set his snifter on the desk.

"He had a rather long list of why we should pay him more."

"How much is he asking this time?"

"An extra hundred a month."

Rosalind's stomach tightened. Yes, that's exactly what they were talking about, bribing the only lawman in Sitka and the one Marshal who was in charge of the entirety of Alaska. There was only one other lawman in Alaska, and that was Yuri's brother-in-law Jonas Redding. But he lived in Juneau, and he worked under Marshal Hibbs as a Deputy Marshal.

She'd heard rumors that Marshal Hibbs was on her father's payroll, but no one could ever prove anything. People just assumed the Marshal was being paid off when charges against her father got dropped after a few months of an investigation that stalled.

Two summers ago, her father had been investigated for falsifying the navigational charts that the ship captains used. The incorrect charts had led to numerous ships running aground or hitting rocks in the islands of Southeast Alaska. The Marshal had dropped all charges against her father last year and instead charged some clerk with the Revenue Cutter Service for making the mistake.

Before that, it looked as though her father might have paid

men to kidnap the youngest Amos boy, Ilya, who had been around ten, but that time Marshal Hibbs hadn't even tried to charge her father. He'd pressed charges against the men who did the actual kidnapping and nothing more.

"That old fool just keeps getting pricier and pricier." Her father's voice took on a sharp edge. "Pay him for now, but maybe it's time we start thinking about a less expensive way to protect ourselves from the law."

"Those were my thoughts exactly," her uncle drolled.

Rosalind swallowed. She didn't want to think about what that meant. In fact, she didn't want to think about what any of this meant. More suffering for the Amoses, more money to a crooked snake who had no business being a lawman, and likely more power for her father and uncle.

She was so tired of all of this. Would the list of crimes never stop?

How could it when the law refused to investigate her father?

But what if there was a way to force the law to investigate her father? What if she found some kind of evidence that would see her father put in prison for good? Something that not even Marshal Hibbs could ignore?

Or better yet, something that incriminated both her father and Marshal Hibbs, and maybe even her uncle.

Her father kept track of every penny spent, both for the Alaska Commercial Company and for their personal family Finnances. If he kept meticulous records of those things, then he would also keep a record of the bribe money he paid to Marshal Hibbs—and anyone else he had a need to bribe.

What if she found that ledger? What if she not just found it but gave it to Yuri to give to his brother-in-law, the Deputy Marshal? That would be enough to get her father and uncle and the Marshal arrested, put on trial, and sent to prison.

And after that . . .

Her throat thickened. She tried to imagine what Sitka might be like without her father lurking in the shadows, trying to manipulate every last shipping regulation or law to his benefit. She tried to imagine how life might feel for the Amoses once they didn't need to worry about her father trying to ruin them.

She tried to imagine what her own life would be like without her father looking over her shoulder.

She could move her money freely, giving however much money she pleased to whatever charities she wished without needing to be sneaky about it. She could leave Sitka and go somewhere she wasn't constantly reminded of her father's presence. She could maybe even look for a husband who would love and care about her the way Mikhail Amos loved Bryony, rather than find herself trapped in a marriage to whatever business associate her father thought most advantageous.

Her father and uncle were still talking behind the heavy wooden door, but she didn't hear a word of it. She was too busy thinking about what life would look like once her father and uncle were in prison.

But first she had to find proof of her father bribing the Marshal. Her father wouldn't store a ledger like that somewhere it could easily be found. Could she do it? What if her father caught her snooping?

Fear thou not; for I am with thee: be not dismayed; for I am thy God: I will strengthen thee; yea, I will help thee; yea, I will uphold thee with the right hand of my righteousness.

The verse flashed through her head, and she straightened. Was this what the Bible was talking about? Maybe she needed to trust God to keep her safe while she searched her father's things. After all, she would be searching them for an honorable reason.

And it might take her a long time to find the evidence she

needed. But even if it took six months, if the evidence was good enough, she would eventually be free of her father—and the Amos family would be free right along with her.

Surely that was worth the risk of her father discovering what she was doing.

———

Rosalind could barely concentrate as she entered the old governor's mansion for the library committee meeting a quarter hour later. All she could think about was where she'd search first for evidence. The most obvious place to start was her father's study, but that would also be the hardest to search, because her father was always in there, and the servants would think it odd if they found her in the office without her father present.

She stumbled on the grand staircase that led to the second floor where the meeting room was located, then forced herself to take a deep breath and focus on the familiar building rather than the ideas in her head. The library committee meeting was being held in the same building that also housed the governor's office, the offices for the Revenue Cutter Service, the Alaskan branch of the Department of the Interior, the Marshal's office, and a number of other Alaskan agencies.

When Sitka had been part of Russian America, the governor alone had lived here, and it had come to be known as the governor's mansion. The rulers of Russian America had all been men of either noble or high-ranking military backgrounds, and only a mansion would do for such a figure.

The Americans, on the other hand, had turned the grand house into an administrative building that included a jail in the basement.

The strange mixture of elegance and efficiency had always

felt odd to Rosalind. The high-arched ceilings still bore intricate Russian moldings, their delicate patterns contrasting with the thin, serviceable drapes the Americans had hung over the windows.

In some places the ornate wooden trim in the hallways gleamed with polish, but in other places, it had been painted a dull utilitarian white, as though the Americans had sought to erase the Russian artistry in favor of something more practical.

When Rosalind entered the room where the meeting was being held, she found the same clash between architecture and furnishings. The room itself was regal, with a grand fireplace, large windows that overlooked the sound, soaring ceilings, and intricate trim that thankfully had not been painted.

The table, chairs, and rug were practical and efficient and devoid of embellishments.

Before heading toward the open chair at the closest end of the table, Rosalind smoothed her glove over her still sore wrist, making sure her sleeve was pulled all the way down and none of her skin was showing.

There were only four people seated at the table, one of which was Mrs. Henrietta Pembroke, whose husband owned Alaska Territorial Bank. Arthur Bixby, who owned the local Sitka newspaper, was also there, along with Angus McCreedy, who owned the largest logging operation and mill in Sitka.

When Rosalind's eyes landed on the man at the head of the table, her feet stilled.

Yuri Amos.

He was leaning back in his chair, arms crossed over his chest, listening to something Mr. McCreedy was saying about the price of lumber. His thick brown hair was slightly tousled, and his eyes were alive with interest as he listened.

Her stomach twisted. Why was he here?

His gaze flicked up to hers, just for a moment, and something soft passed across his face before he looked away.

Her father hadn't known who would be on the committee, that was true, but Yuri Amos?

She wasn't sure whether she wanted to stride across the room and hug him because he was back in Sitka or slap him for not keeping her letters secret.

She drew in a slow, steadying breath and forced her feet forward, then took her seat at the table.

Yuri spread his hands, a wide grin on his face. "I'm sure some of you are wondering what I'm doing here. I promise I'm not here to sabotage the library. Alexei was called out of town, so I'm his replacement. I suspect this is punishment for something, but I've yet to determine what, so I've decided the lot of us should have a grand time planning the library while he's gone. Should we get started?"

Everyone at the table smiled. Or rather, everyone except for her. She still wasn't sure whether she wanted to hug him or slap him, and she wasn't sure how she felt about him being on the board either. Alexei seemed like a much better fit.

Next Yuri launched into what her father had already explained: the library was to be built with a generous donation from Andrew Carnegie and supplemented by additional funding from several of Sitka's leading businessmen.

After that, Yuri went on to discuss the agenda, and Rosalind felt her shoulders relax as the meeting continued. Yuri had a way of talking that put everyone at ease.

About a half hour into the meeting, the topic of whether to use a new building or repurpose an empty one came up.

"I say we build new." Mr. McCreedy slapped the table with his palm. "I have plenty of lumber, and we can hire the Ashtons to erect the building. They do good work and they're fast."

"We should have enough money to purchase land." Mrs. Pembroke looked around the table. "But where do we build it?"

"Somewhere central, I'd imagine." Arthur Bixby, who'd been designated the secretary of the group, scratched his chin. "The closer it is to the heart of town, the more convenient it will be for people to access."

"The main road near the market would be a prime location," Mr. McCreedy suggested. "It would put the library right in the center of daily life."

"You mean right next to your lumber mill?" Mr. Bixby adjusted his glasses and leaned forward. "What about somewhere near the *Sitka Gazette* office? Literacy and news go hand in hand."

Mrs. Pembroke gave a small nod, her back and shoulders painfully straight. "That's a fine idea. It would also be closer to the bank if we put it there, and a library should be built where respectable clientele will frequent it."

"The bank? The newspaper office?" Mr. McCreedy crossed his thick arms over his chest. "The library is for fishermen and prospectors as much as it is for bureaucrats and business owners. If we can't build it next to my mill, I say we build near the harbor, where sailors and dockworkers and their families can make use of it."

"What about near the water, but not by the docks, which are noisy and busy?" The words were out of Rosalind's mouth before she had fully thought them through. But none of the locations that had been mentioned so far felt right. "It could be within walking distance of the sound, though, and maybe somewhere near the school. There are plenty of open plots of land overlooking the sound. If we build the library in such a place, we could design it with large windows so people can read while looking out over the water."

"Oh, well." Mrs. Pembroke blinked, a bit of the stiffness

leaving her shoulders. "That's a rather wonderful idea. The waterfront would make for a beautiful setting."

McCreedy grunted. "I suppose it could be done, but I still think we'd be better off putting it closer to the docks."

"I like the idea." Yuri leaned forward. "If the rest of you are in agreement, I'll reach out to the land office to inquire about available plots."

Murmurs of approval filled the room.

Rosalind drew a breath. She hadn't expected them to like her idea so much. "Since constructing a new building will take time, I'm also wondering if we could use one of the buildings in town now to set up a temporary library? I hate the thought of waiting until October or November for people to start using the library."

The newspaper owner put his pencil down and sat back in his chair. "That's another good idea. I say we do it."

"I like it too," Mrs. Pembroke said. "We'll need to make a budget to decide how much of our funding will be used for the new building itself, and how much for books, and then we can start ordering books for the temporary library."

"We also need to figure out if we will pay the library workers after this is set up." Rosalind shifted. "I mean, Mr. Carnegie's grant is a one-time gift, right? I know my father's is. Does that mean the library is going to be run by volunteers? Or is the town of Sitka able to contribute something for annual salaries? I don't mind volunteering at the library a couple days a week, but it won't work for me to be there every hour that the library's open."

Yuri was nodding. "Perhaps while we're in the temporary building, we can limit the lending hours to only a couple days a week, and we can ask for volunteers." Again, his voice was soft as he spoke, almost as though he had a special tone he used with her alone. "That will at least get people access to books early on. My family has a nearly empty building at the end of Lincoln Street. The second floor is being used for storage, but the first floor is open, and we might be able to move the goods on the second floor to the warehouse. I'll need to check to make sure, but if that's the case, we can use the entire building until the new library is built."

"I don't think there's need for all that. We can have a library built lickety-split." Mr. McCreedy snapped his fingers. "Got plenty of lumber, like I said."

Mrs. Pembroke humphed. "Yes, but no one else here is keen on the idea of putting our community's books into a lickety-split kind of building. If we're going to spend the money on a new building, then I expect it to be rather grand."

"Let's vote on it," Yuri said. "Does someone want to make a motion that we build a new building and set up a temporary library on Lincoln Street in the meantime?"

"I'll make the motion," Mrs. Pembroke said, her gaze still on Mr. McCreedy. "Provided it's not something thrown up in a rush that will have a caving roof after two years."

"I'll second the motion." Mr. Bixby scrawled something in his notes. "I like the idea of a proper building on the waterfront."

"Perfect. I vote yes." Yuri nodded toward the logger. "McCreedy? Yes or no?"

"Yes," he muttered, "though I still think we could put up a building for less—"

"That's not what we're voting on," Mrs. Pembroke cut in.

"Miss Caldwell?" Yuri moved his gaze to her.

Her tongue turned thick, but she forced out the word "Yes."

"Good. The motion passes with a unanimous vote. Now that those details are settled, we have one last thing to decide. What shall we name the library?"

Sweat slickened Rosalind's palms as she leaned forward,

and her tongue once again felt thick and cumbersome, but she forced the words out anyway. "I think the name should pay homage to the most generous of the benefactors supporting the library."

"So Carnagie Library, perhaps?" Mr. McCreedy suggested. "Or Carnegie Sitka Library?"

"I reckon Miss Caldwell is thinking more along the lines of Caldwell Community Library." Mr. Bixby fingered the curled tip of his mustache, his eyes narrowed her direction. "Am I right?"

All four sets of eyes landed on her, and she had to stop herself from squirming. "It makes more sense to honor members living in the community by naming the library after them than by naming it after a man living thousands of miles away that none of us have ever met."

"So you want the library named after your family?" Mrs. Pembroke released a brittle laugh. "My husband is making a donation to the library fund too. Why not name the library after us?"

"My family's making a donation as well," Yuri said, his head tilted to the side.

Rosalind dropped her gaze to the table.

"Well, that settles it," Mrs. Pembroke said. "Let's name it the Amos, Pembroke, Caldwell Community Library after all of us. In fact, do we have a list of everyone who's made donations so far?"

"Right here." Yuri slid the paper across the table.

"There are seven names." The older woman flashed a smug smile in Rosalind's direction. "Why not use all seven of them in the library name? The Amos, Pembroke, Sorenson, Caldwell, Ulbricht, McCreedy, Devereaux Community Library. Then it's fair to everyone."

"No one wants to list seven surnames before they get to the word *library*," Mr. Bixby drawled.

"Well, I don't want it named after the Caldwells." Mrs. Pembroke crossed her arms over her chest. "They already have enough things in this town named after them."

"Fine. We'll call it Pembroke Public Library," Mr. McCreedy snapped. "Happy?"

Mrs. Pembroke glared at Mr. McCreedy. "I didn't say it had to be named after us."

"But you did suggest it." Mr. Bixby made a few more notes on his paper.

"Why don't we take the week to think on it?" Yuri closed his notepad. "We have a meeting scheduled for next week already. I have the budget on the agenda for then, and hopefully we can vote on which parcel of land to purchase at that time too. Let's all take this next week to come up with our top three names, and we'll discuss them at the meeting as well."

It was a logical suggestion, but Rosalind couldn't ignore the feeling of heaviness that settled over her. She didn't know what the library would end up being called, but she wasn't going to be able to convince the committee to name it after her family.

The moment Yuri closed the meeting, she rose from the table and headed for the door, walking as quickly as she could without looking like she was rushing.

She was half afraid Yuri might call after her and try to strike up a conversation. In fact, there was a part of her that very much wanted to ask him why he'd told Bryony about her letters. But Father would want a report on the meeting as soon as she got home, and the last thing she wanted to do was talk to Yuri before she faced her father.

She skedaddled into the hallway, then headed down the stairs and made her way to the front door. Only then did she discover that it was pouring rain. The coach was currently waiting for her, but it was raining so hard, she'd be soaked through by the time she reached it. Father would be even more furious if she returned disheveled, and she'd left her umbrella in the meeting room beneath her chair.

At the very least, she needed to turn around and go back for it, and she should probably wait for the rain to subside a bit too.

She started back down the hallway, passing Mr. Bixby and Mr. McCreedy on the stairs. She expected to pass Mrs. Pembroke and Yuri at some point too, but she made it all the way back to the meeting room before she found them. They were still inside having a conversation.

Sure enough, her umbrella was where she'd left it beneath the chair. She pushed open the door a bit, intending to get the umbrella and retreat without interrupting anyone, but Mrs. Pembroke's clipped words stopped her.

"I don't want her on the board."

Yuri shook his head, one hand resting casually on the back of a chair. "You don't get to choose who your fellow board members are, Henrietta."

"The only reason she's here is because her father bought her position with that ridiculously large donation."

"And the same can't be said for you and your husband?" Yuri nodded at Mrs. Pembroke. "Aren't you here because of his donation?"

The woman stiffened further. "It wasn't as large as the Caldwells."

A rich chuckle filled the room. "No one else's ever is. That family has almost as much money as God. But Rosalind has good ideas. She was the one who suggested putting the library by the water and opening up a temporary location so we can start ordering books."

"She wants to name the library after herself."

"No. Her father wants the library named after him.

Rosalind will get married at some point, then change her name and move away, and nothing about the library will ever be attributed to her. Everyone who hears the name will think of her father or her uncle, maybe both."

The woman gave an indignant huff. "I meant it when I said I don't want it called Caldwell Memorial Library, or Caldwell Community Library, or Caldwell anything."

"Then come up with three good names for next week, and we'll put all the suggestions to a vote."

"Her ideas shouldn't even be included. They'll be exactly what I just listed—Caldwell, Caldwell, Caldwell."

"She deserves a voice as much as you or me or anyone else." There was something hard beneath Yuri's tone, but he kept a pleasant look on his face. "Now be careful on the walk home. It's raining rivers out there."

"My husband sent me with the carriage, but thank you." Mrs. Pembroke turned and strode toward the door, her steps crisp and her back ramrod straight.

Rosalind scampered a few feet down the hall, then ducked into a recessed doorway, pressed herself against the wall, and shut her eyes. Not that closing her eyelids could make her invisible, but it helped calm her breathing and cool the sweat dampening her palms.

Sure enough, the click of the older woman's boots headed down the hall in the opposite direction.

A creak sounded too.

That was odd. Old buildings had many noises, but the creak had seemed close. Perhaps—

"Rosalind?"

Her eyes flew open.

Yuri Amos stood a few feet away, wheeling the large chalkboard from their meeting room.

She unpeeled herself from the wall, then smoothed her

skirt. Not that making sure her skirt was presentable would hide the fact that she'd been pressed flat against the wood paneling, but it at least gave her hands something to do. "I-I'm sorry. I was just . . . I forgot my umbrella beneath my chair."

He raised an eyebrow. "I saw that. But this isn't the room where we met."

Her fingers curled into the fabric of her gloves. "You were talking to Mrs. Pembroke when I returned, and I . . . that is . . . it didn't seem like a conversation that should be interrupted."

Yuri leaned one arm against the chalkboard. "So you decided to hide?"

Something about his words made her shoulders tighten, but his tone wasn't mocking. If anything, he seemed bewildered.

Then the half smile dropped from his face. "How much of the conversation did you overhear?"

She shook her head. "It doesn't matter."

"It matters to me."

"I didn't hear enough to be of consequence."

"If that were true, you wouldn't have hidden so that Henrietta wouldn't see you when she left." Yuri lowered his voice until it took on that soft, gentle tone he always seemed to use with her. "I want you on the library committee, Rosalind."

She blinked. "You do?"

"Of course. You have good ideas, and I'm told you love reading."

She let out a short, breathy laugh. "Evidently I don't have a good idea for naming the library."

Yuri ran a hand through his dark hair. It should have caused him to look disheveled. His hair was already thick and unruly, with several strands falling over his forehead. But somehow the movement only drew attention to the strong lines of his face and the warmth of his brown eyes.

Did he realize how handsome he was, with his easy smile

and tousled, wind-blown hair? With that strong jaw shadowed with just a bit of stubble?

She swallowed. She had no business thinking Yuri Amos was handsome.

"Did your father put you up to suggesting the library be named after the most generous benefactors?" he asked.

"Yes, but it looks as though I'm not going to be able to get the building named after him, am I?"

"I doubt it."

She tangled her hands in her skirt. She could already feel the pain in her ribs, or maybe her other arm, wherever he decided to take out his anger. Hopefully it wouldn't be on her wrist. That was still sore.

She might even have a punishment waiting for her when she got home, since she hadn't gotten the name voted on tonight. She could tell her father they were voting on the name next week in hopes that she'd get only one beating, but there was no saying whether that plan would work.

"Are you all right?" Yuri stepped into the recessed doorway. "You look upset. Do you need something? Is there anything I can do to help?"

She swallowed again and shook her head. "Why are you being so nice to me? I'm supposed to be furious with you, and you're making it impossible."

His brows pulled together. "Furious with me? Why?"

"Because of the letters. Because I told you not to tell anyone. And now your whole family knows."

"You were supposed to meet me before I left for San Francisco, and I didn't . . ." He took a step back and raked a hand through his hair. "I hated leaving Sitka the next morning not knowing what had happened."

"Why? We're not very close friends. You just help me from

time to time. That might make you a good man, but it doesn't make us friends."

"I say it does."

"You don't understand. Your family knowing about the letters increases the chances that my father will find out." She wanted to pace, to release some of the frustration building inside her, but there was nowhere to move. Yuri was still crowding her into the small space between the hallway and the door, and he was so close she could smell the scent of rain on his coat.

And she wasn't scared. Even if she did slap him for betraying her, she somehow knew he wouldn't hit her back, and that just made her want to cry.

Because her father would definitely hit her back. More than once.

"I'm sorry." He stepped closer, crowding her even more.

She couldn't bring herself to care. If anything she wanted him to step even closer, and maybe to wrap one of those long arms around her.

It took all her effort to focus on his words rather than his nearness. Had he just apologized? "What are you sorry for?"

"For causing you to worry. I didn't mean to make things harder by explaining the letters to my family, but I didn't have much choice after Bryony opened one of them and started reading. She showed the letter to Mikhail before telling me what she'd found, and by the time Mikhail asked me about it . . ." He buried his head in his hands. "It was all such a mess."

That's why he was apologizing? She'd told him she was angry, yes, but she hadn't expected him to actually apologize. She thought he'd come up with some sort of excuse. Some reason why he was right and she was worrying over nothing.

That's what her father always did.

"I didn't know what else to do, I promise." He reached out

and gripped her hand, the touch light and casual, almost as though she were one of his sisters and he was giving her fingers a little squeeze.

But it still caused pain to radiate up her wrist. She gasped and tugged her hand back.

"I'm sorry. Did I hurt you?" His brow furrowed. "Wait. Bryony said you hurt your wrist, and that was why you missed our meeting. I take it your wrist is still bothering you? Can I see it?"

She slid her arm behind her back, never mind that the action had to make her look ridiculous. "It's fine. All healed, I promise."

"Then why did you gasp when I touched it?"

Had she? She hadn't meant to show any signs of pain. She'd been successfully hiding those signs from her father all week.

He sighed. "If you won't let me see it, then at least tell me how you hurt it."

"It was nothing. I tripped on the stairs, that's all." She shrugged, but her shoulders felt tight enough to snap.

"You tripped on the stairs?" Yuri's brows pinched together.

"Yes."

"Are you sure you're all right?"

This man. He was so wholesome. So good. So utterly, completely trusting. She wasn't sure whether she wanted to throw herself into his arms and beg him to never let go or tell him she didn't want his help anymore just so that she'd never again find herself in the position of lying to him.

Because he was the very last man in the world she wanted to lie to.

"I really do need to get home. Father won't be pleased if I stay out much longer." She didn't know if that was true or how long her father assumed the committee meeting would take. All she knew was that if she stayed here talking to Yuri, she just might end up blurting out the truth. Or begging him to take her away to San Francisco anyway.

Or both.

And she needed to find proof of her father and uncle bribing the Marshal first.

"It's dark and raining. Do you want me to escort you home?" Yuri's question was filled with so much kindness that she could barely hold his gaze.

But of course he would ask about seeing her home, because that was the type of man he was, kind and gentlemanly and caring, even when he shouldn't be. "Father's coach is waiting outside. Thank you for the offer, though."

Yuri didn't move, still blocking the narrow space between her and the hallway. "If you wait for me to put this chalkboard away, I'll walk you to the door."

"That's not necessary."

But he stayed where he was, looking at her for a long moment, almost as though he could see into the dark places of her life.

That was the last thing she could have, so she stepped forward. "Please, Yuri. I need to get my umbrella."

He swallowed, his throat working for a moment before he moved aside. "Good night, Rosalind."

She turned without saying good-bye, rushed into the meeting room to grab her umbrella, and then headed down the stairs as quickly as she could manage. If she was fast, Yuri wouldn't have time to catch up to her after putting the chalk-board away.

She burst through the front doors, then extended her umbrella, only to find the rain hadn't lessened. It splattered the bottom third of her dress as she rushed toward the waiting carriage. Once inside, she closed the umbrella, sat back on the seat, and stared at her wet hemline.

The trip home was entirely too short. Even with the pouring rain, the coachman reached their mansion in less than ten minutes, and she found Foster waiting for her at the front door.

A worried look filled his eyes when he saw the bottom of her dress, but he blinked and then it was gone, his face as stoic as ever. "Your father is in his study, Miss Rosalind. He asked for you to meet him as soon as you arrived."

Of course he had.

She tried to spin excuses in her head as she followed the butler down the hallway toward the heavy wooden door to Father's study. But much like the carriage ride, the walk was far too short, and her brain was far too tired, and by the time Foster knocked and her father called for her to enter, she hadn't managed to come up with a single excuse that might appease him.

She found him sitting in one of the opulently upholstered armchairs, smiling and sipping brandy as he spoke with another man dressed in an impeccable suit that would have cost every bit as much money as her father's.

She'd seen the other man before, though she didn't recall his name or how he knew her family. The main thing she remembered about him was his size. His frame was so broad it dwarfed the chair, making her father look small across from him. He wasn't as old as her father, but the streaks of gray at his temples and creases around his eyes and mouth told her that he certainly wasn't her age either. She guessed him to be maybe twenty years older than her.

"Rosalind, you're back." Her father waved her closer, a genuine smile filling his face. "Do you remember Leeland Vandermeer? He's part owner of the Northern Pacific Railroad? He's agreed to marry you."

"He what?" she rasped, her breath clogging in her lungs.

Mr. Vandermeer stood, his size expanding as he rose until it dominated every last nook and cranny of the room.

Every instinct screamed at her to retreat as he approached, but she forced herself to stay still.

He stopped in front of her, then reached out and tilted her chin up. "Your father assures me you're obedient."

The scent of brandy brushed her face, and his gaze traveled over her, starting at the very top of her head and traveling down to the soiled hem of her dress.

She tamped down the urge to shiver, but he must have sensed that she wanted to, because he gave a low, amused chuckle.

"You're just as beautiful as I remember too. Yes, you'll do quite nicely." He reached into his pocket, dropped to one knee, and held out a ring. "Rosalind Caldwell, will you do me the honor of becoming my wife?"

11

San Francisco; Four Days Later

Alexei ran his eyes over the smooth hull of the schooner sitting in dry dock. The *Ella Anne*, named after Dwayne Hollister's wife, Ella, and his oldest daughter, Anne. It was a decent ship, sitting in the middle of a decent shipyard that had been well kept and seemingly well run until the death of its owner. Alexei suspected the shipyard had continued to run reasonably well even after Dwayne Hollister's death, right up until Harold Farnsworth had lured away its best workers with higher wages.

It was cheaper to promise higher wages to the foreman and the handful of seasoned workers who could have kept operations going than to pay a fair price for the shipyard. But Alexei intended to pay a fair price.

He didn't care that the few workers attempting to repair the wooden schooner looked more lost than competent. Nor did he care that half the workbenches in the yard sat empty, tools scattered or missing entirely. The dry dock was sturdy, the slipway was more than sufficient, and the lumber yard was well stocked. The two large warehouses that held various shipbuilding supplies and materials were in good repair, and the Hollisters owned enough property that another dry dock could be built and two vessels could be worked on at the same time.

The shipyard could be running at full capacity within two months, possibly sooner.

Sacha strode around the side of the ship, brushing sawdust from his hands. "This isn't nearly as bad as I expected."

Alexei raised a brow. "What did you expect?"

"When I saw the price Yuri offered for the shipyard, and I heard that Mrs. Hollister accepted it, I expected a mess. And Yuri said he nearly doubled Farnsworth's offer." Sacha ran a hand along the hull of the ship. "A few new hands with the right knowledge of shipbuilding, and this place will be running smoothly."

"Those were my thoughts too."

Hollister's widow had met with him briefly when he arrived. She didn't want to sell, but she had four daughters ranging in age from six to sixteen, and she was smart enough to know she wouldn't last much longer without a knowledgeable foreman.

The main thing Mrs. Hollister had wanted to know earlier was whether he intended to honor the price Yuri had offered her.

He'd said no. He'd said no, then added that the shipyard was likely worth an additional two thousand dollars, provided the ship in dry dock was in good condition and could be seaworthy within a few months. If the ship passed muster when he and Sacha looked her over, that was exactly what he planned to give Mrs. Hollister.

"And the *Ella Anne?* What do you think of her?" Alexei stared up at the ship. He knew she was structurally sound, but

Sacha would be better at estimating how long it would take to repair the hole in the hull and the rotting decking.

Sacha just grinned at him. "She's also in better shape than I thought. Looks like they were halfway through replacing the planking when Farnsworth started poaching their workers. I can have her seaworthy in a month."

"A month?" That solved the problem of how he would fill the extra contracts Yuri had procured. In fact, with the *Ella Anne* fit for service and Yuri living in San Francisco, they'd be able to add a sixth shipping route to meet their eleven new contract obligations. They might even be able to add a few more contracts in time.

"What, no interrogation about whether I can truly have her seaworthy in a month, or if it might take a month and three days?" Sacha scratched his temple.

"I assume much of that will depend on how quickly you and Yuri can hire workers, and how much the workers already know about shipbuilding. Other than that, you know what you're doing."

Sacha slapped him on the back. "Now that's something I never thought I'd hear you say."

"Don't get used to it," Alexei muttered.

Sacha chuckled, the sound deep and hearty, then moved his gaze to encompass the rest of the shipyard. "Buying her is a good decision."

"I can't take credit for it. I wouldn't have even had the chance to purchase this without Yuri."

"When Yuri told us he made an offer on this place, I thought he'd lost his mind. Instead, he found a gem."

"He has a better head for business than he lets on. I used to think it was all luck. Now I'm starting to think it's strategy hidden inside so much charm and laughter that people can't tell which direction is up."

Sacha grinned. "Never thought I'd say it, but I think our little brother has finally learned to think rather than leap."

Alexei huffed a laugh. "Or he's still leaping, but at least he's aiming in the right direction these days."

"So what happens now?" Sacha rubbed his beard. "Do we go to the bank and get a nice fat banknote to hand over to that poor widow?"

"Yes, and after that, we're going to visit Harold Farnsworth."

12

Sitka; the Same Day

Yuri tugged at his collar and leaned forward, squinting at numbers on the ledger. A bead of sweat itched at his temple. He ignored it and focused on the ledger, tapping his pencil as he scanned the list of shipping weights, dock fees, and something that looked suspiciously like a misfiled invoice for six crates of salted cod.

"How does Alexei do this day after day without clawing his eyes out?"

Mikhail smirked from where he stood in the open space in front of the windows, swinging his Indian clubs in controlled, rhythmic arcs. Being an explorer in Alaska meant Mikhail didn't have work during the winter, and this was one of the many ways he stayed fit. "Tired of doing Alexei's paperwork?"

He'd grown tired of it after about twenty minutes. On the first day Alexei had left. And that had been six days ago. "No wonder he never smiles. I wouldn't smile either if I had to calculate ledgers and match shipping manifests with warehouse records."

"Don't tell anyone, but I think Alexei likes the paperwork." Mikhail drew one of the clubs forward in a loop across his chest, then guided it up over his shoulder and back down again, not breaking his concentration.

Yuri slid a random envelope into the ledger to mark his place, then snapped it shut. Alexei could sort through most of this after he returned. His older brother might have said he wanted the audit done by the time he returned, but he didn't actually expect Yuri to follow through and have it completed, did he?

Alexei had been gone before, sometimes for as long as three months. But they typically had time to prepare for his absence, to decide which paperwork was essential and which could wait. And Alexei always let the businesses he was working with know when he would be gone for an extended period of time, which cut down on correspondence.

This was the first time Alexei had actually given him a specific task to complete. He could still recall the way Alexei had narrowed his eyes at him, still hear the sound of his voice when he'd said, *I'm in the middle of doing our semiannual audit. . . . You should be able to finish it by the time I return.*

It was an impossible task. Why did the audit need to be done at all? He'd found only a few discrepancies so far, and none of them were significant enough to impact the functioning of the business.

"I need a bit of air." Yuri shoved away from Alexei's desk, the polished surface not even visible beneath the mess of letters and shipping manifests and ledgers. "I'll be back."

Mikhail's muscles flexed as he transitioned into yet another series of movements. This one involved swinging both sets of clubs high above his head before bringing them out in a series of wide circles. "Where are you going?"

"To the post office. I interviewed three men for mining-foreman positions while I was in San Francisco, and I want to see if any of their letters of recommendation have arrived."

"You interviewed mining foremen?" Mikhail stopped, dropping his clubs to his side. "Why?"

"You know why."

"We haven't even filed a claim." Mikhail set the clubs down and grabbed a towel, which he used to wipe the back of his neck and his forehead.

"Correction, you haven't filed a claim here. In Sitka."

"Don't tell me you filed a claim in San Francisco for that gold vein I found in November."

"Of course I filed a claim."

Mikhail had found the vein purely by accident. He'd been sent on a late-season rescue mission to find a team of missing botanists who had gotten lost after their guide had died in a bear attack. He'd returned from the expedition with two things he hadn't expected. A future wife, and the location of a gold vein hidden deep in the mountains of the Stikine wilderness.

After he'd gotten home, the family had talked about filing a claim in Seattle so that no one in Alaska would know about the discovery, but Alexei sent Yuri to San Francisco before anyone had reason to travel to Seattle. Yuri had just assumed he should file a claim there, but Mikhail clearly hadn't been expecting him to do so.

"We're about to buy a shipyard, and after that, Alexei will still want to buy a barge—either that or build one in our new shipyard." Yuri crossed his arms over his chest. "Both of those things will cost money. How better to get it than by mining the vein you found? That will involve hiring a foreman and likely setting up a small stamp mill. I don't know if we'll need an entire refinery on-site or if we can pay another company to process the gold, but I figured the right foreman could tell us that."

Mikhail's face darkened into a scowl. "This is going to get out, you know. Everyone will discover that we own a claim."

"My plan is for no one to know until we start exporting gold sometime this summer. If we handle things right and hire people from California rather than Alaska, we should be able to keep the entire operation secret for a few months."

"I don't like it."

"You haven't liked it from the beginning. But if we don't mine the vein, someone else will." He understood why Mikhail wanted everything in the wilderness left pristine and untouched. But Alaska was over half a million square miles. He wasn't convinced that mining ten or twenty acres of land would make that big of a difference. "This way we can have a say about how the mining is done, how the workers are treated, and how much of the mountainside gets destroyed in the mining process."

Mikhail didn't answer, just wiped the sweat from his hands, his movements slow and methodical.

"You can't be mad that I filed the claim. We talked about this before you got married."

Mikhail still said nothing. Yuri rolled his eyes, then turned his back on his brother and stalked down the stairs and outside into a rare bit of winter sunshine.

Was everyone in his family mad at him right now? It seemed that way. Alexei was upset because he'd saved them money and not bought a sinking pile of rusted metal. Mikhail was mad because he'd done something about the gold vein rather than just talk about it. And Sacha . . . well, Sacha wasn't mad. He probably looked at all of this as some kind of merry adventure.

But still, two of his brothers were unhappy with him, and he hated that feeling.

He strode up the street toward the post office, his boots sinking in the mud from days upon days of winter rain that had preceded the afternoon's small bit of milky sunshine. The air carried the scent of salt and damp timber, mingling with the faint aroma of woodsmoke from the chimneys of shops and houses. Everyone seemed to be outside enjoying the break in the rain. Dockworkers were hauling crates from a newly arrived ship, a group of women stood beneath the porch of the mercantile chatting away, and a pair of fishermen stood near the docks mending their nets.

At least here, outside the office, no one was upset with him.

He turned, leaving the waterfront and making his way to where the post office sat a block inland. The bell above the door gave a hollow chime when he stepped inside, and Mr. Hooper looked up from where he stood behind the counter sorting a bundle of letters.

"Ah, Yuri." He reached beneath the counter. "Got a fair bit of mail for you today."

"Thank you." Yuri took the stack and flipped through the letters. Most of them were for Alexei, but a couple were post-marked from San Francisco. Could they be from the mining foremen candidates?

The bell rang behind him. He tucked the envelopes into the pocket of his coat and turned toward the door, then stopped.

Rosalind Caldwell stood just inside, her hand resting lightly on the arm of a hulking dark-haired man with streaks of gray at his temples. There was something familiar about the giant, though Yuri couldn't quite place where he'd seen him before.

"Mr. Amos." Her voice was perfectly polite when she spoke, without any hint of the vulnerability from their conversation after the library committee meeting. "I don't believe you've been introduced. This is Mr. Leeland Vandermeer, my fiancé."

Fiancé? The breath rushed from his lungs, and for a moment, he could only stare at Rosalind and the man towering beside her.

Alexei would know how to keep his face neutral and his features schooled at a time like this. He would know how to look at the large man and not give away a single thought or emotion.

But he wasn't Alexei, and he hated the man beside Rosalind instantly, if for no other reason than the fact that Rosalind was just as cold and proper around him as she was around her father.

And that wasn't the true Rosalind. It wasn't the woman who could dream up a library by the water so townsfolk could have a pleasant place to read, and a temporary library so that people could have access to books months sooner than they would otherwise.

He didn't know what emotions flashed across his face as he looked between Rosalind and Vandermeer. All he knew was that her fiancé watched him with dark eyes that made the hairs on the back of his neck prickle.

"Your name sounds familiar." Yuri forced himself to extend his hand. "Have we met?"

"Oh, I'm sorry. Mr. Vande— Leeland, this is Yuri Amos." Rosalind nodded his direction. "His family owns both Sitka Trading Company and Amos Family Shipbuilders. Perhaps you've done business?"

"Sitka Trading Company?" The man gave his hand a stiff shake. "I believe we have a contract with your family's company to handle goods delivered by ship and transport them inland on my railroad line out of Seattle."

Something about the man's tone set Yuri's teeth on edge, but at least now he knew why he recognized him.

"How is it you know my fiancée?" Vandermeer looked between the two of them.

Fiancée. Right. Yuri should congratulate Rosalind. That was what a normal person would do.

But the words wouldn't come. Instead, he found himself searching her face for something that might tell him that she wanted this marriage.

But her blue eyes were guarded and distant.

"We serve on the library committee together," he finally answered. "Has Rosalind told you about that? She has some rather good ideas."

A small smile crept across her lips. "Did you find out if we can use your empty building? Or do you need to wait until Alexei returns? I heard he is in California?"

"Yes, a quick trip to San Francisco," Yuri answered. "But Mikhail and I already discussed it, and we're happy to use the building as an interim library while an official one is being built. We can clean it out whenever we wish and start collecting books."

Rosalind's smile grew even larger. "Father said we can donate some of our books that we don't use, and I went to the mercantile yesterday. Mr. Fredricks has a catalog with thousands of books that can be ordered."

"That's good to know." He rubbed the back of his neck. "I wonder if you might recommend a budget to be spent on each category of books, allotting a certain amount for fiction and a certain amount for—"

"Rosalind's going to be rather busy planning our wedding," Vandermeer interrupted. "She'll have limited time to help."

Rosalind's head snapped toward her fiancé. "But Father said he wanted me involved with—"

"That was before our wedding was announced." Vandermeer laid a hand over hers where it rested on his arm.

Something smoldered inside Yuri. "When is the wedding?"

Please, Father, help it be some distant date a year or two away, enough time for Rosalind to come to her senses, or for me to plan a way for her to leave Sitka if that's what she wants.

"It's been set for the last weekend in May." She whispered as if it were an execution date.

Four months. He barely resisted curling his hand into a fist. That wasn't nearly enough time.

"We'll be married in time for me to take Rosalind somewhere new for the summer. The change in scenery will be good for her." Vandermeer patted Rosalind's hand, and Yuri had the sudden impulse to wrench her away from the towering man.

Anyone who really knew her would be able to see that she'd shrunk in on herself while standing beside Vandermeer. She kept staring at her shoes rather than looking at him or her fiancé.

Vandermeer was still speaking, something about travel arrangements and the move down to Seattle after the wedding.

Yuri barely heard him. His eyes remained on Rosalind, and her gaze finally flickered up to meet his.

Their connection lasted only a second before she broke it, but Vandermeer must have noticed, because his grip on Rosalind's arm shifted, his fingers flexing slightly. "Of course, I can always inquire about Rosalind getting a position on our library committee down in Seattle. Once she settles into her new role as my wife, that is. She'll have a household to run, guests to entertain, and children to bear and raise first. And I'll expect my wife to be home when I return in the evenings. I certainly can't have her traipsing about town whenever she pleases. Perhaps the Seattle library committee meets in the afternoon."

Rosalind was still as stone, her head ducked toward the ground once again. The only hint of emotion he could find was that the fingers of her free hand were curled into the fabric of her sleeve. Her hands were gloved, so he couldn't tell if her knuckles were white, but he wouldn't be surprised.

Vandermeer didn't seem to notice.

"Sounds like you have it all planned out," Yuri rasped, the words like gravel in his throat.

"A man has to run his household properly. Women can get all sorts of ideas if you don't set the right expectations. I ran into that a bit with my first wife, but we straightened matters out soon enough." The man sent him a wink, then loosed a low, dark chuckle.

Yuri had to shove both hands into his coat pockets to keep from balling one of them into a fist and sending it flying toward Vandermeer's jaw.

Rosalind chose that moment to look up at her fiancé and give him a tight smile. "We should go, Mr. Van— Leeland. Father will be expecting us soon. Just let me collect the mail."

Vandermeer released her arm only long enough for her to step up to the counter, where Mr. Hooper was waiting with a bundle of mail.

She retrieved it without a word, then returned to Vandermeer and put her hand back on his arm. The bell above the door chimed as she and her fiancé disappeared into the afternoon.

Yuri stared at the door for a few seconds, then let out a slow breath and looked down at his hands. They were shaking.

"Are you all right, Yuri?"

Yuri's gaze snapped up to the postmaster's. Had Mr. Hooper witnessed their entire conversation?

"I'm fine," he muttered, his eyes moving back to the doorway that Rosalind had disappeared through.

It was a lie. He wasn't fine.

And he'd never felt so powerless in his life.

13

That Afternoon

"I can't believe you're getting married!" Millicent threw herself into Rosalind's arms and squealed. "This is so exciting."

Rosalind smiled, not because the idea of marrying Leeland Vandermeer made her happy, but because she had grown so accustomed to forcing herself to smile over the last four days that she could now do so without thinking.

"How romantic." Jane sighed, stepping forward to give Rosalind a hug of her own. "I dream of my wedding day."

"How does it feel to be the first of us?" Freya hugged her, her eyes bright. "Are you excited? Oh, four months seems so far away. How will we ever wait?"

"Will the wedding be here or in Seattle?" Jane clasped her hands together beneath her chin. "Please say it will be here. I'm not sure that Father will want to travel all the way to Seattle for a wedding."

Again, Rosalind plastered a smile on her face. "It will be here." Her father had granted her that much at least.

Or maybe he hadn't granted her anything at all. Maybe he'd always intended for it to be in Sitka because he wanted to make a show of his wealth.

But the one thing she knew he'd granted her because of her engagement was a chance to host her friends for an afternoon tea. In the years she'd been living in Alaska, she could count on one hand the times he'd allowed her to have friends over.

But in this case, he'd been the one to suggest it.

"This is all so romantic!" Freya flounced over to the settee, where a proper English tea had been laid out in the library for them to enjoy, complete with a three-tier tray filled with finger sandwiches and minicakes and crumpets with cream.

"It's really not." Rosalind followed her to the settee. "People get married all the time."

"Oh, don't be ridiculous!" Millicent waved a hand as she sat in one of the armchairs across from the settee. "I hear that Mr. Vandermeer is unbelievably wealthy. Is that true?"

"Yes, I heard he has five houses!" Jane's grin was so large it took up her entire face.

"Uh, I don't know how many houses Leeland has." Though he could well have five. Her fiancé had more money than he knew what to do with, but that still didn't mean she wanted to marry him.

He was stern and short-tempered, and he spent far too many hours in the evenings drinking in her father's study. Her father didn't consume half the liquor Leeland did.

Was that intentional on her father's part? Did he want to get Leeland drunk in the hopes that he'd give away some kind of secret or sign an unfavorable contract while he was inebriated? She didn't know.

The one thing she did know was that, for the first time since her mother died, her father was happy with her. Even though she hadn't managed to get the library named after him yet, he was still pleased. He hadn't struck her once since Leeland arrived.

The least she could do was take advantage of his good mood by inviting her friends over once a week until she married.

Who knew if she'd be able to see friends at all after she married Leeland and moved to Seattle?

If she married him. Because as much as her father wanted it, she couldn't imagine herself walking down the aisle toward Leeland Vandermeer. Nor could she imagine speaking the words "I do" to him.

"Which of us do you think will get married next?" Freya helped herself to one of the crumpets and added a dollop of clotted cream on top of it.

Rosalind busied herself pouring the tea, making sure she poured it evenly into each cup without spilling so much as a drop.

Millicent grinned. "I think we should place a wager on it."

"Millie, that's scandalous!" Jane gasped, but her face had broken out into another smile as well.

Millicent made another swishing motion with her hand. "It's no different than what the men do down at the bar."

"I'd like to say I'll be the next to marry, but I don't even have a suitor." Freya poked out her bottom lip.

"Don't be ridiculous." Jane picked up her teacup. "I saw Yuri Amos walking you home from the mercantile just yesterday."

Rosalind flinched, causing tea to slosh from the pot onto the fancy white tablecloth. She swallowed. Would the housekeeper tell Father she'd put a stain on the tablecloth? Would he give her another—

"Yuri walked you home?" Millicent clasped a hand to her heart. "Why didn't I know about this?"

Freya's shoulders rose and fell on a disappointed sigh. "I don't think he fancies me that way. He was just being helpful. I ended up purchasing more things than I expected for Mother but didn't bring a horse. When he saw me trying to carry four sacks' worth of goods, he offered to carry them."

Millicent sighed, light and dreamy and far different from the way Freya had sighed. "That sounds exactly like something Yuri would do."

"But it doesn't mean he likes her any more than he likes the rest of us." Jane picked up one of the small sandwiches cut into a dainty triangle. "Do you think he fancies one of us but is just afraid to show it?"

Rosalind ducked her head. She was the last person who should try to answer that question. All she knew was that her heart hurt at the thought of Yuri Amos.

Normally she looked forward to seeing him, even if it was for a few brief moments as they exchanged letters each month. They never said much to each other during those exchanges, yet something about him had always felt safe.

But not yesterday at the post office. She'd hated every moment of that encounter.

Had Leeland not been with her, she would have walked home with an extra bounce in her step and a smile on her face. Would have replayed over and over in her head whatever small bit of conversation they'd shared.

But yesterday morning she'd wanted the floor to open up and swallow her.

What must he think, knowing she was engaged?

She stared into her tea. Nothing. He probably thought nothing. It wasn't as though there was something romantic between them. Maybe he was kind to her and listened when she talked, but that didn't mean he had any type of romantic interest in her.

And she wasn't sure she had any romantic interest in him either. She wanted to marry someone like him, true. Someone kind. Someone who listened. Someone who saw her as a person.

But that didn't mean she wanted to marry Yuri Amos in particular, did it?

Of course not. It was a ridiculous notion. Half the women in town fancied themselves in love with him, including her friends.

"Well?" Freya nudged her with her elbow, and Rosalind nearly spilled her tea on her lap.

She pressed her eyes shut when she realized it hadn't spilled. Not a drop.

"Can't you let us see your ring? Please?" Freya leaned closer. "We don't need to give anyone the details if you want us to keep it quiet. We really just want a look."

Was that what her friends had been asking? To look at her ring? She set her teacup down on the table in front of her, then extended her hand toward Freya, ignoring the way her fingers trembled. "Here you go."

A faraway look filled Freya's eyes. "Oh, this makes me dream about what our own rings might look like. If one of us marries a man rich enough to give us a ring, that is."

Jane and Millicent left their chairs and came around the back of the settee for a closer look.

"I've never seen a ring with so many stones in it before," Millicent said.

"It's breathtaking," Jane murmured, tilting her head to study it.

Millicent bent even closer. "It's so big."

"It's heavy." Rosalind blurted.

Millicent's laughter echoed through the room. "Well, I'd rather have a heavy ring than a small one. I'd say your fiancé has excellent taste."

Yes. Everyone who saw the ring said that exact thing. Rosalind looked down at it, trying to see it through her friends' eyes.

Large and heavy, the gold band had been set with a single oval-cut sapphire surrounded by diamonds. She knew it was breathtaking, knew her friends were right about how lovely it was.

Yet she hated it.

The door to the library opened, and the air felt suddenly dark, never mind the giant floor-to-ceiling windows that over-looked the sound.

She didn't need to look up to know her fiancé had just stepped inside.

"Ladies." Leeland's voice was smooth and deep. "I trust I'm not interrupting?"

Millicent straightened, smoothing her skirt and casting an excited glance at Rosalind. "Not at all. We were just admiring the ring."

"Were you now?" He strode toward Rosalind and took her hand, lifting it so he could examine the sapphire. "I chose the largest stone the jeweler had. Only the best for my future wife."

He brushed his thumb over the ring, but it pressed just a little too hard, causing the ring to dig into her skin.

She forced herself not to pull away.

"Has my fiancée been telling you all about our wedding plans?" He smiled at her friends; then his eyes shifted to her.

She opened her mouth, but no words came out.

Because she hadn't told them anything other than that the wedding would be in Sitka.

Because she'd spent most of the conversation thinking

about Yuri Amos rather than the man she was actually betrothed to.

She looked down, never mind her hand was still caught in Leeland's.

For the second time that week, she wished the floor would open up and swallow her, but she settled for pressing her eyes shut instead.

Come to San Francisco.

Oh, drat. Why was that the first thing she saw when she closed her eyes? Why did her mind dredge up the image of Yuri standing in the snow, offering to help her escape her father?

What if she had said yes? What if she had left Sitka right then?

Her father would have tracked her down by now, that's what.

So where did that leave her?

14

Sitka; the Next Morning

Yuri swung the ax harder than necessary, splitting the log with a violent crack. He barely paused before grabbing another log, setting it upright, and swinging again. And again. And again.

Wood chips flew and sweat trickled down his back despite the cold wind off the ocean. He barely felt any of it, barely heard the rhythmic thud of the ax embedding itself in the stump. All he could hear was Vandermeer's voice. All he could see was the smug look on his face as he spoke about Rosalind's future.

She'll have a household to run. Guests to entertain. Children to bear and raise. That deep, grating chuckle. As if he were sharing some kind of secret.

As if Yuri was in on it.

A man has to run his household properly. Women can get all sorts of ideas if you don't set the right expectations.

Yuri's grip tightened around the ax handle, and he swung

harder, the force vibrating up his arms when the ax sliced clean through the piece of wood and landed in the stump. How could she marry a man like that? Didn't she care that she'd be miserable?

He threw the split log onto the growing pile and balanced the next log on the stump.

"You planning to chop the entire woodpile before breakfast?" Mikhail's dry voice cut through the air.

He hadn't even realized his brother had walked up. Yuri swung the ax again, splitting the next log with a single swing. "I don't mind the extra firewood. Just think how happy Alexei will be when he returns home to find it split and stacked. Maybe I'll even get a smile out of him."

Mikhail leaned against the side of the woodshed, which sat just a few feet behind the back door of the house. "But at this rate, you'll have more than enough for our family. You might even be able to heat the entire town."

"Maybe we're in for an unusually long winter." He positioned a new piece of wood on the stump, then swung the ax.

"If you needed to work off some anger, you could have just gone a few rounds with Mikhail's punching bag in the warehouse," Bryony said from where she stood on the stoop outside the kitchen door. He wasn't sure how long she'd been there, but a glance at his sister-in-law revealed that she was dressed in a pair of Ilya's trousers with dampness rimming the neckline of her shirt and sweat trickling down the side of her face.

Yuri just shook his head, then glanced at Mikhail. "I can't believe you're forcing your new wife to train with you. Did you make her use the punching bag this morning?"

"I like it," Bryony said. "But not as much as I like the Indian clubs."

Yuri tapped the ax into the tree stump, letting it rest there before eyeing his brother. "You're making her do the Indian clubs too?"

Mikhail merely crossed his arms over his chest. "I'm not making her do anything, but if she's going to join me on my expeditions, then she needs to be in good shape physically. Surely you don't expect me to take her into the wilderness unprepared."

Most people wouldn't expect a wilderness guide to take his wife with him at all, but Bryony was different. She seemed genuinely excited about heading into the wilderness with Mikhail this spring, and she didn't seem to mind the exercises he'd concocted for her either. If anything, she looked happy standing beside the kitchen door, her cheeks flushed pink and loose strands of copper hair clinging to her temples.

Yuri just shook his head and wiped the sweat from his brow with the back of his arm.

"Tell me, Yuri . . ." Bryony leaned an elbow on the railing beside her. "This wouldn't have anything to do with Rosalind Caldwell, would it?"

"What makes you think that?" Yuri yanked the ax out of the stump and grabbed another log from the pile. Maybe he wasn't done splitting wood after all.

"Oh, I don't know." Bryony cocked her head to the side. "Maybe the fact that there's a rumor going around town about Rosalind's recent engagement to some railroad baron. Or maybe it's that you look like you're imagining a certain someone's face on every log you split."

Yuri brought the ax down harder this time, sending the wood flying once again. "I saw her yesterday."

Mikhail exchanged a glance with Bryony. "Rosalind Caldwell? Where?"

"The post office."

Bryony came down the steps. "Did she seem all right?"

"She seemed . . . proper." Yuri set another log in place. "Polite. The way she always is in public."

Bryony frowned. "That doesn't answer the question."

Yuri blew out a breath. The image of her shrinking under Vandermeer's grip flashed through his mind. "Like I said, she looked and acted like she usually does. I can't tell you whether that means she's fine. I can just tell you she acted normal for the situation."

"How was her wrist?"

"She said it was fine the other night after the library committee meeting, so I didn't ask after it further." He couldn't even imagine how he would have asked, not with Vandermeer glowering at him each time he glanced at Rosalind.

"Did you look at it the other night?" Bryony sounded even more concerned now.

"No. She said it was fine. Why? Don't tell me you think she lied."

Bryony bit the side of her lip.

Yuri narrowed his eyes. "What aren't you telling me?"

"I was . . . ah, wondering if . . . if her wrist had . . . gotten worse." Bryony's words were slow and careful, almost as though she internally debated each one before speaking.

"Why would it get worse? Does she often trip while walking down the stairs? She's never seemed clumsy to me." On the contrary. Everything about Rosalind was poised and refined. Always. She was the most graceful person he'd ever met.

Bryony glanced at Mikhail, and something unspoken passed between them. Then she looked at him with an expression that made the hair on the back of his neck stand up.

"What's going on?"

"You really don't know, do you?"

His hands tightened around the handle of the ax, though he didn't swing it. "Don't know what?"

Bryony and Mikhail exchanged another glance.

Yuri found himself gritting his teeth. "What?"

Bryony let out a slow breath. "He hits her."

The words landed like a punch to his stomach, knocking the air from his lungs.

"He . . ." His voice came out hoarse, so he cleared his throat and tried again. "Who hits who?"

Bryony's hazel eyes filled with something that made his stomach churn. "Her father. He hits Rosalind."

He stared at his sister-in-law, the words refusing to take shape in his mind, refusing to make sense. Surely he'd misheard; surely he was missing something.

Preston Caldwell. Owner of the Alaska Commercial Company. He wasn't a kind man, but surely someone in such a prominent position knew better than to strike his own daughter.

Yet this was the man who was selling her off to Vandermeer like livestock, no doubt in exchange for some sort of business deal that was sure to benefit both parties.

This was the man who had forced her onto the library committee just so the library would bear his name.

The man who kept her controlled, carefully watched, and perfectly in line at all times.

Yuri's pulse thundered in his ears as the pieces fell into place. "I asked her to come with me to San Francisco. To leave Sitka. I didn't even know he was hitting her, and I told her I could help her get away. She refused."

Bryony rested a hand on his arm. "I offered to help her get away as well, before Thanksgiving, when I first saw a bruise on her cheek."

"She said no then too?"

Bryony nodded. "I leave notes for her from time to time through our mutual friend Millicent, who passes them on, and I always make the same offer."

"And she always refuses."

He was going to be sick. Right there. In front of both Bryony and Mikhail. He sucked in a breath, trying to calm the churning in his stomach.

It didn't work. He turned away from Bryony just in time to empty the contents of his stomach on the base of the wood stump rather than all over her feet.

Mikhail wrapped an arm around his shoulders. "Come on, let's get you inside."

He didn't want to go inside. He wanted to march straight up to Preston Caldwell's house and demand he hand over his daughter.

Which the man would never do. Not in a thousand years.

"Why won't she leave?" Yuri gripped the front of Mikhail's shirt. "Why won't she do something to get away? Why won't she fight back?"

"I think it's because she doesn't believe she can get away, not really," Bryony said. "Her father has so many resources, and she's worried fighting him will only make things worse."

He hung his head. She'd told him as much the night of Mikhail's wedding. He was a fool for not putting things together sooner.

"Do you think . . ."—He swallowed, then turned his gaze to Mikhail—"This Vandermeer character . . . How well do you know him? He doesn't seem like the type to treat Rosalind right either."

Mikhail dropped his arm from around Yuri's shoulders. "Alexei invested some money with him a few years ago, then stopped after it became apparent what kind of man he is."

"And what kind of man is that?" Yuri asked, almost afraid of the answer.

"He seems to be a good enough businessman. But . . ." Mikhail grimaced.

"But what?"

"He's a little too fond of drinking, and he's got a reputation for being violent when drunk. He got into a fight in one of the bars when he was here last spring and broke the owner's nose. Marshal Hibbs got called in, but no charges were filed. You know how money has a way of keeping things quiet."

"And Rosalind's supposed to marry him?" Yuri's breath turned shallow. "She's supposed to leave Sitka and live with a man like that? No. I won't allow it." He made a slashing motion with his hand. "There has to be something we can do."

He owed it to God to find a way to help. It was his duty as a Christian.

"We've offered to help her leave multiple times." Bryony raised her hands, palms open, then let them drop back to her sides. "There's nothing else we can do unless she takes us up on it."

He wanted to retch all over again, never mind his stomach was empty. "What if she marries him, and we never see her again? What if . . ." His voice caught. "What if he's violent with her like her father is? What if . . . What if she never gets away?"

Mikhail's expression darkened, and for a moment, neither of them spoke.

"I'll send her a note through Millicent." Bryony stepped closer. "If she's not comfortable with her new fiancé, maybe she'll change her mind now and accept our help."

"I'll talk to her after the next library committee meeting too." They'd already had one impromptu conversation after the last meeting. Surely they could have another one.

It seemed like so very little, but it was the only thing he knew to do.

"Maybe I will go use that punching bag," he muttered, then he stalked off toward the warehouse.

15

San Francisco; the Next Day

"You've got a lot of nerve showing up here."

Alexei hadn't even fully stepped into Harold Farnsworth's shipping office before the man greeted him.

He paused in the doorway, meeting the eyes of the blond-and-gray-haired man whose business dealings he'd spent the last two days mucking up. "I can leave if you'd like, but don't tell me you wouldn't have done the same thing if the situation were reversed."

Harold leaned back in his chair and picked up a glass filled with dark liquid. Cognac, if Alexei had to guess. It had been Farnsworth's drink of choice on Alexei's previous visits to San Francisco.

Usually the man offered him some, but today Farnsworth merely swirled it in his glass, then set it down on his polished desk without taking a sip.

Alexei took Farnsworth's silence as an invitation to step inside. He shut the heavy wooden door behind him and headed toward the upholstered armchair opposite the sprawling desk. "That shipyard is an amazing opportunity for me and my family. You can't blame me for taking it. And I can't even bring myself to feel bad about it, seeing how you were trying to swindle a widow and her four daughters out of an inheritance."

Farnsworth pressed his lips into a flat line. "I was looking for the best possible deal."

"Their most valuable workers are now working for you. That seems like a deal."

Farnsworth muttered something, then shook his head. "Why are you here, Alexei? I thought you too honorable of a man to gloat."

Alexei stiffened. "No. I'm not here to gloat. I'm here to thank you for the business advice you've given me over the past several years, and I'm also wondering if I might call on Laurel before I return home."

Farnsworth had raised his glass of cognac again, but rather than take a sip, he stilled, his golden eyebrows winging upward. "You still want to call on Laurel?"

He steepled his fingers. "I don't see why business dealings between us should ruin the friendship I have with your daughter."

"Friendship? Is that what you call it?"

Alexei shifted. "She's a lovely woman. I consider it a privilege to know her."

Farnsworth finally took a sip of his cognac, then set it down. "Laurel doesn't have many friends, not like her sisters do, and she certainly doesn't have any gentleman friends. Other than you, it seems. But there's part of me that wants to be mad at you, at your brother Yuri—at everybody, really—about losing that shipyard."

"You wouldn't have lost it had you offered them a fair price." Alexei crossed his arms over his chest. "In fact, you could have offered them more than me at any point, and they would've taken your offer over mine. Mrs. Hollister will need to live off what she's made from the sale for the rest of her life."

"You're probably right." Farnsworth took another sip of his cognac. "Though a man can never be too careful with how he spends his money in this economy."

Alexei bit back a laugh. There was nothing wrong with the economy, at least not as far as Harold Farnsworth was concerned. The man was making money hand over fist, and judging by the ship he was building just outside the office, he was going to be making money for a long time to come.

"So, about Laurel . . ." Alexei prompted. "I leave for Sitka tomorrow, and if at all possible, I'd like to see her before I go and continue writing her after I'm gone."

Farnsworth set down his glass with a sigh. "Come over for supper tonight, then, and bring the brother you brought to town too. What's his name? Samson? Samuel? I feel like it starts with an S."

"Sacha."

"Sacha. I should have figured it'd be Russian. I'll send a note around to my wife about dinner. Laurel will be happy to see you, I'm sure. And honestly, as much as I'm mad that you swooped in and stole my next acquisition out from under me, that was well played. Having that shipyard will be a good decision for your business."

Farnsworth paused and tilted his head, and Alexei could almost see the ideas flashing inside his mind. "Of course, you could always move down here and work for me, manage what I have. We might even be able to combine the two shipyards."

Alexei lifted an eyebrow. "You want me to manage your shipyard?"

"You're a naval architect. Seems like it would be a good fit."

"I'm a year short of having my degree."

"You could finish it easy enough if you were living here. I have a foreman who's handy when it comes to swinging a hammer, but he doesn't understand the newest advances in shipbuilding, or how strong steel is, or how the structure of a large metal ship differs from that of a smaller wooden one. He doesn't know much about the boilers that power them either. He's from the era when everything was wood and sails."

"Those are the kinds of ships I build," Alexei pointed out.

"Yes, but only because your supplies are limited due to your location. You understand how the bigger ships work, and I have a feeling that you'll be building one of your own before too long. So, like I said, if you want a job, you can have one. All you need to do is move down here."

"And marry Laurel? Is that the unspoken part of this offer?"

Farnsworth scowled. "I might be a businessman, but I'm not so shrewd that I consider my daughters assets. While I require them to marry respectable men, I won't strong-arm them into marrying one of my associates out of convenience."

Alexei blew out a breath. That was something, at least.

"I'm sure Laurel would enjoy you being closer, for what it's worth."

It was a nice offer. Farnsworth didn't need to start talking about a salary for Alexei to know he'd be paid well. But he wasn't sure he could leave Alaska. Everyone other than Yuri might be married, but it seemed like his family needed him now more than ever. "I appreciate the offer, truly. But I belong in Alaska."

Farnsworth exhaled. "Figured you'd say that, but if you ever get tired of all that rain and snow and wind, there will be a place for you here."

"I'll keep that in mind." Alexei stood. "What time is dinner?"

"Seven."

He turned and headed toward the door, moving quickly through the outer office, where a trio of clerks sat working at their desks. When he stepped out into the shipyard air, the scent of salt and wood and metal filled his lungs.

All too easily he could picture himself living here, working in this shipyard, attending fancy dinner parties, courting Laurel in earnest, maybe even drafting designs for entirely new ships. Ones that were more efficient. Ones that could carry the same load as a barge but moved through the water with the speed and precision of a wooden cutter.

But with the rest of his family living in Alaska, he couldn't picture himself enjoying it.

Or at least, he couldn't envision himself enjoying most of it. But the part where he got to design new ships? He'd wanted to do that since he was a boy.

And really, would it be so hard to have a lovely woman from a wealthy family by his side as he did so?

16

Sitka; the Same Day

Her father had let her leave the house by herself. That's how good of a mood he was in now that she was marrying a wealthy railroad baron. He hadn't even blinked when she'd asked him if she could spend the afternoon in the temporary library building, helping to clean out and organize some of the books people from the community had already donated.

Rosalind didn't care that the building was filled with dust or that cobwebs clung to every corner of the ceiling. It wasn't her father's house, and for a few hours, it was just her and the books and the quiet.

Or rather, it would be quiet if not for the wind howling outside and rattling the windows. Rain streaked the dirty glass, obscuring her view of the road and carriage. The weather had only grown worse in the half hour since she'd arrived. But her father was in such a good mood these days, she wasn't too worried about getting her dress dirty while she worked.

No, the afternoon was nearly perfect, even with the storm. The only thing that would make it better was a fire in the wood-stove that stood in the corner.

The only bad thing about her being engaged was that she hadn't found much time to search for proof of her father bribing the Marshal. She'd been able to slip into his study once when Leeland and her father were meeting with her uncle on Castle Hill, but otherwise she was either with Leeland or Leeland and her father were in his study, making it impossible to conduct her search.

And she still wanted to search for the ledger. She didn't want to marry Leeland, and the best way out of the marriage would be to find that ledger sooner rather than later.

But when she'd left to come to the library, her father and Leeland had once again been ensconced in the study. There'd literally been nowhere for her to search.

Rosalind hunkered into her thick mink coat and ran her fingertips along the spine of a leather-bound volume of poetry, then slid it onto one of the shelves against the wall. She needed to focus on shelving books, not let herself get distracted by the ledger. At the meeting tomorrow night, she intended to bring up the need for more shelves for the temporary library. Fortunately there was plenty of space for her to sort through the books that had already been dropped off.

Perhaps Mr. McCreedy could donate some lumber, and she could get some of the schoolboys to help build shelves after school. Surely whatever they built for this building could be moved to the new one once it was complete.

She bent to pick up a crate that had been set beside the doorway.

"Rosalind?"

She whirled around, her heart hammering against her ribs,

only to find Yuri standing near the storeroom in the back, droplets of rain clinging to his hair and coat.

"What are you doing here?" He came forward, his brow furrowed.

She felt like she should be the one asking that question. A moment ago she'd been completely alone; then he'd appeared out of nowhere. "I've done a little cleaning, but I'm mainly sorting through the books. I underestimated how much dust there would be, though, or I would have brought cleaning supplies."

If she could have found a way to get them out of the house without her father noticing, that is. The idea of her cleaning might have tested his good mood.

Perhaps she'd ask Foster and their French chef to see that cleaning supplies were placed in the coach before she came to the library next time.

Yuri gave his head a small shake. "You shouldn't be cleaning in that, Ros. At least not while I'm here getting the floor wet enough to be mopped."

Ros? Since when did he call her Ros? No one called her that, except maybe her mother when she was a small girl and before Father decided that the nickname didn't sound sophisticated enough. But there was something almost tender in the way it fell from Yuri's lips. What might it be like to hear him say it every day?

Which was a ridiculous thing to think. Goodness. What had gotten into her?

"I'll bring more serviceable clothes tomorrow, if Father gives me permission to come shelve books again, that is. But where did you come from?" She pulled her gaze away from his and peered around his shoulder. "Is there a back door?"

"Through the storeroom, yes." He jabbed a thumb over his shoulder.

"Ah, well . . ." She wasn't quite sure what to say. Had he come through the front door, the coachman would have seen him, and she would need to leave to prevent questions. But since the coachman hadn't seen him and the rain outside was coming down so hard it was impossible to see through the windows, she could stay a little longer.

"Are you here to work? I have permission to stay until five thirty. But do you mind building a fire?"

He just stood there looking at her, the side of his jaw flexing, almost as though there was something he wanted to say. Then he turned and headed toward the stove and the small pile of dry wood.

She bent to pick up the crate she'd been about to move before Yuri had come in. But the moment she tried to lift it, her wrist protested, and she let out a small cry, dropping the crate back to the floor.

"What's wrong?" Yuri was by her side in an instant.

She straightened to her full height, then winced as she stretched her wrist, trying to get the pain to subside. "It's just my wrist. Nothing to be concerned over."

She expected him to head back to the woodstove then, but he didn't. He stayed there, right beside her, so close that she could almost feel the warmth of his body through her coat.

"Can I see it?" he asked, his eyes riveted to her hand.

"I, ah . . ." She slid it behind her back. "That's unnecessary. It's healing just fine."

"If that were true, you would have been able to pick up that crate."

She swallowed and took a step back, but that only caused her to bump against the bookshelf.

"Rosalind . . ." Yuri's voice was calm and patient, but the muscle on the side of his jaw pulsed, a tiny movement she couldn't help but notice given how close they were standing.

It almost made him seem angry. But why would he be angry? She was voluntarily helping with the library. That meant he should be thanking her, didn't it?

"You really don't need to see it. I promise." She slid her wrist even farther behind her back. "The doctor said I could take the sling off after two weeks, and it's been two weeks and three days." What she didn't tell him was that she'd taken the sling off more than a week early, and that she'd convinced her father he didn't need to send for Dr. Hollis to inspect it at the end of the two weeks.

Yuri took another step closer, that muscle still pulsing on the side of his jaw, and suddenly he was too big, too close, too dangerous. His frame loomed over her as she stood against the bookshelf, completely and utterly trapped.

She pressed her eyes shut and sucked in a breath through lungs that felt as though they'd been coated in glass shards.

He muttered a word under his breath, low and harsh, and backed away.

How she could feel such a thing with her eyes closed, she didn't know, but when she opened her eyes, he was standing several feet away, his hands splayed wide in a gesture of innocence.

"I'm not going to hurt you, Ros." The gentleness in his tone contrasted with the stiff way he held himself. "Not today. Not tomorrow. Not ever. Do you understand?"

"Bryony," she whispered. "She told you, didn't she?"

His gaze flicked down to her arm, which she'd dropped to her side at some point. "About your father and how he treats you? Yes. I don't know why it took her so long. I think she assumed I already knew." He scrubbed a hand over his face. "I should have known, shouldn't I? All the clues were there. I'm sorry for being so blind."

Her brows pinched together. "You're not blind." He noticed more about her than anyone.

"Tell me, did your father hurt your wrist because you snuck out to go to Mikhail and Bryony's wedding reception? Did he figure out where you'd gone and punish you for it?"

"Yes," she whispered into the space between them.

His throat worked, his muscles moving as though he'd just swallowed something sharp and painful. "I'd still like to see your wrist, just to make sure it's healing. Do you mind?"

He asked so kindly, it was almost impossible to refuse, so she held out her arm. "If you want to look at it, you can, but it's going to take a dreadfully long time to undo the buttons on my glove without a hook."

He came closer, his steps tentative and cautious, as though taking painstaking effort not to startle her again. Then he wordlessly began undoing the buttons that ran halfway to her elbow, his fingers large against the tiny black beads.

Outside, rain splattered the windows and pounded against the roof, but somehow the room felt small and warm, never mind there was still no fire in the stove. The feeling of her arm in his hands and the way he studied her wrist as he undid each and every button seemed to banish the coldness.

Her throat grew dry and her breath hitched, two sensations she often felt around her father. But this was different.

Far different.

Unlike last time, his closeness didn't frighten her; it made her aware of everything about him. The rhythm of his breathing, the slight brush of his sleeve against hers, the careful way his fingers moved. From this distance she could count the various shades of brown in his eyes and see the shadow of stubble along his jaw.

And suddenly she had the strangest desire to step closer, to feel his arms wrapped around her and lay her head on his chest, just so she could hear the steady thump of his heartbeat.

Oh, what was she thinking? She was engaged, and even if she wasn't, Yuri Amos was the last man she could get any romantic inclinations about.

He released the last button, then slowly tugged the glove off her hand.

His frown deepened as he surveyed the skin. It was ugly and discolored from fading bruises, and even though the swelling had gone down when she'd worn the sling, it was coming back.

She'd looked at it as little as possible over the past week and covered it with a glove from the moment she woke every morning to when she went to bed each night.

Yuri's touch remained gentle as his fingers skimmed over the worst of the bruising, then he rotated her wrist with a slow turn.

She sucked in a breath when the movement sent a stab of pain up her arm.

His eyes flitted briefly up to hers, then he moved his gaze right back to her hand. Next, he took her sleeve itself and slowly slid it a few inches above her elbow, stopping only when the fabric constricted and wouldn't go any farther.

She looked away, toward the bookshelf, the floor, anything that wouldn't allow him to see her eyes.

He was completely silent, but somehow that was worse than facing his anger. Somehow that said more than if he had started yelling or stumbled over himself trying to talk.

<hr>

Yuri wanted to be sick again. The bruising was more severe than he'd imagined. Splotches of purple and green and yellow crept from her wrist halfway up her forearm. And the bruises higher on her arm, away from her wrist, looked newer. They were deep purple instead of fading yellow and green, and some of them were groups of little ovals, the perfect size and shape of fingers.

His pulse kicked hard in his throat. He wanted to tear something apart. Her father. The walls. The world that let men like him walk free.

How had he missed this? How had he met her on the beach for three years without knowing? How many times had he said hello to her in town without the faintest inkling something was wrong? How many other bruises had she been hiding?

And why hadn't she told him?

He drew in a slow breath. "You'll have to forgive me. I usually tell people that a merry heart fixes most things. But no amount of laughter or joking will fix this. You have to let me get you out."

"Get me out?" she whispered. "What are you talking about?"

"You can't stay in Sitka. What if your father does this again? What if it's worse next time?"

She tugged her arm away, her eyes dropping to the floor. "He hasn't touched me since my engagement. Besides, Leeland will take me away from all this in a few months."

Leeland. Yuri raked a hand through his hair. He didn't trust that man to behave himself around Rosalind either. "Is he going to treat you any better?"

Her lip trembled, but all she said was, "He hasn't hit me."

"Not yet. But he's known for having a temper when he drinks. What's he going to do when he takes you to a completely different city?"

"Please, Yuri, this isn't your problem," she whispered, her voice barely audible over the sound of the rain on the roof.

"What if I want it to be?" he rasped, his voice coarse and gritty.

Something flickered across her face—surprise, confusion, hope?—he wasn't sure what to name it.

"I have a plan, but it's complicated."

"How's it complicated?"

A strand of golden hair had come loose from her pins, and she shoved it away from her face. "If I leave, if I run wherever you want me to go, my father will be able to find me. And now he has Leeland to help him."

"No. We'll put you somewhere safe, hide you in a small town where he'd never think to look." He'd put more thought into this than he wanted to admit.

She shook her head. "It won't be enough. He'll still find me."

He raked a hand through his hair. "How? He can't send men to search every town in the country. That's impossible even for him."

"That's not how he'll find me." She turned toward the crate of books again, as though suddenly remembering there was work to be done. "He'll trace me through my money."

"You mean the donations you make to the charities? Isn't that your father's money?"

She bent to pick up one of the books, then frowned at him. "No. It was my mother's. She left me an inheritance after she died, and when I turned eighteen, I got access to the money. I've been investing on my own for the past four years, and I have six places I support. You already know about the charities. Even if I leave, my solicitor will still need to send money to my list of charities, which means I'll have to communicate with him. It's the same solicitor who handled my mother's accounts before she died, and my father knows him. That's how he'll find me."

The money she was donating to charities was hers? Yuri stared at her. Everything he'd thought he'd known about Rosalind Caldwell had just cracked down the middle not once but twice in the course of the same conversation.

"I, ah . . . I assume this is a good amount of money?" It had to be for her to support so many charities.

"Yes." She pressed onto her toes and slid the book she was holding onto the top shelf. "I've managed the investments on my own too, but even though none of it belongs to my father, he's powerful enough to pressure the bank into putting his name on my account. And once he does that, he could take the money from me. Then where would I be?"

"I don't even want to know how much 'a good amount' is in your world."

The town might whisper behind her back about her privilege and her father's power, but she'd really been investing and giving to others, making decisions for herself and growing a future. All while being too trapped to fully make use of her money.

He gave his head a small shake. "I could lend you money to live on for a few months, and surely the orphanages and women's shelters and all the other places you've been supporting will understand if you ceased your donations for a bit so we can get your funds transferred to another bank and moved to a new solicitor that your father doesn't know about."

She turned to him, another book in her hand. "In order to change solicitors, I'd have to go to Washington, DC. But after that, I could leave and disappear rather quickly, couldn't I? I suppose I could send all the charities rather large gifts in February and explain in my letter that I won't be able to send funds for six months. That should be enough time to get my money moved."

"Do it, Ros, and don't wait until February. Do it now. None

of the places you support would want you living in a situation where you could be hurt just so you can send them money."

She swallowed, the delicate muscles of her throat working.

"Promise me you'll do it. Promise me you'll try to leave." He took a step closer, not caring how desperate he sounded. "Before you get hurt worse. Don't let your fear of your father stop you from doing what you need to do most. God will protect you."

"I'm already working on a plan. It will take time, maybe a month or two, but you don't need to worry. Father hasn't been violent lately." Rosalind slid the book in her hand onto the shelf that was even with her elbow. "Father didn't even get angry after I failed to get the library named after him."

"That's why you wanted to . . ." His throat turned dry, memories of last week's library committee meeting flooding his mind. "He's . . . he's going to hurt you if we don't plaster the name Caldwell on the new library?"

"That's what I'm saying. Usually he'd be angry with me, but when I got back from the meeting last week, prepared to give him the news, Leeland was there, and he proposed." She bent down and picked up three books from the crate. "Father wasn't even upset about the library."

"But he will be once we pick a name."

"Hopefully not, since I'm engaged. Like I said, he's been very lenient lately. That's why he let me come here. And a couple days ago, he let me invite Millicent, Jane, and Freya over for tea. The only friend I'm not permitted to see is Bryony."

He didn't trust any of it. "How long will this 'good mood' last? What happens when something makes your father angry again? Will you bear the brunt of it?"

She turned away and slid one of the books onto the shelf at her elbow, right beside the previous book she'd shelved. "Like I said, I have a plan, but it might take a couple months. But you don't need to worry about me, I promise. I'll find a way to survive."

He pressed his eyes shut. "This isn't the kind of thing anyone should have to survive. Your father's first job should be to protect you. You have bruises from his fingers on your arm, and they look fresh."

She slid the other two books onto the second shelf from the top, then rolled her shoulder in its socket. "I've always bruised easy. Not everything is how it appears."

"Are you telling me your father never grips your arm a little too hard? What about your fiancé? Is he gentle with you?"

She was silent.

"Ros, your well-being matters more than the money. Don't let that keep you here." His voice came out rougher than he intended. "We can untangle the accounts later. Right now, you need to be safe. I can have you on a ship headed away from Sitka with two days' notice. I could probably even take the skiff and leave in the dead of night tonight, then take you to a port where your father won't be able to trace you. Maybe Vancouver or Portland? You could get on a train from there, and no one will know you even arrived in town. We can change your name. We can buy you a wig so that your hair's a different color. We can do anything. I'll even go with you to Washington, DC, just to make sure no one your father's hired has found you. Just tell me what you want, and I'll see it's done."

She looked at him for a long moment, her eyes filled with something he couldn't quite name. Then her gaze drifted to the floor and her shoulders hunched in on herself. "Just give me a few more days to work on my plan."

"You don't need a perfect plan to leave. You just have to let me help get you away from here and trust God to keep you safe. Do you remember the verse I shared with you at the wedding reception? 'Fear thou not; for I am with thee: be not dismayed;

for I am thy God: I will strengthen thee; yea, I will help thee; yea, I will uphold thee with the right hand of my righteousness.' That verse is still in the Bible. Those promises are still yours to claim if you want them."

"I'm trying, Yuri," she whispered. "Please believe me when I say I'm trying." Then she turned her back to him and returned to shelving books.

17

San Francisco; the Same Day

Alexei lifted a bite of lobster Newburg to his mouth and chewed slowly, then glanced at Laurel, seated beside him. She was quiet and poised, her light brown hair reflecting the glow from the elaborate chandelier. On his other side, Sacha was working through his plate of food with mechanical efficiency, his usual smile nowhere to be found.

Across from him sat Beatrice and Genevieve, Laurel Farnsworth's younger sisters, each flanked by their husbands, who wore suits every bit as tailored and unwrinkled as Farnsworth's.

Alexei swallowed his food, trying to pay attention to the conversation.

"The fund has already surpassed thirty thousand, and the board expects a full expansion by early spring." Edward Banning, one of Laurel's brothers-in-law, dabbed at his face with his napkin.

Alexei took another bite of food, which at least prevented him from yawning. The pastry that the rich lobster sauce had been ladled over was light and flaky, perfectly balancing the denseness of the brandied cream and chunks of lobster. Getting the lobster from New England all the way to California wasn't cheap. The shellfish would have had to be packed in ice and hauled by rail for days.

Even though, as the owner of a trading company, he could ship delicacies for virtually nothing, he'd never bothered importing food like this. Maybe he'd been wrong not to splurge every so often, though, because the meal was excellent.

"Personally I think the municipal bonds are the smarter long-term play, but one can't have his way with everything when dealing with a board of directors," Banning continued, sending his wife Beatrice a tight smile.

"If you want the highest return, real estate is where you ought to be investing," Dwayne Everett, Genevieve's husband, responded.

While Alexei didn't know all the details of Everett's holdings, he was aware the man had amassed a rather impressive number of rental and business properties in the city.

"There's nothing like bricks and mortar to solidify a reputation in this town," Everett added.

"I think both have their merits." Farnsworth took a sip of wine from where he sat at the head of the table. His wife was directly across from him, at the opposite end of the long table, in a dark green gown with a dyed ostrich feather sticking out from the side of her carefully piled hair. "Buildings can burn, ships can wreck, and markets can crash. A wise man hedges his investments and doesn't rely too heavily on any one thing."

"Even if that man happens to own a shipping company?" Alexei asked.

Farnsworth eyed him. "Especially then. One storm can drag multiple vessels to the sea floor."

He agreed. "I'm sorry to say our father had no desire to diversify his holdings."

Farnsworth shook his head. "A pity, that, but I've heard it's something you're trying to correct."

"Indeed." Alexei took a bite of food, then looked at Laurel seated beside him, hoping his full mouth and the fact he'd just turned his attention elsewhere would prevent the man from asking any specific questions. He had no desire to explain his holdings and investment strategies to two men he barely knew and another he'd just cut out of a business deal.

Banning quickly filled the silence, pulling the conversation right back to his defense of bonds, which only seemed to irk Everett.

Sacha muttered something. When Alexei glanced at him, his face was an emotionless mask. But the way he sat, with his shoulders stiff and his back tight, told Alexei enough. That and the fact his brother's plate was nearly cleaned, never mind they'd only been served the main course ten minutes ago.

It really was a shame neither of them was enjoying himself. The dining room itself was far nicer than anything they had in Sitka, with mahogany wainscotting, gilded-mirror frames, and hand-painted wallpaper. The chandelier overhead was large and intricate, showering them in light that glinted off the cut crystal goblets and the porcelain dishes on the table.

But given the choice, they'd both enjoy a simple bear roast or borscht served on plain dishes while his family was crammed around the scarred kitchen table back in Sitka. That would have been far more appealing than this meal, even with the lobster.

"Is the food to your liking?" Laurel asked quietly from beside him.

He turned toward her. She really was quite beautiful, with clear green eyes set into a delicate face and her soft brown hair pulled into an updo that looked both simple and elegant. Everything about her was finely composed, from the graceful slope of her neck to the faint color in her cheeks to the smooth gown draping her frame.

Her brows knit together. "Or is something not to your liking?"

The food. Right. She'd asked him about it, and rather than answer, he'd ended up staring at her like a besotted fool.

"Forgive me. The food is quite delicious." He cleared his throat, then raised his eyes to Laurel's mother. "Mrs. Farnsworth, please give my compliments to your chef."

Laurel's father waved his hand absently. "Of course. We brought him in from France last year, and we've already decided we're never letting him go. His cooking is truly extraordinary."

"I just love hosting dinner parties now that he is the chef. His dishes are the envy of all our guests." Mrs. Farnsworth gave a delicate laugh and lifted her wineglass, the trio of rings on her hand catching the light. "Gertrude Downing is fit to be tied that we have a better chef than her. It makes me want to invite her over for luncheon once a week."

"Mother? You've had the Downings over for lunch? Next time invite me as well." Genevieve adjusted the heavy pendant at her neck—a pendant that looked to be three times the size of the modest one Laurel wore—then leaned forward, her eyes gleaming with a look of excitement Alexei didn't quite trust. "I heard they are going to have to close their garment factory. They can't compete with the prices of ready-made dresses from out east."

Beatrice wrinkled her nose. "Serves them right for wanting

to get into such an industry. Can you imagine wearing a dress made in some dirty factory and not by a dressmaker who measures and fits you and then makes the dress to your exact size?" She smoothed a hand over the bodice of her sapphire-colored gown. "It took Madame DuBois two weeks to make this dress."

Genevieve sniffed. "Mine took nearly three weeks. The lace was imported from Bruges. But that's not the point. Can you imagine the money their father will lose, needing to close everything? I don't even know that they'll be able to keep their French chef. They might be forced to settle for an American one."

"That would serve Meredith Downing right." Beatrice tapped a finger against the stem of her wineglass, not seeming the least bit concerned about the potential Finnancial ruin of the Downing family. "Do you know what she told me at the Wentworth wedding? She had the audacity to assume that my dress was out of style. She said something about it looking like something she'd seen in *Harper's Bazaar* three years ago. Three years! Can you imagine? I felt amply justified in informing her that it had been in December's edition, and I had promptly commissioned Madame DuBois to make one for me, with a few enhancements, of course."

"The nerve of that girl." Genevieve huffed, then looked across the table at Laurel. "Did she say anything about *your* dress? It likely *was* from three years ago."

"Oh, heavens," Mrs. Farnsworth sighed and pressed a hand to her chest. "Do not remind me of that atrocity. Laurel, I told you to pay a visit to Madame DuBois in December to have a new dress made for the Wentworth wedding, but there you were, wearing that same dress you wore to the spring ball at the Mercers. I still don't know what you were thinking."

All eyes at the table turned to Laurel. She shifted in her chair, staring down at her plate with her lobster Newburg only half eaten. "It was a perfectly good gown that I'd only worn once. I saw no reason not to wear it again."

Beatrice dropped her head into her hand. "She's hopeless, Mother. I don't know what to do with her."

"Honestly, Laurel." Genevieve waved a hand at her sister. "Why do you complain about not having a husband? No man will want to marry you if you don't even try to look presentable."

Alexei glanced at Farnsworth, waiting for him to put a stop to the conversation. For a family so concerned about appearances, disparaging a family member during dinner with guests hardly seemed proper. But Farnsworth simply took another bite of food.

"I don't complain about not having a husband," Laurel said, her brows drawing down. "That's Mother. And I *do* try to look presentable."

Beatrice shook her head. "That's the fifth or sixth time I've seen you wear that dress, and it doesn't even have any embellishments. Genevieve is right. You don't even try."

"And I know for a fact," Mrs. Farnsworth added with a disapproving glance, "that you only gave your lady's maid a half hour to dress you and do your hair before dinner. That's not trying to make a good impression."

Alexei set down his fork, the clink of silver hitting the china plate resonating through the room. "I think Laurel looks lovely. Perhaps the fact that she only needs a half hour to ready herself for dinner is a testament to her natural beauty."

Beatrice coughed into her wine. "You do know Laurel's twenty-five and hasn't yet been able to find herself a husband? Daddy's been trying to find her one for years."

Alexei stiffened. Beside him, Laurel had hunched her

shoulders, her whole body seeming to shrink in on itself. Did the women in this family have no shred of decency? He couldn't imagine what he would do if one of his sisters said such a thing about another sister, and in front of company, no less.

But neither Beatrice's husband nor her father seemed inclined to put her in her place.

Alexei opened his mouth to say something on her behalf, but Sacha spoke first. "Perhaps she hasn't met the right man yet."

Beatrice set down her wineglass with a thud. "Or perhaps none of the right men want anything to do with a woman who spends more time in the kitchen like a servant than she does making herself presentable. Did you know that's where I found her when I arrived earlier, Father?"

"You were in the kitchen?" Farnsworth's voice was cold.

Laurel's cheeks colored.

"This is so embarrassing," Genevieve muttered.

"I told you to stay out of the kitchen." Farnsworth pinned his gaze to Laurel. "Have I not made myself clear on that?"

"You did," Laurel whispered, staring down at her plate.

"What did you make?"

"The pastry and the dessert."

"The pastry?" Her father probed the last remaining bite on his plate with a fork as though it was suddenly now worthy of the waste bin.

"I wasn't trying to be obstinate. I just wanted to help. I've been working on a new tart recipe and—"

"What do you suppose Mr. Amos thinks, seeing my daughter behaving like one of the housemaids?"

"I think she's skilled and generous," Alexei ground out. "And I thought the pastry was a delicious complement to the lobster sauce."

Across the table, Genevieve huffed. "And I say it makes her little better than a scullery maid."

"It's highly inappropriate, to be sure." Genevieve's husband agreed.

Beatrice pressed a hand to her chest. "Just think, what if word of this spreads?"

"It won't spread," Farnsworth snapped. "Because no one here is going to speak of this." He ran his eyes around the table, then sat back and tossed his napkin onto his plate, the last two bites of the lobster pastry untouched.

"Are you going to have the dessert served?" Genevieve slanted a glance at Laurel. "After she disobeyed you?"

"We have to bring something out." Beatrice's eyes grew round. "It would make us little better than paupers to end a meal without dessert."

"I agree, but not what Laurel made." Mrs. Farnsworth pressed a hand to her chest. "Surely there's something else in the kitchen that will suffice."

Farnsworth snapped his fingers, and one of the servants appeared by his side. "Have the chef send something other than Laurel's tart out for dessert. See what he has on hand."

"Yes, sir." The servant gave a nod, then headed through the doorway.

Beside Alexei, Laurel's head bent to the point that she could see nothing beside her lap, and she didn't seem to have any intention of looking up any time soon.

The servant returned a moment later and moved straight to the host. They exchanged a few words, and then Farnsworth gave a subtle nod. Two more servants stepped forward and began clearing plates. No one spoke. Even Beatrice and Genevieve had reverted to taking polite sips of wine.

Beside him, Sacha sat with his arms crossed, his face like

stone. Alexei couldn't blame him. He probably looked as serious.

"Well," Banning said, folding his napkin and glancing down the table, "I for one wouldn't mind seeing your chef's dessert menu make its way into the hotel kitchens. I hear the Fairmont is still hiring."

"Hotels are a passing fad," Everett replied, swirling the wine in his glass. "No one wants to live like a transient forever. You want stability? Own the buildings people rent."

"Not this again," Beatrice muttered with a sigh. "It's the same argument every meal."

Farnsworth gave a faint smile. "That's what happens when one son-in-law owns buildings and the other owns bonds."

Genevieve leaned in toward her husband. "I do hope you're not still invested in that cannery down by the harbor. The newspapers say it smells dreadful."

"It smells like money," Everett said smoothly. "But I appreciate your delicate nose, darling."

THE DOOR to the dining room opened, and two servers returned bearing dessert trays that held chocolate pudding.

A crystal dish was set before Alexei, and he picked up his spoon and took a bite. Rich cocoa flavor spread across his tongue. It tasted excellent as far as chocolate pudding went, but he'd bet every last cent in his bank account that Laurel's dessert would have been better.

He glanced her way. She still hadn't moved from her hunched position, but he caught the slight tremble in the lace cuff at her wrist.

He lowered his spoon to the saucer and leaned close. "What kind of tart did you make?"

Laurel shook her head, not even trying to meet his gaze.

"Lemon cream and sugared orange peel, topped with candied ginger and raspberry syrup."

His mouth turned moist just hearing it. "It sounds delicious."

She peeked up at her father, her teeth sinking into her bottom lip. "I can have two of the tarts sent over to your hotel later, if you're serious about trying it, that is."

"Actually," he said, his voice low and steady, "I was thinking you could come visit me in Alaska and make it there."

Her eyes jerked over to his. "You . . . you want me to go to Alaska?"

He wanted her to go anywhere that wasn't here. He had for as long as he'd known her. She didn't fit into the gilded life her family lived.

"It would be my honor to host you. Sacha and his wife, Maggie, share a house with me, and they would make perfectly acceptable chaperones. It would give you an opportunity to see whether living in Alaska might suit you."

Laurel's breath caught, her fingers curling gently around the stem of her water glass. "I don't know if I would suit Alaska. I've never been farther north than Seattle."

"That's all the more reason for you to come see Alaska for yourself and find out if it suits you."

When she looked up at him again, a small, shy smile curved her lips. "It would be quite the adventure."

"I imagine you'd handle it better than most." He ran his eyes over her. "And I want you to know that you look lovely tonight. I don't care how many times you've worn your gown, it suits you well."

Color bloomed across her cheeks. "Thank you."

Alexei studied her a moment longer, letting the silence settle comfortably between them while the rest of the table continued to chatter on about investments, property lines, and the latest gossip from Nob Hill.

If only he could snap his fingers and have this be the last dinner Laurel Farnsworth ever had to spend pretending to belong in a place she so clearly didn't.

He didn't have the power to whisk her away just yet. But maybe he would soon.

18

Sitka; the Same Day

Rosalind returned home to find a sapphire necklace waiting on her vanity. Much like her engagement ring, small diamonds formed a ring around the circular stone pendant. A note was scrawled beside it, not in her father's handwriting, but in Leeland's large, sloppy script.

Wear this to dinner with the dark blue satin.

She didn't want to wear either, but what would happen if she didn't?

Maybe Yuri was right. Maybe she should just leave without trying to find proof of her father bribing the Marshal.

She absently brushed her bruised wrist. It wasn't healing as it should. She probably needed to go back to using the sling, but not when her father might see her, or he'd pull her off the library committee and refuse to let her friends visit again tomorrow.

She rang for her maid and walked into her dressing room, filled with gowns of all colors and fabrics. She preferred light colors and material. Lavander chiffon or pale blue silk, but Leeland always seemed to want her in heavy fabrics and dark tones, like royal blue velvet or jade green satin. The requests became more frequent with each day he stayed in Sitka.

Her maid appeared in the doorway, and she tried to say that she wanted to wear the dark blue satin, but her mouth didn't want to work, and her tongue felt as though it had been wrapped in cotton.

She didn't want to change, not really. She'd much rather wear the dress she'd been wearing all day. It was light and comfortable, with soft yellow tones that matched her hair and reminded her of spring.

But her maid was already moving toward the dark blue dress. She pulled it from the hanger, then turned and smiled. "Mr. Vandermeer requested that we recurl your hair for dinner tonight. And did you see the necklace he left on your vanity? It's lovely. You're blessed to have such a thoughtful fiancé."

Was she blessed, though? Truly?

Her mother would tell her to rejoice in the Lord despite her circumstances, but surely this wasn't what God wanted for her life. Surely she was missing something. Should she really be thanking God because her father hadn't hit her since the night he sprained her wrist?

She sat silently as the maid went through the motions of removing her walking dress and putting on the dinner gown, then curling her hair for the second time that day and piling it atop her head. Finally, the maid added the sapphire pendant around her neck, then stood back so Rosalind could stare at her reflection.

A poised, elegant woman looked back at her. Was this what Yuri had seen when he'd looked at her so intently that afternoon? When he'd begged her to find a way to leave Sitka? A mannerly woman who was a perfect example of femininity? Or had he seen beneath the shell to a woman who liked to read books and visit with friends? Who would gladly volunteer time to help any of the charities she supported, if only she lived nearby. Who was quite good at managing Finnances and investments and even enjoyed reading the business section of the newspaper.

She'd bet Yuri Amos had never in his life told a woman what clothes to wear—and that he never would, not even after he married.

She suddenly wanted to be having dinner at his house, not her father's. And she suddenly didn't want to marry a tyrant or someone her father picked for her. She wanted to marry someone kind. Someone who smiled. Someone who asked her what she would like and listened when she answered.

Someone like Yuri Amos.

It was a ridiculous notion. She could never actually marry Yuri himself, and not just because their families were enemies but because every girl in Sitka wanted to marry him. He was the most eligible bachelor in town, and half a dozen women, if not more, were already in love with him, Freya, Jane, and Millicent included.

And why wouldn't every single woman in Sitka want to marry him? He was charming and kind and helpful, never too busy to stop and lend a hand or give an encouraging word. He was probably the most wonderful man in all of Alaska, or maybe in all of America.

She hoped that one day God might bring someone similar to him into her life. Someone who would love her for who she was and not marry her because of who her father was or the business connections she would bring into a marriage.

She lifted a hand to the necklace at her throat, fingers brushing the sapphire as she stared at her reflection. She couldn't stay in Sitka or marry Leeland.

Which was all the more reason she needed to find proof of her father's illegal activities. She couldn't let Leeland's desire to be either constantly by her side or with her father deter her from the task that needed doing.

She went downstairs and forced herself to sit beside Leeland at dinner, smiling politely and listening while he and Father and Uncle Simon talked about requiring traders to become Indian agents.

After dinner, she slipped into the kitchen and asked the chef to send a maid to wake her first thing in the morning, then retired to her room for the evening.

Part of her hated herself for creeping down to her father's study after the maid woke her in the morning. It felt sneaky and dishonest, but not more sneaky than bribing Alaska's most powerful lawman and trying to swindle the Amos family out of sixty thousand dollars.

Her heart pounded the entire time she was in the study, each creak of the house and gust of the wind somehow making her believe her father was in the hallway headed to his study hours earlier than usual.

It was all a bit ridiculous. She knew he'd stayed up late with Leeland. She didn't have the faintest idea what the two of them had been discussing, but they would both sleep until nine or later.

But after spending three hours searching his study, she came away empty-handed.

19

Sitka; the Next Day

By the time Yuri strode into the meeting room at the old governor's mansion the next evening, his eyes felt as though they'd been coated in sand.

It probably had something to do with how late he'd stayed up the night before, first reading his Bible and then poring over every last paper in the office to see if it might give him some clue as to how he could get Rosalind away from her father. Or better yet, give him some clue regarding a crime her father committed that could get him locked in a jail cell so he couldn't hurt Rosalind.

He'd come up with nothing.

He knew Preston Caldwell had done underhanded things over the years. His brother, the governor, was no different. But proving it in a court of law was something else entirely.

Everyone that family hired to do their dirty work was paid too well to ever confess the Caldwells' involvement, even men who were currently sitting in prison.

Mikhail and Bryony had both joined him after dinner last night, all of them wanting to find some way that might prevent Caldwell from going after Rosalind if they helped her get away. After he'd returned home from the temporary library, he'd told them everything about his conversation with Rosalind in the empty building, her bruises, the source of the donation money, and the real reason Rosalind wouldn't leave Sitka. All of it.

The only part he'd left out was how badly he'd wanted to pull Rosalind against his chest and hold her, just so she could know what it felt like to be safe, even if the embrace lasted only a few minutes.

"Sorry I'm late." Yuri opened his satchel and pulled out the agenda and his notes from last week.

"It's all right. We were just talking about shelves." Angus McCreedy rubbed the back of his neck. "Rosalind says she's been to the temporary building, and we need more in there, so—"

"Actually, the first thing I want to discuss is the name." Yuri set his papers down and plopped into the chair at the head of the table. "We're going to temporarily name the library after its largest local contributors, Preston and Simon Caldwell. Meaning the library will be called the Caldwell Memorial Library."

"We're what?" Arthur Bixby's pencil clattered to the table.

"I thought you said we should bring our list of names and vote." Mrs. Pembroke sniffed. "That's the fair way to do it. I have mine right here." She patted the folded sheet of stationery in front of her.

"I changed my mind," Yuri snapped, his words causing the room to go still. "Once we have a plot purchased and construction on the new building is underway, we can revisit the subject."

"How much is Caldwell paying you to do this?" Bixby growled.

Yuri didn't meet the other man's gaze. Instead, his eyes drifted to Rosalind. It was the first time he'd dared to look at her since walking into the room. He expected her to be sitting there with her head ducked and hands hidden on her lap, just as she had for the previous meeting.

But she was looking straight at him, a panicked look in her eyes. "No. You can't do this. You said we would vote. It needs to be fair."

That's what he'd thought too, until he realized there was a very good chance Rosalind would end up with more than just an injured wrist if the library wasn't named after her father.

"See?" McCreedy slapped his palm on the table. "Not even Rosalind wants the library named after her family."

"I wouldn't say that." Mr. Bixby had leaned over next to Rosalind and was looking at the paper on the table in front of her. "All three of the ideas listed on her paper here have Caldwell in the name."

Mrs. Pembroke tilted her nose in the air, somehow managing to look down at Yuri and glare at the same time, never mind he was a good eight inches taller than the petite woman. "And here I thought you would be a fair and honorable president of the library committee. Mr. Bixby already asked how much Preston is paying you to do this, and I want to know the same thing."

He pressed his lips together. The others could think whatever they wanted. The truth was, he had a biblical obligation to help Rosalind. Psalm 82:3–4 was clear. *Defend the poor and fatherless: do justice to the afflicted and needy. Deliver the poor and needy: rid them out of the hand of the wicked.*

The Bible itself asked that he do justice and rid the needy out of the hand of the wicked There were only a handful of ways he could do that when it came to Rosalind, and he was going to take full advantage of each and every one of them.

Later, after Rosalind was far away from Sitka, the library committee could revisit the name issue in earnest. Hopefully Rosalind would have decided to leave Sitka on her own, but if not, at least she would be married and far enough away from her father that he couldn't hurt her.

In the meantime, he didn't care whether everyone else argued or assumed Caldwell had paid him off.

———

Rosalind gripped her hands together under the table. She'd come to the meeting tonight with so many ideas, and now she couldn't voice a single one of them, not when everyone was mad at her.

But they weren't nearly as mad as she was. Fury boiled in her chest every time she looked at Yuri.

What did he think he was doing, barging in late with red-rimmed eyes and a stubbled jaw that made him look like he hadn't even bothered to shave, then announcing that the library would be named after her family?

Except she knew what he was doing. Of course she did.

He was trying to protect her.

And maybe she should thank him for that, but somehow that only made her angrier.

Because now the rest of the committee wouldn't even look her in the eye, and no one was inclined to listen to a word she said.

All she'd wanted was for them to consider her ideas, like they had at the last meeting when she suggested purchasing a waterfront plot. But Yuri's pronouncement about the library name set everything off on the wrong note, and now no one could agree on anything. They argued over chairs and shelf height and donation lists, and Rosalind didn't get more than two sentences out the entire time.

When Yuri finally ended the meeting, she shot to her feet, ready to bolt toward the door, but Yuri's voice stopped her.

"Rosalind, can you stay back a moment?"

More heat filled her veins, but she stilled.

Mrs. Pembroke sniffed again, then headed for the door, her nose high enough that she just might drown if it started raining.

Mr. McCreedy and Mr. Bixby followed without appearing to think much of the two of them being left alone.

The second the door clicked shut behind Mr. Bixby, she whirled on Yuri. "How could you?"

Yuri blinked. "How could I what? Name the library after your family? You know very well why I did it."

"Now everyone hates me." She despised the tremble in her voice, but she didn't know how to get rid of it.

"They don't hate you. They hate me." Yuri jabbed a thumb at his chest. "I'm the one who did it."

"You might be the one who forced everyone into giving you your way, but I'm the one they blame for it." Tears filled her eyes, but she pushed them away. It was ridiculous to want to cry. Yuri hadn't hurt her, so why did what he'd done feel more painful than her father's fists?

"Hey, don't cry." He crossed the distance between them in two large steps.

"I'm not."

"There's a tear streaking down your cheek, Ros."

Confound it! She pressed her eyes shut, but that only caused another tear to slip from her eye.

He lifted a hand to her cheek and swiped at her tear with his thumb. "Will you let me take you away from here yet?" he whispered.

She shook her head. "No, but I'm working on it. I promise."

"That's what you said yesterday. How are you working on it? Did you write your charities and tell them they wouldn't be receiving money from you for six months? Do you at least have letters for me to mail?"

"No."

He dropped his hand. "I'm going to get you away from here, Rosalind. I don't care how many times I have to ask or how much nagging I have to do. I don't care if I have to storm into every library committee meeting for the next four months and do something outlandish and embarrassing. You need to escape your father, and marrying the fiancé he picked for you isn't a good way out."

She licked her lips. "I know. I just . . . There's something I have to do first."

He narrowed his eyes. "What?"

"You don't want to know."

"I absolutely do."

She looked away, her gaze fixed on the ornate molding of the fireplace. "I overheard my uncle and father talking about increasing the amount of bribe money they give to Marshal Hibbs every month. I know there's proof of it somewhere inside my father's study. I want to find it and turn it over to your brother-in-law, the Deputy Marshal."

"What?" Yuri nearly shrieked the word, but when she turned back to face him, she found him stock-still.

"You might be confident that I can escape my father simply by leaving, but I'm not so sure. The fact that he's bribing Alaska's most prominent lawman feels like something I should prove before leaving. If my father's in prison, he can't steal my money or force me to marry Leeland."

He shoved a hand into his hair. "You can't tell me there's a safe way to get that kind of information from your father. What if he finds you searching his study? What if he hurts more than just your wrist?"

"You're the one who told me to ask God for strength and not to let my fear control me. What do you think I'm trying to do? Don't attempt to scare me out of what I need to do. My father bribing the Marshal needs to be brought to light."

He opened his mouth, then closed it. That's what she'd taken the verse from Isaiah 41 to mean? That God would protect her from her father while she tried to prove his involvement in a criminal activity?

He'd told her that verse to encourage her to leave Sitka, not to give her a reason to stay longer. But should he really try to stop her from proving the bribery? The entirety of Alaska suffered whenever Marshal Hibbs looked the other way for influential people committing a crime, and he'd done so more than once.

"Is there something specific you're looking for?" he finally asked. "Or are you searching for a random slip of paper he accidentally left lying around?"

"My father records everything in ledgers. I'm sure there's one that contains not just a record of the Marshal's bribe money but a list of other people who have been bribed too. All I can tell you at the moment is that it's not in his desk."

She's already searched her father's desk? He fisted his hands at his side. "Rosalind . . ."

"You won't get me to change my mind." She lifted her chin.

He swallowed, every muscle of his body still tense. "No. I don't suppose I will." He ran his eyes down her before bringing his gaze back up to meet hers again. "At least promise me you'll be careful. And if you ever feel like you're in danger, or if your father catches you and figures out what you're doing, I can have you away from Sitka within an hour. We'll leave on our skiff and go to Wrangell or Petersburg or Ketchikan, some small village where we can hide for a few weeks before taking you to a larger port."

"All right," she whispered in return. "If I need to leave on short notice, I'll send word through Millicent."

"You promise?" he asked.

She pressed her lips together and sucked in a long breath before finally forming a reply. "Yes. I promise."

His shoulders lost a bit of their tension, and the lines around his mouth softened. "Just don't make me come for you too late."

She nodded, then fled before she found herself accidently stepping into his arms and begging him to take her away from Sitka that very moment.

20

She couldn't sleep. The fire had long since dwindled to embers, but Rosalind lay awake beneath her quilt, her eyes fixed on the shadows dancing across the ceiling. She could still recall the way Yuri's hand had felt on her cheek, soft and warm as he'd wiped a tear away with his thumb.

And she could still see the look of worry that had crept into his eyes when she said she was searching her father's study.

Her stomach let out a low growl, reminding her of the hunger pains she'd ignored for most of the evening, including during the library committee meeting.

She had Leeland to blame for them. He'd decided to start serving her food at meals. At first it had seemed thoughtful and gentlemanly—until she'd realized exactly how little food he planned to let her eat.

He'd barely set any food on her plate for both breakfast and lunch, so she'd been starved by the time dinner had rolled around. But Leeland had dished food onto her plate then too. When she'd reached for the platter of turkey for a second helping, he'd gripped her hand and told her she'd had plenty. And when the servant had come around with slices of pie for dessert, he'd told the servant that she didn't need any pie either.

Father hadn't said a word, and neither had Uncle Simon. All Father had talked about was their marriage contract and how it couldn't be finalized until some unnamed associate arrived from San Francisco or Seattle or maybe even from Washington, DC.

She hadn't quite caught where. She'd been too focused on the heaping platters of food in front of her that she could no longer help herself to.

Hopefully Leeland wouldn't try to restrict her portions again tomorrow. She wasn't sure she could endure another day of eating only bread, a small bowl of soup, and half a serving of turkey for dinner.

Her stomach growled again, and she threw off her covers. That was it. She was going to the kitchen. She padded across the floor and opened the door, then made her way down the familiar hallways and stairs despite the darkness.

When she reached the kitchen, she didn't even need to light a lamp. Dim light emanated from embers in the stove's hearth, allowing her to make her way across the flagstone floor to the pantry.

A plate sat waiting on the shelf at eye level, with pie and stuffing and two slices of cold turkey wrapped loosely in a linen cloth. Had Foster said something to the chef about how little she'd gotten to eat at dinner? She'd have to thank him in the morning.

She took the plate and set it on the table that the chef used for rolling out dough, then dragged a stool as close as she could to the hearth.

The house was cold at this time of night, but she'd been so

hungry, she hadn't thought to put on slippers or throw a wrapper on over her nightgown. She sank her fork into the pie first, never mind the turkey and stuffing on the opposite side of the plate.

Flavors exploded on her tongue. She didn't know how their chef did it. All she knew was that pie wasn't supposed to be this good. It seemed like it should be a sin, really, for pastry to melt in her mouth and berries to taste like they'd been sweetened by sunlight instead of sugar.

She closed her eyes as she chewed, letting the warmth of the embers in the stove and sweetness of the food ease some of the hunger gnawing inside her.

THE HOUSE REMAINED SILENT, the walls thick enough to muffle the wind, and even if Father discovered her here, he likely wouldn't be angry over a quick visit to the kitchen. But she still ate her food as fast as she could, finishing the pie before moving on to the turkey and stuffing.

Once she was done, she pumped water into the sink and washed her plate, then dried it and put it away, removing all evidence that someone had visited the kitchen in the middle of the night.

She should probably go back to bed and catch a few hours of sleep before the scullery maid woke her early to search her father's study. Except she still felt wide awake, and she had little desire to stare at the ceiling for several more hours until dawn lit the sky.

Should she try searching her father's study now? It was half past two in the morning. No one was up. And this would give her an even longer amount of time to search than usual. She still hadn't looked through the large cabinet with her father's property ledgers and land deeds. Perhaps he'd hidden his bribery records in there.

Rather than take the stairs when she left the kitchen, she padded softly down the hallway and turned right. She was nearly to the study when a shadow separated itself from the wall.

"Well, well, well," Leeland's low voice echoed through the hallway. "This is a pretty sight."

She froze. Could he tell she'd been to the kitchen? Would he be angry about her eating?

He stepped closer, then reached out and settled his large hand on her shoulder, letting his thumb stroke the skin of her neck. The scent of brandy clung to his breath, but his movements were too steady for him to be drunk. "This is a rather lovely nightgown. White, too. Nice and virginal." He raked his gaze down her and smiled, but there was nothing kind about the curve of his mouth. "I'll have more made before our wedding."

Her stomach churned, and she tried to shrink against the wall. He was too large and too close. Too powerful.

He chuckled, low and deep, then his thumb settled over the hollow of her throat. "What's wrong, love? Does the thought of being dressed in white when I bed you for the first time make you uncomfortable?"

The thought of him bedding her at all made her beyond uncomfortable, though she didn't say so.

"My only problem with your outfit is that you're not wearing your sapphire necklace." His voice grew lower. "Whyever not?"

She swallowed, but it did nothing to alleviate the growing pressure of his thumb against her throat. Did he realize how hard he was pressing? That his thumb was positioned right over her windpipe? It wasn't that she couldn't breathe at all, but she certainly couldn't breathe as easily as usual.

"I asked you a question." His eyes hardened. "Why aren't you wearing your sapphire necklace?"

"I . . . haven't been wearing it to bed. I would hate for the chain to break in my sleep."

"I can buy you a new chain." His thumb pressed harder against her throat until it cut off her air. Her breath stopped. Her mouth opened instinctively, but no air came rushing in. Then her lungs began to burn under the sudden starvation of air.

She flexed her fingers at her sides, but he only held her tighter.

The seconds dragged—one, then two, then three—before he released her with a low chuckle and stepped back.

She heaved in a breath, her lungs aching for air, then pressed a hand to her tender throat.

Leeland's eyes raked down her again, pausing on her heaving chest, then continued down the rest of her body in a way that felt both mortifying and indecent. Never mind that the fabric of her nightgown covered everything from the top of her ribs down to her ankles.

"You're wearing my ring on your finger. Next time I see you, my sapphire better be around your neck too. And every time after that. I don't care if it's the middle of the night and you're in your nightgown. Do you understand?"

She forced herself to nod.

"Good." He watched her for another moment, then turned and stalked down the hallway, his frame so large the floorboards creaked beneath his weight.

She stood against the wall, hand still pressed to her neck, until his footfalls disappeared into the dark.

He hadn't hit her, hadn't even hurt her, really. There might be a small bruise on her neck come morning, but it was nothing she couldn't conceal with some powder.

And yet, she couldn't stop shaking. If this was how Leeland treated her before the wedding, what would happen after, when it was too late for her to get away?

21

Yuri couldn't stop himself from whistling as he let himself in the back door of the temporary library building. Not only had McCreedy dropped off lumber for shelves first thing this morning, but the sun was shining today. Actually shining. In the middle of winter. It was a rare day indeed, and he planned to spend as much of it as possible outside.

If he worked quickly, he might be able to mount shelves on two walls before lunch. He reached for the toolbox in the storeroom, but a series of thuds echoed from the front.

Had McCreedy returned, thinking he would help? Hopefully so. The work would go twice as fast with an extra set of hands.

He headed through the storeroom, with its adjoining office at the back of the building, then entered the storefront. But Angus McCreedy wasn't the one making noise. Rosalind stood by the shelves against the wall. Sunlight caught the golden tones in her hair, and the light green shade of her dress made her look like spring itself had walked in early.

She moved briskly between the boxes and shelves, putting

away books with a speed that bordered on careless. A spine caught against the edge of the shelf, and she shoved it in anyway. Another book slipped from her hands and landed on the floor. She muttered something under her breath, crouched to pick it up, then stood and smoothed her skirt in one long, distracted motion before resuming her work.

"Good morning."

At the sound of his voice, she jumped, then whirled toward him, a hand pressed to her chest. "Yuri, you scared me."

He nodded toward the toolbox in his hand. "I didn't mean to. I'm here to build shelves, which it appears we're going to need before lunch at the rate you're working."

Her cheeks turned a faint shade of pink. "Am I working too fast?"

"I doubt there's such a thing as working too fast. The sooner the books are ready, the sooner we can open. But don't feel as though you need to spend every waking hour here. I'm certainly planning to enjoy the sunshine later."

"The sunshine. Right." She gave a sharp nod, then turned to start shelving the books again.

Yuri set the toolbox down and came closer. "Is something wrong? You seem . . ." He wasn't sure quite what word to use. *Nervous* maybe? *Flustered?*

She put another book on one of the shelves. "I've decided to take you up on your offer."

"My offer?"

"To help me leave Sitka."

"You have?" He should have been happy to hear such a thing, but something in him ached at the way she said it. Her voice was flat and her eyes dull. It didn't seem like she was asking for help so much as surrendering. "What happened to change your mind?"

Her hand moved to the pendant lying against the base of

her throat. It was large and dark and blue, a lovely necklace that matched her engagement ring, even though both items looked a bit too big and gaudy with the simple dress she was wearing. "I can't marry Leeland, which means I need to get away. But I still need time to see if I can find proof of my father bribing Marshal Hibbs."

He took a step closer. He should probably care more about the bribes, but at the moment, he just wanted to keep her safe. "How soon can you go?"

She pressed her lips together. "A week from today? Does that work? I . . . I think I should do as you said and try to figure out the money part after I'm somewhere safe."

He was glad to hear it, though a week felt like an unreasonably long time. Each day she lingered increased the likelihood her father would find out what she was up to, but he'd make it work. "I'll make the arrangements. We'll go to Seattle and from there take a train to Washington, DC." He didn't care how badly he needed to strong-arm Alexei. He'd make sure they had a ship available to leave that night, which would get them away from Sitka hours before anyone realized she was missing.

"Thank you," she whispered, turning back to the books, her hand still clutching the pendant in a way that made him frown.

Had something happened last night? What wasn't she telling him?

And what if she was in more danger now than she had been before?

SHE STILL HADN'T FOUND anything.

Rosalind wandered into the library of her father's mansion, her neck aching from spending the past two hours searching his study. Normally she wouldn't be able to search it in the evening, but both her father and Leeland, along with her uncle, had been invited to a meeting at the hotel with the owner of a shipping company from San Francisco. Snow had started falling shortly after they'd left, and she didn't know whether that would keep them away longer or cause them to head home earlier, or if it wouldn't affect things one way or the other.

She still hadn't found any record of her father bribing the Marshal—or anyone else—over the years. She knew he had a ledger of transactions somewhere, but she'd told Yuri that she would leave Sitka a week from today.

What if she didn't find the evidence before then? Was she supposed to leave without any proof of her father's criminal activity? How many more people would her father hurt if she couldn't find evidence that would land him in prison?

She let the library door fall shut behind her, then leaned her weight against it and tilted her head toward the ceiling. *Dear God, please help me find evidence before I leave.*

But no answer seemed to come. The only thing that greeted her was the ticking of the mantle clock and the low crackle of the fire. She sighed and crossed to the table near the window where she'd left her knitting, then sat down and stared at the yarn.

There had to be proof of the bribes somewhere. It wasn't as though her father was an honest man. If he was going to forge numbers and bribe officials and steal land from native communities, there had to be a record of it somewhere.

Dear Father, what am I missing?

She fingered the scarf she'd been working on but didn't pick up her knitting needles.

Maybe she'd be better off sorting books for the town library. Father had said they could donate some of the older books they no longer used, but if she didn't get things donated before she left, the books would probably never make it to the library.

At the very least, it would give her something to think about besides how big of a failure she was.

She stood and crossed to the tall bookshelf nearest the door. Most of the titles were older. There was a smattering of every-thing—travelogues, religious commentaries, and even a few well-worn novels from when her mother had been her age. She started pulling books from the top shelf, careful to check the condition before stacking a few into a pile on the floor.

She worked her way down the shelf, selecting books that might be of interest to others, but that she hadn't read in several years and her father didn't use for business. When she reached the lowest shelf, she crouched down, the spines of the books all but invisible in the shadows.

She pulled out a dusty copy of *The Marble Faun*, then flipped it open before closing it and setting it back on the shelf. Her father wouldn't want her to give away a Hawthorne novel.

When she went to slide the book back into its slot, it wouldn't go all the way in, almost as though something stopped it. She never would have noticed how the spine stuck out had she not been holding the book, but now that she knew how deep the shelf was, its position on the shelf seemed odd.

The book beside it seemed to stick out a bit more than necessary too, and the one beside that. Had something gotten caught behind them?

She pulled the trio of books out and felt behind them. A warped section of wall met her hand, or maybe it was careless patching from years ago.

Wait. It didn't seem like the wall was warped at all. It was every bit as smooth as the shelves themselves. It was almost as though a wooden panel had been deliberately placed at the back. She pulled on the board, wriggling it backward and forward until it gave way. Two small leather-bound books rested flush against the wall behind it.

She pulled them out, her pulse quickening and blood rushing in her ears. The books looked similar to the ledgers in her father's study. Had she just found what she'd been looking for?

Please, Father, help these be what I need.

She undid the clasp on the first ledger and flipped it open.

Her blood turned cold.

These were the seal-harvest totals from last summer. The date was written clearly on the top of the page. The trouble was, the brief summary of seals harvested didn't match the US government quota. Everyone knew the Alaska Commercial Company had the ability to kill two hundred thousand seals per year, a number scientists had said wouldn't damage the population. The number was hardly a secret. But the summary on the first page of the ledger made it look like the ACC had killed over three hundred thousand seals.

She flipped to the next page, where the number of seals killed was meticulously tallied and broken down by date, location, and kill crew.

She turned the page, and the pattern repeated. The ledger had week after week of detailed counts, locations, and notations, often with little side marks like an asterisk beside unusually high yields, a small *p* to indicate pelts shipped, and in some cases, a check mark next to tallies that had clearly been adjusted downward in the public-facing reports.

There was no mistaking what she was looking at. This wasn't a rough estimate. It was an internal account of every seal harvested, including the ones never declared to the government. And it meant the ACC had never paid the government bounties on over one hundred thousand seals. How could they, when they were allowed to kill only two hundred thousand?

She flipped forward several pages, her chest tight. At the

end of the ledger, a neat table compared three columns—*Total Harvested, Reported Harvest,* and *Government Bounty Paid.*

Her pulse quickened as she studied the numbers. The totals didn't add up. The difference between what had been harvested and what had been reported was staggering. She traced the columns with her finger, doing the math in her head line by line.

The unreported kills amounted to about one hundred thousand seals. If each pelt carried the usual bounty, then the government was owed more than two hundred thousand dollars. And her father's company had kept nearly that much in profits—almost one hundred and eighty thousand—by lying on their reports.

She blew out a breath. God had answered her prayers after all. This wasn't the bribery list she'd been looking for. It was much more.

The northern fur seal was going extinct, and poaching at sea was rampant. Yuri's older brother Sacha had commissioned a report about how the quota for harvesting two hundred thousand seals was far too large given how quickly the population was dwindling, and newspapers had printed the report in every paper along the Pacific Coast after it had been released, sparking a debate about just how many seals should be harvested.

Her father and uncle had naturally insisted that taking two hundred thousand seals a year wasn't harming the population, but even she had noticed a decline in the number of seals in Sitka Sound, and she'd only been here four years. People like Freya who had lived in Sitka their whole lives couldn't stop talking about how they never saw seals anymore.

She opened the next ledger, then swallowed as she stared down at the tally of names, dates, and monetary amounts. Some names she recognized, like the foreman who managed the Saint

George Island seal camp and the accountant who oversaw shipments out of Dutch Harbor, but most she didn't. Still, the pattern was clear. These were bribes labeled as either "special allowances" or "discretionary bonuses." She opened the first ledger again and quickly saw that the payment tallies coincided with harvest spikes and false reporting periods noted in the first ledger.

Every payout was tied to someone who had the power to overlook a discrepancy, such as a local inspector, a ship captain, or a government clerk.

She flipped through page after page, watching the sums rise. Some payouts were as small as fifty dollars, but a few crept into the thousands.

Once again, she tallied the numbers in her head and calculated that the ACC had made a profit of nearly two hundred and twenty thousand dollars after all the bribery payments.

She sat back on her heels, the two ledgers heavy in her lap.

If she turned this information over to the authorities, it just might be enough to ruin the Alaska Commercial Company's standing with the US government. It would certainly be enough evidence to land her father and uncle and anyone else who'd had a hand in running the company in prison permanently.

And she knew exactly what she needed to do with it.

"So there we were, eating dinner, and Alexei couldn't keep his eyes off her." Sacha waved his fork over his plate, never mind he nearly ended up flinging a piece of baked salmon across the room.

"Yes, but did he smile?" Yuri leaned back in his chair, soaking in the fun of having Sacha and Alexei sitting around the cramped table. They'd arrived that morning, but this was the first meal they'd sat down to as a family.

"I could keep my eyes off Laurel perfectly fine." Alexei scowled at Sacha, who sat around the corner from his place at the head of the table. "It just so happened that there was nothing else in the room worth looking at."

Mikhail slapped him on the back. "Are you falling in love, brother?"

"I am not falling in anything." Alexei stabbed a piece of salmon on his plate with unnecessary force. "Laurel Farnsworth and I are just friends."

"That's why he took her for a walk after dinner." Sacha winked. "Because they're just friends."

Laughter erupted around the table.

Or rather, everyone except Alexei laughed. He just sat there with a deepening scowl.

"I can already see it in my mind." Yuri took a sip of water. "Alexei will fall in love with this woman and move to San Francisco, where he wanted to be all along."

"I just told you I'm not in love with her." Alexei set his fork down with a thud. "And I told her father no to the job too. Times change."

Yuri's laughter died so fast, it felt like the air had been sucked from the room. Across the table, Sacha stopped eating mid-bite, a piece of salmon dangling from his fork. Even Maggie had stilled with her teacup halfway to her mouth.

"What job?" Mikhail leaned forward in his chair, his golden eyes pinned to Alexei.

Alexei pinched the bridge of his nose and sucked in a breath. "Sorry. I didn't mean to say anything about it. I'm tired and being careless with my words."

"Farnsworth offered you a job?" Sacha frowned. "When was this? You didn't say anything to me about it."

Alexei shrugged. "Because it doesn't matter. I'm not going to take it."

"Is it what Sacha said? Would you be working for Mr. Farnsworth at his shipyard?" Maggie asked.

"It's managing his shipyard, yes." Alexei shoved another bite of food into his mouth.

"Would it pay well?" Mikhail had gone from leaning forward to sitting back in his chair as he analyzed Alexei.

"Like I said, it doesn't matter. I'm not going."

"Let me try to understand. One of the wealthiest shipbuilders on the Pacific Coast offered you a fancy job filled with money and invited you to move down there where you'll be near the daughter he can't seem to marry off?" Mikhail crossed his arms over his chest. "Don't tell me I'm the only one who sees where this is going."

Alexei threw up his hands. "It's not going anywhere because I'm not going to take it. I'm not leaving Alaska or any of you."

"There was a time when that was the only thing you wanted." Sacha wiped his beard with his napkin.

Alexei just shook his head. "That was a lifetime ago."

"Well, that's a relief." Yuri leaned back in his chair. "I was already trying to picture you in one of those San Francisco suits with a stiff collar, shiny shoes, and no wood chips in sight. I doubt even a merry heart could survive that."

Mikhail snorted into his coffee, and Bryony tried to hide a grin behind her hand.

"Don't worry," Yuri added, eyes dancing as Alexei scowled at him. "We'd have sent care packages—bits of sawdust and sea salt—just to remind you where you belong."

Alexei just shook his head. "They'll be no need for care packages filled with sawdust, I assure you. I was never meant to have what I wanted to have in San Francisco with Clarise. I have no desire to move down there now. I feel bad for Laurel more than anything. I can't promise there's something romantic there, but I can't promise there's not." He moved his hand to his chest, rubbing his palm back and forth over his breastbone. "That will take some time to figure out, but the one thing I know is that I'm not leaving Sitka."

He took a sip of water, then raised his eyes and moved them around the table. "But there is something of interest all of you should know. While I was in San Francisco, I sent a telegram to Secretary Gray about the villages of Klawock and Kasaan being forced to relocate and Governor Caldwell requiring anyone who trades with an Indian village to register as an Indian agent. The secretary sent me a telegram back almost immediately. He had no idea any of this was happening, and he'll be returning to Alaska to look into these matters himself."

"He will?" Yuri raised his eyebrows. "I didn't think he cared what happened here, as long as it doesn't mess up something he's trying to do in Washington, DC."

"He cares if he thinks whatever's happening will lead to poorer relations with the tribes," Alexei answered. "He wants them to relinquish their claim to tribal lands and move to larger cities and villages. He's likely concerned that whatever the new governor is up to will hinder that."

"Wonder what the governor will say when Gray arrives." Mikhail took a sip of coffee.

"He'll probably find a way to impound another ship or take away another one of our contracts," Alexei muttered.

"Let's hope that's all he does." Bryony had gotten up from the table and was starting to dish out cake.

"Enough about this mess." Alexei took the cake Bryony handed him and cut into it with the side of his fork. "What happened here while I was gone? Anything I should know about?"

"Nothing." Yuri scooped up his last bite of potatoes. "It was nothing other than boring."

Mikhail smirked. "Yuri didn't even try to finish your audit, and I think he only answered half of your correspondence. I hope you're planning to work twelve hours or better for the next week."

Yuri held up his hands. "Look, I'm happy to help with the family business. Really. I'll move down to San Francisco and manage the new shipyard, and you can send me to Portland or Seattle to see if I can procure shipping contracts there. Just don't ask me to check shipping manifests against warehouse inventory. All those numbers are enough to drive a man insane."

A knock sounded at the back door. Yuri exchanged a glance with Mikhail. It was strange to have someone knocking in the middle of dinner, and especially at the kitchen door. A person would have had to cross through the tree-lined backyard to reach it.

The knock sounded again, and Sacha started to push back his chair. "Let me see—"

"It's probably for me." Alexei was already standing. He was seated closest to the door anyway, and he reached it in only a few seconds.

But despite the fact everyone was curious about their unexpected visitor, he only opened the door partway, his body blocking their view.

"Can I help you?" Confusion laced Alexei's voice.

Yuri was half tempted to stand and go to the door, just to see who it was, rather than eat his cake. Then the person at the door spoke.

"Is Yuri here?"

Rosalind. He dropped his fork and sprang to his feet. Was something wrong?

"Is this about the letters?" Alexei asked.

A hard ball formed in Yuri's stomach. He hadn't yet told Alexei about his plans to help Rosalind escape. In fact, Alexei hadn't been home long enough for anyone to tell him about what Rosalind was suffering at the hands of her father. That wasn't exactly the type of thing they'd discuss at the dinner table where little ears were present.

Alexei stepped to the side so Yuri could greet her.

"Is everything all right?" He couldn't think of a single good reason that would propel Rosalind from her house after dark and cause her to sneak up to their back door at a time of day when her father might very well notice she was gone.

"Would you like to stay for dinner?" Bryony came up behind him. "It's been too long since we visited."

"I can't stay." Rosalind stood just beyond the doorframe, her chest heaving and eyes glancing around without settling on any one thing. Snow dusted the top of her hatless head, and wisps of hair had come loose around her face. It was the most disheveled he'd ever seen her.

"I just . . ." She licked her lips, then glanced around again before she opened her cloak and shoved two slim journals at his chest. "Can you give these to your brother-in-law? The Deputy Marshal?"

Then she turned and fled into the night.

"Ros! Wait!" he called, but she was already gone, leaving only a set of footprints behind her in the snow.

"What is it?" Alexei asked.

"I don't know." He handed one of the journals to Alexei, not sure whether he should be chasing after Rosalind.

Alexei opened it and scanned the page for a moment, his eyebrows pinched together. "Is this . . . Is this what I think it is?"

"What did she give you?" Mikhail asked from behind them. "Come inside and shut the door so we can see."

Alexei shook his head, his eyes still pinned to the page. "It appears to be proof of Preston Caldwell falsifying the number of seals harvested last year."

"What?" Sacha jumped up from the table so quickly, his chair nearly toppled backward.

Yuri opened the ledger he was still holding. It wasn't a record of the number of seals killed, not like Alexei's ledger. This one was filled with names and dates and payment amounts.

"This isn't right," he whispered.

"Obviously." Alexei flipped a page. "Secretary Gray will want to know about it. Immediately. If only there was a way to send a telegram straight from Sitka. The best I can do is write one and send it with the *Alliance* when it leaves in the morning. The captain can wire it for me when he gets to port, but that's a three day delay."

Alexei was right. While telegraph lines connected most major cities in the United States, there was no telegraph cable that ran from Seattle to Sitka, meaning that any telegram they sent needed to travel by ship to Seattle or San Francisco or Portland before it could be sent via wire.

"We should use the mimeograph in the office to make copies of this," Mikhail suggested.

Conversation swirled around Yuri, but all he could think about was how Rosalind was supposed to have brought him proof of bribing Marshal Hibbs. It would be condemning evidence, but not exactly a large scandal that people in Washington, DC, would care about.

Did her father know she had these ledgers? This was the type of thing men would commit murder over to keep quiet.

Why had she left to go back home rather than stay with him? He could have spirited her away on the *Alliance*.

A hard ball formed in his stomach. He shoved his ledger into Sacha's hands and raced toward the door.

"Where are you going?" Bryony asked as he stormed past her.

He didn't answer, just wrenched the door open and ran into the night.

"Yuri!" Mikhail called after him.

He didn't stop to answer his brother. If he was fast enough maybe he could catch Rosalind before she got home.

His boots pounded against the snow and mud of the back lane as he ran, cold air slapping his face and tearing at his shirt.

He barely felt it. Barely even noticed he'd darted outside without his coat.

All he could see was the way Rosalind had looked standing in the doorway. She'd been pale and her hands had been shaking, and she hadn't even tied her cloak properly.

Did that mean she was in danger?

Of course she was in danger. She lived in constant danger.

But bringing him those ledgers had put her in even more danger.

The houses along Lincoln Street blurred as he raced toward the hill where the Caldwells' mansion sat. He rounded a corner too fast and skidded, nearly losing his footing. A startled man tipped his hat and stepped back out of his way, but Yuri didn't slow.

He pushed past the dark windows of the mercantile and bakery and *Gazette* office before turning onto the final stretch of road, where the hill climbed toward the Caldwells' mansion.

Her house came into view and a shape moved near the stoop. Was it her?

"Rosalind!" he shouted.

"Yuri!" Mikhail's voice echoed from behind him, but he kept running, never mind the footsteps pounding behind him.

"Yuri, stop!"

He made it a few more steps before Mikhail caught him. One hand closed hard around his arm, and the other braced against his chest like a wall.

"Let go of me."

"No. You need to think, Yuri, with your brain. If you barge into that house, what are you going to do? Reveal to Caldwell that you have proof of his fraud? Do you think Rosalind will be safer if you do that?"

"She asked me to find a way to help her, and now she's in

more danger than before. I can't let her go back into that house."

"She's trusting you to help with the ledgers, you dunderhead. And here you are about to blow everything to pieces."

Yuri shoved at his brother's arm, but Mikhail didn't budge. He was too strong and athletic, and trying to fight him was useless.

"Do you think I don't want to break that door down myself?" Mikhail growled. "She's my wife's friend too, and her father won't even allow them to exchange letters. But charging up there is only going to make things worse."

"Then what do we do?" Yuri tried to shove Mikhail's hand away. "Sit around while her father gives her more than a sprained wrist?"

More footsteps thudded behind them, then Alexei and Sacha rounded the corner, both breathing hard.

"Somebody better tell me what's going on." Alexei strode toward them, his eyes moving between the two of them.

"Fine. I'll explain it." Yuri shoved away from Mikhail and told Alexei and Sacha all of it, from the bruises Bryony had discovered Rosalind hiding, to the day he saw her wrist for himself, to the fact her father was trying to marry her off to a man who was just as dangerous and violent as he was, if not more. Then Yuri explained that Rosalind had finally agreed to let him help her escape, and they planned to leave Sitka in a week's time, but first she wanted to find evidence of her father bribing Marshal Hibbs so that the corruption could stop and he could be put in prison.

But the evidence she'd just brought him was far bigger and more involved than that.

Alexei stood silent for a long moment, his head turned toward the grand house at the top the hill while his hands clenched at his sides. Then he turned back to them, and his gaze found Yuri's. "You did the right thing, Yuri. I'm proud of you."

Yuri blinked. "You are?"

Alexei rarely gave away compliments, but then, he shouldn't be surprised his brother would support his helping Rosalind, not when Alexei himself had sacrificed so very much for their family.

"'Defend the poor and fatherless,'" he whispered. "'Do justice to the afflicted and needy. Deliver the poor and needy: rid them out of the hand of the wicked.' That's in—"

"Psalm eighty-two, verses three and four." Alexei slung an arm around his shoulders. "I know those verses well."

Of course Alexei had those verses memorized. How could he not?

Alexei used the arm around Yuri's shoulders to turn him away from the Caldwells' mansion and back toward home. "And now that we know we have a responsibility to defend Rosalind, we need to figure out the best way to do it. That means deciding what ship to use to get Rosalind away from here, what port you should dock at, and where to hide the ledgers until Secretary Gray gets here. We're not simply going to take these to the corrupt Marshal we know Caldwell is paying."

"Like I said before, we should use the mimeograph to make copies of what we have." Mikhail strode in front of them, moving gracefully through the mud and snow on the road. "Or at least we should copy the most incriminating pages, then hide them in two separate spots in case Caldwell comes looking for his ledgers."

"What if Caldwell figures out we helped Rosalind after she leaves?" Sacha asked from where he walked behind them.

Alexei shrugged. "I don't see how that would change anything. He wants to destroy us already, and he'll want to destroy us all over again after we turn over evidence of him falsifying his seal numbers to the secretary of the interior. Why not give him a third reason to hate us?"

"If those ledgers are enough get Caldwell thrown in prison, we won't need to worry about him anymore." Yuri heaved out a breath.

"I hope we can get the charges to stick this time," Sacha muttered.

"The government isn't going to like that they got cheated out of two hundred thousand dollars in bounties last fall," Alexei said. "It will stick, both for Preston and his brother. The question is, how much damage can the two of them do before the authorities come?"

Yuri grimaced. "Did Secretary Gray say how soon he was coming to look into the issue at Klawock and the new Indian agent requirement?"

Alexei shook his head. "He did not."

Yuri looked down the road at the snow falling over the harbor. "I hope it's soon."

23

The Next Morning

Rosalind tried to keep the knife from trembling in her hand as she spread marmalade across her toast, but she couldn't quite manage it. A quick glance at her father told her he hadn't noticed, which was good, because it was all she could do not to spring out of her seat and ask if he'd discovered his secret ledgers were missing.

He hadn't said a word about her being in the library or even going out last night. He'd still been gone by the time she got back to the house, and she'd hoped the servants wouldn't say anything about her quick trip down to the harbor, but she could never be sure whether they would talk.

But so far that morning, neither her father nor Leeland had even acknowledged her existence. All they'd done was talk about their meeting last night at the hotel.

"McCrae seems eager to help." Leeland shook the salt-shaker over his eggs, dumping three times the salt Rosalind would have used. "I hope your brother can work something out."

"He will. McCrae will make the perfect business associate." Her father took a sip of his coffee. "His familiarity with Alaska rivals the Amoses', but he has more ships, and he might even be able to undercut their rates. If Simon gives him the contracts he just took from them, it could be the beginning of the end for the Amoses."

Leeland shoved his toast into his egg with a satisfied grunt, causing the orange yolk to smear across his plate. "It's a clever strategy. Starve their business slowly enough, and no one can blame you when it dies."

"It's one strategy." Her father took another sip of coffee, a bored look on his face. "Though I'm starting to think ridding Alaska of the Amos family might require a multipronged approach."

Rosalind's stomach clenched. Just what did her father have planned now?

She didn't want to know. She just wanted to leave Sitka and disappear, but she should probably tell Yuri about this McCrae man and the shipping contracts next time she saw him. Then at least his family would know what was coming.

Leeland loosed a dark chuckle. "I'm sorry I won't be here to see what unfolds next, but I really do need to get back to Seattle."

Rosalind set down the toast she'd been about to take a bite of. "You're leaving?"

"The day after tomorrow." He reached out and settled his hand across the back of her neck. "Don't be too disappointed, darling. I'll be back in time for our wedding."

She stilled beneath his touch, then took a small bite, trying to ignore the way the toast turned to sawdust in her mouth.

He leaned close until his lips were next to her ear. "Will you miss me?"

She nearly choked. "I . . . Of course. Very much."

He chuckled and sat back, moving his gaze back to her father. "She's not very good at lying, is she, Caldwell?"

Her father sent her a brief glance. "No, but you'll find that's to your benefit. It's impossible for a person who can't lie to hide anything from you."

The toast she'd just swallowed churned in her stomach. Was it impossible for her to lie? Or at the very least, to cover something up? Did her father know about the ledgers, and this was his way of leading into the conversation? Her abdominal muscles tightened, as though already anticipating the pain of his fist connecting with them.

"See that?" Her father nodded her direction. "Look how she squirms after being caught in a lie."

Leeland turned to her again, his gaze heavy as he ran his eyes over her.

If only the floor would open up and swallow her. But it didn't, so she forced herself to take another bite of her toast.

Her father dabbed his face with his napkin. "I noticed you were going through the bookcases yesterday, Rosalind."

She froze, her breath suddenly feeling like it scraped over a thousand jagged shards of glass as she sucked it into her lungs.

"I assume the books sitting in a pile on the floor are for the library donation," he went on. "I trust you weren't being careless with what you chose to donate. Some of the books in the library are quite valuable."

"I only took ones that I know neither of us have any interest in." She tried to keep her voice neutral, tried not to give away any of the fear roiling inside her, but she wasn't sure she succeeded. "Would you like to go through them before I donate them?"

"That won't be necessary. Just avoid sorting through the books on the bottom rows. I've had the servants shelve some of my personal favorites there, and I don't want those donated. Understood?"

The bottom rows? So he hadn't noticed she'd removed some of the books, taken the ledgers from behind them, and then put them back? "Yes, sir."

"Make as large a donation as possible. Perhaps the library can even shelve the books we donated in its own section with our name on it."

Her fingers clenched beneath the tablecloth. The library was already getting named after them. Wasn't that enough? "I'll bring it up at the next board meeting. I'm not sure getting our own section of the library will be possible, but I could probably talk the board into placing a stamp on the inside fold of the book stating who donated it."

As long as the library also placed similar stamps on the books that came from donors. But she wasn't going to tell her father that.

"Books," Leeland muttered around a mouthful of food. "Not much good unless they're ledgers or legal records."

"You think that because you're a man of business, but my daughter prefers stories. Most of them are nothing but dreams."

Rosalind took a slow sip of tea. The ledgers she'd touched last night certainly weren't a dream, even if she'd found them hidden behind a stack of novels.

Avoid sorting through the books on the bottom rows, he'd said. As in, all of the bottom shelves?

She had looked through the books on only one bottom shelf, but the library was filled with wall-to-wall shelves. What if there were more records hidden behind the other shelves? What if her father had been falsifying seal-harvest numbers for more than just past year? Or what if there were records of other illegal activities, like bribing the Marshal?

She needed to search all the lower shelves in the library, and maybe some of the upper ones too. But that shouldn't be hard. She often sat in the library. With its soaring windows that overlooked the town and the harbor, it was the most peaceful room in the house.

She just needed to make sure her father was distracted and the door was locked before she looked.

She picked up her toast and lifted it to her mouth.

A meaty hand gripped her wrist. "Don't take another bite."

She looked up to find Leeland glaring down at her. "I'm sorry?"

"You've eaten enough." He tightened his grip on her wrist until it hurt. "It's unbecoming for a woman to overindulge."

Heat crept up her neck. She hadn't even touched the ham on her plate. Only the slice of toast and half a poached egg.

"Leeland," her father said mildly, "you'll have her for a lifetime. Let her enjoy breakfast."

Leeland gave a slow shake of his head. "She'll thank me when her corset closes without a struggle. No man such as myself should accept a bride with anything more than a sixteen-inch waist. I'm sure you'd expect the same if you were to remarry."

"My corset closes just fine," Rosalind breathed.

"Only because it's not laced tightly enough." He glared down at her. "A woman of your station is expected to have an hourglass figure."

Rosalind shifted. "I have an hourglass figure."

"Not one with a small enough waist, which is why you need to restrict your food intake."

Rosalind stared down at her plate, trying to ignore the pangs of hunger in her stomach. She'd had friends back in

Washington, DC, who insisted on having tiny waists, some of them even insisted on getting their waists down to sixteen inches. It was quite fashionable in the city, but those friends would get the worst stomachaches after eating a fancy meal, and the laces on their corsets were drawn so tight around their ribs, she swore half of them had trouble breathing. She didn't need to be a doctor to know that forcing a woman to maintain such a small waist wasn't healthy.

If she married Leeland, would she be expected to maintain that shape for the rest of her life? Even after bearing children?

"Well?" Leland said.

She looked up and realized he was still watching her with those hard eyes that never expressed anything other than displeasure.

"What do you say? Will you work on trimming down your waist by the time I return?"

"I . . . yes. I'll make it my top priority."

"Good." Leeland took another bite of his eggs and toast, ignoring the yolk from the egg that dribbled down the side of his chin.

She lowered her gaze to her untouched ham and folded her hands in her lap. Two days. That was all she had to endure of the horrid man beside her. Then she planned to never see him again in her life.

24

Sitka; the Next Day

Done at last. Yuri stepped back from the bookshelf and arched his back, stretching out his muscles as he surveyed his work. The final two bookshelves stood finished, filling up the last wall of the temporary library.

He didn't want to think about how long he'd spent yesterday and today measuring, sawing, and hammering, all while hoping Rosalind might stop by the library. He'd even worked through lunch earlier, just to make sure she didn't show up during the short time he would have been gone.

But she hadn't stopped by, not even for a few minutes.

Yet someone from the Caldwell household had been here. The floor was filled with crates of books, and the inside folds on over half of them were stamped with Preston Caldwell's name. Yuri had found them there when he'd walked into the library that morning. Did that mean Rosalind had stopped by after he left yesterday?

Clearly he'd missed her, and that rankled, because all he

wanted to do was ask her why she'd turned those ledgers over to his family.

He stared at the front door, willing it to open and her to walk inside wearing both a smile and a dress that reminded him of spring.

Over the past week, Rosalind had swept the floors of the building and cleaned the windows and scrubbed the old wood-stove in the corner. Plus, she'd shelved all of the donated books as soon as they arrived.

He'd assumed it wouldn't be difficult to find her here this week, but clearly he'd been wrong.

He glanced at his pocket watch. A quarter past four. But he wasn't ready to give up just yet on the possibility of Rosalind stopping by. Maybe he'd start shelving books. He wasn't sure quite how Rosalind had the books organized, but surely he could figure it out.

He headed to the closest crate and bent to pick up the first book.

It was a biography of English abolitionist William Wilber-force. Did Rosalind have a section for biographies?

It took him only a few seconds of searching to find the biographies and set the book in its proper place. Then he bent to pick up the next one.

The door creaked open, and he snapped his head up. "Ros—"

The name died on his lips when he saw Alexei step inside.

His brother raised his eyebrows. "Expecting someone else?"

"I was hoping for it, at least." He nudged one of the crates with his foot. "Rosalind had these donations sent here, and I was expecting her to stop by and shelve them."

Alexei ran his eyes around the room, then let out a low whistle. "The library committee was busy while I was gone."

"Most of it was Rosalind, though Angus donated the lumber and helped build some of the shelves."

"And you built the rest? You did a good job." Alexei bent to pick up a book from the crate, then turned it over in his hands. "It's hard to imagine Caldwell letting his daughter get involved with something like this, or letting any of his books go, really."

"She said we could have the books her father didn't use. I don't think he'll notice most of them are gone."

"Still . . ." Alexei shelved the slim volume in the poetry section. "I take it you haven't seen her since she dropped off the ledgers?"

"No. I've been watching for her." He picked up another book and turned it over without really seeing the title. "I don't like it."

They worked in silence for a few minutes, sliding books into place. Even though it was still afternoon, darkness had already fallen, giving him even less hope that Rosalind would arrive.

Had her father discovered what she'd done with the seal ledgers? Was she lying injured in her bed, perhaps this time with her wrist fully broken? Or maybe a broken leg?

"I wasn't sure what to expect when I left you in charge of the library committee, but you've done well." Alexei slid another book onto the shelf. "Or rather, mostly well. I've gotten several complaints about the library's name."

Yuri grimaced. "Caldwell wanted it named after him."

"Preston Caldwell wants everything named after him."

"I know, but he tasked Rosalind with making sure it got done, and I was worried . . ." His throat closed, leaving the words to hang between them.

Alexei turned to him. "Are you saying you think her father would have hurt her if he didn't get his way?"

"I'm sure of it. Besides, I said the name was temporary. I plan to change it the second Rosalind is away from here."

"We need to talk about that."

"Me helping Rosalind?"

"More like how long it's going to take you to help Rosalind, and whether you head straight to San Francisco after you're done, which would probably be best, because if Caldwell's not behind bars by then, he'll be out for your head."

His stomach suddenly felt as though a lead ball had lodged inside it. "What do you want to know?"

"The shipyard transfers to us on February fifteenth. Originally I wanted you down there next week, at the beginning of the month, but that was before I knew about Rosalind. How long will it take for you to get her somewhere safe?"

Yuri shelved a copy of *The Lives of the Twelve Caesars* with more force than necessary. "First we need to go to Washington, DC, to see if we can change solicitors and get her money moved to a bank her father doesn't know about. But after that . . ." He licked his lips.

"What?" Alexei raised his eyebrows. "Is there a relative she can live with?"

"Not if she wants to stay hidden."

Alexei reached for the last book from a crate, then scooted the crate to the side and slid another crate over so both of them could reach it. "So what's the plan? To leave her in a large city where she can blend in?"

"That's one option."

Alexei pinched the bridge of his nose. "Just don't say it will be San Francisco where you'll be."

Yuri's throat felt gritty as he shelved another book. "I've considered it."

"Her father will find her there, especially once he learns you're living there too. But even if you weren't going to be there, San Francisco is still too close. You need to put her somewhere in the middle of the country, away from water. Maybe Saint Louis? Or better yet, Omaha? It's big enough for her to blend in, but landlocked and small enough that it won't be high on Caldwell's list of places to search."

"Actually, I want to take her to Belton, Texas."

Alexei blinked. "Where?"

"Belton, Texas. It's between Dallas and Austin. Rosalind supports a Woman's Commonwealth down there. She sends them a hundred dollars every month."

Alexei frowned. "A Woman's Commonwealth? What's that?"

"It's a community where women and their children live and support each other, away from abusive husbands. They work, raise their kids, sell things they make on their farm, and protect each other. Rosalind's been supporting the community for a few years, but I didn't know much about it, so when I was in San Francisco, I hired an investigator to find out more. Just got his letter the other day."

Alexei sat back on his heels. "And you want to take Rosalind there?"

Yuri rubbed the palm of his hand over his breastbone. "It seems like a place she might be able to heal. And like a place her father won't think to look for her."

Alexei gave a sharp nod. "It's a good plan."

It was. In fact, maybe it was too good of a plan, because he couldn't think of a way to talk himself out of it—or of a way to somehow have her closer to him, since he was going to be stuck in California.

"How long do you think it will take to escort her to Washington, DC, and then take her to Texas?" Alexei shelved another book.

Yuri shrugged, sliding the book in his own hand onto the

shelf in the novel section. "It's two weeks just to get to Washington. But hopefully once we're there, the banking details will only take a day or two, and then we can board a train to Texas. So maybe a month, but possibly less."

Alexei rubbed his jaw. "The moment the deed to the shipyard transfers, someone needs to be on-site in San Francisco."

"I intend to run the shipyard like you said, but I won't be able to get there by the beginning of March. But maybe Sacha is the best man to get things started. I know what a dry dock in need of repair looks like, but if you expect me to catalog the supplies needed to fix it, I'd get it wrong ten times over before I got it right. Sacha will know right away, and he'd be able to interview new workers and figure out who knows a thing or two about working on wooden ships."

"Sacha has two adopted children and a baby on the way. I don't want to uproot him from his family."

"Then send everyone down there with him for a few weeks. Ainsley and Finnan will think of it as an adventure. And Maggie can still return here in plenty of time to have her baby." Yuri slid yet another book onto the shelf.

"Maybe that will work." Alexei gave a small nod, then turned to him rather than reaching for another book. "Oh, I almost forgot to tell you, I just received word from Jonas. He's coming to Sitka with Kate and Nathan. There's been an incident in Unalaska, and the judge, Marshal Hibbs, and Dr. Hollis are all headed there for an investigation and trial. Jonas will fill in for the Marshal while he's gone, and Kate and Nathan will fill in for Dr. Hollis. Evelina is staying in Juneau to continue running the Indian school and trading post."

"It will be nice to see everyone, plus we can give Jonas the seal-harvesting ledgers while we're waiting for Secretary Gray to arrive. When is everyone supposed to get here?" Yuri bent down to retrieve another book, then paused. He was nearly to the bottom of another crate, but the books at the very bottom didn't look like normal books. They looked like journals or ledgers, nearly identical to the ones Rosalind had given him two nights ago.

Alexei was busy giving him some kind of estimate about when the others would arrive, but Yuri nodded toward the crate. "Alexei . . ."

"Are those more ledgers?" Alexei crouched beside him, then picked up one of the books and opened it. "This one is for two summers ago."

Yuri opened the other one. "So is this. It has more seal tallies."

"And mine has the bribe amounts and dates." Alexei rubbed his jaw. "She must not have had a way to get them to us directly, so she hid them here."

"Or meant to give them to us and didn't get the chance." Yuri swallowed as he flipped through the ledger. "Do you think her father knows? Do you think that's why she's not here today? Because he found out what she did?"

Alexei just shook his head. "I don't know, Yuri. I'm sorry."

"Could we . . . That is . . . do you think it's possible to . . ." Yuri licked his lips. "To send someone to check on her somehow?"

"And just how are we supposed to do that?"

"Perhaps someone can drop off donation forms from the library for Rosalind to fill out? I bet Caldwell will want credit for giving the library so many of his books, and we need an official way to track who gave what."

Alexei blew out a breath. "We could probably send Bryony over. Caldwell might even let her talk to Rosalind for something like that."

"I hope so." He had to at least know she was safe—and that she was still planning to leave Sitka with him in a few more days.

25

"Rosalind?"

The door to the library creaked open, and Rosalind slammed the book she'd been holding shut, her heart hammering against her chest. Never mind that she wasn't snooping on the bottom shelves any longer. She'd stopped that ten minutes or so ago, about the time she guessed her father and Leeland might want a break from whatever they'd been discussing in his study for most of the morning.

But the copy of *The Last of the Mohicans* still felt like fire in her hands, and she couldn't stop her heart from pounding against her ribs as Foster nudged the door open and poked his head inside the room.

"Ah, there you are. Your father needs you in his study."

"He does? Are you sure?" Her heart hammered harder. What could he possibly need her for? Unless . . .

Her eyes drifted down to the three crates sitting on the floor, each one filled with books.

And each one concealing a set of ledgers at the very bottom.

"Are these crates ready for the library?" Foster asked, following her gaze. "I can have them loaded into the carriage if you'd like to drop them off after dinner."

She swallowed. "Yes. Yes, they are. Please see that they're loaded."

"Very good, Miss Rosalind. I can take one of them now, unless you need me to escort you to your father's study?" He headed toward where the crates sat beside the set of shelves she'd just finished sorting through.

"Oh, take it now, please. I can see myself to the study."

Though she was nervous, there was something satisfying about watching Foster glance at the novels on the top of the crate, then pick up the whole thing and start for the door. He wasn't the least bit suspicious. No one likely would be. All three sets of ledgers that she'd pulled from the hidden crevices on the bottom shelves had been dusty, indicating that once her father hid them, he was unlikely to go back to look at them again.

She followed Foster out the library door, then headed down the stairs behind him. When he turned toward the kitchen, she went the opposite direction, not stopping until she stood in front of the study's large wooden door. She paused for a moment, sucking in a breath that would hopefully calm her nerves.

Three voices spoke from behind the door. Two she recognized as belonging to her father and Leeland, but the third voice was unfamiliar.

She knocked twice, then waited for her father to call for her before she entered. Her eyes immediately went to the stranger. He was seated in one of the chairs opposite her father's desk, a ledger open across his knees and spectacles perched on the bridge of his nose.

Tall, wiry, and perhaps in his early fifties, he stood as she entered. "Ah, Miss Caldwell. It's an honor. I'm Mr. Dunning, vice president of District National Bank in Washington, DC. I was just reviewing some of your investment summaries with your father."

Washington, DC? The breath clogged in her lungs. *District National Bank?* That was her bank, the one where she kept the money her mother had left her, but also where her father, her uncle, and the Alaska Commercial Company did most of their banking. What was the vice president doing here? And had he just said he'd been reviewing her investments with her father?

Even though she was over eighteen and a legal adult woman?

She pressed her eyes shut for the briefest of moments. *Please, God, don't let him find a way to take my money from me.*

"I'm sorry. Can you explain that again? I thought you said . . ." She twisted her hands in the folds of her skirt. "That is, I thought Mr. Holloway handled my accounts."

And he never would have done something like this, at least not unless her father paid him an exorbitant amount of money —which he might well have done with Mr. Dunning sitting before her.

"Mr. Holloway is still your official solicitor, yes." Mr. Dunning offered her a quick smile. "But we conduct periodic internal reviews, and your portfolio caught our attention. In a good way, I assure you. You've had quite remarkable growth these past several quarters."

He flipped a page and adjusted his spectacles. "High-risk rail bonds, two early stage shipping ventures, and even a timber acquisition in the Yukon. Your account is one of the fastest growing at our bank."

"Then why are you here? Does fast growth pose some sort of problem?" She shifted, her eyes flicking to her father.

He sat behind his desk, his face a mask that didn't give

away any emotion, let alone a clue as to what he might be thinking. He hadn't said a single word yet either, but his fingers tapped on the polished surface of his desk.

"I'm here at the request of your father, of course." Mr. Dunning's eyebrows furrowed. "I come twice a year to review his accounts, but this time he asked me to bring the necessary documents to transfer your accounts to your future husband as well."

That's what had caused her father to get his hands on her banking information? After how cautious she'd been to only communicate with her solicitor every few months so her father never thought it necessary to read the letters from the solicitor; after she'd been so careful to never mention the money her mother left her, agreeing to marry Leeland had caused her father to look at her Finnances?

"Wait. Did you just say you were going to transfer my money somewhere?" Her throat grew thick. What was Mr. Dunning talking about?

"I wasn't aware you were investing at this scale, Rosalind." Her father's voice was ice cold. "Or with this degree of success. Why didn't you tell me?"

She swallowed again, her mouth seemingly unable to be anything other than dry. "I didn't think it mattered. Mother left the money to me, and I inherited it when I turned eighteen. I assumed that meant I could do with it as I please."

"It meant you could leave it in a savings account where it would earn a modest income, not invest it." Her father reached for his glass of bourbon and took a long sip. "You should have told me what you were doing."

She clamped her mouth shut, not quite able to bring herself to agree with him. Perhaps she should have tried moving her money to a different bank sooner.

There was no saying that would have worked, though. Her

father likely would have found out what she was trying to do, put a stop to it, and made her pay for her actions.

Father set his bourbon down with a dull thud. "I would have negotiated your marriage contract differently had I had all the information."

Her marriage contract? What did that have to do with anything?

Leeland snorted from where he was sitting near the bookshelf. "Is that your way of saying you didn't intend to give me thirty-five thousand dollars when you said you'd have Rosalind sign her accounts over to me?"

"Why would you tell Leeland he could have my money?" The words were out before she could think better of them. She should probably be afraid to speak to her father in such a manner, but this was her money, which she'd saved and invested and grown. She couldn't just let Father hand it over to someone else without trying to advocate for herself.

"This is a normal aspect of any marriage." Her father didn't so much as flinch at her question.

"So you what? Asked the bank to prepare some type of contract that will give away everything I've earned?" She knew she was being too bold, knew her father would probably punish her for her outburst later, but she still couldn't seem to stop herself, not with so much at stake. Her father didn't think she was just going to hand over her money, did he?

Dear God, please give me strength, she prayed. *Please help me not to be afraid and to stand up to what they're doing.*

"Your father's simply being efficient." Leeland leaned back in his chair and crossed his arms behind his head. "A woman's Finnances naturally become the husband's concern after marriage. Your father was being proactive by making sure the details were settled before we wed."

Mr. Dunning cleared his throat and gestured toward the

open folder on his lap. "I assure you this is standard, Miss Cald-well. Upon marriage, assets can be legally consolidated. The contract we've put together ensures clear title and establishes Mr. Vandermeer as trustee in matters of long-term planning."

"Trustee?" She twisted her hands together. "I think you mean owner."

Mr. Dunning shifted in his chair but didn't deny it.

"I don't understand." She turned back to her father and Leeland. "Why this? Why now?"

"I'm leaving tomorrow morning." The condescending smile that had been curled across Leeland's lips since the beginning of this conversation dropped from his mouth. "This needs to be settled before I go."

"I thought you said it won't go into effect until we're married."

"We need time to organize the transfer of funds." Leeland flung a hand toward Mr. Dunning. "I don't use the same bank or the same solicitor as your family, so there is much to be done, and it's not the sort of thing that should be rushed."

"Leeland is correct." Her father was back to tapping his fingers on the desk, his rhythm more impatient than before. "You'll be married in under five months. There's no harm in beginning the transition now."

It felt as though the room was closing in on her, or maybe the whole world. She wasn't going to have a choice about signing the horrendous contract Mr. Dunning was holding. Not given how her father's eyes were growing narrower and narrower. Not given the small muscle that was pulsing on the side of his jaw. He was probably already thinking of ways to punish her for her obstinance as soon as Leeland left.

"Sign the contract." Her father pointed at Mr. Dunning. "Now."

She stared at her father, panic rising in her chest. She

couldn't do this, couldn't sign away something she'd worked so hard for. Here she'd been worried about what her father would do with her money if she left, but she hadn't once considered what he might try to do with it when she married. How could she have been so foolish?

"Would you like to review the contract for yourself, Miss Caldwell? It outlines the asset transfer." Mr. Dunning took one of the folders from his lap and stood, then removed a packet of papers and set them on her father's desk. He waited for her to approach before continuing. "You'll retain a personal allowance with minor discretionary access to the funds, but investment decisions and access to the whole of the account will fall to Mr. Vandermeer after the marriage."

"And the charitable donations?" she rasped. "Will those be allowed to continue after the wedding? The same amount each month to the same organizations?"

Mr. Dunning glanced at Leeland. "That will be up to your future—"

"Certainly not in their current state," Leeland cut in.

"About that, Rosalind." Her father pinched the bridge of his nose. "What were you thinking? Six thousand dollars a year in donations? This is the exact reason you shouldn't be managing your accounts without oversight."

She wanted to tell him that had he been overseeing things, he would have balked at her purchase of railroad stock and timber tracts, and the account would have grown only by about a quarter of its current rate. But she held her tongue.

"I might permit you to make a few small contributions each year, once I've had time to evaluate which of these institutions are reputable." Leeland lumbered to his feet and approached the desk. "But five hundred dollars a month is excessive."

"They're orphanages and schools and relief programs for women without husbands." She didn't add that the women without husbands she supported were single because they'd been abused.

Leeland's jaw hardened. "I won't have my wife throwing money at street children for the sake of her conscience. We'll make donations when they benefit our name, like your father has done with the new library."

A scream built inside her chest, but she forced it down. She had to stay calm, had to keep thinking, had to make sure she understood as much as possible about this horrible contract—if for no other reason than knowing how to get out of it.

"What about if you die?" She slanted a glance at Leeland. Her fiancé was twenty-three years older than her. It was reasonable to think she'd outlive him. "Does the money revert to me then?"

"Your fiancé has grown children from his first wife," her father answered. "They will naturally be entitled to their own share of Leeland's assets, and control of his business will go to his oldest son. A dower arrangement has been laid out in the contract."

"Wait. Are you saying that after Leeland dies, my mother's money will go to his children?"

"You'll get an annual salary of five thousand pounds," Leeland snapped. "That's plenty for you to live on."

She was making that much off her investments right now, year over year, on top of her giving.

Mr. Dunning cleared his throat and tapped the top piece of paper. "If it pleases you, Miss Caldwell, I can draft an additional clause specifying charitable intent, and you can initial it. Mr. Vandermeer will still have final approval of spending once the accounts are merged, but the clause will be on record."

On record. It was a meaningless promise, one Leeland wouldn't bother to honor.

"This doesn't go into effect until we're married, correct?"

She studied the first page of the contract, slowly reading the clause at the top. *Upon the union of Leeland Russell Vandermeer and Rosalind Marie Caldwell in holy matrimony . . .*

"Yes." Mr. Dunning gestured to the first line. "It takes effect on the day of your wedding."

"I see. Thank you." She drew in a breath. She wasn't going to get out of signing this contract, not with how all three men were watching her. But there was still a chance it might never go into effect. If things went her way. If Yuri helped her escape, and she managed to stay hidden. If her father ended up in prison for his crimes.

Dear Father, please let Yuri's plan work.

She uttered the prayer, then took the pen, blinked the burning away from her eyes, and signed.

26

Sitka; Three Days Later

"How many of the Caldwells' ledgers do we have in all?" Sacha asked as they climbed the steps to the office on the second floor of the warehouse.

"Eight," Yuri answered, striding up the familiar stairs despite the darkness shrouding him, his brothers, and Jonas, who had finally arrived from Juneau. "Two a year, going back four years."

"One records the actual number of seals taken versus the number reported, and the other details who was paid to ignore the discrepancy." Alexei closed the outside door behind them, shutting out the winter chill. "You have to give them credit for keeping meticulous records. I'm almost envious."

Sacha let out a low whistle. "Four years is a long time to steal over two hundred thousand dollars a year from the government and not get caught."

"Looks like they're about to get caught now." Mikhail reached the top of the stairs first.

"I expect to be up late tonight taking a nice long look at everything, but no one else has to stay," said Jonas, Evelina's husband and the Deputy Marshal for Alaska.

He was right about it being late. The children were all in bed, but Jonas had wanted to see all the ledger information, and Alexei had wanted to wait until everyone was in bed to discuss it. This wasn't the type of thing they could have someone overhearing.

More and more ledgers had trickled into the stream of donations coming from the Caldwells over the past few days. Rosalind had never once shown up at the library, so Yuri hadn't had a chance to ask her about them. They did manage to send Bryony up to the governor's house with a book-donation form for Rosalind to fill out.

She only saw Rosalind for a few minutes but said that she looked unharmed. Other than that, Yuri'd had no contact with her, and that still made him worry.

When no ledgers had come in the crates today, Alexei had said they should have a meeting. Jonas had arrived in town yesterday with Kate and Nathan. Jonas had been largely quiet since they'd told him about the ledgers, only saying that he wanted to see everything together before deciding the best course of action.

"Has Rosalind sent over evidence of anything else?" Mikhail asked. "I find it hard to believe this is the only area in which the Caldwells are trying to circumvent the law."

"The seal-harvesting ledgers are all we have. If she finds something more, she might keep it for herself in case her father tries to find her after she leaves. That was the original plan." Yuri reached the top of the stairs and looked for the lamp that usually sat on the windowsill of the second-floor office of their warehouse, but it wasn't there.

"I left the lamp at my desk last night. Let me light it." Alexei's shadowed form headed deeper into the office.

"How many days until you and Rosalind leave?" Mikhail nodded toward the harbor, his shadowed form still visible beneath the thin layer of clouds only partially concealing the moon.

"Two." At least that's what they'd agreed on last week, but it would help if he could actually talk to her and make sure that was still the plan. What was he supposed to do, just stay up all night on Friday, waiting for her to arrive at their house so they could sneak her onto the ship and leave before dawn?

He'd like to have things a bit more organized than—

Something caught his eye outside the window that overlooked the shipyard. "What's that?" It almost looked orange.

He went for a closer look.

"Just a minute," Alexei called. "I found the lamp. Now I just need to light it."

"No, keep it dark." Yuri spoke quietly, just loud enough for Alexei to hear him across the office. "Someone's down there."

"Where?" Mikhail was instantly by his side, surveying the shipyard.

"There." Yuri pointed. "Behind the dry dock."

It was hard to make out the figures beneath the hazy light of the moon, but three shadowed forms eventually came into view, moving between the dry dock and stacks of timber stored beneath the dry dock's roof that kept the ship from getting too wet when they were working on it.

That flicker of orange appeared again, and only then did Yuri realize one of them was carrying a lantern.

Except the flame looked too large and wild for a lantern. Could it be a torch? Yuri's heart thudded against his chest.

· · ·

T‍HE THREE FIGURES joined together underneath the post holding up one corner of the dry-dock roof, and suddenly, the one flame turned into three.

"Fire!" The word left Yuri's mouth like a gunshot. "They've got torches, and there's three of them!"

Mikhail bolted for the stairs.

"Let's split up and see if we can stop them before they burn anything." Alexei followed Mikhail to the stairs.

"I'll take the one by the dry dock," Mikhail called from the stairway.

"I'll circle around the back of the dry dock and make sure no one burns the lumber." Yuri raced after his brothers.

"I'll start the sea pump and grab the hoses." Sacha thundered down the stairs behind them. "Just in case they manage to light something."

"Am I the only one that's armed?" Jonas called over the noise of their racing footsteps.

There was no time to answer. Mikhail opened the door, and they burst outside, scattering. A shipyard didn't run without its own emergency system. Years ago, they'd installed a manual water pump and hose system that drew seawater directly from the harbor, more to clean bilges and hulls than fight fires, but it worked for both.

Yuri raced across the muddy ground, veering behind the dry dock until he spotted a figure heading toward the lean-to where they stored dry lumber for their ships.

Yuri lengthened his stride, trying to keep his steps as light as possible so the arsonist didn't realize he was there. He closed the gap until only twenty feet separated them, then ten, then five.

He must have made some kind of noise, because the man turned.

"Drop it!" Yuri growled.

The arsonist whirled back around and ran faster.

Yuri surged forward and tackled him before he could reach the lean-to. They crashed to the ground, the torch skittering into a patch of mud, where it flickered and died. A punch landed against Yuri's jaw, but he swung his fist right back, using twice the force of his assailant. The man grunted but twisted beneath him and caught Yuri in the ribs with his elbow. Yuri shifted and drove his knee into the man's side. Another punch flew toward his temple, but this time he saw it coming and ducked, then swung his own fist toward the man's face. It met his cheekbone with a satisfying crack, and the man grunted.

The fight left him for a fraction of a second, but that was all Yuri needed to pin the man's wrists above his head.

He thrashed and tried to twist free.

"I don't think so," Yuri muttered, tightening his grip and pressing his weight downward until the struggling slowed. "One down!" he shouted to his brothers.

"The other two are running!" Mikhail's voice rang out from the opposite side of the dry dock.

Yuri glimpsed two shadowy figures vaulting the fence next to the lean-to. Alexei and Mikhail raced to the fence, but the arsonists had been too far ahead.

"You got one?" Jonas sprinted toward Yuri, his pistol drawn.

"Yeah." Yuri stayed on top of the assailant until Jonas arrived and trained his pistol on the man. "The others hopped the fence just over there." He nodded toward the spot.

Both Alexei and Mikhail were heading his direction.

Alexei reached them first, his eyes still surveying the fence. "I'm tempted to try chasing them even though we don't know which direction they went."

"Do you want me to?" Mikhail heaved out a breath, his chest rising and falling from whatever chase he'd given to the other men.

"No," Jonas said. "We don't know anything about them. They could be armed."

Sacha arrived with a length of hose slung over his shoulder. "Pump's running, just in case we need it."

Alexei wiped his forehead with the back of his arm. "At least we stopped them before they could light anything."

Yuri pushed himself to a standing position, giving Jonas a chance to handcuff the arsonist and ask his name.

The arsonist refused to give it, but Yuri didn't care. The man would spend at least one night in jail, and Jonas was quite good at interrogating criminals. They'd likely have the man's name before morning.

"I'm just glad we were in the office when they came." Yuri tried to brush the mud from his sleeves. "Can you imagine if we had been in bed?"

Alexei rubbed his jaw. "I was thinking the same thing."

"I'll give you one guess who's behind this," Mikhail muttered.

"Maybe so, but let me take this one to the prison to see how much information I can get out of him." Jonas hauled the arsonist to his feet and jerked him forward. "We'll handle the rest in the—

Whump!

A burst of light flared in the back corner of the shipyard, flames erupting from the base of the lean-to.

"No!" Mikhail yelled.

The fire caught fast, racing over the dry stacks of wood with a crackle that soon turned to a roar.

Sacha ran toward the blaze, uncoiling the hose over his

shoulder as he went. Yuri raced to help him, then grabbed the end of the hose and aimed it at the base of the flames.

Sacha released the lever on the nozzle, and seawater gushed out, causing the lumber to hiss and smoke.

But the fire had already spread to the next stack of lumber.

27

"You have the most beautiful hair."

Rosalind felt a tug on the back of her head, then turned to look over her shoulder at where Freya sat behind her, running a brush through her dark gold tresses. She still couldn't believe her father was allowing her to be here, but he hadn't even hesitated when she'd asked for permission to pack an overnight bag, walk to Millicent's, and stay the entire night.

Millicent had transformed the parlor at the top of the stairs into a girlish dream, with pillows scattered across the floor, a roaring fire in the hearth, and a tray of pastries and hot chocolate resting on the low table between them. At the moment they were taking turns brushing each other's hair, something that made the time it took to brush their usual one hundred strokes go faster.

"Thank you, Freya." Rosalind glanced over her shoulder again at her friend. "But your hair is far prettier than mine. It's so light."

"It's lighter, but it's fine and thin. Yours is wavy and thick."

Freya's brows furrowed as she worked through a snarl near the bottom of her hair.

"She's right, Rosalind," Millicent said from where she sat braiding Jane's already-brushed hair. "It's prettier than all of ours combined. Mr. Vandermeer is going to melt when he sees it down for the first time."

The warmth that had been filling her chest evaporated, never mind the heat from the fire. What would her friends say if they knew Leeland had already seen her with her hair down?

If they knew he'd been more taken with the idea of stopping her from breathing than he had with the thickness of her hair? She pressed a hand to her throat, where her bruise hadn't quite faded.

"Oh yes," Freya agreed. "He'll love your hair."

"Are you counting down the days?" Jane asked.

Rosalind blinked. "Until my wedding?"

"Until your wedding. Until your fiancé returns. Any of it."

"I know Mr. Vandermeer is older than you, but he's so big and strong. He's almost like one of those characters from a dime novel." Millicent sighed dreamily.

A hard ball settled in Rosalind's stomach. He was big and strong, yes, but he didn't remind her of some dashing hero in a novel. If she had to pick someone who reminded her of that, it would be Yuri Amos.

After all, he was the one who agreed to get her away from Sitka, and now she only had two days to go.

"Oh, some of these dresses are so pretty, I swear you could wear one for your wedding. Here." Jane handed her a magazine opened to a fashion plate. "What do you think of this one?"

Rosalind took the magazine and studied the page. The bride wore a fitted bodice with pearl buttons, and the skirt was layered in delicate lace that trailed into a long train. "It's lovely, but I don't think it would survive Sitka's muddy streets in May."

Jane laughed. "Well, maybe you'll ride in a carriage the whole time. A white one. With roses pinned to the door."

"Ooh, and ribbons." Millicent reached for a pastry. "Pink ones, like in that issue of the *Ladies' Gazette*. Wouldn't that be dreamy?"

"I think I'd rather ride in a sled pulled by huskies," Freya said, tossing the brush aside and grabbing a cup of hot chocolate. "If I ever get married in Sitka, I want a winter wedding, and that's how I want to arrive. Then I won't need to worry about getting mud on my dress—just snow, and that melts."

"Dog sleds aren't romantic," Millicent said, licking raspberry filling off her fingers. "They're just cold."

"And you'd have to get married halfway up a mountain if you wanted to make sure you had snow," Jane said. "Everyone in California thinks Alaska is full of snow, but it mostly just rains in Sitka and Juneau, even in the dead of winter."

Freya's lips turned down into a pout. "I still want snow and a dogsled for my wedding."

"Then maybe you should marry a trapper from the interior." Millicent spoke around her mouthful of pastry. "They get more snow away from the coast, and there are plenty of dogsleds that run along the Yukon River once it freezes."

"What about your wedding cake?" Jane nudged Rosalind's shoulder. "Have you thought about what you want? There's a drawing here of a cake with three tiers and sugared violets."

Rosalind glanced at the magazine, then nodded absently as she reached for a pastry. She hadn't given a moment's thought to cake. Leeland would probably order it. Just like he'd ordered her gown to be made down in Seattle—and followed it with a reminder that he expected her corset to be laced to sixteen inches on their wedding day.

She took a large bite of the pastry, purely out of spite. She'd lost track of how many sweets she'd snuck from the kitchen since Leeland had left. She didn't even know why she was worried about how tightly she was going to lace her corset. It wasn't as though she was planning to actually marry the man.

"I want a lemon-flavored cake for my wedding. But rather than talk about cakes, there's something else I want to know . . ." Millicent leaned in close, a wicked grin on her lips.

"Don't ask it," Jane warned.

"Have you thought about your wedding night?" Millicent blurted.

Rosalind nearly dropped her pastry. "I . . . ah . . ."

"Millicent!" Jane hissed. "It's not proper to ask such a thing."

"We were all thinking it!" Millicent grinned. "Don't blame me for being the only one brave enough to ask."

"I *was* thinking it." Freya giggled, then looked at Rosalind.

In fact, all the girls were looking at her.

She opened her mouth, never mind that she hadn't the faintest idea what to say. But before she could utter a word, clanging split the air.

They all froze for a moment, looking around the room.

"Is that . . . Is that the fire bell?" Millicent finally asked.

Shouting sounded from outside, and Rosalind's heart thudded against her chest. Where had the fire started? Was the town in danger of burning?

Freya bolted toward the window and pressed her face to the glass. "I can't it see from here."

A door shut down the hall, and Millicent's father charged through their cozy little parlor, his shirt not tucked fully into his trousers.

"Come on, girls. Get your coats on and come help," he called as he thundered down the stairs.

"Your father's right." Millicent's mother appeared next, her hair pulled into a sloppy bun. "You're old enough to carry water, all of you."

They jumped from their spots and rushed down the stairs behind Millicent's mother, pausing just long enough to pull on their boots and coats. The scent of smoke greeted them the second they stepped outside, and dozens of people had already flooded into the street, running toward the harbor at various speeds.

Rosalind's nightgown whipped against her legs as she kept pace with Millicent, Jane, and Freya. Was one of the warehouses on fire? Hopefully not. Not only was a warehouse large and likely to catch other buildings on fire, but there would be thousands of dollars of valuable inventory lost with such a blaze.

They kept running, passing houses with doors thrown open and people rushing into the night, all while the fire bell continued to toll over the chaos. Shouts rang out from the harbor, first someone shouting for more men, then another voice asking for more buckets. The crackle of flames hadn't yet reached them, but the smoke thickened until it stung her eyes.

Millicent split off from the main road, taking a less crowded side street that ran parallel to the harbor. Rosalind didn't know if she was wheezing from running too hard or from the smoke, but she could barely breathe as they raced closer to the giant plume of smoke billowing into the sky.

She didn't like how far they were running either. Even without being on the road that ran along the harbor, she could tell they were moving farther and farther away from the commercial harbor and closer to the Amos family's warehouse and shipyard.

Please, God, don't let it be the Amoses.

It might not be them. There were a few buildings past

where their facilities sat on the water that could have caught fire too.

But what if it was?

"Here." Millicent reached a street that connected the road they were on to the harbor and pointed, her chest heaving for breath. "It's the shipyard."

"No." Rosalind slid to a stop beside her, following the line of friend's finger. Flames clawed at the side of a wooden building, climbing toward the roofline, while smoke billowed overhead.

She couldn't tell which building it was, didn't even know how many buildings the Amoses had inside their shipyard, but she recognized the fencing. There was no question about the building on fire belonging to the Amoses.

Men had taken axes to the fence, and a line had already been formed, with people handing buckets inside the fence.

"Let's go." Millicent started toward the blaze, and Jane raced to catch up.

Rosalind stayed rooted to the ground. What could cause such a fire in the middle of winter, when all they got was rain and snow?

What was the chance of this being an accident?

"Are you coming?" Freya paused beside her.

Rosalind only shook her head, acrid air pressing against her face. "I . . . I'm sorry. There's something I have to do first."

Was her father behind the fire? She had to know.

"Come back as soon as you can," Freya called over her shoulder as she rushed toward the blaze.

Rosalind turned on her heel and ran, racing up the side street until it ended, then turning down another street and running back the direction she'd come. Her feet pounded over the uneven road and her breath burned in her lungs, but she pressed forward, higher and higher up the hill.

Had her father done this? Had he targeted the Amoses?

Why? Did it have something to do with her? Had he discovered the missing ledgers and figured out what she'd done with them? Was this some kind of retaliation?

She passed two boys with buckets sprinting the other direction, then an old man with a wet rag wrapped around his face. None of them spared her more than a glance.

It was just as well, because tears were pricking the corners of her eyes, blurring the street ahead. She blinked, but they wouldn't stop as she raced up the muddy road, the slope of the hill growing steeper and steeper.

Why did her father hate the Amoses so much?

They were everything she wished her family was. United. Decent. Kind. They didn't threaten and scheme. They didn't control people through fear. They didn't leave bruises on their children or manipulate their daughters into marriages. They loved justice and wanted fairness and didn't think the person with the biggest pocketbook should get to make all the decisions. Was that really such a crime?

By the time she turned onto her street, she was openly crying. But she didn't care.

It wasn't until she reached the walkway to her house that she finally stopped and bent over, her chest heaving as she gasped for breath. Her face was soaked from her tears, and she swiped at them furiously, then paused.

What if the dampness wasn't just tears?

A fat, heavy drop of water hit the back of her neck.

Then another struck her shoulder.

She tilted her face up only to find rain meeting her skin. Not mist. Not drizzle. But thick, fat drops of rain that increased in intensity with each second she stood there, until they hammered the road and rooftops with full force.

Dear Father God, please . . .

She didn't know what she was praying for.

Please help the rain be enough to stop the fire.

Please let the rain protect the town.

Please allow only one section of the Amoses shipyard to have been destroyed and not the entire thing.

She stood there for a long moment, staring up into the sky, trying to tell herself that everything would be all right, and the entire town wouldn't burn because of her father. Then she tromped up the front steps and reached for the door.

Foster wasn't waiting for her. She hadn't expected him to be there at such a late hour, but she also hadn't expected to find voices coming from the sitting room off the foyer either.

It wasn't a room her father used often, only when he was hosting guests whom he didn't want in his study. And he never used the room at this time of night.

The door was cracked open just enough to let sound spill out, and lamplight flickered inside the sitting room, throwing warped shadows across the Persian rug. She peeked through the small opening to find her father standing near the fireplace, still dressed in his formal coat and cravat, though the top button of his shirt was undone and his usually slicked-back hair fell haphazardly across his brow. The two men seated across from him were nothing like the gentlemen he typically entertained. Dressed in ragged coats and muddy boots, they slouched in the parlor's expensive leather chairs. One of them had a rag tied around his wrist, and she could smell traces of smoke even from the hall.

"Only one building?" Her father made a slashing motion with his hand. "I paid you to burn the entire thing to the ground! What about the ship in the dry dock? Did you at least burn that?"

The thin man closest to the fire shifted in his seat. "They

was there. It was like they was expectin' it, like they was waitin'. No sooner did Billy pull out his torch than we heard shoutin'.'"

The second man, broader and wearing a felt hat, leaned forward and rested his elbows on his knees. "The lumber was the only thing we was able ta burn, and that was sheer luck. Frank 'ere tossed his torch over the fence after we ran. We didn't think it would hit nothin', but it caught the lumber shed on fire."

"And that was when we left and came here." The skinny man shoved a hand into his hair. "You owe us the rest of the money. Where is it?"

Her father didn't move from his position near the fire. "I said half upon accepting the job and half upon completion. Seeing how ninety percent of the shipyard is still standing, I wouldn't call that complete."

"But we started a fire." The wiry man threw up his hands. "Got the whole town down there right now tryin' ta put 'er out."

"And in the morning, the whole town will be looking for the arsonists." Her father stared straight at the arsonist. "I suggest you leave town now, as discussed, before anyone finds you."

The two men exchanged a look, then the big one stood, his body looming over her father. "Not without our money."

Her father maintained his stance, not seeming to care that the other man had six inches on him. "I'm not paying you anything more for a job that wasn't even half done, and I won't change my mind. But if you want to stay and take your chances with the Deputy Marshal—who just so happens to be related to the Amoses—be my guest."

Rosalind straightened, ready to head back out into the night. She knew enough to incriminate her father and warn the Deputy Marshal about the arsonists who would surely try leaving the island before dawn. But the small movement caused her elbow to accidentally bump the door.

The broad man turned. "Well, well, well, who's this charming lass, Caldwell? She wouldn't happen to be yer daughter, would she?"

"Out," her father snapped. "Both of you. Now."

"But you still haven't—"

"Get out of my house." Her father shoved a finger toward the door. "And I suggest you get off the island before you're caught."

The skinny man stood, and Rosalind used the time to slip inside the room. She ignored the lecherous way both men looked at her as they shoved their way past her, and she pinned her gaze on her father.

"How could you?" she spat the moment the front door slammed shut.

"What are you wearing?" Her father barked in response.

She knew she looked affright. Her hair was windblown and damp, her face wet from the rain, and her nightgown half sodden beneath her open coat. But she was too angry to care. "Paying men to burn down someone's business, Father? Really? You could have caught the entire town on fire."

Her father's jaw clenched. "Do you know how many difficulties that family has caused your uncle and me?"

"No." She stalked toward her father. "All I see is a wholly good family trying to do what's best for Alaska, and you trying to destroy them for it. Why did you do it?"

His eyebrow quirked, and he loosed a cruel laugh. "Can't you guess?"

The sound of his laugh caused her anger to drain away. What was she thinking, coming here by herself and confronting her father? Her heart pounded against her chest, not because her blood was racing, but because it had turned icy cold.

Her father had discovered the missing ledgers. That had to be it. He'd found out what she'd done with them, and now he was trying to burn everything the Amoses owned to the ground so the evidence would be destroyed.

"Did you know they contacted the secretary of the interior and reported your uncle for resettling the village of Klawock?" He sneered.

She blinked. "What?" The village of Klawock? What was he talking about?

"And now the secretary of the interior is coming to Alaska to look into the matter himself."

"I . . . ah . . . That's why you hired the arsonists?"

Her father took a step closer. "It's one reason. The other had to do with what I found when I searched your room."

"You . . . you searched my room?" The breath whooshed from her lungs.

"I got a little curious when I learned you'd been donating hundreds of dollars a month to charities without my knowing." He sent her a sharp smile. "After all, I keep close tabs on your mail, and I certainly would have noticed letters sent to charities on a monthly basis. Imagine my surprise when I pulled up a loose floorboard and found a stack of notes from the charities. Those letters all thanked you personally, but do you know who they were addressed to?"

She closed her eyes.

Her father slammed his fist against a small table beside one of the chairs. "Look at me when I'm talking to you!" He waited until she opened her eyes before continuing. "I asked if you knew who they were addressed to. And don't try lying."

"Yuri." She nearly choked on his name.

"That's right. Yuri Amos, brother of Alexei and Sacha, both of whom have caused nothing but problems since we moved to Sitka. So, yes, I burned their shipyard. That family deserves to be ruined, and I won't stop until they are." Her father took a step toward her, the anger on his face replaced with a cold, controlled rage. "You're going to pay for your part in this, Rosalind. You're going to pay very dearly."

He pulled back his fist and slammed it into her ribs before she had a chance to curl in on herself.

28

Yuri couldn't remember the last time he'd felt so tired. It was almost as though his entire body was ready to collapse into sleep, and yet his mind wouldn't let it. His hair was still damp from the bath he'd taken, but the scent of smoke still clung to his hair and skin, and judging by the way the kitchen smelled, the whole family would probably need to take baths for a week straight before the stench of smoke dissipated completely.

"At least it was only the lumber." Sacha ran a hand through his damp hair from where he sat directly across the table from Yuri.

"What are we going to do?" Kate rubbed a hand over the bulge in her belly, as though the gesture might somehow protect the child growing inside her.

Yuri glanced around the table, where his siblings and their spouses had gathered. They should probably all be in bed. The children certainly were. But here they were, seated around the same table they'd gathered at after they'd buried their mother, then their father and his second wife, and then their brother, Ivan.

It only seemed fitting to sit here now.

"I'm sure Jonas will launch a full investigation," Alexei said from where he slouched at the head of the table. "This wasn't an accidental fire, and we captured one of the arsonists. He'll talk eventually."

"The other two probably left the island while our building was still burning." Sacha grabbed one of the teacakes from the platter at the center of the table, then tossed it into his mouth, swallowing so quickly he couldn't possibly have tasted it.

"How badly did this fire set us back?" Mikhail picked up a cup of tea, only to set it back down on the table without taking a sip.

"Several thousand dollars in lumber." Alexei blew out a breath, his shoulders sagging. "Like you said, it's a setback, but it didn't ruin us."

"It could have," Nathan gritted, his jaw hard. "Had you not been there when the arsonists came."

"And had it not started raining." Sacha tossed another teacake into his mouth, once again swallowing after barely chewing. "I know the entire town was trying to prevent the flames from spreading anywhere else, even in our shipyard, but without that rain, I'm not sure we would have been successful."

"The Caldwells are mad that Secretary Gray is coming for a visit," Alexei said flatly. "They blame me. The governor said something to me about it just yesterday. I bet that's why they did it."

"I was wondering if they did it because they found out we have their seal ledgers and they wanted to destroy the evidence." Mikhail picked up a teacake but didn't eat it.

Yuri hadn't thought of that, but a chill traveled through him at the idea. "I don't think they know. I saw Rosalind in town today with Millicent and Jane and Freya. If her father knew about the ledgers, I can't imagine he'd let her out of the house."

And Rosalind's father definitely would have injured her, but he wasn't going to think about that. Two more days. That's all the longer they had to keep the ledgers secret before he could whisk Rosalind away.

Pounding sounded on the front door. "Is anyone there? I need help."

Alexei met Mikhail's gaze; then they both stood from the table and rushed to the door.

Yuri didn't recognize the voice, but he couldn't say whether his brothers did. All he knew was that both Alexei and Mikhail strode down the hallway as if flames were still licking at their shoes.

Yuri scooted his chair back and followed them, right along with everyone else.

Another round of pounding sounded. "Hello? Is anyone awake?"

"Can I help you?" Alexei opened the door to reveal a vaguely familiar man standing on the porch wringing his hands.

"I heard the woman doctor is in town. Is she here?"

"I am." Kate stepped forward. "Where are you injured?"

The man shook his head. "It's not me. It's Miss Rosalind. She's in the carriage."

Miss Rosalind? Everything inside Yuri turned hot.

The man was pointing to the carriage, but Yuri lunged forward and grabbed him by his collar. "What did he do? What did her father do to her?"

The man, whom he now recognized as the Caldwell's butler, just shook his head. "I don't know all of it, but it's not good. She needs a doctor."

"Then stop standing there and bring her to the kitchen. I'll get my medical bag." Kate was already dashing up the stairs, her steps fast despite her protruding belly.

Yuri released Foster, who turned back toward the carriage, but Yuri was faster and raced ahead of the older man.

He reached the carriage door first and wrenched it open, then flinched. Rosalind was curled into a heap on the bench seat, eyes closed. Her face was pale though otherwise untouched, but her breathing was choppy and uneven.

His heartbeat doubled. He didn't have to be a doctor to know something was very, very wrong.

"Rosalind?" he asked gently.

Her eyes fluttered open. "Yuri." She licked her lips. "It hurts. Make it stop hurting."

"What hurts, sweetheart?"

"My ribs . . . I can't . . ." A breath shuddered from her lungs, followed by a squeal of pain.

"I'm going to carry you inside. Kate and Nathan are waiting."

Rosalind whimpered and pressed her eyes shut, then gave a subtle nod.

He tried to be as careful as possible picking her up, but the moment he slid an arm behind her back, she gave a sharp cry.

"I'm so sorry, but I have to get you to the kitchen." His voice broke on the words.

"Do you need me to help?" Sacha asked from behind him.

Yuri shook his head. "Handing her to you will only cause more pain."

"How do you know?"

Maybe it was because of the tight way she was curled against his chest, or the short, panicked gasps coming from her lungs. He wasn't sure. All he knew was that he wasn't going to hand her off to another person, not even Sacha.

"What did that monster do to her?" Alexei came up beside Sacha, his dark eyes sweeping over Rosalind.

Yuri just shook his head. That was yet another thing he didn't know. In fact, he wasn't even sure that he cared. All he cared about was getting Rosalind to breathe normally. Was that something Nathan and Kate could fix?

He carried her toward the house, but she made tiny whimpering sounds with each step, and when she tried to suck in a deeper breath, a strangled wheeze escaped.

"Just a minute, love. We're almost there."

She didn't respond. Instead, her body loosened in his arms, and another chill swept through him.

"In here." Kate met him in the doorway, then gestured to the hall that led to the kitchen. "Is it her lungs? Does she have a broken rib?"

"I don't know. She was conscious in the carriage, though she couldn't seem to talk. But now . . ." He glanced at her white face resting limply against his shoulder, and a fresh wave of terror coursed through him.

"Set her down gently. Don't move her shoulders if you can help it." Nathan held the kitchen door open, his sleeves rolled up and his hands stained with the dark orange liquid that he and Kate used to disinfect things.

Yuri set her down on the scarred wood as gently as he could manage. She didn't make a single sound, but that only made everything seem worse. "She was in a lot of pain before she went unconscious."

Yuri stepped away from the table, and Nathan slid a pair of scissors straight down her nightgown from collar to hem.

Yuri looked away. As a doctor, Nathan might have to examine an exposed woman, but he wasn't about to look. But the gasps from both Nathan and Kate had his eyes flickering back toward Rosalind for the briefest of seconds.

Just long enough to see that her chest and abdomen were covered in black and blue bruises, and that there was one place near the bottom of her left side where her ribs bulged and then caved inward.

He ran to the waste bin and retched.

"I'm going to kill him," Bryony said. "I'm going to take one of Mikhail's guns and march straight up there and—"

"No, you're not," Jonas said. "This is grounds enough for me to arrest him. No killing necessary."

Yuri wiped his mouth and then straightened, turning to find that every one of his family members had poured into the room, including Jonas.

When had he gotten back from the jail?

Never mind. It didn't matter. What mattered was that there was a lawman here to record things, and he could also testify in court later, if needed.

His brothers were all like him, trying to find something to look at that wasn't Rosalind's black-and-blue body, but the serious looks on their faces told him that they'd glanced at her for long enough to understand what had happened.

Jonas, on the other hand, had stepped even closer to the table and was vigorously writing notes on the pad he always kept tucked into his breast pocket.

Yuri turned to Kate, but she wasn't flying into action or calling for a long list of medical tools. She'd covered the bottom half of Rosalind's body with a blanket, but now she was standing next to the table with one hand resting on her stomach and a tear streaking down her cheek.

"Don't tell me you can't help. You have to do something, please. You have to try!" Yuri lunged forward, about to grip Kate by the shoulders. Why wasn't she moving?

Sacha hooked an arm around his waist before he reached

her, pulling him backward. "She's doing everything she knows to do, but she's not God. She can't heal everyone."

Tears scalded his eyes. "I should have forced Rosalind to leave sooner. I shouldn't have let her wait for a full week. I should have . . ."

"Stop talking," Nathan snapped. He was moving at least, even if he was pressing on her misshapen ribs in a way that surely would have caused her pain had she been conscious.

His ministrations weren't helping, though. Each breath Rosalind drew seemed weaker and weaker.

"Do you know what a needle thoracostomy is, Kate?" Nathan glanced at his wife.

Kate shook her head, then wiped another tear away from her cheek. "I've never heard of it."

"I need the large-bore trocar and cannula from my medical bag."

"The what?" Kate moved to the medical bag and pulled out a scalpel.

"No. The long needle and— I'll get it." He rushed to the bag sitting on the hutch, then started rummaging around, not remotely bothered by the fact he'd just bumped his pregnant wife out of the way. "We know from autopsies that if a rib or multiple ribs get broken, they can puncture the lungs. There's evidence that the lungs can seal themselves if the puncture isn't too large. But if air leaks into the pleural cavity, it creates pressure that prevents the lung from expanding."

"And you think that's what's happening to Rosalind?" Kate ran her eyes down Rosalind's form.

"It's my best guess. See how the right side of her chest is rising and falling, but the left side is barely moving?" Nathan stepped away from his bag with a chillingly long needle and a small metal tube in his hand. He sterilized them both with carbolic acid, then inserted the needle into the tube. "It's dangerous. I can't promise it will work, and the risk of infection is great, but—"

"Try it," Yuri croaked. "She'll die if you don't, won't she? She's dying right now."

Kate met Nathan's gaze, then gave a small nod.

That was all Nathan needed to start probing her ribs again. What he was looking for, Yuri didn't know, but Nathan stopped after just a few seconds. "Someone, hold her down. Tightly."

Yuri raced toward the table, right along with his brothers. Jonas was there first, since he'd been taking notes.

But Sacha beat him to her other shoulder, and Alexei and Mikhail were both holding her feet, which were closest to the end of the table where they'd been standing.

Yuri looked around for a moment, then settled for holding her hand on the opposite side of the table from where Nathan was working.

"It's going to be all right, love." He pressed his lips to her knuckles. "Just hang on for a few more seconds."

Nathan cleared his throat. "Actually, I don't know that any of this will be all right, Rosalind. You're going to feel pressure between your ribs. I need you to try to stay still."

She didn't respond.

Nathan counted under his breath, then slid the needle and tube into her skin. Rosalind didn't even try to move, never mind that four large men were prepared to wrestle her down.

Nathan waited for a moment, then withdrew the long needle from the center of the tube, leaving the tube itself inserted into her side. A faint hiss filled the room.

"Does that mean it's working?" Yuri blurted.

Nathan gave a curt nod. "It appears so, yes. But something like this is difficult to regulate. I wish we were at the hospital in a proper surgical room."

Just then Rosalind let out a deep breath.

Nathan adjusted the tube slightly, and a bigger hiss followed. Her chest rose again, this time without even a stutter.

She was breathing.

Yuri closed his eyes and bowed his head, not realizing he'd started to cry until a thumb brushed weakly against his knuckles.

"Yuri?" Rosalind rasped.

"I'm here." He placed a kiss against her knuckles.

"Rosalind, your lung should begin to re-expand now that the pressure's relieved." Nathan stared down at the tiny tube poking out of her ribs. "But I don't know how bad the damage to your lungs is. I'd like to keep the cannula in overnight to prevent pressure from building again. Kate, wash the wound carefully with carbolic acid. We'll try binding the ribs in the morning."

"What's wrong with me?" she whispered. "What happened?"

"It doesn't matter." Yuri clasped her hand tighter, then held it up to his cheek. "You're safe now. Do you hear me? You're safe, and we're going to make sure you stay that way."

A tear slid down her cheek. "My father was behind the fire."

Yuri stilled. Was that why her father had beaten her so badly?

"How do you know?" Jonas stepped forward, his notebook back in his hand.

"They were there. The arsonists. In the house. Asking for money."

"And you confronted him?" Yuri gritted.

Another tear fell. "I didn't . . . I didn't . . ." Her breaths quickened, turning short and choppy. "I didn't feel like I had a choice."

"I'm going to arrest him now." Jonas tucked his notepad back into his shirt pocket. "Both for what he did to you and the arson."

Yuri expected Rosalind to thank him, but her eyes had closed again, her breaths coming shorter and shorter.

"No more talking," Nathan pronounced. "You need to rest."

Rosalind's eyes opened into two tired slits. "Am I going to . . . die?"

Nathan's throat worked. "I don't know. If your left lung is so damaged it can't repair itself, then yes. There's nothing I can do other than this."

"But we're going to do our best to make sure you recover." Kate scooted to Rosalind's other side and picked up her free hand. "We'll keep the wound clean so infection doesn't set in and bind your ribs as tight as we need to so the broken bones can heal."

Rosalind didn't respond. She'd already fallen asleep on the table, her breaths back to stuttering.

29

Pain. It covered her body, starting in her lower ribs and radiating outward until it felt like fire consumed everything but her legs and arms. Rosalind groaned, then rolled to her side, trying to find a way to relieve the stabbing sensation above her stomach, but the movement caused an even worse flash of white-hot pain to sear through her.

"Rosalind?"

Even through her pain, she recognized the voice, kind and understanding and gentle. She whimpered, then opened her eyes. "Yuri?"

"I'm here." A hand stroked hair away from her forehead.

He was at her side, sitting beside the bed with shadows beneath his eyes and his hair hanging over his forehead in disheveled tufts.

He reached out and clasped her hand in his, then laid a gentle kiss on her knuckles. "Do you need something? How can I help?"

She shook her head, then whimpered when another flash of

pain knifed through her. "It hurts. Everything hurts. I . . . What's wrong with me? And why are you here?"

She tried to look around the room. She couldn't see much without moving, but she could tell she wasn't in her bedroom or even at home. There were no silk draperies, no fireplace, no gleaming mirror over the mantle. Instead, she was in a small room with fading wallpaper, and a soft, worn quilt draped over her. A modest chest of drawers stood against the wall over Yuri's shoulder, and dim light seeped along the edges of the simple curtains hanging over the window.

"Why . . . Why am I here?" she rasped. Her lungs burned each time she tried to talk, as though she couldn't afford to expel the breath needed to form words, and there was still that terrible searing pain in her lungs.

Was she bleeding? What was wrong? She reached down to touch the spot with the sharpest pain.

"Don't touch your ribs, Miss Caldwell, please." A figure surged away from the wall.

It was the doctor. The young one that Yuri's sister had married. She didn't quite remember his name. Nicholas, maybe or Nigel. How long had he been in the room? "What . . . What happened?"

The doctor exchanged a glance with Yuri. "Don't you remember?"

She pressed her eyes shut, trying to recall what events could possibly have led to her being inside the Amoses' house. There had been a house visit at Millicent's with hot chocolate and pastries; then the fire bell had rung, and they'd all run outside to help. Then she'd realized the Amoses' shipyard was burning, and she'd run home.

She could still see her father's irate face, still feel the pain that radiated through her body when his first blow landed against her ribs. He'd followed it up with another blow to the same spot just seconds later, then another and another until she'd crumpled to the floor, begging him to stop. That's when he'd started kicking her.

She gasped and opened her eyes, only to find them wet with tears. "He said he'd keep kicking me until I stood up and quit crying."

That was the only way she could get him to stop. She certainly hadn't been able to fight him. The pain had been so bad, she'd nearly retched, but somehow she'd managed to suck in her tears and force herself to stand. "Then he . . . he punched me in the ribs and watched me crumple back to the ground before leaving."

"I'm going to kill him," Yuri growled.

"No . . ." She reached out and clasped his wrist. "He'll only hurt you."

"He's not going to hurt anyone." A deep voice spoke from somewhere in the room.

She had to shift to see who was speaking. The movement caused her eyes to flood with tears, but at least she was able to follow the direction of the voice to where Deputy Marshal Jonas Redding stood in the doorway, arms crossed over his broad chest. Yuri's oldest brother, Alexei, was in the room too, leaning against the wall with one foot crossed over the other.

"Your father's in jail," the Deputy Marshal continued. "When the judge returns to Sitka, I'll be asking him to deny bail."

"You arrested my father?" She licked her lips. "Because . . . because of what he did to me?"

"Do you understand the damage to your left lung, Miss Caldwell?" The doctor took a step closer. "Do you realize the gravity of your situation?"

She looked back to Yuri, only to find his eyes had grown redder, and moisture was welling in them.

"You have five broken ribs," he whispered.

"Yes, and at least two of them are broken in multiple places," the doctor spoke in a clinical, matter-of-fact voice. "That in itself is painful and would take weeks to heal, but one of the ribs punctured your left lung."

It had? She pressed a hand to the upper part of her chest and sucked in a breath, only then did she realize that breathing seemed to hurt. She couldn't take a full breath without pain slicing through her. She had to keep her breaths short and shallow just to tolerate the pain. "Am I going to be all right?"

The doctor's throat worked, and for a moment it almost looked like he, too, might be fighting tears. "I don't know. Your lung was collapsing when your butler brought you to us, and you were suffocating. I inserted a small steel tube between two of your ribs to relieve the air in your lungs, but we need to take it out this morning. The problem is, we don't know if the damage to your lung was minimal and it will repair itself, or your chest will fill back up with air once the tube is removed."

"And if it fills back up with air, does that mean . . ." She sank her teeth into her bottom lip, trying to understand despite the fiery licks of pain that refused to leave her alone. "Does that mean I'm going to die?"

"We'll do everything in our power to make sure that doesn't happen."

"That doesn't mean no."

"No, it doesn't." The doctor dragged a hand over the front of his face, his eyes bloodshot. "I might be able to insert the cannula once more, but if that doesn't provide enough time for your lung to repair itself, there's nothing more I can do."

"And if my lungs heal? How long until I fully recover?"

The doctor just shook his head. "It will be a long process, and I can't guarantee success even with that. We know your ribs will heal if we bind them, but there's a correlation between binding ribs tightly and pneumonia. On top of that, we have infection to worry about from the cannula being inserted. I'm sorry, Miss Caldwell. I wish I could give you better news. Truly I do. But I also want to be honest."

Her throat suddenly felt dry. "What's my chance of survival?"

He ran his eyes over her in a manner that felt detached and clinical. It wasn't cold, but it was nothing like the way Leeland looked at her, and it was different from how Yuri looked at her too. "The fact you made it through the night and are now awake and talking is a very good sign."

"I like numbers. Give me a percentage, doctor."

"Forty percent."

Yuri jerked, his hand tightening around hers. "Forty percent? But she survived the night. I thought—"

"We've yet to see how she does with the cannula out, but her breaths are awfully shallow. That alone makes contracting pneumonia a near certainty. Then it becomes a question of whether her body is strong enough to fight it off." The doctor held up his hands. "There's only so much I can do."

Yuri turned back to her, then raised her hand to his lips and pressed a kiss against her knuckles. "You'll fight it off, Ros. You're strong enough to fight it off. I know you are."

She wanted to say he was right, that she would fight no matter what lay ahead, but she was so very tired, and in so much pain, and the idea of even getting out of bed and walking on her own seemed impossible.

"Is it all right if I ask you a few questions about last night, Miss Caldwell?" The Deputy Marshal moved closer to the bed.

She nodded.

"Do you want me to get Bryony while Jonas talks to you?" Yuri asked. "Would it help to have a friend?"

"No, I'll . . . I'll be all right." At least she hoped she would.

The truth was, the longer she talked, the harder it became. It seemed like something stole even more breath from her lungs each time she spoke.

"Not too many questions, Jonas. She needs rest." The doctor stepped away from the bed, giving Deputy Marshal Redding room to come to her side.

The lawman pulled a small notebook and pencil stub out of his shirt pocket. "Do you know why your father attacked you?"

She swallowed and looked away. "It was my fault."

"None of this is your fault," Yuri snapped, his hand tightening around hers.

"No. It is . . . I should have known better than to confront him after the arson."

"Why would you confront him without anyone there to protect you?" Yuri growled.

"I couldn't help it." She paused, sucking in a few more shallow breaths, trying to get enough air to continue speaking. "I was spending the night at Millicent's, and we all came running when we heard the fire bell. But when I saw the fire was at your shipyard, I just knew."

"Did you ask your father directly if he set the fire?" the Marshal asked.

She shook her head, again trying to avoid words. "When I got to the house, two of the arsonists were there . . . My father agreed to pay them half the money when they took the job . . . and half upon completion. But he refused to give them the second part of their payment. He said . . . he said the job wasn't complete because they didn't burn the entire shipyard to the ground."

"And you asked him about it? On your own? Ros . . ." Yuri's throat worked.

She pressed her eyes shut. "That's why I said it was my fault . . . I should have known better than—

"No. None of this is your fault. Do you understand me? The blame for this lies entirely on your father."

"But—"

"But nothing. He's the one who hit you. He's the one who couldn't control his temper. He's the one who . . ." Yuri just shook his head, but she could see him fighting off more tears.

Deputy Marshal Redding looked up from his notebook. "I'll have the prosecutor add arson to the attempted-murder charge."

"Attempted murder?" She blinked. "Is that what you charged him with?"

"You were minutes away from dying last night, Miss Caldwell. I would never consider charging him with anything less." The Deputy Marshal flipped to another page in his notebook. "Now can you describe the two arsonists for—"

Knocking sounded from somewhere else in the house. "Rosalind? Are you in there?"

Rosalind recognized the voice all too well.

The knocking turned to pounding. "Let me in, Amos. My niece is missing, and I need to know if she's here."

"I'll take care of him," Alexei muttered. "The rest of you stay here."

The oldest Amos brother strode out of the room and pulled the door shut behind him.

ALEXEI COULDN'T QUITE STOP his hands from clenching into fists as he headed across the small parlor toward the front door. He wasn't the type to throw punches or shout across a room, but Simon Caldwell was the last man he wanted to see this morning.

Or rather, the second to last man. He wanted to see Preston Caldwell even less.

But the man was still the governor, and it was reasonable for him to want to know where Rosalind was.

"Amos? Are you there?" More banging sounded, the newest round louder than the rest.

Alexei reached the door, then paused and drew in a breath before opening it. "Governor, good morn—"

"Is she here?" The governor jabbed a finger into his chest. "This is an outrage, Amos. You can't have my brother locked up on exaggerated charges and force—"

"Yes, she's here. Follow me." Alexei stepped back and let the man in, then shut the door with a click that sounded far too soft. He turned and headed toward the formal parlor on his left.

The governor didn't follow. He took one look at the doorway and headed the other direction. "I want to see my niece, not have a fireside chat with you. Where is she?"

"Wait." Alexei rushed after him, but the governor was too many steps ahead, swiftly moving across the entryway toward the hallway on the opposite side of the stairs. "She's injured, and I refuse to let you storm through my house, shouting the first thing in . . ."

It was too late. The man reached for the first door he came to, which just so happened to be the sickroom, and opened it. "Rosalind?"

Alexei rushed into the room in time to see Rosalind jerk upward in her bed, then cry out in pain.

She tried to rise, but Yuri pushed her shoulders down and placed himself between her and her uncle. "She's barely breathing. Get out."

Jonas placed a hand on the butt of his gun and moved to stand behind Yuri. "Governor, I'm going to need you to step back. Your niece is being treated for injuries."

"What do you mean 'she's barely breathing'?" The governor ran his eyes over his niece, concern creasing his brow.

"Father lost his temper last night." Rosalind spoke from the bed, where she now lay with an arm curled protectively over her ribs.

"I know. I've been to see him. He feels badly about what happened and fully intends to apologize once he's been released from jail."

"He feels badly?" Yuri's voice turned deathly low. "He nearly killed her."

"Stop being dramatic." The governor waved his hand dismissively. "Everyone knows the attempted-murder charge is ridiculous. Nothing more than an attempt to take revenge out on our family. It will get reduced to a misdemeanor as soon as Marshal Hibbs returns to town."

"There's nothing dramatic or vengeful about that charge. Your niece almost died last night, Governor." Alexei crossed his arms over his chest. "You have Dr. Reid to thank for saving her life."

The man turned to face him, his mouth set in a grim line. "I have no doubt she was scared, but Preston would never—"

"Perhaps you should look at Rosalind's ribs and see the damage." The words were out of Alexei's mouth before he could think to stop them. "Then tell me whether you still think we're being dramatic."

"You saw my niece's ribs?" The governor's face turned red. "Of all the dishonorable, lecherous—"

"It was medically necessary." Nathan pushed himself away from the wall where he'd been standing, watching the interchange. "Your brother left Rosalind with a collapsed lung. She was seconds away from suffocating when a servant brought her here. I have over half a dozen witnesses that can testify to that fact in a court of law, should the need arise. I also have the testimony of my wife, who is a doctor and can support the medical veracity of my claim."

The governor's lips curled. "This house is the last place Foster should have brought her."

"This house is currently the only place in town with a doctor." Alexei could only shake his head. Did the man even realize what he was saying?

"I want to inform you, as her next of kin, that there's still a good chance your niece will not live." Nathan moved closer to the governor, his voice professional and void of any emotion. "The damage that the broken ribs did to her lungs might be too great for her to survive."

The governor's shoulders loosened, some of the fight draining away from him. "Is it really that bad?"

"Look at her and tell me what you see." Nathan extended his hand toward Rosalind.

The man moved his gaze back to his niece, who was wincing in pain and taking increasingly fast and shallow breaths. "Very well. I'll hire a nurse to see to her needs as she recovers. How soon can she be ready to leave?"

"She's not leaving," Alexei gritted.

"You just said Preston would be facing charges. Surely it's safe for me to bring her back to her house while—"

"No." Alexei made a slashing motion with his hand. "She'll stay here, under the same roof as the two doctors who have been caring for her, until they deem her ready to be released."

The governor narrowed his eyes. "You can't keep my niece confined here against her will."

"Just how long have you known about the abuse?" Yuri stepped closer to the governor, his shoulders set in a tight line. "Did you know about her sprained wrist before this? What other injuries did you overlook and fail to report to the Marshal?"

The man stiffened. "I don't see what a hurt wrist has to do with this."

"It proves you knew your brother was abusing her and did nothing to prevent it," Yuri snapped. "We're not letting her leave with you. You'd have to murder everyone in this room before we'd let you take her."

The governor's lips pressed into a flat line. "Fine. I'll send word to her fiancé about what happened last night. He should be here in a week, maybe less. Then he can marry the girl and be done with it."

A chill ran down Alexei's spine. "If you think there is any chance I'll turn an abused woman over to a man known for having a temper, you are sorely mistaken."

The governor whirled on him. "You don't have a say in this, Amos."

"Why don't we ask Rosalind what she wants?" Yuri nodded toward the bed.

Rosalind moved her hand up to clutch the sapphire necklace lying against the hollow of her throat. Somehow it had stayed around her neck all this time, even through the procedure Nathan performed last night. "No . . . I don't want anything to do with Leeland. I won't marry him. Not while I recover, and not in May when the wedding is scheduled. The Amoses are right . . . He's violent, and he won't be a good husband to me."

There was something about how she clutched the necklace against her throat that made Alexei frown, but before he could ask about it, the governor turned back to him, angry lines contorting his face.

"Why are you doing this? Haven't you done enough already? First the seals, then the harassment lawsuit, then informing Secretary Gray about relocating those backwater

Indian towns. And now you're interfering with my family? Why?"

Alexei leaned forward, crowding the governor's space. "Because you ordered our shipyard burned to the ground last night."

"You're fortunate it was only one building," he growled, his eyes flashing. "You deserved to have everything burned."

"And I deserved that because of the seals?" Alexei leaned even closer, until he could feel the governor's breath on his face.

"And the lawsuits."

"So you're not denying you were behind the arson attempt?"

"We were both behind it!" the governor shouted.

Alexei stepped back and glanced at Jonas. "Is that enough to arrest him?"

Caldwell let out a low guttural sound, then lunged.

Alexei didn't have time to brace himself before the governor's hands slammed into his shoulders. The force of the impact drove him backward a few steps, but he regained his balance and shoved the man away.

It was enough to send the governor crashing into the doorway.

"Enough!" Jonas was across the room in an instant. He wrenched Simon backward, hooked one arm around the man's chest, and yanked his arms behind his back in a clean, practiced motion.

"I demand you release me immediately!" Caldwell twisted, but Jonas forced his face against the wall and kicked his feet apart. "I'm the governor."

"And I'm the acting US Deputy Marshal." Jonas's voice was as hard as the steel Farnsworth used to build his massive ships down in San Francisco. "And I just witnessed you assault a civilian inside his own home after admitting to conspiracy to commit arson. You're under arrest."

"You can't arrest me! You have no authority to—"

"I have every authority," Jonas snapped.

Caldwell tried to lurch away, but Jonas slammed him flat against the wall.

Alexei met the man's gaze. He hadn't known for certain that the governor had been involved in the arson, only his brother. So Alexei had made a series of calculated statements to see if he could get the truth, and they had paid off.

The governor seemed to realize that, because even from his position against the wall, he narrowed his eyes at Alexei. "Just wait until I get released from jail, Amos. I'm going to use every last resource I have to destroy—"

"Stop talking, Governor." Jonas hauled the man upright. "Unless you want me to add threatening an individual to the list of charges against you."

That was enough for the governor to finally shut his mouth.

Jonas used the few seconds of silence to march the man toward the door and out of the house.

30

Sitka; Two Days Later

"So there's no lasting damage to my lung?" Rosalind sat with her arms raised, trying not to wince as Kate wrapped a bandage around her chest.

"There doesn't appear to be, no." Dr. Reid stood beside the bed, scrawling notes onto the pad he'd used to track her respiratory rate and symptoms for the past two days. "Your trouble breathing now has to do with pain from your broken ribs, not because air from your lung is leaking into your pleural cavity."

"I see." Or at least she tried to see everything that he was explaining, but all she knew was that every breath still seared the bottom of her chest.

"There, how does that feel?" Kate pinned the end of the bandage to the top of her chest, then sat back. "Does it hurt less when you breathe?"

Rosalind took a slow breath, dragging air partway into her lungs. "The pain feels duller now, though it's still there."

Dr. Reid gave a short nod. "That's to be expected. We'll

keep your ribs bound constantly for the next few days, but I'd like to move toward unwrapping them at night as soon as possible to prevent pneumonia. We don't know exactly why restricted breathing leads to pneumonia, but you've been through enough already."

Yes, she had been through quite a bit, hadn't she? She pressed her eyes shut, memories of the past three days filling her mind.

Both her father and Uncle Simon were in jail, and they must be furious. This wasn't the first time they'd done something illegal, but it was certainly the first time they'd been arrested for it, and without a judge on the island to set bail, they would be there for a few more days at least.

Deputy Marshal Redding said he was going to petition the judge to deny her father bail because of the severity of the charges, but the judge might let him post bail anyway. What would happen once he was released? Would he come to the Amoses' house and try to get her?

The Deputy Marshal was less optimistic about the judge denying her uncle bail. He was only facing arson conspiracy charges, and it would take a good bit of nerve for a judge to force the governor of Alaska to stay in jail until trial.

She looked up at Dr. Reid. "How long until my ribs are healed?"

"Usually about six weeks." He wrote something down on one of his charts. "But yours could take longer given the severity of the damage."

She couldn't stay here six more weeks. Her father would surely find a way out of jail by then, and her uncle had already said Leeland was coming back to Sitka.

She clasped her hands together, trying to ignore the gnawing sensation that had lodged itself beneath the pain in her ribs. "I can't stay here that long. What's the earliest I can travel?"

"I suggest staying here until you are fully recovered." The doctor sent her a stern look.

"I can't. It's not safe." She'd been supposed to leave Sitka yesterday with Yuri, and though they'd clearly missed that ship, she had to get away from Sitka before Leeland came for her or her father got out of jail.

Was Yuri even planning to take her away from Sitka anymore? Would it be possible for them to sneak away now that the entire town knew she was staying with the Amoses?

Or perhaps it was still possible for her to sneak away, but it would be impossible for the Amoses to appear as though they had nothing to do with her leaving.

A brisk knock sounded on the door; then it cracked open.

"Can we come in?" Alexei poked his head inside and looked at Dr. Reid.

"Yes, as long as Miss Caldwell is feeling up to visitors?" The doctor looked at her.

She nodded, and Alexei stepped into the room with Yuri following behind him.

Something in her chest loosened. Yuri hadn't left her side that first day after she'd been injured, though she'd barely been awake long enough to recall anything other than her uncle's visit. But every time she'd awakened, she'd found her hand in his and heard his gentle voice trying to soothe her through the pain.

But yesterday, Bryony had taken over most of her nursing. The doctors made regular visits, of course, but she'd seen Yuri only a couple of times.

"Rosalind?" Yuri must have sensed her worry, because he crossed the room in three strides and gripped her hand.

"What's wrong? Is it the bindings? Are they too tight?" He sent a glare his sister's direction. "I told you to be gentle with her."

"She has five broken ribs." Kate threw up her hands. "Even if I wrapped her in clouds, she'd be in pain for weeks."

"It's not the bindings." Rosalind tightened her hand around Yuri's.

"Then what, Ros? What can I do to help?" He bent down until his face was even with hers, then he smoothed her hair away from her forehead. "Tell me, and I'll make it better."

Her eyes filled with tears. Oh, why did Yuri have to be so kind? It was almost too much.

"Rosalind?" he asked again. Then he straightened and sent another angry look across the room, this time glaring at both his sister and brother-in-law. "What did you do to her? Bryony said she was fine after lunch."

Dr. Reid shook his head. "We didn't do anything. I was answering questions about her recovery timeline when you came in."

"If you told her she won't recover, I swear I'll—"

"I can't stay here," she blurted before Yuri charged across the room and throttled his brother-in-law. "Everyone in your family has been so kind and wonderful, but I need to go, before my uncle and father get released from jail. Before Leeland comes to Sitka."

"Absolutely not." Dr. Reid made a slashing motion with his hands. "Your ribs cannot handle anything other than you lying in bed, not to mention the incision from your cannula insertion still isn't healed, and we need to monitor you for signs of infection and pneumonia."

Yuri and Alexei exchanged a glance, then Yuri blew out a breath. "That's actually what we were coming to talk to you about."

"You were?" She swiped a tear away from her cheek. "Does that mean you have a way for me to leave?"

"Not quite," Alexei said, his voice low and serious. "It means we learned this morning that your uncle was released from jail."

"But how? Is the judge back? Is he going to release my father too?"

"The judge isn't back yet," Alexei answered. "The head jailer decided to release him last night anyway."

Her hand fisted in the fabric of her quilt. "Why?"

Alexei shrugged. "Probably because your uncle threatened the man to within an inch of his life, or maybe he bribed him. Whatever the case, the jailer doesn't know about the seal-harvesting ledgers and probably thought it unlikely your uncle would end up in prison long-term, meaning your uncle's threats carried enough weight that he got released."

"Did he come looking for me again?" She glanced at the door. "What does he want?"

Alexei shook his head. "Nothing, apparently. He left Sitka on the first ship out of the harbor this morning."

"He . . ." She lay back on her pillows. "But why did he leave? Where is he going?"

"Nobody seems to know."

"Could he go to Washington, DC? Could he be after my mother's money?" She sprang into a sitting position, ignoring the fire in her ribs, and threw off her covers. "I have to leave."

Yuri moved to stand directly in front of her, blocking her ability to stand, never mind that she wasn't sure she could stand in the first place. "You're not going anywhere like this."

"But I have to."

Yuri gave her a stern look. "You're too unwell to travel."

"But what if—"

"No. You're staying here."

"For today, yes, and probably tomorrow too," Alexei said. He'd taken a position against the wall, arms crossed as he surveyed the room. "But she needs to leave as soon as possible, Nathan."

Dr. Reid scowled at Alexei. "That would be six weeks. Maybe eight."

"No. It has to be sooner." Alexei scrubbed a hand over his face. "We don't know how long her father will be in jail. We have another week at best until the judge and Marshal Hibbs return, and there's no saying what will happen after that. If we knew when Secretary Gray would be arriving, that might help. Both Caldwells will likely be arrested again as soon as we show him the seal-harvesting ledgers. But in the meantime, we don't know what her uncle is up to or how long he'll be gone. And we don't know when her fiancé will return either."

"There is no way Rosalind can get the medical care she needs on a ship or train." Dr. Reid slung a hand on his hip.

Alexei shook his head. "Rosalind was injured three days ago. The longest we can risk keeping her here is another four, maybe five days. Teach Yuri how to do anything that will need to be done after that."

Rosalind's mouth fell open. Teach Yuri how to care for her? Did Alexei realize she'd just had her ribs wrapped? That not even Dr. Reid had been involved in the process? Kate had done it. She wore only her chemise and bloomers beneath the bindings. It wasn't exactly the type of thing a woman wanted a man to do.

Kate must have been thinking the same thing, because she stepped forward, her brows pinched. "Are you sure you want me to teach Yuri how to wrap her ribs? That isn't exactly . . . er . . . appropriate for a couple that isn't married."

Dr. Reid arched an eyebrow at Alexei. "Sending the two of

them across the country together isn't exactly appropriate either."

"I'm aware." Alexei looked between her and Yuri. "That's why they're going to get married."

"No." The word erupted from Yuri's mouth.

Heat pricked Rosalind's eyes. She wasn't sure how she felt about marrying Yuri, but did he have to reject her so quickly? He hadn't even taken a full second to think about the idea.

Or maybe she did know how she felt about marrying him. He was kind and loyal and generous. He got upset from time to time, but never so angry that he would hit her or choke her or harm her in any way. She'd been telling herself for months that she wanted to escape her father and find a man like Yuri to marry.

But to marry Yuri himself? That almost seemed like too much to hope for, like she was being given a blessing that was too big and too good and something she didn't deserve.

She tucked her knees up to her chest and wrapped her arms around them, trying to focus on the pattern of the quilt despite the tears blurring her vision. Did nobody want her? Was she only ever resigned to being a burden? Or if not a burden, then a bargaining chip in some kind of business or political marriage?

Was she asking too much to be wanted? To belong some-where? To be loved for who she was?

And she'd never met a family so good at loving others as the Amoses—or a man so good at making people feel loved and accepted as Yuri.

"Can I have a word with you, Alexei?" Yuri snapped. "In private."

He stalked toward the door without waiting for his brother to follow, and all Rosalind could do was sit there and watch the man she just might be in love with walk away after refusing to marry her.

———

"WHAT ARE YOU THINKING?" Yuri whirled on Alexei the second the door to Rosalind's room closed behind him.

"I'm thinking we had better move away from the door unless you want your future wife to overhear everything you're about to say." Alexei stalked down the hallway toward his study.

"I can't marry her." Yuri stormed into the study and slammed the door shut behind him. "Why would you suggest such a thing?"

"Oh, I don't know. Maybe because she needs legal protection from her father before he gets out of jail and tries to kill her again or forces her to marry a monster. I don't understand why you're upset. You're clearly in love with her."

"That's not the point." Yuri shoved his hand into his hair and fisted it at the roots. "You never should have suggested I marry her, and in front of her no less. Why didn't you talk to me first?"

Alexei crossed to the fireplace and leaned against the mantel. "I thought you would jump at the opportunity. In fact, I don't understand why you're not. You just admitted that you love her."

Yuri paced from one side of the office to the other, then whirled and paced back the other direction. "She's had every choice in her life taken away from her, and you want me to take away yet another choice? I don't care if it's under the guise of trying to help her. I won't do it, not for something that will affect the rest of her life. She deserves to have a say in who she marries."

A muscle pulsed on the side of Alexei's jaw. "Marrying her is the best way to protect her from her family and her fiancé. Keep in mind we don't know what her uncle is doing right now."

"I still refuse to force her into marriage!"

"I don't see what choice you have." Alexei crossed one of his legs at the ankle, still leaning against that dratted mantle, every inch of him controlled.

It was almost enough to make Yuri scream. He balled his hands into fists and turned away, lest he end up hurling something across the room.

How could his brother be so calm right now? He might have feelings for Rosalind. He might even love her. But this was not the time to ask her to make such a weighty, long-lasting decision.

And yet Alexei had a point. Marriage was a good way to keep Rosalind safe. It would legally remove her from anything having to do with her father or uncle or Leeland Vandermeer, and it would put her under his protection.

Oh, why did all this have to be so complicated? "If we marry, what would the plan be after we go to Washington, DC?" He turned to face his brother. "Is Rosalind supposed to come to San Francisco with me? Do we live together as husband and wife there? Her father will find out where she is after a few weeks, and so will Vandermeer. It's not like my presence is going to be a secret, and ships sail from San Francisco to Seattle and Juneau and here all the time."

Alexei sighed and pressed his fingers to his temple. "I don't know. I haven't thought that far ahead."

"You want her to bind herself to me for the rest of her life, and you don't even know how to keep her safe a month from now?" He was shouting again. Maybe they should go back to the beginning of this conversation, and he should start it by knocking some sense into his brother.

"Don't look at me as though you want to kill me," Alexei muttered. "She'll be safer married to you than not."

"She'll be safest down in Texas at the Woman's Commonwealth, like we talked about."

Alexei pushed himself off the mantle. "Likely so, but I can't send you across the country and have you tend her medical needs unless the two of you are married. Before she was hurt, you wouldn't have needed to share a cabin aboard a ship or a private train car, but now you will. There's no way for her to travel otherwise."

His brother was right. This marriage was a good idea in so many ways—but not in the way that mattered most. "What if we get an annulment?"

Alexei quirked an eyebrow. "What?"

"An annulment. What if I don't touch Rosalind other than to wrap her ribs or tend to her medical needs? What if I act as though we're not married and do my best to keep my distance, and then once we get to Texas, we petition the judge for an annulment?"

"I suppose that could work, though I think the annulment will need to be filed here, where the marriage takes place. You can check with Evelina on the particulars."

"Fine. I'll check with her, but if an annulment is the way to make this work, I want the papers drawn up before we leave. That way I can send you a telegram as soon as I get to San Francisco. You can file the papers immediately, and Rosalind will be both safe and free to finally live her own life down in Texas."

Alexei studied him for a moment, shadows smudging the skin beneath his eyes. "Are you sure about the annulment? I understand why you're doing this, but are you certain it's what you want?"

No, he wasn't. He really just wanted to scoop Rosalind up, marry her, and take her somewhere far away, where the two of them could be together and wouldn't need to worry about anyone or anything.

But that would involve taking choices away from her, which had the odd effect of making it one of the last things he wanted to do, along with being one of the things he wanted most in the world. "I have to let her make these decisions for herself. If she still chooses me after I take her to Texas, and she sees what it would be like to live among other women who have experienced abuse similar to hers, then . . ." He shook his head and swallowed the lump that had lodged itself in his throat.

"I want you to know I'm proud of what you're doing. I know I told you I was proud of you when we got the first ledger, but I wanted to tell you again." Alexei looked down and shook his head. "I spent years telling you to stay away from Rosalind Caldwell, but only because I didn't know what her father was putting her through. Had I realized it—"

Yuri reached out and patted his shoulder. "Don't feel guilty over it. I didn't realize it either. I mean, I saw more of it than you did. There was always something about her that nagged me, that made me want to slow down and take extra time to be kind to her. But even after I started helping with the letters, I still didn't realize her father was hurting her. Bryony was the one who figured it out, and only because she stayed with the Caldwells for a few days last fall."

"You still did the right thing by helping her, even though I didn't see it. And I want to . . ." Alexei's shoulders rose and fell on a shrug. "I want to apologize for not seeing it sooner."

Were they really having this conversation? Him and Alexei? Usually their conversations were filled with Alexei griping because he was too friendly or having too much fun or had messed up some paperwork, and then he'd turn around and tease Alexei for being too serious and never smiling.

But not today. "Everything I'm doing for Rosalind, I'm doing because I learned it from you."

Alexei's brows drew down. "I don't understand. I had nothing to do with Rosalind. That's what I just apologized for."

Yuri swallowed. "I'm not talking about Rosalind. I'm talking about how you sacrificed your dream of living in San Francisco and marrying Clarise so you could come home and take over the shipyard and trading company after Father died. James chapter one, verse twenty-seven says, 'Pure religion and undefiled before God and the Father is this, to visit the fatherless and widows in their affliction.' And I watched you do just that after we were left fatherless. You raised five siblings, took on a business you never wanted, paid for medical school for Kate and law school for Evelina. Did you think I didn't notice? Of course I noticed. You've been defending the fatherless and delivering the afflicted ever since I was a boy.

"And you don't just do it for our family," Yuri continued. "You do it for the tribes too. Most traders would have stopped by the village of Klawock, realized they were moving, then sailed down to San Francico to try and procure a shipping contract for the new cannery going in there. Instead you came straight back to Sitka and confronted the governor, then sent word to the secretary of the interior. That's seeking justice for the afflicted."

Alexei stared at him for a long moment, his eyes misting for a fraction of a second before he blinked the moisture away. "I don't suppose I ever thought of it that way. The Bible says to protect the needy, and so I do. It says to clothe the naked and feed the hungry, so I do. That's all I can say."

"Well, I've noticed what you do. So have the rest of us.

Look at Evelina taking free cases for the Tlingit or that woman whose husband was hitting her. Look at Kate administering medicine to anyone and everyone, regardless of whether they're white or Indian or if they can pay. Even now, you wanted me down in San Francisco by early March, and yet you're letting me take Rosalind to Washington and Texas first. And all I have to say is just . . ." His throat felt scratchy, and confound it, his eyes felt hot too. "Thank you. Just thank you. You're the best big brother a person could ask for."

He threw himself at Alexei, wrapping him in a hug and not letting go as the burning sensation turned into tears.

Alexei stood there for a moment, not quite stiff but not exactly warm either. He awkwardly patted Yuri's back then tried to extricate himself.

Yuri just held on tighter.

"'Bear ye one another's burdens, and so fulfil the law of Christ,'" Alexei finally whispered, a bit of the stiffness leaving him. "That's the verse I try to live by. I know of the one about defending the fatherless and delivering the afflicted from the hand of the wicked too, but 'Bear ye one another's burdens' is the verse I pray over every morning. I took it to heart after Father and Amika died, and that's all I'm trying to do is bear the burdens of you and others in our family. I must have taught you well, though, because now you're doing the same thing for Rosalind."

"Yes. I suppose I am." Yuri leaned back, then dropped his arms from around Alexei. "The only thing I can say is that you do all of this out of duty. And I understand that. You're one of the most responsible people I know. But I don't just want to act out of duty. I want to act out of gladness too, because 'a merry heart doeth good like a medicine.' There's so much darkness and hurting in this world, and I want to give people merry hearts almost as much as I want to solve their other problems.

Look at Rosalind. It will feel amazing to take her away from her father and put her somewhere safe. But the thing I want most is to see her smile. She didn't do it nearly enough before she was injured, and she's smiling even less now. I'll know I've helped her the way God wants when she starts smiling freely again. And if I can spend my life helping people like her, people who no one else sees, then maybe I'll have lived it well."

"You'll have lived well indeed." Alexei exhaled, and the action seemed to lift something in both of them. Then he clasped Yuri's shoulder and turned him toward the door. "Now dry your tears, and let's go tell your temporary wife about the plan you've come up with."

31

"Ros? Are you awake?"

Rosalind blinked at the crack in the door, then raised herself up higher onto the bed.

Yuri stepped inside, closing the door behind him with a quiet click. "I was hoping we could talk, but I can wait if you're tired."

She yawned into her hand. "It's all right. I can talk."

"Did I wake you?" His brows pinched together with that familiar look of concern she was becoming accustomed to seeing.

"No. My mind was too busy to sleep."

She wasn't sure how long ago Kate and her husband had left the room so she could sleep. All she knew was that sleep wouldn't come. Alexei's suggestion that she and Yuri marry—followed by Yuri's swift refusal—had been the only thing she could think about.

Yuri pulled the chair that was sitting against the wall over to the bed and sat down. "Alexei and I talked about his idea, and we came up with a plan that we think might suit the two of us a little better than rushing into a marriage."

She swallowed. Did he realize they were discussing marriage as though it were some sort of business contract? It almost seemed like something her father might do. "What's your plan?"

"After we go to Washington, DC, and straighten out your money, I was planning to take you to the Woman's Commonwealth down in Texas. The one you support that Mrs. McWhirter runs?"

Her mouth opened, but it took a few seconds before any words would come out. "You are?"

His shoulders rose and fell on a loose shrug. "It seems like a good place for you to go and recover, not just from your father's most recent beating, but from spending so many years of your life with a man who thought so little of hurting you. I doubt your father would think to look for you there either, and we can't have him finding out where you are until after he's put in prison for his seal-harvesting crimes."

"All right. Yes, that makes sense. I'd like to go to the Commonwealth, actually." She'd never once seen any of the charities she supported. To spend time at any of them seemed wonderful, but to specifically see one that helped battered women? That was better than anything she could have hoped for.

Yuri sent her a tender smile. "That's what I thought. But in the meantime, we still need a way to protect you from your father and Leeland, to legally make it so they can't do anything to harm you or find a way to take your money. And the best way for us to do that is to temporarily marry."

She searched his face. What was he saying? "So you want to marry me now? I thought you said you didn't want to marry me? And what do you mean by 'temporarily marrying' me?"

He reached out and wrapped her hand in his, his palm large and warm. "We'll marry in a private ceremony before we leave Sitka but have everything set up so we can file for an annulment as soon as you're in Texas."

"Oh." She carefully eased her body back against the pillows, once again not certain what to think. "That's . . . That's awfully . . ." She wasn't sure what word to use. *Severe*, maybe. *Calculated? Well planned?* "What if—"

She clamped her mouth shut before her next thought spilled from her mouth.

"What if what?" he prodded.

She licked her lips. What if there were feelings between them after spending so much time together traveling to Washington, DC? What if she wanted to stay married to him?

But she couldn't ask him that. And honestly, what was she doing letting her mind wander to such a place? Yuri didn't want to stay married to her. He'd said as much when he refused to marry her after Alexei first suggested it.

And she couldn't blame him. Her family had done nothing but harm his since they'd moved to Sitka. The thought of him permanently binding himself to a Caldwell probably made him sick.

"Do you have a question, Ros?" he asked, his voice gentle in the dim room. "Does something about the plan not work? We don't have to do it if you don't want to. The last thing I'd ever do is force you into a marriage that you don't want."

All she could do was shake her head, then squeeze her eyes shut against the tears suddenly threatening to spill onto her cheeks. "No. This is a good plan, the best plan, really. I can't think of a better one."

"So you'll do it?" He stroked a thumb over her knuckles. "You're all right with temporarily marrying me with the understanding that the marriage won't last more than a few weeks."

"Yes," she spoke past the lump in her throat. Because as far as she was concerned, the problem wasn't the marriage; it was all the things her father had done to his family, and how quickly Yuri wanted their marriage to end because of it.

Alexei dipped his pen into the small bottle of ink, then stared at the paper in front of him, still not able to come up with a single word. He didn't know how long he'd been sitting there staring at what should have been his letter to Laurel, but so far he'd only managed to write two words. *Dear Laurel* . . .

Nothing else would come. He set his pen down and stared out the window, where darkness blanketed the world. He didn't know how late it was, only that it was past midnight, and trying to sleep would be useless, just like trying to write Laurel.

He hadn't been able to get anything at all done since his conversation with Yuri.

Everything I'm doing for Rosalind, I'm doing because I learned it from you.

Had he really made that big of an impact on his siblings? That hadn't been his goal. After their father and stepmother had died at sea, he'd just done what he considered to be his duty.

He could still remember the day twelve years ago when he left San Francisco for Sitka. He'd been at naval architecture school, bent over a drafting table with two other friends, working on a sail plan for a three-hundred-and-fifty-foot, five-masted barque. The vessel had over an acre of sails that needed to be positioned. His friend Howard had burst into the room. One look at Howard's face, and he'd known something was wrong. He could still recall the sound of Howard's voice and see the large whites of his eyes as he had come toward them, saying that a telegram had arrived from Alaska.

Just like he could still recall the six words that had changed his life.

Come home. Father, Amika, Ivan dead. —S.

Alexei had left San Francisco on the first ship north, hoping and praying that Sacha was wrong, that somehow there'd been a mistake, that maybe one of their ships had been delayed, and everyone was presumed lost at sea only to arrive safely home by the time he reached Sitka.

That had been Alexei's prayer the entire way north, but the moment he stepped foot in Sitka, he'd known there'd been no misunderstanding. The somber faces of his siblings had told him everything before he debarked the ship.

They'd all sat around the familiar, old table in the kitchen as Sacha and Mikhail explained that their father and step-mother had been lost at sea, caught in a wild storm that had dashed their small boat against the rugged coastline about a mile north of Sitka Sound.

It was tragic, but it was fairly common, especially for traders. People died at sea every year.

But the circumstances of Ivan's death had ripped a hole in his heart. Twenty-year-olds weren't supposed to die, and they especially weren't supposed to be killed by the brother of a man's fiancée. But that's exactly what happened. Ivan had been mistaken for a robber during the same brutal storm when their parents' boat had gone down. When he'd opened the back door to Clarise's house with news that her parents' ship had returned safely to the harbor, he'd been greeted by a blow to the back of his head. That had caused him to fall forward and hit the front of his head on the corner of the hutch near the door. He'd lost consciousness as a result of both head injuries and never regained it.

Dr. Hollis had been called, and Ivan had been moved to a bedroom in Clarise's house, but his breaths had grown weaker and weaker throughout the night and ceased before lunch the following day.

Nathan and Kate had since explained to Alexei that a blow to the head can cause a person's brain to swell, and surgery could be performed to relieve the pressure by drilling a hole into the skull. Sometimes it worked and saved a person's life. Sometimes it didn't. And sometimes the person lived but was never the same. In severe cases, the person might not be able to walk or talk after the surgery, in spite of not dying.

But Dr. Hollis was an older doctor who hadn't bothered to keep abreast of the newest advances in medicine. Either he hadn't known about the surgery or didn't feel comfortable doing it.

Ivan had died, and so had Alexei's plans for the future.

The first thing he did was move home. He had seven siblings to care for. An eighteen-year-old, a sixteen-year-old, and two fifteen-year-old twin sisters, followed by Yuri, who'd been ten, and Inessa and Ilya, who'd been four and one. All of them had needed a parent. He'd made an extremely poor replacement for their father, but somehow they'd all survived.

The businesses had survived too, slowly and surely, never mind that Ivan had always been the one with the head for business. Alexei had been the dreamer who'd wanted to open a second shipyard down in Seattle and design and build steel-hulled ships. Ivan had been the planner who was going to make it all happen.

Alexei stared down at the blank paper in front of him and rubbed a hand over his breastbone. It seemed ridiculous, but he still missed his brother, even after all this time.

Just like he still missed Clarise.

Or rather, he missed the life he was supposed to have with Clarise.

Her brother, William, had stood trial for involuntary manslaughter. In those days Alaska was run by a navy general who acted as governor, and that governor just so happened to be Clarise and William's father. And governors' children were rarely convicted of intentional crimes, and they certainly didn't get convicted of crimes they accidentally committed.

It was true there'd been a rash of robberies in Sitka for about two months leading up to Ivan's death. The thief had been caught the very next week, and the jury had ruled that William Rothley had been defending himself, his sister, and their property when he struck Ivan. They declared him innocent.

William's trial and acquittal had felt like reliving Ivan's death all over again. Alexei hadn't been able to truly grieve Ivan's death until it was done.

After the trial was finally over, what should have been a time of clinging to Clarise and making plans for their life together had instead been marked by her slowly withdrawing from him. At first she'd been insistent that he could never forgive her, but he'd been just as insistent that there was nothing to forgive. William, not she, had killed Ivan, and it truly had been an accident. And even though he still felt frustration and anger and sorrow when he thought of Ivan's death, he'd still fallen in love with a flaxen-haired, blue-eyed woman who had a smile for anyone and everyone.

He'd taught her to sail a boat and tie a sailor's knot. And she would tease him into smiling when he was too serious or beg him to take breaks from the office and go for a walk around the harbor. She could see the light from the office above the warehouse from her own house, and when he worked late, sometimes she would come over with a batch of cookies—ones she'd baked herself, not asked their cook to bake. They would stay up until the wee hours of the morning, talking and dreaming and planning and kissing.

After the trial, they moved up the wedding, since Alexei wouldn't be returning to San Francisco for his last year of school and set a date for October. But one day Clarise didn't come to meet him for their walk by the harbor. He'd thought it odd but decided to wait, certain something had come up and that she would stop by the house as soon as she was able.

But one hour turned into two, and two turned into three, and three turned into four.

He'd finally headed over to the Rothleys' after dinner.

He could still recall the paleness that had crept over the butler's face when he asked after Clarise. Still see it slowly dawning on the servant that Clarise had left without saying a word. She'd left a letter for the housekeeper to give him that the butler hadn't known about. The letter explained that she'd gone to Washington, DC, with her brother and mother to stay with her mother's sister, and that her father, General Rothley, would be joining them in the spring when he finished his service to the navy.

And that had been the end of it. He'd spent four years of his life falling in love with a sweet girl-turned-woman, only to have her jilt him.

Earlier that afternoon, Yuri had spoken of all the ways he'd helped him and Kate and Evelina, the native tribes, and anyone else who had a need.

But none of that made his heart hurt any less when he thought of how he'd lost the woman he'd once loved so dearly.

32

Inside Passage; One Week Later

The pain was worse than she'd expected. Rosalind squeezed her eyes shut, waiting for the rocking of the ship to ease, but no sooner had the ship straightened than it was caught up on another wave. Up and down, up and down. Each movement jarred her ribs and sent flashes of agony through her body. She wasn't one who typically got seasick, but the pain was bad enough that her stomach was starting to feel queasy.

She whimpered, then tucked her knees against her chest, curling herself into a ball on the bed in the captain's cabin. And to think that Dr. Reid had said the ship would be the gentler part of the journey. He was more concerned about the train, but she couldn't imagine being in more pain. The constant moving was causing more agony than when her father had nearly beaten her to death ten days ago.

"Rosalind?" The door to the cabin creaked open, and Yuri's voice filled the room, but she didn't acknowledge him.

"Sweetheart, what's wrong?" Hurried footsteps approached

the bed, but she wasn't going to roll over and look at him. That would only hurt more.

Oh, heavens, she was such a child, not even able to roll over in her bed.

"Rosalind, darling?" Yuri stroked her hair away from her face, then settled a hand on her shoulder. "Do you need help? What can I do?"

"It hurts," she rasped. "Nathan was right. I'm not strong enough to make the journey, and this was supposed to be the easy part."

"There's a storm coming, and the sea is wild. Normally I would tell Captain White to ride it out, but we can seek shelter off one of the islands until it passes."

"No. Don't make the whole ship wait on me. We've already booted the captain out of his cabin, and the ship is making an extra stop in Portland just for me. Tell Captain White to keep going. I'll be— Ah!"

The ship came down hard off a particularly large swell, causing her to bounce against the mattress. Flames licked the lower part of her chest, and she curled herself into an even tighter ball.

"Hang on. Let's see if this helps." Yuri kicked off his boots and climbed onto the bed behind her. Careful not to touch her ribs, he slid his arm over her lower stomach and hips.

It would have been a wholly inappropriate position had they not been married, but the Russian Orthodox priest had come to the house yesterday evening to marry them before they left. They'd also signed paperwork to annul the marriage and even had the priest sign it, along with writing a statement that claimed she'd been under duress at the time of the marriage.

"Does this feel better?" He spoke into her hair. "Are you moving less with me behind you?"

She drew in a shallow breath, and only then did she realize

the pain had lessened right along with the pleasant warmth filling her chest. "I . . . It doesn't make any sense. Why is there less pain?" It was still greater than when she'd boarded the ship, and she could still feel the rising and falling of the vessel as it bobbed on the water, but this was certainly better.

"Nathan told me I might need to try this. Having something firm against your back can lessen how much you move, but a wall or board would be too firm and an unnatural shape, so he suggested I lie behind you and brace your body so that I absorb most of the movement."

"It's nice." Too nice, really. She could get a little too used to feeling Yuri's arms around her.

She'd longed for this very thing more than once before she'd been injured. Now he was here doing it as her husband— a husband she couldn't keep. "You don't have to stay, though. I'm sure there are other things you should be doing."

"Taking care of you is my priority. Everything else can wait." He smoothed another strand of hair away from her cheek and tucked it behind her ear, then nuzzled his face into the hair hanging wild and free behind her.

She pressed her eyes shut and relaxed into him. She could stay like this forever, curled in Yuri's arms and letting the heat from his body seep into her back. It made her feel like she was the most cherished, protected person in the world.

And it made her wonder how she was going to be able to watch the person who made her feel so cherished walk out of her life after he took her to Texas.

Washington Coast; One Night Later

"I can't breathe . . . Let me go. I can't breathe!"

Yuri sat upright on the pallet where he'd been sleeping on the floor of the cabin.

"Please, you have to let me go."

"Rosalind?" Yuri looked in the direction of the bed, but inky blackness filled the ship's cabin.

A weak cry sounded next.

He threw off his covers and stood. "Rosalind, what's wrong?"

Panicked breathing met his words, followed by the rustle of sheets and the thump of a hand hitting the wooden headboard.

"No— Please— Stop—I can't breathe. Let go of me! I can't breathe!"

Yuri felt his way toward the bed in the darkness, then reached out, blindly trying to find his wife. "Rosalind?"

She was facing the opposite direction, hunched in on herself as sobs shook her shoulders.

"Ros?" He gave her a gentle shake. "What's wrong? Are you in pain? Did something happen?"

She jerked, and the sudden movement was followed by an immediate whimper. "Yuri?"

"What's wrong, darling? Are you in pain?"

"I was having a nightmare." Tears clogged her voice. "Did I wake you? I'm so sorry."

"It's all right. I don't mind being woken. Do you need anything? Is there something I can get you? I can go down to the kitchen and brew some willow-bark tea if you're in pain."

"No." She clasped his hand, and only then did he realize she was trembling. "No. Don't leave. Please."

"I won't. Here, let me onto the bed. You can rest your back against my chest until the pain calms down." He climbed onto the bed and lay down, just like he had yesterday during the storm.

"How do you know I'm in pain?" she whispered into the darkness.

"How you were moving had to have jarred things. Was it that bad of a dream?"

She seemed to be crying an awful lot for a nightmare, especially one that had ended.

He wrapped an arm over her lower stomach, then slid his body fully behind hers so she didn't have to move.

But she didn't relax into him, not like last time. She stayed stiff and tense in his arms. "I'm sorry. You said we're passing Seattle tonight. I know I'm in a ship, and I know Leeland's not going to row out and get me, but I . . ."

She'd been dreaming about Leeland? He wrapped his arm more tightly about her. "You kept saying you couldn't breathe."

"I did?"

He stroked a strand of wayward hair away from her cheek. "Do you want to tell me what happened?"

Part of him wanted to demand an answer. She was clearly terrified. The fact she'd been pleading for breath—and that it had somehow been related to Leeland—made him want to swim to shore and strangle the man in his bed. But he was trying to give Rosalind as many choices as possible, which meant he was going to give her the choice to talk to him.

"He didn't strangle me, not exactly. But he knew right where to put his thumb. One moment I was breathing just fine, the next I could only get half my air, and the next . . ." A shudder wracked her body, and she let out a small whimper. He had no way of telling if it was because of her ribs or the memory. "I wasn't wearing his necklace, you see. I had his ring on, but not the necklace. He said I needed to wear it all the time, and then he cut off my air and told me it would be worse if he found me without it again."

"The sapphire one? The one you didn't take off until after we were married?"

"Yes." Tears choked her voice.

"Why didn't you tell me?"

"I did."

"You didn't. I would have remembered."

"I didn't tell you about my throat, but I told you I wanted to leave. I went to the library the very next day and worked until you showed up, waiting to tell you that I wanted you to take me away. Remember?"

That's what had prodded her to finally accept his help? Why hadn't she told him everything? He wouldn't have let her return to her father's house to look for evidence against him. He would have gotten her away from Sitka that night.

"I was in my nightgown too," she continued, her voice still trembling. "It was late at night when he found me. I'd sneaked down to the kitchen to get some food, because he wasn't letting me eat much . . ."

Vandermeer wasn't letting her eat much? Yuri's hand tightened into a fist against her stomach. Just how much of a monster had her fiancé been? And why was this the first time he was hearing about it?

"I was going to search my father's study, but then Leeland was there in the hallway, and he made some kind of comment about me being in my nightgown and our wedding night, and . . . and . . . How come your entire family saw me in my nightgown—or less than my nightgown, really—but that never made me feel ashamed? How come lying here with you in my nightgown with your arm wrapped around me doesn't make me feel dirty, but after one second in Leeland's presence, I felt like a prostitute?"

"I don't know, darling, but I'm so very sorry. No man should ever make you feel dirty. And no man should ever cut off your air to teach you a lesson. And no man should ever tell you how much food you can or can't eat."

These all seemed like statements that shouldn't need to be said, like things that should be fundamentally understood. But he wasn't sure that Rosalind knew them, which made him wonder just how much his wife had endured before God had brought her to him.

"He wanted me to be thinner for our wedding. That's why he wasn't letting me eat much food," she added. Almost as though another person trying to starve her was some sort of afterthought. "He said my corset needed to be laced tighter for the wife of someone with his social standing."

Yuri pressed his eyes shut and buried his face in her hair. "I hate him. I absolutely hate him. I didn't want you to marry him even without knowing this, but now that I know it . . ." His throat became hoarse. "You listen to me. You have nothing to fear anymore. Do you understand that? You're my wife now, and I'm going to take care of you, and you have nothing to be scared of."

"'Fear thou not; for I am with thee: be not dismayed; for I am thy God: I will strengthen thee; yea, I will help thee; yea, I will uphold thee with the right hand of my righteousness.'"

"Yes, exactly," he whispered through a thick throat.

"Do you remember when you told me that? It was the night of Bryony's wedding reception, when you found me standing outside in the snow and offered to take me with you to San Francisco. I've used it a lot since that night. So many times, really."

"I'm glad that verse gave you strength, but I'm also going to use every last bit of effort and leverage I have to make sure you're never again in a position where you feel afraid. Do you understand?"

She nodded, the back of her head bumping against his chest as she moved. "Yes."

"Good. Now get some rest." He tightened his grip on her, then paused to see if her body tensed with pain. It didn't, so he kept her pressed tightly against him, then nuzzled his mouth beside her ear and prayed, hoping it would be enough to soothe her mind from the horrors she'd endured in Sitka.

33

Portland, Oregon; the Next Morning

"We didn't need to book a hotel room. We're only going to be in Portland for part of a day." Rosalind shifted closer to Yuri as the elevator began climbing to the fifth floor of the Merchant Hotel, where he had just paid for a room.

The elevator was one of the new hydraulic kinds, complete with an iron gate the attendant had drawn closed before starting their ascent. Ornate brass fixtures gleamed along the paneled walls, and a leather-covered bench curved against the back wall. A polished dial above the gate marked their progress by floor, and the attendant controlled the movement with a lever, occasionally adjusting pressure as the elevator gave a slight groan with each passing level.

She'd ridden in an elevator such as this a few times in Washington, DC, but she hadn't been there in four years. She wasn't sure which unnerved her more: how quiet the ascent was or the sensation of rising off the ground without any visible stairs.

Or maybe she was most unnerved by the fact they were in the elevator at all, heading to a room they were only going to use for eight hours in the middle of the day. The train east was scheduled to leave just after dinner that night, but it was just past ten o'clock in the morning. The first thing Yuri had done after making sure their private car would be ready for the evening train was to hire a coach and take her straight to the fancy new hotel that had recently opened in Portland.

She hated the thought of him paying so much money just so she could be comfortable for half a day. She could have wandered the streets of Portland instead. Yes, her ribs still pained her, but maybe a short time out of bed would do her good. It wasn't like she needed to stand and walk the whole time. They could have shared a long lunch and then had an early supper before the train left. Then she would have needed to spend only a few hours on her feet.

She tugged on Yuri's sleeve and leaned close enough that the elevator attendant wouldn't hear their argument. "It's not too late for you to get your money back for the room."

Yuri just shook his head. "I have enough money to pay for a hotel room."

"Yes, but you don't need to. I'm fine, see? I'm standing completely by myself."

"And how badly do your ribs hurt?"

She winced. Quite a bit since leaving the ship. All of the moving from the ship to the carriage to the hotel was taking its toll, but Yuri didn't need to know that. "They're fine. They're still bound from when we left Sitka two days ago."

"Exactly. We need to rewrap the bindings somewhere private that doesn't involve a rocking ship or moving train. I also just might happen to want my wife to rest for a few hours on a bed that's not moving too. You can't convince me you slept well last night after your nightmare."

"But . . ."

"But nothing. You can argue all you want, but I'm not going to change my mind."

The elevator creaked to a halt, and the attendant slid the gate open and unlatched the outer door, revealing a carpeted hallway lined with crown molding and tall windows.

Yuri extended his arm and she took it, but he led her only a short distance before stopping in front of a heavy wooden door and inserting a key into the lock.

The room was just as well appointed as the hallway and lobby downstairs. A velvet chaise sat angled near a window framed by brocade curtains, and an intricately carved walnut bed stood in the center of the north-facing wall, dressed in crisp white linens and a satin coverlet. A marble-topped washstand gleamed in one corner, and beside it was a small writing desk and padded chair.

Her eyes moved back to the bed, and she let out a small whimper. Maybe Yuri was right. Maybe spending the day here wasn't such a bad idea after all.

"I want to take your bandage off and let your ribs rest for a few hours, like Nathan said." Yuri had moved farther into the room and had already set their suitcase on the stand beside the dresser. "You're supposed to practice breathing too, remember?"

Breathing. Right. She pressed a hand to her ribs. They were painful even now, but not nearly as painful as they would be with the bindings off. Nathan had been right about them helping with the pain. Before Kate had bound her ribs for a final time, Nathan had forced her to take a few deep breaths. Yuri hadn't been in the room, so he didn't understand how excruciating the pain had been.

Still, if taking those deep breaths would prevent her from getting pneumonia, she would do it.

Yuri took a few items out of his suitcase and set them on the polished dresser.

"I'll step into the hall while you change out of your dress, and then I'll come back to help with the bandage. After that, you can lie down under the covers, and I can leave again as long as you're not in too much pain."

She didn't want him to leave, pain or not. They might not be in Seattle—where most people probably assumed they'd be headed after leaving Sitka—but they were close enough for her to be nervous, especially without knowing where her uncle was or if her father had been released from jail. In fact, she didn't think she'd stop being nervous until she left Washington, DC, for the hiding place Yuri had promised to take her, somewhere her father would never find her.

Yuri headed for the door, his back stiff and his steps quick. Was he mad at her? For what? Objecting to the hotel room? She'd already changed her mind about that.

He'd reached the door and was in the process of opening it before she told him to wait.

He paused and turned to her, the door open a couple of inches.

"I . . . ah . . ." She licked her lips. "I can't get out of the dress by myself. Do you mind helping with that too."

He should have known as much. He'd helped her into the dress that morning before she'd left the ship and out of it after they'd boarded in Sitka. But for most of the trip, she'd worn only her nightdress, yet another thing Kate and Nathan had told her to do. She hadn't left the captain's cabin on the ship once, but she'd likely need to wear a dress on the train, even with their private car.

"Right. I'm sorry." He turned and rubbed a hand over his face. "I don't know what I was thinking. I just want to give you privacy, but I suppose that's not always possible."

"It's the reason we're married, remember? Because it wasn't going to be possible for you to tend to my needs and me to have privacy on this trip."

His Adam's apple bobbed. "Right. Of course." He marched back into the room, his gait still stiff.

She turned and presented her back to him, standing right there in the middle of the room. Her hands trembled slightly as she gathered her hair to one side, and she had the sudden urge to look at anything and anyone other than her husband.

Which was ridiculous. He'd helped her button her dress that morning.

But he hadn't helped her step into it. She'd been able to take off her nightgown and pull her dress over her head by herself. It was just the buttons at the back that she couldn't manage.

Yuri came up behind her, and she almost swore she could feel the heat from his chest radiating into her back, never mind that they weren't even touching. Then his fingers brushed the base of her neck. It was all she could do not to flinch.

It's just a dress. A dress and a fake marriage that will only last for a few weeks. He doesn't want me forever. He's only helping me now because he knows there's no one else I can ask. He's the one who asked for an annulment, the one who refused the idea of a real marriage with me in under a second.

She repeated the words in her head, trying to remind herself of her situation. She couldn't afford to get caught up in any fancy ideas of a future with Yuri. Everything he'd done so far—including holding her last night after her nightmare—had all been done out of kindness, nothing more. Yuri might well be the kindest person on the Pacific Ocean, but that didn't mean he had feelings for her like she had for him.

He worked in silence behind her, his movements careful and slow. The first button slipped free. Then the next.

She closed her eyes. Maybe it was a blessing she couldn't see his face.

His breath brushed the back of her neck as he undid more buttons, but he didn't speak. He didn't even clear his throat. Just kept going, one button at a time, until the bodice loosened and sagged around her shoulders.

She gripped the front of the fabric to keep it in place. "You can turn your back now. I'll get the rest."

"And then what? You'll have me turn around and see what removing the dress has revealed so I can unwrap the bandage? Just let me help with the whole thing. You shouldn't have to fight with your dress while I'm standing right here."

How did he know she'd fought with it earlier?

Never mind. It didn't matter. What mattered was that he was right. It would be much easier to let him finish helping, and the end result would be no different. In a few minutes he'd see her with her bindings undone, wearing nothing but her bloomers and chemise.

Heat filled her chest, then rushed up to her cheeks.

"So do you want me to help? You can do it yourself if that's truly what you want."

"You can help," she whispered.

He moved around in front of her. She kept her eyes on the carved detailing of the washstand behind him, refusing to meet his gaze as she loosened her fingers from the front of her gown.

He eased the sleeves from her arms, and the bodice dropped away, falling halfway down her hips, where the flair in her petticoat caught it. The action revealed her bindings down to her waist. Normally she'd be wearing a corset, but her bindings disappeared beneath the waist of her petticoat instead.

He reached for her waist, then stopped, his hands pausing midair. "It, ah . . . it looks like I'm going to need to unfasten your petticoat. Is that all right, or do you want to do it?"

"You can do it," she muttered. She'd spent ten minutes fighting with the dratted thing that morning, too embarrassed to ask for Yuri's help with it. But she couldn't imagine being any more embarrassed now, and just like with the dress, he'd have to see her without her petticoat to help with the bindings anyway.

He moved around to her back again, his movements gentle as he tugged at the waist of the garment, probably trying to find the hidden hooks that held it up. It took him maybe half a minute, and then he slowly peeled it back, letting both the petticoat and her dress fall to the floor and pool around her feet.

Yuri stepped back around to her face, then reached for the loose end of her bindings near her side and undid the pin. "Tell me if anything hurts."

"It all hurts," she whispered, her throat tightening. "Even with the bandage on, but I don't want pneumonia."

He didn't respond, just began to unwind the bandage. His movements were so slow and careful, it almost seemed he was afraid the fabric itself might break her if he tugged wrong or moved too fast.

He moved from her front to her back, then around to her front again, following the path of the bandage. She wasn't going to think about how the movement gave him a full look at her body from every angle as she stood there in nothing but her bloomers and chemise and a quickly disappearing bandage.

The longer he worked, the more the pressure around her ribs began to ease. She wasn't sure if she liked the sensation. The pain at the bottom of her ribs turned sharper, but the rest of her body seemed to relax, almost as though her muscles themselves had needed to breathe.

She stared straight ahead at the curtains as he reached the final turn, not wanting to look down to see what her wrinkled, sweaty chemise might have revealed, and certainly not wanting to meet his eyes.

Was she being ridiculous? There was a medical reason for what Yuri was doing, and it was nothing to feel embarrassed about. Nathan had seen her in her bloomers and chemise numerous times.

But it had never felt this intimate.

Maybe because she didn't fancy herself in love with Nathan, and Kate had been there every time they'd removed her nightgown and rewrapped or adjusted the bindings.

Yuri pulled the last of the bandage away, then walked to the dresser and set it down. "Where do you want to practice your breathing? Do you want to do it in bed?"

"Nathan and Kate said I should be able to draw more air into my lungs while I stand." She didn't wait for him to return to her side. She simply sucked in a breath, as big and as large as she could.

Oh, heavens, it hurt. Pain seared her lower ribs, and a whimper escaped her lips. But she didn't stop, not even when tears stung her eyes. She forced as much air into her lungs as possible, then blew it out.

"Rosalind?" Yuri was by her side in an instant, rubbing a small circle in the center of her upper back. "Are you sure you're doing it right? I don't think it's supposed to be so painful."

"It is," she rasped. "At least this is how it felt before. Nathan said I need to do it as much as possible."

She repeated the breath, dragging as much air as she could into her lungs for as long as she was able, then blowing it all out.

Yuri gripped her forearm, then placed her hand on top of his own arm, giving her something warm and solid to grip when she drew the next breath. A tear slipped down her cheek, but she just squeezed her eyes shut and kept going, in and out, in and out, trying to get the trapped, foul air out of her lungs.

"Ros, stop. You're hurting yourself. I don't like this."

She shook her head. "I have to. I'm not going to let myself get pneumonia."

"Then use my other arm too." He slid his second arm beneath her free hand, and she gripped it before dragging in another breath, and another.

"How long are you supposed to do it for?"

"As long as possible. My breaths are getting deeper. Can you tell? It's like I can get more air into my lungs now than before."

"The only thing I can tell is that your pain is getting worse."

He wasn't wrong. Fire engulfed her ribs, but the pain would pass. It was only for a few weeks. It didn't have the ability to kill her the way pneumonia did.

Yuri didn't say anything more, only stood beside her as she finished the final set of breaths, his arms still beneath her hands.

When she was done, she sagged forward and pressed a hand to her ribs.

Yuri stepped behind her and gently placed his hands on her shoulders. "That's enough for now. Come lie down."

She didn't move right away. Her chest ached too much, but she eventually let him guide her to the bed. She climbed onto the mattress with slow, careful movements, wincing as she lowered herself onto her side.

Yuri pulled the covers over her, then hesitated, hovering at the edge of the bed. "Do you need anything before I go? Some food or water, perhaps? Maybe a snack?"

There was something she needed, though it had nothing to do with food, and she felt like a fool for asking it.

But what was a little more embarrassment after Yuri had

already undressed her? So she forced the words out. "Will you hold me?"

"You want me to . . . to get into bed with you?"

"Like on the ship, yes."

"But you're on land. You're not moving."

"That's not why I'm asking." With her back to him, she couldn't see him to even guess what he was thinking.

He stood beside the bed for so long, she was certain he'd refuse her. But then she felt the bed dip.

Little rustling noises sounded next, likely him untying his boots. A moment later, she heard them drop to the floor with a thud. Then he crawled into bed behind her, moving slowly as he scooted closer and curled one arm around her middle. His chest pressed lightly against her back, warm and strong and steady.

She let out a shaky breath, tears leaking from her eyes, even though she had no reason to shed them.

"I have you now." His breath brushed the back of her neck. "You don't need to worry about anything anymore. Just rest and get better. I'll take care of the rest."

Tears flooded her eyes anew, because she knew she could believe him. Knew he'd do everything he'd just promised.

But the tender, loving man who was holding her was still planning on dropping her off in Texas, then filing annulment paperwork and walking out of her life forever.

34

Washington, DC; Thirteen Days Later

"What if the money's gone?"

Yuri reached over to where Rosalind's hand rested on his arm and squeezed. Once again they were riding in a hydraulic elevator, but this time they were at District National Bank in Washington, DC.

"It won't be gone," he told her softly enough that the elevator attendant couldn't overhear them.

"How do you know?" she whispered back.

He squeezed her hand again. "'God hath not given us the spirit of fear; but of power, and of love, and of a sound mind.' But if we get inside that building and find that the money *is* gone, I'll charm the banker into finding it for us. You'd be surprised what a merry heart can do."

She shook her head, the smile falling from her face as worried lines reappeared on her forehead.

Oh, well. At least he'd gotten her to smile for a few seconds.

They'd been over this time and again. They didn't know if

the money was there, but the likelihood of it being transferred out of her name without her father going to Washington, DC, directly was slim. And the likelihood of her father beating them to Washington when he'd been stuck in a jail cell the day they'd left Sitka was even slimmer.

Rosalind might have signed a contract allowing her money to be transferred upon her marriage to Leeland, but that wedding date was months away, meaning the money should still be secure.

On their second day in DC, they'd learned that her uncle was meandering around the city, schmoozing politicians. They didn't know why, but the likelihood that he'd be able to access her funds was even slimmer than Leeland getting ahold of them.

Though Rosalind was nervous today, she'd been disciplined and logical about her money ever since arriving. Had it been his money, Yuri would have barged through the doors of the bank the moment it opened on his first morning in town and demanded all the money be immediately transferred.

And if he'd done that, anyone wanting to follow the money would have been able to figure out exactly where it went.

Rosalind had been much smarter about things. On their first day in the city, she had set up a business and declared herself the sole proprietor, using only her first initial, then her middle name, then her new surname Amos. The owner of the Ladies Literary Society was R. Marie Amos, not Rosalind Caldwell.

Then she'd gone straight to a bank and opened up an account under the business's name. Then she'd walked five blocks and opened another account at a second bank—this one under her full married name, Rosalind Amos. A third account followed that afternoon, this time under R. Caldwell, the name that her mother had once used for her banking and charitable contributions. Fortunately Rosalind's mother had been named Roberta, and they shared the same first initial. The banker had asked no questions after seeing her marriage certificate, and Rosalind had made sure none of the accounts could be traced to the same address.

By the end of the third day, she'd secured four separate accounts across four banks, and she'd had Yuri secure an account at one of the banks as well. She deposited only small amounts in each. They were never enough to raise suspicion, but enough that once the full sum of money she intended to transfer arrived, she could quietly redistribute the funds without triggering alarms. One account would appear to belong to a widow managing her late husband's inheritance and interested in promoting literacy. Another to a schoolteacher saving to open a finishing school. Another to a church sewing circle.

She never went to the same bank twice in the same outfit. She wore different hats, adjusted her posture, and even took her hair down one day so it hung in a braid beneath a shawl. Once, she sent Yuri in alone while she watched from a carriage window. Another time, she wrote out instructions and stayed back at the hotel altogether. That was for the one account that they shared, but he was on the account under his middle name, too, as Y. Isaiah Amos.

His wife had thought of everything, down to the last cent.

But none of that stopped her fingers from trembling now as the elevator slowed to a stop and the attendant unlatched the gate, revealing the quiet, marble-tiled lobby of the District National Bank's private banking floor.

Yuri reached out and squeezed her shoulder. "You did everything you could. Whatever happens next, God will help us handle it."

"Miss Caldwell!" A balding man with a friendly smile greeted her the moment she stepped out of the elevator. "I could hardly believe it when the clerk rang up to my floor and said you were in the lobby. What a pleasant surprise!"

"Mr. Holloway. How nice to see you in person." She extended her hand, and he bent to kiss it briefly before letting it go.

"Come into my office." Mr. Holloway motioned for them to follow him on the short walk down the hall, then held the office door open, ushering them both inside. "I must say, your accounts have kept me busy over the last few years, with all the things you've invested in."

She smiled politely at the solicitor. "You've done a very good job directing my money as I've instructed, despite my being so far away."

"It's been a joy to watch your assets grow, especially knowing how dedicated you are to extending the extra you earn to those in need." The man turned to Yuri. "I assume this is your fiancé? Mr. Vandermeer?"

Rosalind bit the side of her lip and sent Mr. Holloway a nervous glance. "Actually, this is my husband, Mr. Yuri Amos."

"Amos?" The man's brows pinched together, but he extended a hand for Yuri to shake.

"I must have misunderstood something." Mr. Holloway left them standing near the door and headed to his desk, where he pulled open one of the drawers and began rummaging through papers. "I thought we were preparing your assets to be transferred to a Mr. Leeland Vandermeer in Seattle? Upon the event of your marriage to him?"

"Yes, well . . ." Rosalind sunk her teeth into her bottom lip again.

Yuri reached out and gave her hand a little squeeze, then bent down and spoke in a low voice. "'Fear thou not; for I am with thee.'"

Rosalind drew in a breath and straightened. "I called off that engagement and married Mr. Amos instead."

"I see." The man studied him a bit closer, then scratched the back of his head. "Ah, was there a particular reason that your engagement was canceled? Mr. Dunning returned from Alaska only recently, and he seemed quite certain that there would be a wedding to Mr. Vandermeer. I've already begun liquidating some of your assets at his request."

Rosalind took a few steps forward, then winced, likely because the movement had caused her ribs to hurt. "What assets?"

"Let's see." The man sorted through the small stack of papers in his hand. "It looks like he wanted you to sell off your timber tracts in the Yukon, along with your holdings in the Southern Pacific Railroad and the silver-mining shares in Colorado." Mr. Holloway's brow furrowed as he scanned the page. "There's also a note here about divesting from the orphanage endowments and reallocating the returns to municipal bonds."

"He wants the orphanage endowments reallocated?" Rosalind reached for the sheet of paper in Mr. Holloway's hand, then studied it, all signs of nervousness disappearing as she scanned the page. "The lumber tracts and silver mine have been our biggest earners. What was he thinking?"

"I wondered the same thing myself. In fact, I sent a wire to Seattle just last week, making sure he was aware that your account growth would likely drop by a rather large percentage if you divested those two assets. I asked him for confirmation before I proceeded further."

"Did he send it?"

Mr. Holloway shook his head. "No, I haven't heard back from him."

"He was planning to take a trip to Alaska," Yuri interjected. "Perhaps he's there."

Rosalind's head whipped his direction, her eyes widening before she turned back to Mr. Holloway. "Yes, I'm afraid he and my father are quite cross about my marriage to Yuri, but Yuri and I have known each other for four years. He's been helping with my charitable contributions for nearly as long, and the two of us are much happier together than Leeland and I would ever have been."

"Is that so?" The banker asked, his eyes moving between the two of them.

Rosalind cast her gaze to the ground, as though suddenly ashamed that she'd married someone who made her happy rather than the monster her father had picked.

It was almost too much for Yuri to watch. She'd been so strong earlier that day when they'd visited a different bank and met one of Rosalind's friends for lunch. But now that she stood in front of Mr. Holloway, she was wilting.

He stepped closer to her, then reached out and gripped her hand. A small stroke of his thumb over her knuckles was all it took for her to blow out a breath and raise her head. "I'm also more Finnancially astute than Vandermeer and don't believe my wife should rid herself of her most profitable investments merely because we're married. Rosalind has done such a good job of managing her accounts that I see no reason to take over her investments as her husband."

Rosalind looked at him, a small smile creeping across her mouth. "Yes, that's it exactly. I assume you can see why I'm much happier being married to a man like Yuri."

The older man sent them a smile that was just as soft as Rosalind's. "Yes, of course I can see it. And I'm happy for you, Miss— I mean, Mrs. Amos." The man moved his gaze to Yuri. "Do you own a company too, Mr. Amos?"

"My family has two shipyards, one in San Francisco and another in Sitka, Alaska, plus a trading company. We compete a bit against the Bering Shipping Company, which Rosalind's father owns."

"Ah, I'm beginning to things understand now." The man's smile grew even larger. "And you said you've known each other for four years? So you must have met shortly after Rosalind moved to Sitka?"

"Yes," Yuri answered.

"Exactly," Rosalind said at the same time.

"Well, then, it seems I owe you a congratulations on your nuptials." Mr. Holloway sat, then gestured for him and Rosalind to sit in the chairs across the desk. "Now, what can I do for you today? I'm assuming you want your husband's name added to your accounts, Rosalind?"

"Actually, I want everything liquidated." Rosalind pulled a sheet of paper from her satchel, then fiddled with it for a second before handing it over to him. "I'd also like all nonliquid assets transferred to the care of Mr. Gerald Rupert at Riggs and Company here in Washington."

The man froze. "I'm sorry. I think I misunderstood something."

"My instructions are written down on the paper. I need my cash assets divided into three equal sums and transferred into bonds made payable to bearer, and I want my investment hold-ings all transferred to the account listed below, at Riggs and Company."

The man's mouth opened, then closed, then opened again. "Surely you don't expect me to let you walk out of here with fifteen thousand dollars' worth of bearer bonds. You could be robbed on the street and your money stolen forever."

Rosalind twisted her hands in her lap, but that was the only sign she was nervous, and Mr. Holloway couldn't see them from where he sat behind his desk. All he could see was the way Rosalind met his gaze directly. "I'll take my chances."

"Did I do something to offend you, Mrs. Amos?" The banker rubbed the back of his neck, his eyes drifting back to her paper with instructions. "Have you deemed me inefficient at handling your funds? Because if that's the case, District National Bank can move you to another solicitor who—"

"No. You've been very faithful with my money, just as you faithfully served my mother before me." Her shoulders deflated. "Please understand this has nothing to do with you personally. My father wasn't aware of how large my accounts had grown, but when Mr. Dunning came to Sitka, he freely shared my Finnancial information with my father after my engagement to Mr. Vandermeer."

"Ah." Mr. Holloway shifted in his chair. "I'm sure Mr. Dunning didn't intend to offend you. Your father and the Alaska Commercial Company are rather large clients here at District National Bank, and we are on good terms. When your father asked Mr. Dunning about your accounts, he probably saw no reason to withhold the information."

"Yes, I'd estimate the ACC alone brings in about a million and a half dollars in revenue each year," Rosalind responded.

Mr. Holloway gave a short nod. "You've seen your father's books, I take it."

"No, those are just estimates based on the little I've put together. With my father being such a large client, though, I can see why Mr. Dunning wouldn't want to offend him. The problem is, I want my banking information to be private, which means now that I'm married and leaving Sitka, I need my money in banks that won't disclose my personal Finnancial information to my father. And I want the funds moved secretly so that no one at any of the new institutions is tempted to do what Mr. Dunning did and share the state of my investments without my consent."

Mr. Holloway's shoulders slumped. "I'm starting to understand."

"Good, then make out my bearer bonds, please. And see that my other investments are transferred to Mr. Rupert the day after tomorrow. I'll be staying in town until all the Finnances are settled. If you have any need to reach me, I can be found at the address on the bottom of the paper through the end of the week." Rosalind nodded toward the paper she'd given him.

"Very well, Miss Cald— Mrs. Amos. The man looked almost pained as he studied the instructions. Then he slowly opened the top drawer of his desk and began filling out slips of paper, which he soon handed to Rosalind.

Yuri didn't know how bankers made money, but he had a feeling Mr. Holloway would be losing a decent chunk of commission money with Rosalind closing her accounts.

After a few minutes, the banker stood to his feet and came around the desk. "It's been a pleasure doing business with you all these years, Mrs. Amos, and with your mother before you. I'm sorry to see our relationship end."

Rosalind stood, and Yuri stood immediately afterward, extending his arm to support her. He had a feeling her ribs were rather painful.

"Thank you, Mr. Holloway. Have a good day." She settled her hand on Yuri's arm.

"Have a good day as well," he mumbled as they let themselves out of the office.

The moment they closed the door behind them, Rosalind released a breath and reached for her ribs. "It hurts, Yuri."

"Let me take you back to the hotel. You can rest for the remainder of the day."

She clutched his arm tightly through the sleeve of his suit-coat, leaning her weight on him as they started toward the elevator.

"You were amazing in there," he whispered low enough for no one else to hear.

She slanted him a worried glance. "I was so nervous."

"I know, but you were also brave."

She pressed her lips together. "I don't know how you can say that when I feel like I might fall apart."

"You might feel like falling apart, but you never do. I haven't seen it happen once," he murmured. "You're one of the strongest people I've ever known."

And he meant it. His wife might not have marched into this bank with the same level of confidence that Kate had performing surgeries, but she'd gone in with a solid plan and let the banker know her wishes even though she'd been nervous and in pain and had endured years of abuse.

He wasn't lying when he said she was one of the strongest people he'd ever known.

35

Rosalind sucked in a breath, trying not to wince as the carriage hit a bump in the road.

Yuri frowned from where he sat across from her. "I thought you told me the pain was getting better?"

"It is." Or rather, it had been. Until she'd decided to overdo it today. Her ribs had been screaming at her for the past several hours, and in a single afternoon, it felt like she'd lost all the progress she'd made after three weeks of healing.

But at least her money was safe. A bit of pain was a small price to pay for that, wasn't it? Now the only thing she was waiting for was the transfer of her stocks and ownership shares. That would take a few days, but as soon as everything had been moved to Riggs and Company, she'd be able to go anywhere in the country without worrying about her father having access to her money.

It almost seemed too good to be true.

Still, she'd rather not have the pain. She pressed a hand to the bottom of her ribs, where the pain was always the worst, then looked up to find Yuri watching her.

The moment their eyes met, he stood and moved to the other side of the carriage, positioning his warm body right next to her.

"Don't tell me you're fine." He wrapped an arm around her, tugging her against him. "I can see the pain on your face. How bad does it hurt?"

She didn't answer. Instead, she pressed her eyes shut and settled into his warmth.

He held her there for a few seconds, his fingers stroking idly up and down her arm as the carriage rattled and bumped its way toward their hotel. When he finally spoke, his voice rumbled out of his chest, low and deep. "I wish you would have gone back to the hotel to rest after you finished at District National Bank."

"Mr. Holloway was right. Having my money converted into bearer bonds was a huge risk. Anyone could have taken the bonds from me and put my money into their own accounts. I wanted to see that they were deposited before the banks closed."

"I could have made the bond deposits for you, at least for the two banks that have my name on the account. And you could have waited until tomorrow morning to take the other bond to the third bank."

She stared out the window. Of course he would say such a thing. He was too sweet, so sweet, in fact, that she couldn't imagine saying good-bye to him once he'd taken her to Texas.

They hit another bump, and she grimaced.

"We're almost there," he whispered against the top of her head. "I don't like how shallow your breathing is. We'll get you out of this monstrosity of a dress as soon as we're back; then you can lie down and rest."

She looked down at her dress, which truly was a monstrosity. She'd worn a fancy gown of midnight blue faille, with a tightly fitted bodice and rows of decorative buttons down the front. It was elegant and respectable, but the high collar pressed against her throat, and the corset beneath it dug mercilessly into her ribs. Even the narrow-cut sleeves felt too snug now, as though her body had grown too weary to bother maintaining good posture.

They'd met one of her old friends and her husband for brunch before she'd headed to the bank to meet with Mr. Holloway, and she'd known what would be expected of her both with Agnes and at the banks.

She'd also known the dress was too tight and that she'd have trouble breathing before Yuri had even finished buttoning it that morning, but she hadn't said anything.

That had been foolish, because her ribs had been getting steadily better, and she didn't remember them hurting this bad since they'd left Portland.

The carriage slowed, but it still managed to hit a bump before stopping, and she couldn't help the whimper that escaped her lips.

Yuri moved to the door and opened it before the driver climbed down from his perch. He stepped out first, then turned and held out his arms. "Come here."

She didn't want to even breathe, much less climb out of a carriage in full view of the busy Washington street, but she forced herself away from the seat anyway and reached for Yuri's hand. He helped her down the steps, taking a bit more of her weight than was customary, then steadied her against his side before they entered the grand marble lobby of the Arlington Hotel.

Fortunately the lobby was too busy for anyone to pay them much mind, and Yuri guided her straight to the elevator, where he gave their floor number to the attendant.

He kept her tucked against his side as the elevator jerked,

then groaned, then started to move. She rested her cheek against the soft wool of his coat and closed her eyes, trying to suck deep breaths of air into her lungs, but the dress was simply too tight for that, and the bindings beneath it didn't help.

Yuri thanked the man after the elevator stopped and he opened the gate, but he kept his arm tucked firmly around her as he guided her to their room.

The moment the door closed behind them, he swept her into his arms.

She gasped. "What are you doing?"

"Carrying you to the bed. You're about to fall over."

She probably could have made it to the other side of the room, but she didn't argue, just let herself rest against him until he set her down at the edge of the bed.

He moved to undo the top button at her neck next, but she stilled, the breath freezing in her lungs. "Yuri, I can do the front buttons."

She didn't have a lot of dresses with the buttons on the front, but she had enough that most days she could manage dressing without Yuri's help.

"Just let me get you out of this, Ros. Then I'll have hot water sent up from the kitchen and make you some willow-bark tea, and you can rest."

She settled her hand over his. "I can do it."

He looked up at her. "Are you sure? It will take you twice as long."

She nodded.

"Very well." He stood, then glanced around the room, raking a hand through his hair. "I'll . . . ah, I'll give you some privacy and see about the hot water myself."

"Thank you."

He gave a short nod, his eyes moving to her face but not

drifting lower to the handful of buttons he'd already managed to undo; then he walked to the door.

It took her a ridiculously long time to undo the rest of the buttons, just like it had taken her a ridiculously long time to button them that morning, but Yuri wasn't knocking on the door after two minutes or even five.

No, she had the buttons completely undone and the dress off, and was fumbling with the bindings around her ribs before a soft rap sounded on the door.

"Are you decent?" Yuri poked his head inside. "Can I come in now?"

She was the farthest thing from decent. Her dress and petticoat were both pooled at her feet, and she was sitting there in nothing but her stockings, bloomers, and chemise, with only a few layers of her bindings unwrapped.

But Yuri only briefly glanced at her discarded clothing and the way she was sitting there in her undergarments as he entered with a cup of steaming tea. His eyes found her face in less than half a second, and he kept them there.

"I would have helped with the bindings had you waited." He set the tea on the bedside stand and then sat beside her, still keeping his eyes on her face.

"I got it tangled." She tugged on a twisted length of cotton at her side.

"Here. Let me help." Yuri's voice was soft, his movements slower than before as he brushed her hands aside. His fingers were steady as they found the knotted edge and began to loosen the worst of the twists. "You must have been in agony walking around with both the bindings and the corset and the tight bodice on that dress."

She swallowed. "I needed to look professional."

"You needed to let your body heal."

Agnes hadn't thought much of Yuri when they'd met for

brunch. Her new husband, Arnold, worked for the Treasury Department. Both Agnes and Arnold had asked the same types of questions as Mr. Holloway about what Yuri did for work and whether he owned a company. And though Agnes hadn't found anything she could outright criticize about Yuri, Rosalind had been able to see the judgment in her friend's gaze. He wasn't wealthy enough, he didn't wear a fancy enough suit, he didn't refer to politicians by their first names or belong to any of the prominent clubs for gentlemen in the city. But perhaps his worst offense had been not treating their waitstaff with condescension, or Agnes and Arnold with the deference they would have believed was theirs.

No. He was simply kind and polite to everyone, and extra attentive to her in a way Arnold hadn't been with Agnes. Yuri hadn't said anything about Agnes and Arnold's probing questions or the smug looks on their faces when he gave them an answer that displeased them. He'd simply supported her throughout the entire meal, leaning his head close and asking if she was in too much pain, watching her carefully to see if he could spot anything amiss.

Just like he was supporting her now by helping with her bindings without ever looking at her in a way that made her feel ashamed.

She'd known for months that if she ever married, she wanted to marry someone like Yuri Amos. But somehow, over the past few weeks, he'd gone from being the kind of person that she wanted to marry to being the one and only person she wanted to spend the rest of her life with.

Or rather, to stay married to.

Because they were married. And the longer she was married to him, the more she didn't want their marriage to end.

A lump rose in her throat. She hadn't meant for this to happen. She'd signed those annulment papers with the full intention of granting him the annulment once she'd moved her money and was safely in Texas.

And she'd known she had feelings for him even then, but having a bit of attraction wasn't the same thing as love. She couldn't quite say when her feelings turned to something more, but now she'd gone and fallen in love with the man beside her in a way she couldn't ignore.

"Yuri," she whispered, leaning close.

His eyes met hers. He was nearly done with the bandage now, but when she spoke his name, his eyes moved immediately to hers, and he paused. "Is something wrong?"

Was it just her imagination, or did his voice emerge lower and more gravely than usual?

But nothing was wrong. Her ribs still hurt, but she barely noticed the pain, because for the first time, it seemed like everything in her life might finally be right.

She was married. To a man she loved and wanted to spend the rest of her life with. To a man she knew would spend his every last breath taking care of her the way a husband was supposed to care for a wife.

There was only one more thing she could possibly ask for. Her gazed dipped to his lips, and she leaned closer, then pressed her mouth to his.

The warmth of his lips flooded through her like sunlight after winter. He let out a small sound, then moved his hand from the bandage up to the side of her neck and pulled her closer.

He kissed her slowly, but it was so very tender, as if he was putting every last bit of energy he had into memorizing the shape of her mouth. His thumb brushed the hollow behind her ear, and her hands curled into the front of his shirt, where his heartbeat thrummed steadily beneath her palms. She leaned even closer, the ache in her chest melting into a pool of warmth.

And then he was pulling back. He gave no warning, just wrenched himself away from her and jumped off the bed.

"I'm sorry, Ros. I shouldn't have done that. I don't know what I was thinking." His eyes were closed, as though he couldn't quite manage to look at her.

"Don't say that. I liked it."

"I did too." He raked a hand through his hair. "That's the problem."

"I don't understand. We're married. There's nothing wrong with us kissing or . . . uh, doing more than kissing."

His jaw clenched. "There is when we're getting an annulment."

"But what if I don't want an annulment? What if I want—"

"It's not safe for us to openly be married until we know your father is in prison." He opened his eyes and held up a hand, then backed farther away from the bed, as though standing any closer to it might catch him on fire. "And I'm not going to do anything to compromise you either. We got married knowing that what we have wouldn't last, that it was just a legal way to protect you for a few weeks until you can hide in Texas. That's all our marriage is, and it needs to stay that way. Now I'm going to go for a nice long walk and let you rest without me being around to distract you."

He was out of the room before she had time to tell him not to go, the door closing behind him with an unmistakable thud.

She sat there for a moment, staring at the door in nothing but her undergarments, willing it to reopen and him to walk back inside.

But he didn't. And why would he? He might be right about it not being safe for them to be married until her father was in prison. But her father had kidnapped his youngest brother, for heaven's sake. Then her father had the Amos family's ships searched and one of them had even been seized. He'd brought ridiculous charges against both Sacha and Mikhail for things they weren't guilty of, and attempted to have their shipyard burned down. And now he and Uncle Simon were trying to steal shipping contracts out from under them.

She'd never had anything to do with her father's vendetta against the Amoses, but Yuri probably thought of the cruel things her father had done every time he looked at her. How could he not?

Oh, it was a miracle Yuri had agreed to help her as much as he had.

What he'd said about their marriage was right. They'd been wed with the understanding that it was nothing more than a short-term, legal formality.

Which meant she needed to resign herself to the fact that there could be no future for the two of them—no matter how badly she wanted one.

36

Sitka; Three Days Later

"I don't care whether you're the one in charge." Alexei whirled around and glared at Mortimer Quimby, the territorial secretary of Alaska.

They were in the governor's office, where, since the moment Simon Caldwell had left, the scrawny little man had set himself to running the territory as if it were one of his ledgers.

"You can't give the Alaska Commercial Company sole fishing rights to the waters surrounding Prince of Wales Island." Alexei jabbed a finger at Quimby. "The Tlingit have been fishing that land for centuries."

"He can and he will," Preston Caldwell said in a bored tone from where he sat in a chair near the wall of books. "He's acting governor, and the contract has already been signed."

Alexei kept his gaze pinned on the territorial secretary, a skinny man who sat in his office from sunup to sundown and had never once been to the island whose fishing rights he was giving away. "I wouldn't listen to his advice. He'll be going to prison soon, and he won't be able to bribe you anymore."

"I won't be going to prison." Preston fanned his fingers out in front of him, studying his nails. For what, Alexei didn't know. As far as he was concerned, the man appeared far too haughty and indifferent about the legal battle ahead of him. "Everyone knows my attempted-murder charged is a farce. I'll never be convicted."

Alexei clenched his hands into fists. "A farce? I watched your daughter nearly die on my kitchen table."

Preston stifled a yawn. "No one will believe your word over mine."

"They won't have to." Alexei stalked closer to where the arrogant man still sat in the richly appointed chair. "Or did you forget that Alaska's medical director is the one who saved your daughter's life?"

"It was an accident." Caldwell brushed an imaginary speck of lint off his suitcoat, still not bothering to look at him. "She fell down the stairs."

"You kicked her until you broke five ribs, and the fact you're out of jail for so much as a day makes me sick."

Caldwell's head jerked up at that and he stood, eyes flashing. "Be careful, Amos. Unlike the Russians, we don't have an antiquated judicial system. Americans are innocent until proven guilty."

"And I have no doubt you'll be proven guilty," Alexei growled.

The first thing the judge had done upon returning to Sitka was release Caldwell on bail, just like Jonas had predicted. No judge wanted to hold a man as powerful as Preston Caldwell in prison for a crime he had yet to be convicted of. The judge had made Caldwell promise that he wouldn't leave Sitka, but the man clearly wasn't worried about his day in court.

Probably because he planned to bribe the district attorney to reduce the charges. Alexei hadn't officially heard of that happening yet, but he was waiting for it.

He'd long suspected both the Marshal and the district attorney had been in the Caldwell family's back pocket. Now he could prove it for the lawman, but not for the attorney. Hibbs was listed as a bribe recipient on every single ledger Rosalind had given them about the seal-harvesting numbers.

If the secretary of the interior ever arrived in Sitka, that would be one of the first things Alexei showed him. He was beyond ready to end the corruption that had plagued Alaska for the last four years.

The territorial secretary cleared his throat. "I appreciate your concern, Mr. Amos, but we're not here to discuss the charges against Mr. Caldwell. The agreement I signed—"

"What agreement are you talking about this time?" The office door banged open, and Alexei found himself looking at none other than Jacob Gray, secretary of the interior.

The snowy-haired man stepped inside the office and looked around, his brows pinching before his gaze settled back on Quimby. "Please tell me you're not trying to give away hunting or fishing rights that could be sold for a reasonable fee."

"You came." Alexei spoke the words to himself, but Gray must have overheard them, because he shifted his walking stick to his other hand and reached out to clasp Alexei's shoulder.

"Of course I came. I sent you a telegram saying I would. Didn't you receive it?"

"I'm sorry, Secretary Gray, but there was no need for you to make the trip all the way from Washington." Caldwell stepped forward and shook the older man's hand. "Whatever Amos told you to bring you here, I'm afraid he misrepresented it. Everything is under control."

Gray's bushy white eyebrows rose, and he planted the tip of

his cane against the carpet with a tap. "That's interesting information, because I made a point to stop by the village of Klawock on my way up here. Or rather, what was once the village of Klawock. Imagine my surprise when I found a large cannery under construction instead. Now where is Simon? I need to have a word with him."

"He's, uh . . ." Quimby stuck a finger in his collar and tugged. "He's not here."

"Then send someone to get him," the secretary boomed, banging his cane on the floor again.

Alexei winced. "That's not what he means. The governor fled Alaska."

"What? Why?" Gray's bushy white brows shot up. "Did something happen?"

"Yes," Alexei answered before Caldwell tried explaining. "He and Preston paid three men to try to burn down our shipyard. They're both facing arson charges. I don't know if that's why he fled, or if it had something to do with him moving the Indian village of Klawock, or something else entirely."

"Arson, you say?" Secretary Gray's gaze swept the three of them. "Someone better go back to the beginning and start explaining. I want to know everything, and I strongly suggest you tell me the full story."

Washington, DC; the Same Day

Yuri watched Rosalind curled on the bed, her blond hair fanning out over the pillow as she slept.

They'd had a busy few days, going from bank to bank to make sure Rosalind's Finnances were sorted before they left town. But they'd learned all their work had been worth it just after lunch, when they'd gone to Riggs and Company and received confirmation that her nonliquid assets had been transferred.

That meant they could leave for Texas tomorrow. Yuri had brought Rosalind straight back to the hotel and then left her to pack and prepare herself for the trip. Evidently she'd been tired, because she'd somehow managed to remove her shirtwaist and skirt and was now curled on the bed with random items of clothing strewn about the room.

She was so peaceful as she slept, with her long lashes casting shadows across her cheeks and the faintest flush of pink lingering on her skin. Her chest rose and fell in a steady rhythm, and she had one hand tucked beneath her cheek.

Oh, how was he going to travel five days across the country with her and not have his heart wrenched out of his chest?

After their kiss three days ago, he'd thought he'd handled the situation by telling her they couldn't kiss—or do anything more than kiss—and then going for a nice long walk, eating dinner at the restaurant across the street, and not returning to the room until he'd known Rosalind would be asleep for the night.

He'd been determined to sleep on the floor so they couldn't accidentally bump or touch while they were in bed together. But somehow she'd woken while he'd been making up a pallet with extra blankets, and she'd begged him to sleep beside her, promising she wouldn't try to kiss him again.

So he had. It had been a long, sleepless night, lying there with the heat from her body radiating into him. The next two nights had been equally long and sleepless.

Rosalind hadn't said anything about the kiss, but for the past two days, it seemed like she'd stood closer to him than necessary, accidentally brushing against him whenever they walked side by side or sat waiting in a lobby or carriage. She'd touched his arm and shoulder so many times he'd lost count. Once, while they waited for the elevator in the hotel lobby, she'd laced her fingers with his. It had just been for a moment, then she let go, but the touch had him recalling their kiss and wishing he could feel her body pressed against his again.

Just that morning, she'd adjusted his cravat. It shouldn't have felt romantic. The cravat had been crooked, and his sisters and brothers had all helped him with crooked cravats numerous times before. But it had almost seemed like Rosalind made a game out of seeing how close she could stand to him and how near she could bring her lips to his before reaching up. Her fingers had grazed the skin of his neck as she'd straightened it too, and not just once.

If her goal over the past three days had been to have him constantly replaying their kiss in his mind, she'd succeeded. It was all he could think about, that and the series of other small touches she was constantly giving him.

And it was all a giant mess. He wasn't supposed to have these feelings for her, and she certainly wasn't supposed to be returning them.

He'd known the fake wedding would be hard on him, but he'd been certain it wouldn't be so hard on Rosalind, that there was no way she'd develop feelings for him. He didn't have anywhere close to her family's wealth and influence, and she'd grown up in a world where status was the most important thing a man could offer his wife. He expected her to marry in truth one day, someone who could give her the life she was accustomed to but also treat her with kindness.

So he'd tried to keep everything between them kind and friendly, but not too personal.

But all that had blown apart when she'd initiated their kiss. Oh, he'd been tempted to kiss her a dozen times during their trip from Alaska to Washington, but he hadn't ever tried it.

He'd focused his efforts on being respectful and gentlemanly when their situation required them to be personal with each other, like helping her undress and wrapping and unwrapping her ribs. He always made sure to keep his eyes on her face, not allowing himself more than a passing glance at her curves or the shape of her body beneath her undergarments. He'd left the room and given her privacy on multiple occasions. He'd done everything he could think of to preserve her dignity and never make her feel unwelcome or ashamed.

And then she'd up and kissed him, which brought him to where he was now, watching her sleep while trying to figure out how he was going to spend five days on a train with her and not kiss her again.

She'd shifted at some point since he'd entered the room, and now her shoulders peeked above the quilt. The edge of her nightdress was pulled down on one side too, revealing a creamy patch of skin.

She'd get cold if she slept like that too long, so he hung his coat on the hook beside the door and headed toward her.

He was just about to pull the quilt up over her when her eyes fluttered open.

"Yuri?" She blinked, one hand still tucked beneath her cheek.

"I'm sorry. I was just trying to straighten your covers." He pulled the cover up, then stepped away from the bed. "Go back to sleep. I'll head out for a walk."

"No, that's all right." She yawned, then pushed herself up on the bed, the action causing her golden hair to cascade about her shoulders. "I think I've been sleeping for a while. What time is it?"

"Half past four."

Her eyes widened. "Apparently I've been sleeping for a

long while." She let out a small wince as she stood from the bed, but otherwise gave no indication of pain.

Yuri swung his gaze away from her. It was almost too much to look at her with the shadow of her body visible beneath her nightgown and her hair long and free at her back.

But she came toward him anyway. "You have a smudge."

She pressed onto her tiptoes, bringing their mouths mere inches from each other. She wiped at something on his cheek next, but the feel of her thumb on his skin sent warmth throughout his entire body.

He stepped away, nearly causing her to stumble, since she was still on her tiptoes. "You can't keep touching me like that."

She blinked, almost as though she found his words confusing. "What?"

"We're getting an annulment, remember? None of this between us is real." He shoved a hand into his hair. "I should be able to message Alexei and tell him to file the paperwork in another week."

"After we get to Commonwealth?" Her brows pinched. "Is that when you're going to send a message to Alexei?"

"Yes."

"Are you sure we need to get an annulment?"

He squeezed his eyes shut. Why did she have to ask that? Did she realize how hard this was on him?

"I mean it, Yuri." She reached out and gripped his hand. "What if we stay married after we finish here? What if I go to San Francisco with you and help run the shipyard? What if—"

"No. It won't work. I told you why last time you asked." He shook his head. "Your father and Vandermeer would figure out where you were after a month or two, and then what? It's too risky."

"My father might already be in jail." She stepped closer to him, her bare feet silent on the hotel rug. "We know that Secretary Gray left for Alaska over two weeks ago. He has to be in Sitka by now. Maybe my father and uncle have already been charged with fraud and are sitting in a jail cell awaiting trial as we speak."

"I sent Alexei a telegram our first day here, letting him know we'd arrived and where he could reach me with news of your father. I've heard nothing other than that the judge released him, but he can't leave Baranof Island to come look for you."

"But there's always a delay in telegrams." A strand of golden hair caught on the shoulder of her nightgown, but she didn't brush it away. "It takes several days for a ship to reach Seattle. He might be behind bars, and we simply don't know yet."

"And if he's not?" He folded his arms across his chest. "It's too risky. Besides, we know the law hasn't caught up to your uncle yet. He was just here in Washington last week. Even if he's left town, he won't be back in Alaska yet."

"But my uncle's not the threat. Leeland and my father are, and if my father's in jail and I'm already married, Leeland will leave me alone. I'm only in danger from Leeland if the marriage gets annulled. Then he could force me to marry him, which is all the more reason to keep our marriage intact." Her voice broke slightly on the last word, and she released his hand and wrapped her arms around herself.

Yuri just shook his head. "Leeland would have to figure out where you are before he could force you to do anything."

Her brows pinched. "And you're that confident he won't?"

"He'd never think to look for you at the Commonwealth, just like your father. Besides, it seems like a good place to let you heal."

"I don't need to go into hiding to heal." She pressed a hand to her ribs. "I'm healing fine. There's less and less pain every day, I'm taking deep breaths, and I'm going longer and longer without wearing the bindings."

"Yes, but what about the healing you need to do on the inside? You have nightmares multiple times a week, and sometimes when I take off my belt or turn around too fast . . ."

He didn't need to finish the sentence. She knew what he was talking about and had dropped her gaze to stare at her toes.

Just yesterday, she'd let out a gasp and shrunk against the wall, and all he'd done was take off his belt. Granted, he'd taken it off quickly, yanking it from his waist in a way that caused the end to snap. But it was an everyday, mundane movement that shouldn't have provoked any type of reaction from her. She'd done the same thing one other time when he'd taken off his belt, but sometimes she even cowered when he turned around abruptly.

He couldn't claim to understand it. All he knew was that it was some kind of reaction she couldn't fully control, and it made her suddenly experience random, intense bouts of fear.

Hopefully the women at the charity in Texas would know how to help her through it.

"Do you want to go to Texas and see the Woman's Commonwealth? Do you want to try staying there for a few days?" he asked.

She pressed her lips together, her eyes still riveted on the ground. "Yes, I want to go see it at least. I don't know if I'll want to stay, though."

"Then let me take you. You can see how you like it, and that will allow more time for things to get settled in Sitka."

"And if they're not settled by the time you need to leave for San Francisco?" she whispered. "Does that mean I have to stay behind in Texas?"

"I swore a vow to love and protect you, and those are the first things I'm going to do as your husband. Once your father is locked up, things might change, but we need to start by going to Texas. Because the truth is, even though you're standing here asking if we could not file for an annulment, once you're at the Commonwealth, you might want to stay forever and want nothing to do with me, and there won't be anything wrong with that decision. Do you understand?"

She nodded. "Yes."

He turned back to the half-packed room. "Now let's get back to packing so we can leave in the morning."

He turned and took one of the shirtwaists she'd left lying on the bed, then folded it for her. If only her father had already faced trial and was sitting in prison. Then maybe the two of them could . . .

No. He couldn't let his mind wander that direction. Because as far as he knew, her father wasn't sitting in prison, and he might not ever be. He might find yet another way to weasel out of what seemed like a sure criminal conviction.

Besides, Rosalind had just told him that she wanted to go to Texas and see the Commonwealth for herself. How could she really know whether she wanted to stay married to him when she hadn't yet seen the other option she had?

Telling her that they could stay married without letting her see the Commonwealth first felt like it would be taking yet another choice away from her, and he loved her too much to put her in that position.

37

Sitka; the Same Day

"Two hundred and twenty thousand dollars?" Secretary Gray blinked through his monocle, then leaned closer to the ledger splayed open on Alexei's desk.

The secretary, Mikhail, and Jonas were all in his office above the warehouse, their bellies full from the meal Bryony had cooked earlier. Alexei had invited Secretary Gray over for dinner before he'd left Castle Hill that afternoon. He'd made the invitation look casual, like little more than a friendly offer, but had fully intended to spend most of their time together showing the other man the seal ledgers.

"They hid two hundred and twenty thousand dollars' worth of seals from the Department of the Interior last year?" Secretary Gray dropped his monocle, letting it dangle on its chain as he looked at Alexei.

"Technically it was from the Bureau of Fisheries." Alexei nodded toward the ledger. "But yes. At least, that's how it appears."

"There are four years' worth of records." Jonas rapped his knuckles atop the stack of ledgers they'd piled onto his desk.

Gray's frown deepened. He picked up the nearest ledger and flipped a page with more force than necessary. "Are they all as bad as this one?"

"No. The earliest one starts off with only a few hundred extra seals harvested." Jonas slid the ledger from 1884 out from the bottom of the stack and opened it. "It appears that once the ACC—or Caldwells, whoever you want to say is responsible—figured out how easy it was to take the extra seals and pay a few bribes, they scaled up their operation rather quickly."

"Scaled it up?" Gray slammed the ledger shut, the crack echoing off the walls. "Do you have an estimate of how much money they cheated us out of in total?"

"They illegally harvested about three hundred and fifty thousand seals," Jonas answered. "And with the US government's bounty being two dollars per seal pelt, that means they kept about seven hundred thousand dollars by evading the bounties."

"I have the exact tallies here." Alexei slid the secretary one of the papers that he'd run a series of calculations on.

Gray snatched the paper, scanned it, then flung it back down on the desk. "Three-quarters of a million dollars. Do you understand what this means? They didn't just cheat the Bureau of Fisheries. They cheated Washington. They cheated the whole of the American people." He turned to Jonas, his voice trembling with rage. "Arrest Preston Caldwell. Immediately."

Jonas held up his hands. "I'd love to arrest Caldwell, but I don't have the authority to make any arrests. Marshal Hibbs stripped me of my position and badge."

"He what?" Gray's face reddened beneath his snowy hair. "I thought you were the Deputy Marshal?"

"I was." A muscle pulsed on the side of Jonas's jaw.

"Until Hibbs returned to Sitka and realized I'd arrested Caldwell for attempted murder and arson, and that I was planning to arrest the governor for arson as soon as he returned to the island."

"Hibbs is one of the people listed in the payout ledger." Mikhail flipped through a couple pages of the ledger still splayed on the desk, then pointed to one of the lines. "He's right here."

Deeper furrows grooved the wrinkled skin of Gray's forehead. "Is he listed just for this year or for other years too?"

"He's listed all four years," Alexei answered. "And we suspect Caldwell has paid him to make other investigations and charges disappear, like when we caught Caldwell distributing false navigational maps two summers ago."

The secretary's head snapped up, and he narrowed his gaze on Jonas. "Redding, I hereby reinstate you, not as Deputy Marshal, but as the sole acting Marshal for Alaska. I'm relieving Hibbs of his position. Now go arrest Caldwell and Hibbs."

If Jonas was happy to get his job back with a promotion, he didn't show it. In fact, he didn't even shift his stance. His jaw tightened for a brief moment, but all he said was, "We need warrants first."

"Then get me the judge. And the district attorney too." Gray stabbed the air with his finger. "I want a list of every person who was paid in these ledgers arrested immediately. And if the governor steps foot back in Sitka, I want him arrested immediately too."

"I have a list here of others involved in the falsified seal numbers, as well as their bribe amounts." Alexei handed him another piece of paper.

Gray took the list, then just shook his head. "I knew I should have made you governor last fall."

"What?" Mikhail's head jerked up, and he looked between him and the secretary.

"Did you just say you almost made Alexei governor?" Jonas had been heading toward the stairs, but he paused and turned back.

Heat crept up the back of Alexei's neck. Nathan was the only one in the family he'd told about that conversation, mainly because the man had caught him in a moment of weakness. He hadn't intended to tell anyone else. Ever.

Alexei shot Gray a dark look, hoping it would cause the secretary to shut his mouth, but the man barreled on. "Of course I almost made him governor. I'm not a fool. It's plain to see that he's the most qualified person for the job."

"So why didn't you give him the job?" Jonas cocked his head to the side.

The secretary thrust a hand toward Alexei. "He refused it!"

"You refused the governorship?" Mikhail swung his golden gaze to Alexei, his eyes filled with questions. "And then you let him bring in Simon Caldwell?"

"I didn't realize who his second choice was." Alexei crossed his arms, more to keep his hands from fidgeting than to look intimidating. Most of the time staying quiet and sending people a stern look would get them to leave him alone, but Jonas and Mikhail weren't going to let this go.

The next question came from Mikhail, who was suddenly all sharp edges and angles. "Why did you refuse the governorship?"

"Because the lot of you are a bunch of Indian lovers, and we have a federal policy to uphold." Secretary Gray absently waved his hand at Alexei. "But I might offer you the job again, if you think you can enforce the policy on hand."

"You mean refuse to acknowledge the native tribes have any rights to the land and put my two half-Aleut siblings into an Indian boarding school?" Alexei clenched his jaw. "I told you before that I won't do either of those things. That hasn't changed."

"Fine. Then I'll find another corrupt idiot in Washington to send up here." Gray rubbed a hand over his snowy hair. "He'll last two years, and you'll send me telegrams complaining about him the entire time. And who knows how much money he'll try to swindle away from the government. This sounds like a brilliant plan."

"You said Alexei had to put Ilya and Inessa into one of those boarding schools?" Jonas's face hardened. "How could you ask such a thing? Have you ever even visited one of them?"

The secretary blinked, a confused look crossing his face, as though he thought asking him to visit one of the schools where he insisted on sending Indian youths was ridiculous. Then he shook his head and jabbed a finger at Jonas. "Aren't you supposed to be getting the district attorney and the judge? We'll deal with this governor business later. I need Caldwell and Hibbs arrested tonight."

38

Sitka; Two Days Later

"So that's it? Everyone is in prison?" Bryony took a sip of water, then helped herself to a second piece of bread sitting in the basket on the kitchen table.

"Yes. At least everyone I could find." Jonas plunged his spoon into the bowl of borscht in front of him and took a hearty bite.

Alexei watched his family from where he was seated at the head of the table, which seemed a bit too empty, even if they were enjoying a pot of Evelina's borscht.

Kate's twin, Evelina, and their two half siblings, Inessa and Ilya, had been in Sitka for about a week and a half. Usually Evelina taught a half-day school for the Tlingit children in Juneau, but when she'd learned there was trouble with Preston Caldwell and Jonas was needed in Sitka until Secretary Gray arrived, she'd given the students a break and come to Sitka. Of course, she hadn't been expecting Jonas to lose his job when

Marshall Hibbs arrived before Secretary Gray, but she'd been here when it happened.

But regardless of what had brought Evelina and his half siblings to Sitka, it felt nice to have them home again. Getting everyone together was becoming more and more difficult. Going forward, Christmas might be the only time all seven of his siblings and their families were together each year, especially now that they were opening a shipyard down in San Francisco.

The table had felt painfully empty since Sacha and Maggie, and Maggie's younger siblings, Ainsley and Finnan, left for San Francisco.

And confound it. Alexei missed Yuri more than he wanted to admit. He couldn't remember the last time Yuri had been gone for so long. It felt almost wrong to go through the day without anyone teasing him about how rarely he smiled.

But this was going to be their new version of normal now, because as soon as Yuri had dropped Rosalind off in Texas, he'd be moving to San Francisco for good.

Alexei pressed his palm to his breastbone. It didn't seem fair that he should miss the hooligan so much.

"Not everyone was in Sitka," Jonas continued, still answering Bryony's question about the arrests. "And some of the officials and hunters who work for the ACC are only here in the summer. Warrants for their arrests have been sent to the various locations where they live, but we have no way of knowing if anyone else has been arrested yet."

Alexei didn't want to think about how long that list of people would be. They'd spent the past two days poring over the ledgers with Secretary Gray, researching each and every name. It seemed like the Caldwells had been willing to pay off anyone and everyone to keep their extra seal-harvesting efforts a secret. But what Jonas said was true, anyone in Sitka involved in falsifying the numbers was now sitting in the jail beneath the old governor's mansion on Castle Hill, and that included Preston Caldwell and Marshal Hibbs.

"I'm just glad Mr. Caldwell is in prison. He should have been sent there years ago." This from Ilya, the youngest sibling in their family. He was a child of their father's second marriage. Half Aleut and half white, he hadn't even been two when his parents died. Raising him had been one of the biggest reasons Alexei had left San Francisco and returned to Sitka—along with keeping the family's businesses afloat.

"I don't know that I'll be able to rest easy until Simon Caldwell is in prison too," Mikhail muttered. "I don't like the fact that he's gone."

Jonas shrugged his broad shoulders. "A warrant for his arrest has been sent to Washington, DC. It's only a matter of time before he's either caught there or shows up back here, thinking he's still the governor."

"Yes, we'll all rest easier once we know Simon has been arrested." Evelina dropped her spoon into her borscht with a plunk, her gaze moving to Alexei. "But I think we should stop talking about the Caldwells, and Alexei should tell us about the letter that arrived in the mail today."

Alexei tried to scowl, but he wasn't quite sure he managed it. "There were several letters. Since when do you care about shipping-contract extensions?"

Evelina settled a hand over her growing stomach and glared right back at him. "I was referring to the letter written in a feminine hand."

"Did Laurel write him?" Bryony's eyes lit with excitement, and she turned his direction, her red braid swinging over her shoulder. "What did it say?"

"Let's see. Does this make the third or fourth one you've received since returning from San Francisco?" Mikhail grinned at him.

"I hardly see why it matters." Alexei wasn't about to admit that it was, in fact, the fifth letter he'd received.

"So when do we get to meet this woman?" Jonas pinned him with his serious lawman gaze, one that had probably caused a couple dozen criminals to confess on the spot.

Alexei kept his mouth shut.

"Perhaps we should all take a trip down to San Francisco." Mikhail shifted into a comfortable position on his chair. "To visit Sacha, of course. We'll probably be expected to invite the Farnsworths to dine with us at that new hotel down there, which means we'd be forced to meet Laurel. What a shame."

"Perhaps you should schedule your trip to start in a month or more, maybe you could go down there for Easter," Alexei suggested.

Mikhail narrowed his eyes. "What are you up to?"

"Wait. Is Laurel coming here?" Bryony nearly dropped her water glass. "Is that why you want to send Mikhail away? Do we get to meet her?"

"Don't tell me she's going to be here for Easter," Mikhail drawled.

Alexei smirked. "She's aiming to arrive around the middle of March and stay through at least Easter."

Evelina squealed, the sound so high-pitched he winced. "This is wonderful! Jonas, we have to come visit while she's here."

"Is there anything specific she wants to do while she's here?" Bryony cut in. "Mikhail and I will have several weeks before we have to leave on our next expedition. I can't wait to meet her."

"Does this mean Alexei's getting married?" Ilya plunged his spoon into his soup with a scowl.

"Yes!" Bryony and Evelina shrieked in unison.

Alexei resisted rolling his eyes. Barely. "No. It means I invited a friend for a visit."

Jonas sent Ilya a wink. "They'll be married before summer ends. Just watch."

"They better not be," Mikhail snapped. "I've been present at every single one of my siblings' weddings so far. I don't plan to miss Alexei's."

Inessa jabbed her spoon at Mikhail. "You weren't at Kate's."

"And Alexei got an earful for it, allowing her to be married while I was on an expedition, believe me." Mikhail sent Alexei a glare.

Alexei threw up his hands. "She was married within eight hours of being trapped in that cave with Nathan. No one was there for the wedding unless they happened to already be in Juneau."

Mikhail tapped his fingers on the table. "Either you marry Laurel before Bryony and I leave, or you wait until we get back. None of this getting married over the summer while we're gone."

He was tempted to try telling Mikhail that he was getting riled up over nothing, but the truth was, there might be a wedding sometime over the summer. He could see himself being happy married to Laurel. She didn't necessarily inspire the same whirlwind of emotions that his former fiancée, Clarise, used to, but maybe that would change with time.

"He can't get married." Ilya's scowl deepened. "Then I won't have any brothers left."

Evelina dabbed her face with her napkin. "You can't expect Alexei to stay single forever. He was engaged before any of the rest of us."

"Is Laurel coming to visit because she thinks you might be the next governor?" Inessa asked, her dark hair falling over her shoulder.

"Not that I know of." Though he could certainly see Laurel's parents supporting the marriage if he were indeed the next governor. "She doesn't know that I was offered the position last summer, so I doubt she thinks it's possible for me to become governor now."

"Are you sure?" Jonas asked. "I bet the paper in San Francisco has run half a dozen articles about Preston Caldwell being charged with fraud, and there being a warrant out for the current governor's arrest."

"I still doubt she knows I'm in the running to be the next governor." Though Jonas brought up a good point. Her father had many connections, and if he'd heard rumors about the next governor, this could be maneuvering on her parents' part.

But he still remembered the flare of excitement in Laurel's eyes and the soft curve of her lips when he'd invited her to Alaska. Maybe this was what had been needed to get her parents' permission for the trip?

"Has Secretary Gray offered you the governorship again?" Inessa asked, now evidently wanting to talk even though she'd remained silent for most of the meal.

"No. I have a meeting with him in the morning, but I don't know if he intends to discuss that or something else." He wasn't sure when Gray would be returning to Washington. There were still a lot of things to be sorted through. The village of Klawock and the new cannery owned by the ACC and fishing rights around Prince of Wales Island were just a few of those things. Alexei couldn't begin to imagine how many more messes Simon Caldwell had made that would now need to be cleaned up.

"If he doesn't ask you, who do you think he'll ask to be the next governor?" Inessa pressed.

Alexei ran his eyes over his youngest sister, with her dark hair and dark eyes and brown skin. She was lovely and athletic, moving with a grace and ease that few women possessed. And she was suddenly awfully interested in who the next governor of Alaska would be. If only he knew why.

"I don't know." He scrubbed a hand over his face. The whole family now knew why he'd turned down the governorship over the summer, but it wasn't something he'd ever intended to share, especially not with Inessa and Ilya. This conversation was turning awkward fast.

"Do you think he might ask you to be governor again in the morning?"

Alexei just shook his head. "I already said I don't know. Do you have another question to ask? If so, get to the point." He shoved a spoonful of borscht into his mouth.

"It's just . . ." Inessa licked her lips. "If Secretary Gray says you need to send Ilya and me to an Indian boarding school to be governor, I'm willing to go. In fact, I want to go."

He choked on his borscht. "You don't mean that."

She raised her chin. "I mean every word of it. I want to see what they're teaching my mother's people firsthand. The entire point of these schools is to assimilate us so we can learn the ways of the Americans. And I want to learn their ways. I want to see what they are teaching and doing. And then I want to go to college and learn law like Evelina, so that I can help the Aleut in court. I want there to be a day when the ACC refuses to pay my grandfather for the seals his village kills, and I file a lawsuit in court. Or file a lawsuit for the Tlingit down in Klawock, saying they shouldn't be forced from their homes and shouldn't have to give up their ability to fish in the waters around Prince of Wales Island."

"That doesn't mean you should be that person," Alexei growled.

On the other side of the table, Evelina sat quietly, tearing off a bit of bread and dipping it into her borscht.

Alexei narrowed his eyes at her. "You don't look surprised by this."

Neither did Jonas.

Evelina exchanged a glance with Inessa. "We've been discussing the boarding-school idea for a few months, actually."

Alexei pressed his eyes shut. "Does Kate know too?"

"It was her idea," Inessa said.

"Of course it was." He should have seen this coming. His first two sisters had insisted on being educated in men's professions, so why would Inessa be any different? "Wait, you discussed going to a boarding school on your own, without knowing about the ultimatum Secretary Gray gave me?"

Inessa nodded. "I hadn't thought of it at first. I just asked Lina if she could start teaching me law so I'd have less to catch up on when I went to Boston to study, but once I told Kate why I wanted to study law, she suggested I go to a boarding school for a year."

"Right." He pressed his fingers to his temple.

"I know you've done a lot for my grandfather, Alexei, and my mother's people. You do a lot for the Tlingit and Inupiat and Athabaskans too, but they need more than you stepping in and starting an argument when they're about to be taken advantage of. They need actual laws on their side, and who better to find a way for them to have those laws than someone who understands both ways of life?"

"They won't let you speak your native language." It was the first thing that came to mind, one of the largest objections he had to the boarding schools. Indian youths were forced to speak English, even if they didn't know a word of it upon arrival. And they were treated cruelly each time they spoke in their native tongues.

But Inessa was only shaking her head at him, her long black hair shimmering beneath the lamplight. "English is my native language. We both know I'm more American than Aleut. Or maybe I'm more Russian. I don't exactly know what I am, but I do know that my people need a voice, and I want to be that voice. Going to a boarding school is a good place to start, and if it helps you procure the governorship, then that's even better."

He swallowed. "Are you sure?"

"Very sure."

"I don't want to go to a boarding school." Ilya scowled at his sister. "I think it's a terrible idea."

"It would be a terrible idea for you." He wouldn't send Ilya under any circumstances, no matter what Secretary Gray said about the country's Indian policy and him being governor. But it might not be a terrible idea for Inessa. "Secretary Gray might not offer me the position of governor again. He hasn't brought it up since that first night in the office, and I can't in good conscience ask tribes to leave the land they've been hunting and fishing for centuries and move into towns. That leaves me in nearly the same place I was in last summer."

"Can you find a middle ground?" Inessa leaned forward, her dark eyes shining. "Some way to compromise? Because if you don't take the governorship, it will go to someone else who will want to exploit the native tribes all over again."

"She's right." Mikhail rested his back against the chair. "You would do a better job as governor than anyone else. I think you should find a way to take the position, even if you have to do a few things that don't align with your views. You'll be able to do far more good as governor than you will as a business owner who's always fighting with the governor."

Alexei tilted his head back to stare at the ceiling, though the wooden beams gave nothing away. Could he find some type of compromise with Secretary Gray? Was there a way for him to be governor and do good for Alaska without having to pursue policies that would harm the native tribes?

It seemed like something he should at least think about.

39

Rosalind scanned the sun-bleached hills and golden fields as the buggy carried them farther and farther from town. The road curved gently between pastures edged with live oaks and barbed wire, while the wind stirred the tall grass. She'd never been to Texas before, but it seemed peaceful, like the type of place a person could come and enjoy the feel of sun on their face or lie down for a lazy nap beneath a tree.

They'd left the little town of Belton nearly twenty minutes ago. Yuri had rented a buggy from the livery after the stagecoach had arrived in town. But she hadn't expected the Commonwealth to be this far outside of town.

"Don't be nervous, Ros. I've exchanged several letters with Mrs. McWhirter. You're going to like it here." Yuri reached out and settled his hand over hers.

It was a simple touch, but it still felt entirely too nice. There'd been precious few touches on the train ride from Washington, DC, to Waco, and just as few on the stagecoach ride from Waco to Belton. It almost made her wish for the days when her ribs were so injured she could barely breathe. Yuri hadn't thought twice about touching her then, but he was being much more circumspect about things now.

It wasn't that Yuri had been cold toward her on the trip, exactly, but there was certainly a distance between them that hadn't been there on their trip to Washington or during their stay in the city.

Which was ridiculous, because it shouldn't be possible to miss a person she was constantly with.

Yet it seemed like the gulf between them widened with each passing day.

A windmill creaked up ahead, and a pair of cattle lifted their heads as the buggy rolled past. They passed a clothesline next, and Rosalind could see glimpses of a white clapboard house set back from the road. It was likely situated by a creek, given the trees and other vegetation that grew near it.

The driveway to the house soon came into view. She licked her lips. "Is this the Commonwealth?"

"Yes. What do you think?" Yuri nodded toward the house and field that spread beyond it.

She looked around. There were several women moving about the property. One was hauling a basket toward steps on the side of the house, another was tending a garden tucked neatly beside a low fence, and a third drew water from the well beneath the windmill. Children played in a patch of shade near the clapboard house, their laughter mingling with the cluck of chickens pecking in the dust.

Beyond the main house, more buildings came into view— long, low structures with tin roofs, a small barn, a shed, and a laundry yard strung with fresh linens fluttering in the sun. A series of fences framed everything from animal pens to fields.

Something about it still felt familiar, almost like this place was a memory she couldn't quite catch. "It seems pleasant," she finally answered. "Like a nice place to live."

Yuri sent her a lopsided smile, but it didn't quite reach his eyes. "See? I knew you'd like it."

She did like it. She just wasn't sure that she liked it more than she'd like spending her future with Yuri. But that wasn't an option they had at the moment, and from everything she could see about the Commonwealth, it seemed like a wonderful place to live until her father was in prison.

Yuri slowed the buggy, and the front door to the house opened to reveal a portly woman with a wide smile.

"Miss Caldwell, is that you?"

"Mrs. McWhirter?"

"Yes, I'm Martha McWhirter." The woman came down the steps to stand beside the buggy. "Founder and proprietress of the Woman's Commonwealth. I want to start by thanking you for your generous donations to our organization all these years."

"Oh, you're welcome, but I'm actually Mrs.—"

"She's still Miss Caldwell." Yuri cut her off, then hopped down from the buggy and came around the back of it to greet Mrs. McWhirter.

The woman watched Yuri's movement's with narrowed eyes, almost as though she distrusted something about him wanting to greet her. "I've explained the rules to you by letter, Mr. Amos. No men are allowed on the property. If you'll kindly empty Miss Caldwell's things from the wagon and deposit them here, the women and I are perfectly capable of seeing they are delivered to her room."

Yuri wasn't allowed on the property? At all? Rosalind's eyebrows winged up.

But Yuri was already nodding his head at Mrs. McWhirter, clearly unsurprised by her instructions. "Of course. Just give me a minute."

He climbed into the back of the wagon and slid her trunks to the edge, then grabbed the smaller suitcase she'd carried with her on the train. Rosalind used the time to climb down from the wagon, careful not to do anything that might aggravate her ribs.

She would have stepped to the back of the wagon next to pick up her suitcase, but Mrs. McWhirter reached out and gripped her hand.

"I want to thank you again for your donations. We've been able to finish the new dormitory so every woman has her own room. The windmill you paid for last year keeps our laundry yard supplied with water, and we've added more troughs and clotheslines so we can take in work from Belton. We used some of your funds to purchase barbed wire too, so we now have enough fencing to keep the entire property fenced in, plus have pens for all the livestock."

She smiled. "I'm so glad to hear it. I can't wait to see everything for myself."

The portly woman smiled right back at her. "I'm more than happy to give you a tour."

"Here's the last of everything." Yuri set the final trunk on the ground, then glanced up at the white clapboard house. "Are you sure you don't want help taking her trunks to her room?"

Mrs. McWhirter bristled. "Quite sure. Thank you."

He cut his gaze away from the other woman and took a step closer to Rosalind. "How are your ribs?"

"They're all right." She pressed a hand to the worst of her injuries. It still wasn't fully healed, but it was getting better every day.

He handed her smallest suitcase to Mrs. McWhirter. "She'll need some extra tending until her fractures heal fully. The doctors say it should be at least two more weeks of rest and binding, but she might need longer."

"We're careful with all of our women, Mr. Amos." Mrs. McWhirter took the suitcase, her voice clipped. "Now if you'll kindly vacate our premises. You're making some of our residents nervous."

Once again, Rosalind felt her brows pinch. She looked around the property, which now held even more women, many of them trying to look busy while pretending not to watch them.

She might not have met the women yet, but she wanted to call out that they had no reason to be nervous around Yuri. He was the kindest, most gentle man she'd ever known.

But Yuri didn't defend himself. He merely stepped back from the luggage, wiped his hands on his trousers, and nodded once more.

It shouldn't have hurt, the way he stood there silently, so close and yet so distant, but it did.

His gaze finally drifted to her, and he gave her a small nod. "Good-bye, Ros."

"Wait." She rushed to his side before he could climb onto the wagon. He didn't intend to say good-bye to her like this, did he? Without so much as even a hug? "Where are you going? You're not headed back to San Francisco yet, are you?"

"The stage comes twice a week. I'll be at the boarding house for two more days."

Her throat turned dry. "What if I don't want you to leave?"

He shook his head. "You know that's not possible."

"And the annulment?"

"I doubt there's a telegraph line that runs to Belton, but there should be one in Waco. I'll send a telegram from there when I travel through on my way to San Francisco. The papers should get filed sometime next week."

It all felt so final. She couldn't stand the thought of saying good-bye, not to the one man she'd been able to trust back in Sitka, not to the man who'd taken time to see her as more than just the daughter of the richest person in town. Not to the man who'd crawled into bed with her and held her tight for nearly three weeks.

She couldn't say good-bye to him. Not yet. Not like this. She reached out and fisted a hand in his shirt. "Will you come back? To say good-bye at least?"

He pressed his eyes shut. "Rosalind . . ."

"Please, Yuri." She took a step closer, near enough that she could smell the scent of sunshine and dust on his skin. She could feel Mrs. McWhirter's glare boring into her back, but she didn't care. "You said that we could still be together after my father is in prison, remember?"

He opened his eyes, and the gaze he sent her was so very familiar, filled with softness and tenderness that she wanted to wrap herself in. "If that's what you want, then yes."

"What if I don't want to say good-bye just yet? Will you come back again before you leave? Please?"

"Oh, I nearly forgot." Mrs. McWhirter patted her pocket, then pulled out an envelope. "This came for you yesterday, Mr. Amos. I assume whoever sent it knew you'd be stopping here."

Yuri took the envelope but didn't bother to look at it. He merely thanked Mrs. McWhirter and slid it into his pocket, then turned back to her. His eyes searched her face for one long moment, but he didn't reach out to touch her. "Good-bye, Ros."

He climbed into the buggy, flicked the reins, and turned the team toward the gate.

Rosalind stood there, an ache forming in her chest as she watched the dust rise behind him.

It wasn't until he'd turned off the drive and was making his way down the road that she realized he'd never given her an answer about coming back to say good-bye a final time.

40

She was going to like it here. At least that's what Rosalind told herself as she stood in the quiet of her room, finally unpacking her things. The view of the setting sun outside her window was perfect, with rolling hills and tall grass swaying in the fields and cows bedding down for the night.

If she looked out the window on the other wall, she'd see the laundry yard where Commonwealth women earned money by doing laundry for local townsfolk. The day's wash had already been taken in for the night, but a young girl pumped water from the windmill, her braid swinging with each pull, and two women knelt in the fading light to weed the vegetable patch before darkness fell.

It wasn't the quiet, lonely refuge she'd imagined when Yuri spoke of "somewhere to heal." It was a working community, and everyone seemed to have a place in it. She'd met most of the women earlier while touring the grounds. Some had been milking the cows and goats, others had been turning the milk from that morning into cheese, and some had been seated at the mending table, which was yet another source of income for the Commonwealth. Everyone had welcomed her, though some women had certainly been more standoffish than others, and some of the children especially seemed scared of strangers.

Mrs. McWhirter had told her that the women here were in various stages of healing. Some had just left terrible situations, and others had been in residence for over five years and focused on helping the new residents as well as selling goods in town. Mrs. McWhirter had explained that the longer the women stayed, the more comfortable they became with life away from their violent husbands.

Rosalind had asked if anyone ever left, but the woman hadn't wanted to speak much about that.

A knock sounded, followed by the creak of hinges, and Rosalind looked up from the shirtwaist she'd just placed in the dresser to find two women she recognized.

"Rosalind?" Lydia stepped inside, her sleeves rolled to the elbow and her hair pinned in a tight bun.

Margaret stepped into the room behind Lydia. She was taller and quieter and had lines around her eyes and mouth that made her seem older than she probably was. "We thought you might want help settling in." Margaret headed straight for the open trunk.

"And Mrs. McWhirter—or Martha, really—asked us to bring you a towel." Lydia set a towel and washcloth on the bed, then put a small sewing basket on the dresser. "We have a bathing room downstairs, if you want to wash off the traveling dust before bed. There's already water warming on the stove. If you don't use it, someone else will."

Rosalind smiled. "A bath sounds lovely, thank you. In fact, I think I might stop unpacking and take you up on the offer right now. Do you mind helping me with my dress?" She touched the back of it. "It's not the easiest thing to get out of on my own, though I've gotten pretty good at managing my own bindings over the past week."

"Bindings?" Lydia's hands paused where they had already started undoing the long string of buttons at her back. "What do you mean bindings?"

"I . . . er . . . I was injured before I came here."

"Did your husband hit you?" Fury laced Lydia's voice as she undid another button. "My husband hit me too, and—"

"No. He didn't hit me."

"Lying about what happened won't do you no good," Margaret snapped from the wardrobe where she'd been hanging dresses, her entire body stiff. "Best thing a woman can do is face it, if you ask me."

"I agree." Lydia's hands kept going, farther and farther down her back.

The woman could surely see her bindings at this point, and Rosalind found herself wishing she had worn one of the shirtwaists that buttoned down the front.

Did they really think Yuri was responsible for the injury to her ribs? And if that's what Lydia and Margaret believed, how many others thought the same thing?

Oh, Yuri, how can they think such a thing about you? She'd been trying to put him from her mind all afternoon and focus on the new life she could have at the Commonwealth. But he had risked so very much to bring her here, and now these women—these strangers who knew nothing about her—were assuming he was just like her father and Leeland and the men Lydia and Margaret had fled.

"It's safe here. There's no reason to lie to protect your husband." Lydia finished the last of the buttons. "Besides, your husband can't exactly come here and take you away. Martha's got plenty of shotguns, and she trains the women who stay here how to use them."

Lydia untucked the bandage and started unraveling it. The movements were similar to what Yuri had done countless times since their wedding, but with Yuri, the action had always felt tender and gentle. There was nothing gentle in Lydia's practical, no-nonsense touch.

"Not the boys," Margaret added. "Boys are allowed to stay here with their mothers until they turn twelve. After that, they need to go live with their fathers or find a job."

"Twelve?" Rosalind turned her head slightly. "That seems awfully young."

"Not when you consider every woman here has been hurt by a man." Lydia tugged off the last of the bandage, then set it on the bed. "That's why Martha doesn't teach the boys to shoot."

"Just the women and girls learn?"

"Exactly. Can't have any of them boys gettin' their hands on a gun. There's no saying what they might do. I mean, look at what your husband did to you." Lydia nodded toward her ribs.

Rosalind slid a hand over the bottom of her ribs. "I already told you it wasn't my husband. He's the kindest man I've ever met."

The frowns on both women's faces deepened.

"It was my father," she whispered, ducking her head. Hopefully they'd believe her now. "And it wasn't his hand. It was his foot. He broke five of my ribs, and one of them punctured my lung. I almost died, but my husband's sister and brother-in-law saved me. They're both doctors. And then Yuri married me to protect me from him."

Silence settled in the room, long and heavy. Rosalind kept her head down, staring at a rather large crack between two of the floorboards. The sound of crickets chirping filtered through the window. Rosalind couldn't say how long the room was quiet for, only that Lydia was the first to speak, and her voice emerged a bit lower and rougher than before.

"Well, you're safe here, no matter what man hurt you. That's what matters."

Rosalind managed a small smile. She was safe.

She knew that. But the safety here didn't come with Yuri's arms wrapped around her, or his words of encouragement whispered in her ear, or his quiet way of making the air around her easier to breathe.

It came with dour looks and distrustful glares whenever she spoke of the man she loved.

41

Belton, Texas; Two Days Later

Yuri tilted his head toward the ceiling of the boardinghouse room and drew in a breath. The telegram sat unfolded and open on the desk beneath the window. But he didn't need to look at it again to remember what it said. He'd memorized it when he'd stopped partway into town to read it after leaving Rosalind at the Woman's Commonwealth yesterday.

P. Caldwell arrested and in jail. Awaiting trial without bail. Warrant issued for S. Caldwell's arrest. I'm new governor. —A.

Yuri still didn't know what to think of the last sentence, only that he was sorry he'd missed whatever had transpired to cause the secretary of the interior to offer Alexei the governorship.

As for the rest of the telegram, he needed to tell Rosalind. The stage would be here just after two that afternoon, which gave him about six hours to ride out to the Commonwealth and give Rosalind the news. She'd said she wanted to know the instant her father was in jail, and she'd said she wanted to stay married to him too.

But did she really? She might have changed her mind over the past two days. That's why he hadn't turned around and ridden back to the Commonwealth after opening the telegram. If she was going to choose him and living in San Francisco over spending her days on a peaceful farm surrounded by kind women who'd understood what she'd gone through, then he wanted to make sure she fully understood the choice she was making. He refused to pressure her into any kind of choice she might regret later, and that included staying married to him.

He'd watched the way her eyes had lit up when they'd turned into the drive at the Commonwealth and noticed the way she'd looked around, as though wanting to explore every inch of the property. He'd seen the eagerness on her face when Mrs. McWhirter had offered to introduce her to the other women too.

There was no question the Commonwealth was the right place for her, but he still needed to tell her what the telegram said. And she'd wanted him to come say good-bye anyway.

Dear Father, give me strength. This is going to hurt. It wasn't the type of situation he could smile or joke his way out of. It was the type that called for Alexei's version of seriousness.

Defend the poor and fatherless: do justice to the afflicted and needy. Deliver the poor and needy: rid them out of the hand of the wicked.

When he'd first befriended Rosalind and God had given him that verse, he'd had no idea how far God would ask him to go to deliver her from her father, or how deeply he would fall in love with her along the way.

But the verse was still true. He wasn't sorry that he'd helped her. He was only sorry that he now needed to say good-bye.

But Rosalind was safe and making her own choices and no longer living in fear. She'd stood up to the solicitor in Washington, DC, and found her father's seal-harvesting ledgers, then turned them over to Yuri to give to Jonas. She'd made so much progress.

That was what he needed to think about as he said goodbye. The good things God had in store for her future, not the things he would lose by not having her in his life.

He grabbed his hat from the hook on the wall and settled it on his head, then latched his suitcase. He could leave it at the livery for a few hours while he rented the horse and pick it back up before the stage came.

He picked up the suitcase and headed toward the door, but knocking sounded on it, followed by the sound of a familiar voice.

"Yuri? Are you in there? Can you open up?"

Rosalind? He wrenched the door open.

"I can't stay at the Commonwealth." She brushed past him and stalked into the room. "I mean it."

He scratched his head. "Is something not to your liking? If someone treated you poorly I'll ride out to the property myself and give Mrs. McWhirter a piece of my mind."

"It's not that." She spun and faced his direction, and she was a mess. Her shirtwaist was crooked where it tucked into her skirt, her updo was disheveled and sliding to one side, and golden whisps of her hair poked up every which way. "The Commonwealth is lovely, really. It's a nice, peaceful place for women who need a better life."

"Then what's the problem?"

"You're not there."

"I'm not—" His throat closed, and any words he had shriveled on his tongue. "Are you saying . . . "

"I'm saying that I still want to stay married to you." Her

voice grew hoarse, and moisture crept into her eyes. "I know you must hate me for what my father did to your family. I know you can barely stand to look at me and will probably turn me away. But I also know that the coach comes this afternoon, and I had to tell you how I felt before you left. That I can't imagine my life without you, nor do I want to. So if you can find it in your heart to forgive me for what my father did, then I want to be by your side. I don't care where we go or what we do."

He dropped his suitcase to the floor with a *thunk.* "Is that what you think? That I don't want to stay married because of your father? I don't blame you for what he did, Ros. Those were his actions, not yours."

"You don't?" A tear slipped down her cheek. "Then why did you pull away when I kissed you? Why have you been so distant from me?"

He reached out and pulled her into his arms, then dropped his forehead down until it touched hers. "Because I was worried about your father finding you if we stayed married. And because I wanted you to see the Commonwealth. I wanted you to know what your choices looked like, not blindly choose me. I can't offer you much more than a rented apartment in a dirty city while I work far too many hours trying to get my family's new shipyard operational."

"You've offered me more than that from the very beginning." She reached up and rested a hand on his cheek. "You're the kindest person I've ever met, and I love you for it. Just like I love you for the way you helped me with my charity letters even though you barely knew me when we started, and for the way you insisted on naming the library after my family to try to protect me. For the way you asked me to leave Sitka and go somewhere safe time and again, and for the way you sat by my side the day after I was injured. Or how you dropped every-thing to take me to Washington, DC, and then here, never mind that you're supposed to be in San Francisco right now helping your family. You promised to love and honor and cherish me on our wedding day. But the truth is, you were loving, honoring, and cherishing me long before we got married, and I'm taking you up on that promise in earnest. I won't let you get out of it so easily."

He opened his mouth, then closed it, not quite sure what to say. "I'd hardly call what we had a wedding day. You didn't have much choice about marrying me."

She blinked. "Is that what you've been telling yourself? That I married you because I felt like it was my only choice? I *wanted* to marry you. Back in Sitka. I didn't agree to a rushed wedding because of my father or Leeland or my ribs. I agreed because I was already in love with you, and I wanted nothing more than to spend the rest of my life by your side."

Once again, his mouth opened, but no words came out. Had she truly felt this way about him? All this time? "Why didn't you say something?"

"Because you didn't want to marry me."

"Not want to marry you?" He scrubbed a hand over his face. "Why would you think that? Wait. Was it because of the things your father tried to do to my family?"

"Of course. Like I said, I can't blame you for not—"

He stepped close to her again and pressed a finger to her mouth. "That was never it. I never blamed you for what your father did. Not once."

She stepped away from him. "But you didn't even have to think before you shot down Alexei's idea that we get married. You told him no before he even finished talking. Then you left the room to talk to him, and when you came back, it was with a plan for a temporary marriage."

He'd never meant to give her that impression. All he'd done

was set his own feelings aside and try to protect her first and foremost.

But he'd been so fast to quash Alexei's initial suggestion that they marry. If she'd had feelings for him—if she loved him—how must that have looked to her? And then when she'd asked if they could stay married in Washington, DC, he'd been fast to tell her no again.

But he'd left her at the Commonwealth for two days, and somehow she'd found a ride to Belton and sought him out entirely on her own.

He'd just been praying that God would give him strength while he said good-bye to her a final time, but then she had appeared before he could even rent a horse, answering his prayer in a way that was entirely different from what he'd expected, and telling him that she was choosing him freely—not out of fear or duty or obligation.

He reached out and stroked one of the wayward wisps of hair away from her face, tucking it behind her ear. "Are you sure you want to stay married and come to San Francisco with me?"

"San Francisco, Sitka, Juneau, Washington, DC. I don't care where it is. I just want to be with you." She reached up and laid a hand on his cheek, their faces so close that their breath mingled. "I love you, Yuri Amos."

"I love you too." He pulled her into his arms, savoring the familiar way she fit against him. "I've loved you for years, ever since you moved to Sitka, really."

Tears filled her eyes, and she sniffled. "Then why did you tell your brother no when he first suggested we marry? Why did you insist on an annulment?"

He leaned down and rested his forehead against hers. "Because you're the only person who should get to decide your future, and I didn't want you to feel trapped for the rest of your life."

"And you set up things so we could get an annulment so that I'd have a choice about marrying you in the end?"

"I wanted to bring you to the Commonwealth. I thought you'd love it. I assumed you'd want to stay and . . ." He shook his head. "I suppose that wasn't fair of me, was it? Even though I said you could have your own choice, I assumed you'd want to stay here with women who've been through similar things."

"I'm glad you brought me here. I mean, Mrs. Mc— Martha had written me about improvements they'd made to the property with my donations, but seeing it and meeting the women I've helped was so much better than I could have imagined. I hope my investment accounts do even better next year, simply so that I can raise the amount I donate every month."

Of course she'd say that, this dear, sweet, generous woman God had given him. He couldn't stop his lips from forming a gentle smile. "I hope that happens too."

"But none of what I saw here makes me want to stay. I still want to be your wife, but do you think San Francisco will be safe for me?"

He released her, but only so that he could pick up the telegram from the desk. "Very safe. The envelope Mrs. McWhirter gave me when I dropped you off was a telegram from Alexei. Your father is in jail awaiting trial, and I can't imagine Leeland will want anything to do with your family after a scandal as big as this."

He handed her the paper. She took a moment to scan it, then squealed and launched herself back into his arms. A moment later, she pressed up onto her tiptoes and settled her lips on his.

He moved his hands up to frame her face, then brushed the tear tracks on her cheeks with his thumbs as he deepened the kiss. She melted into him, her fingers curling into the fabric of his shirt. He tasted salt, whether it was from her tears or his own, he didn't know. All he knew was that he kissed her until the taste of salt faded, then rained kisses across her cheeks and neck before finally dragging his mouth back to hers.

When he finally pulled away, she looked at him through wide, shining eyes. And then she smiled. A real, true smile. The kind that could only come from having a merry heart. The kind of smile he'd been waiting to see on her face for years.

Bear ye one another's burdens. Do justice to the afflicted. Fear thou not, for I am with thee.

All three of those verses were coming together in the woman before him, a woman he'd almost missed out on making his.

"I love you so much," she whispered.

He planted a kiss on the soft place where her neck and shoulder met. "And I love you just as much, maybe even more."

And he planned to spend the next fifty years of his life making her smile.

But he wasn't going to tell her that. He was going to show her. Every day. Until she figured it out for herself.

42

Sitka; Two Weeks Later

A lexei spied the ship entering the sound from his position behind his desk. His monstrously large desk, which was situated near the back of his monstrously large office, inside the monstrously large former governor's mansion atop Castle Hill.

But even from this distance, he recognized the sails of the *Alliance.*

He set the map he'd been studying down on his desk and stood, then took a few steps closer to the window overlooking the sound. The wall to his left held another window that overlooked the town, giving him a full view of all the goings-on in both places.

He'd been governor for less than a month, and every minute of it had come with an endless list of things to do. He'd been staring at a map of Alaska, trying to figure out where a company from California could put a cannery without forcing the Tlingit clan in the town of Petersburg to relocate like the clan in Klawock had. He had yet to come up with a solution, but he had to think of something.

That was one of the things he'd had to agree to before Secretary Gray was willing to appoint him governor. He had to acknowledge the US government's official stance that none of the Alaskan tribes had any claim to the land, that the US government had paid Russia for the land, and that Russia had taken it from the various tribes by force.

It wasn't true and he didn't agree with it, but he'd had to agree on paper; otherwise Secretary Gray would have appointed someone who was just as intent on trampling the rights of the natives as Simon Caldwell had been. So he was trying to use his position of power for good. So far it hadn't been easy, but he hadn't given up hope of finding a solution that would prevent the town of Petersburg from relocating.

The other concession he'd had to make was about Inessa. She would be attending Reverend Jackson's industrial boarding school in Sitka in the fall. The only concession he'd received regarding the government's Indian policy was that Ilya could continue learning at Evelina's school in Juneau.

It seemed like a small victory, but it was enough. As Mikhail had pointed out, even if he had to make a few compromises, Alaska would do better under his governorship than under any of the previous governors.

Or at least he hoped it would do better under him. But if he thought the paperwork involved in running a trading company and shipyard was cumbersome, then the paperwork he faced as governor was enough to bury him whole.

The ship sailed deeper into the sound, its nose pointed toward the wharf in front of his family's warehouse. It was close enough now for him to make out the sailors working on deck and a family of four standing on at the railing. Sacha and Maggie had finally returned from San Francisco, along with

Maggie's younger siblings that Sacha had adopted, Ainsley and Finnan.

He turned and strode toward the door, then yanked it open. "I'll be back in an hour," he told Lyle, the clerk who had outlasted Alaska's past three governors. "I'm going down to the harbor to greet my brother."

The thought of Sacha returning put a smile on his face, but so did the thought of Yuri and Rosalind being settled in San Francisco.

If there was ever a woman who deserved to be well cared for and happy, it was Rosalind Caldwell Amos. Even though he'd suspected Yuri's feelings for Rosalind for over a year, he never would have thought there was a way for the two of them to end up happy and married, but God had other plans.

Alexei took the stairs down to the foyer two at a time, then barged through the giant wooden doors of the mansion and started down Castle Hill at a brisk trot. People nodded and called out to him as he passed, but he kept his gaze pinned on the harbor, only waving back and nodding on occasion.

He reached the wharf about half a minute before the sailors slid the gangway down from the ship and was the first one up it.

Even with all the movement on deck, it wasn't hard to spot Sacha. His big, burly brother simply had a way of commanding space.

"Sacha." Alexei clasped his arms around him, hugging him tight. "I missed you."

Sacha squeezed him tight enough to push the wind from his lungs, then released him too quickly, and Alexei nearly stumbled backward.

"Uncle Alexei! Uncle Alexei!" Finnan tugged on the edge of his coat, and Alexei bent down and clasped the six-year-old to his side.

"I want a hug too." Ainsley elbowed her brother out of the way, then pressed up on her tiptoes and gave Alexei a hug.

Alexei smiled, squeezing her tight. He turned to fold Maggie in his arms next, but his gaze snagged on a familiar shade of flaxen hair.

He'd seen that shade only once in the past ten years, but he'd recognize it anywhere.

"Clarise?" The word was more of a whisper than anything. She was talking to one of the deckhands, giving instructions about a large trunk that had been hauled up from belowdecks.

He cleared his throat and turned to Sacha. "What's Clarise doing here?"

Sacha scratched his beard. "Ah, about that. She and her children boarded in Seattle."

Her children? He turned back to study Clarise, and sure enough there was a toddler tucked against her hip and a young girl standing quietly at her side. "Where's her husband? The senator?"

"So you didn't know either?" Maggie came up beside him and gave him a side hug.

Alexei hugged her back but couldn't tear his gaze away from Clarise. "Know what?"

Sacha scratched his beard. "He died last fall shortly after he returned from Alaska. Apparently he suffered from a weak heart."

"I'm sorry to hear that." Alexei knew the right words to say, but they felt empty and dry. At the same time, his brain was scrambling to make sense of everything he'd just heard. "That still doesn't tell me what she's doing here."

Sacha looped an arm around his shoulder. "She's moving back."

Alexei froze, every muscle of his body growing tense. "What? Why? It doesn't make any sense. Why would she come back here? Now? After all this time?" Laurel was coming to visit soon.

"I don't think she's coming back for you, brother. I think she's coming back to get out of Washington."

Maggie offered him a small smile. "She told me that out of all the places she's lived, Sitka is the place she felt most at peace."

"Does she . . . Does she know I'm governor?"

"She does now." Maggie nodded in Clarise's direction. "I told her yesterday. She bought the bakery in town."

The bakery? "Since when does Clarise know how to bake?"

Maggie shrugged.

He licked his lips. This was wrong. All wrong. Clarise had left him twelve years ago, just after his brother died and without having the courage to tell him her plans to his face. She'd left him a letter and then she'd gone to Washington and married a senator.

When she'd returned to Alaska on a visit with her husband last summer, it had been apparent that she wasn't happy, but she hadn't complained to him. If anything, she'd seemed resigned to make the best of the life she'd chosen.

Seeing her again had helped him finally forgive her for leaving as she had, and it had also helped him realize he was ready to move on from his memories of their time together and find another wife. He'd looked at the fact he'd met Laurel only a few weeks before seeing Clarise again as a sign God was pointing him in a new direction. And Laurel and her father were coming to Sitka before the end of the month.

Clarise couldn't just return to Sitka and walk back into his life.

That was the last thing he was ready for.

A note from Naomi

I'm so glad that Rosalind and Yuri fell in love and found a way to stay together forever. I'm sure there are many happy things in store for them down in San Francisco. And I'm equally happy that Rosland's father and uncle are finally facing justice for their crimes.

But even though Rosalind and Yuri already have their happy ending, I couldn't resist writing a bonus scene about their new life together down in San Francisco. (Hint: Rosalind just might be pregnant in this scene!) I think you'll love seeing how happy and contented the two of them are a year into their marriage—and you'll like seeing what's happening with the shipyard too.

If you want to read it, follow the link below and type in your email, so I know where to send it. https://geni.us/ AK5Bonus

Author's Note

For most of history, women facing domestic violence (either from husbands or fathers) had very little legal protection. This was true in the United States as well as everywhere else in the world. During most of the nineteenth century, American courts upheld a husband's "right of chastisement," and while some states began prosecuting severe assault within marriage in the 1850s and 1860s, these cases were rare.

In 1871, the Alabama Supreme Court ruled that a man had no legal right to beat his wife. This case, *Fulgham v. State,* marked the first major legal victory for what we now call domestic violence. But even after this ruling, enforcement remained inconsistent, and most states still required evidence of "extreme cruelty" before granting a divorce or legal separation.

But even though the law offered still offered women little protection, support for domestic violence still started to emerge. One of the most notable examples came from Martha McWhirter of Belton, Texas. Beginning in the 1870s, McWhirter led a women's prayer group that gradually became a refuge for those leaving violent marriages. Over time, this group formed the Woman's Commonwealth, the first legally recognized women's cooperative in the United States. They purchased property, ran small businesses, and even won several court cases affirming their right to live independently from abusive husbands.

Unfortunately, it would take another hundred years before formal domestic-violence laws, restraining orders, and shelters would become part of American legal practice, but Ms. McWhirter's efforts were at least a start.

I wrote Rosalind's story in *Against the Rain* to reflect these historical. Rosalind lived in an era in which a woman's safety depended far more on private courage, personal networks, and local intervention than on any legal protection.

Thank you so much for allowing me to highlight this lesser-known part of nineteenth-century history in her novel. I hope that you enjoyed it, just like I hope that you'll enjoy Alexei and Clarise's story, which will highlight yet another area where women of this era were starting to take a stand for themselves.

It's coming next in *Beyond the Dawn,* where you'll not only get to see Alexei in his new role as governor, but you'll finally discover what went wrong between him and Clarise all those years ago. (Warning: it's probably not what you think.) You can order your copy on Amazon or my website (www.naomirawlings.com).

Other Novels by Naomi Rawlings

Dawn of Alaska Series

Book 1—*Written on the Mist* (Jonas and Evelina)

Book 2—*Whispers on the Tide* (Sacha and Maggie)

Book 3—*Above all Dreams* (Nathan and Kate)

Book 4—*Echoes of Twilight* (Mikhail and Bryony)

Book 5—*Against the Rain* (Yuri and Rosalind)

Book 6—*Beyond the Dawn* (Alexei and Clarise)

Texas Promise Series

Book 1—*Tomorrow's First Light* (Sam and Ellie)

Book 2—*Tomorrow's Shining Dream* (Daniel and Charlotte)

Book 3—*Tomorrow's Constant Hope* (Wes and Keely)

Book 4—*Tomorrow's Steadfast Prayer* (Harrison and Alejandra)

Book 5—*Tomorrow's Lasting Joy* (Cain and Anna Mae)

Eagle Harbor Series

Book 1—*Love's Unfading Light* (Mac and Tressa)

Book 2—*Love's Every Whisper* (Elijah and Victoria)
Book 3—*Love's Sure Dawn* (Gilbert and Rebekah)
Book 4—*Love's Eternal Breath* (Seth and Lindy)
Book 5—*Love's Christmas Hope* (Thomas and Jessalyn)
Book 6—*Love's Bright Tomorrow* (Isaac and Aileen)
Prequel—*Love's Violet Sunrise* (Hiram and Mabel)

Belanger Family Saga
Book 1—*The Lady's Refuge* (Michel and Isabelle)
Book 2—*The Widow's Secret* (Jean Paul and Brigette)
Book 3—*The Reluctant Enemy* (Gregory and Danielle)

Acknowledgments

Thank you first and foremost to my Lord and Savior, Jesus Christ, for giving me both the ability and opportunity to write novels for His glory.

As with any novel, an author might come up with a story idea and sit at his or her computer to type the initial words, but it takes an army of people to bring you the book you have today. I'd especially like to thank my editors. Erin Healy's keen insight and ability to understand my characters and their worlds have made my novels shine in ways that I had never thought possible, and I count it a privilege to work with her. Jennifer Lonas's eye for detail helps me to deliver a polished, professional book to you every single time.

Many thanks to my family for working with my writing schedule and giving me a chance to do two things I love: be a mom and a writer.

Also, thank you to the hospitable people of Juneau and Sitka, Alaska, especially Rich Mattson with the Juneau-Douglas City Museum, and Hal Spackman and Nicole Fiorino with Sitka History. The three of them answered question after question and provided numerous images and book recommendations to help me bring this small slice of Alaskan history to life. And finally, thank you to Susan Gorrilla Benton, a resident of Alaska for over twenty years, who preread this novel looking for any mistakes or inaccuracies.

About the Author

Naomi Rawlings is a *USA Today* bestselling author of over a eighteen historical novels, including the Eagle Harbor Series, which has sold more than 500,000 copies. She lives with her husband and three children in Michigan's rugged Upper Peninsula, along the southern shore of Lake Superior, where they get two hundred inches of snow every year, and where people still grow their own vegetables and cut down their own firewood—just like in the historical novels she writes.

For more information about Naomi, please visit her at www.naomirawlings.com or find her on Facebook at www.facebook.com/author.naomirawlings. If you'd like a free novel, sign up for her author newsletter.

Bonus Scene

San Francisco; One Year Later

Rosalind woke to the sound of hammering. She didn't need to look out the window to know what she'd see. The workers were already hammering away at the first steel-hulled ship the Amos Family Shipbuilders were building. They'd scrimped and saved for an entire year, forgoing profit payments that all of the siblings got twice a year so they could put the money into a steel-hulled vessel. And rather than buy a used ship, they were building a new one.

They'd spent the past year mainly repairing wooden ships, for which there was a large market in San Francisco. As more and more companies moved toward iron and steel ships, there were fewer and fewer shipyards willing to repair wooden vessels, but there were still plenty of wooden vessels sailing the seas, which meant the shipyard had been constantly busy.

Of course, some of their business was due to Yuri. He'd

never met a stranger, and moving to a city as large as San Francisco had catapulted the Amos family name to the top of the harbor master's books and most captains' good graces.

Wealthy businessmen didn't exactly seek them out, but they were the shipyard of choice for everyday merchants and laborers, and these days, warehouse owners were walking all the way to the shipyard and approaching Yuri when they had extra cargo to be shipped or wanted an updated contract.

She rolled onto her side, settling her hand on her belly. It was starting to grow round, but if she wore a large enough skirt, she could still hide the fact she was with child.

Not that she wanted to hide it. She was thrilled to be bringing a child into the world, and she knew for a fact that the baby would have a much better father than she'd had growing up.

Kate said the baby was due to arrive in early August, which meant she was just over halfway along with her pregnancy, but most of the time, August felt unbearably far away. She couldn't wait to hold the little one in her arms. Or better yet, to hand the child to Yuri and watch him cradle it to his chest. She could only imagine the look of love and tenderness that would creep across his face the first time he held—

The door to the room swung open without so much as a knock, and Yuri entered, balancing a tray in his hands.

"You're awake?" He blinked when he saw her staring at him from the bed. "And here I was hoping to surprise you with breakfast in bed."

"You are surprising me. I expected I'd need to come down and make myself breakfast." She ran her eyes down him. "It looks like you've already been to the shipyard. How early did you get up?"

"Early enough to get a few hours of work in—and to get a telegram from Alexei." He set the tray on the nightstand. "It seems the Marshals assigned to your father's case have found another bribery scandal that involves your father, your uncle, and several politicians. Alexei is guessing that your father will face an additional ten-year sentence if he's convicted."

Rosalind drew in a slow breath. "Ten more years?"

"Assuming he's convicted, yes."

"I'm sure he will be." Her father and uncle were both already serving fifteen-year sentences after being convicted of poaching, falsifying their seal-harvesting numbers, bribery, and tax evasion. Now it looked like they would be facing some of those charges all over again for a different crime. Part of her wanted to ask for more details about the charges, but the other part of her just wanted to move on with her life. She slid a hand over her stomach.

"What are you thinking?" Yuri brushed a strand of hair from her cheek.

"That twenty-five years is long enough for our baby to grow up without ever feeling threatened by his or her grandfather."

"It sure is."

Rather than sitting up to eat, she shifted over on the bed and opened her arms for Yuri. "Hold me."

He looked down at her. "I have my shoes on, Ros."

"Then take them off."

He didn't need to be told twice. He had his boots unlaced in a matter of seconds and slid into bed beside her. She snuggled into his warmth as his arms settled around her.

Then she promptly sneezed. "Ugh. You smell like sawdust."

Yuri grinned and tightened his arms around her. "That's the scent of a successful shipyard."

"It's the scent of my pillow too, apparently."

He laughed softly. "Can you imagine it? One day our child will grow up thinking sawdust smells like home."

"Heaven help us."

"He already has." Yuri bent down and kissed her forehead.

She smiled and let her head rest against his chest, the rhythm of his heart steady beneath her ear. She couldn't argue with him. God truly had helped them through what had once seemed like a terrible, hopeless situation. She was grateful every day for the new life he'd given her, a husband who loved her, and a new life the two of them were bringing into the world.

Outside, the hammering carried on, but inside, Rosalind snuggled deeper into her husband's arms—the one place that had always made her feel safe.

About the Author

Naomi Rawlings is a *USA Today* bestselling author of over a dozen historical novels, including the Eagle Harbor Series, which has sold more than 500,000 copies. She lives with her husband and three children in Michigan's rugged Upper Peninsula, along the southern shore of Lake Superior, where they get two hundred inches of snow every year, and where people still grow their own vegetables and cut down their own firewood—just like in the historical novels she writes.

For more information about Naomi, please visit her at www.naomirawlings.com or find her on Facebook at www.facebook.com/author.naomirawlings. If you'd like a free novel, sign up for her author newsletter (http://geni.us/35Yn)